I0841071

BOATS ON A RIVER

ISBN: 979-8-218-27136-7 (Paperback Edition)

Boats On A River / Dennis Balk / Literary Fiction

Printed and bound in the United States of America

Published by Channel 171

Photos: National Archives and Records Administration

dennisbalk.com

DENNIS BALK
B-3351

BOATS ON A RIVER

CHAPTERS

Chapter One

On the Road

"Is that the Armani?"

"Of course it's the Armani."

"Take that jacket off."

"What are you talking about? Take it off. They want the look of success; it's what they elected."

"Take it off, Franklin. They elected the Brooks Brothers, and you know it."

The Armani is impressive. It's the fit more than anything. Perfection. But with the amount of highway junk food over the past few days, Franklin Knight feels the need for one last waistline check. In the cramped quarters of the Winnebago, he has to stand a little too close to the tall, thin mirror to get a decent assessment, especially the waistline. Knight gives one quick tug on the bottom of the jacket to tighten the tailored fit, then brushes it smooth. He considers the front acceptable, which it is. A quick look over his shoulder. The back? It'll have to do.

Newly elected to the House of Representatives after a relatively drama-free campaign, the look he studies in the mirror has to at least resemble the image he's projected across social media for months. Maybe kick it up a notch. Maybe obscure any nagging suspicions the voters might harbor following their vigorously apathetic approval.

Without a shadow of a doubt, Franklin Knight is the perfectly packaged politician of this cycle. He's one of the popular standouts with relatively competent capabilities in the cyclical revival of Washington's history makers. During his years in the DC lower circuits, he perfected his particular expertise: the ability to conjure respectful appreciation among his peers and envious notoriety from the competitors. Franklin Knight wholeheartedly embraces the challenge of performing his personal image as a winning strategy. As far as

Knight's concerned, wardrobe gets you the part.

The deep charcoal blue, impressive Armani with thin black pinstripes has got to be the way to go. It's a gorgeous suit, and it perfectly accentuates his six-foot frame and impressive and expertly trimmed head of gray hair. The suit completes the character of the accomplished, worldly intellectual. But is it too "bookish-cultured" and not enough "down-in-the-trenches, man-of-action?" Is that even still a thing?

"What time in the morning is the Memphis stop?" Knight calls to the back of the Winnebago. He straightens the lapels and adjusts the tie, looking for that perfect symmetry in the knot. It's a process. But in all honesty, it's mostly a pleasant distraction from the long hours on the road. Memphis, in the morning, is the next scheduled event on his cross-country press tour. Maybe the Armani is a little too dark. Too much contrast in the mid-morning sun is a rookie mistake. This can go on for hours. "Tell me you packed the navy tie."

The Interstate offers up yet another bump in the road. They're violent and deafening. The Winnebago rattles like ball bearings in a tin can. Thankfully, it's over in a flash.

In the mirror, Knight's focus shifts to the trees whizzing by behind him, framed in the Winnebago's windows. He has no idea where he is, with only the bright sun of the day. It's an intriguing thought, not knowing where you are.

"Franklin." Alfred willfully inserts himself into the reverie. "We've had this discussion," he says without looking up. "Forget about the suit right now. As your senior staffer and reliable better half, I'm telling you I have a very busy schedule. You know this. We meet the press in the morning. Getting you prepared is a challenge, and my patience is running thin. I insist we get to the business of the day."

Alfred's forte is his ability to pander to the Representative's pronounced vanities and still manage the details of a politician's schedule. Alfred Benson worked his way up to the Representative's senior staff position through a myriad of tedious personal assistant jobs. For the forty-three-year-old African American from Buena Park, California, organizing a politician's agenda isn't terribly taxing. Attention to detail—his best quality—will serve him well in the DC circuit. As fond as he is of Franklin, he is still managing his own career.

Alfred takes balanced steps over to Knight as the Winnebago sails down the highway. He slips his forefinger and thumb under the jacket's collar to gently lift it off Knight's shoulders. Franklin brushes off Alfred's hand and holds his position in front of the mirror. He won't be pulled away from this. It's part of the process.

"Franklin," Alfred says with increasing annoyance. "You may be on the victory lap, but you don't change the uniform until after the after party."

Both are holding on to steady themselves, one hand on the wall, the other on each other's arm. The two of them bicker like cantankerous old friends, which they are.

"This is what you do, Franklin." He puts his hands to his waist. "You find anything to distract yourself. You have this; you have that. We have Memphis at nine in the morning and you need to read over the press script. At the very least once more." He drops his hands to his sides and looks straight up at the ceiling. "Instead, you sift through any and all of your many indulgences to find one distraction after another."

"I would hardly call the wardrobe a distraction."

"We've discussed the press wardrobe numerous times already."

"First of all, you're exaggerating, and second, Memphis is not Phoenix."

"Okay," Alfred says, now demonstrating his irritation. "Let's review." He takes two steps back from Knight to be in a better position to lecture and admonish, and picks up his iPhone from the top of the mini-fridge. He scrolls through a number of bookmarked sites, which isn't easy in the rattling Winnebago. "Okay, here we go. Are you listening? A reporter from the Signal... Please listen to this, Franklin. I beg you. This was Phoenix yesterday afternoon." Alfred does a mock throat clearing for effect. "The newly elected Democratic Representative from the 29th Congressional District, Franklin Knight, appears to be another elected politician without the slightest clue how to deal with any of the real issues in his hometown district." Alfred milks the pause. "Representative Franklin Knight appeared at the Hyatt in Phoenix with other newly elected or reelected officials, or otherwise notables, on their way to Washington for opening day of the joint session."

Alfred looks across to Franklin with a dramatic cold blank stare, waiting for the slightest amount of recognition, possibly a negligible admission of guilt. Knight keeps his poker face. Alfred continues. "At the Phoenix event, one of several stops on his 'No One Left Behind' press tour—an outrageously bankrupt slogan—Representative Knight was asked about health-care for undocumented immigrants.”

Alfred clears his throat again and again. It's carefully crafted, a touch more drama each time. “Franklin? Are you following this? The reporter's follow-up question: How do you register immigrants who are in the state illegally? Representative Knight's response is clearly the typical politician's dodge: All humans have inalienable rights to health care.'” Alfred is now pointing a finger in the air to make the point. “Clearly, in California, they love him, and they elected him for his simple-minded slogans.” Alfred drops both hands to his sides. “Do I have your attention, Franklin? Can we put the Armani back in the closet and get back to work?”

“The question was designed as a trap, which I skillfully avoided. Unblemished,” Franklin responds.

“The question begged a talking point synopsis, which we have rehearsed. Blemished,” Alfred's response.

“And God dammit, this is a good idea and it's important.” Knight takes a step toward Alfred. “This trip across this country is a profound gesture. It's not a gesture; it's an awakening. A tribal… a communal… a convening of spirits. What's the word I'm looking for?”

“Franklin, you are so far out on the limb of your own making, I can't imagine what it is you're looking for.”

Admittedly, one of Knight's pronounced skills is his ability to promote a populist ideal with just the right recipe of inspiration and stretch. Knight's determined agenda to grab an audience and preserve their admiration, at any cost, will almost always drive him precariously close to the proverbial rails. Alfred knows it. Managing the subtleties of Knight's intellect has become a big part of the job.

Of course, the cross-country trip was Representative Knight's idea. A profound gesture, a hoorah of grand theater designed to attract benevolent editorials with the attention he deserves. The idea occurred to him when he was calculating the right configuration of a newly re-energized image he could project into the stale air, corrupt idealism, of the same old cheap-suits Washington crowd. A late-night stroke of inspiration.

In tune with the current trends of media savvy, Knight scripted his road trip as a sojourn, a poetic-nostalgic trip to connect the unrecognized visionaries spread across the country, in small towns and big cities, or something close to that. Representative Knight's sketchy composition of a Kesey or a Kerouac at the wheel is about all he could manage. He was a little lost in the conflicting metaphors of the romantic, dusty sunlight visuals of one decade, layered with important authors and famous beats from a decade earlier, reconfigured with perfectly recorded celebrity voices from a decade later, now vintage. To be honest, Knight would hardly be considered one of the best minds of his generation. To be fair, he's gifted in other areas. Oblivious to the awkward cliché, Knight's quest was set in motion. The Winnebago hit the road.

The Armani moment has finally passed, and Knight is putting the jacket back on its hanger. He catches a quick glimpse of the mirror, the tired lines on his face, the tired eyes. There's a lingering smell of diesel in the Winnebago, but it's too loud and windy to open the windows out here on the road.

"The history idea... alright, I'm willing to admit that might be overplayed." Knight is thinking out loud, with not a lot of conviction. "No one left behind. Maybe it's not the best slogan, but it resonates. If people in this country are unaware of their own history, how can we ever hope to move forward into the future?" He's ready for a nap. "Regardless, no one is perfect, and I will work hard for the people in my district. I believe in hard work!"

"You hate to work," Alfred says as he takes the hanger and jacket from Knight.

"You have to represent the everyday people who elect you," Knight pontificates.

"You never lived in San Fernando. You live in Anaheim."

Resigned to Alfred's business of the day, Representative Knight steps over and takes a seat on the built-in couch next to the young boy who everyone calls Hardy. Hardy's dad, Buddy, is driving. Knight puts his arm up over the back of the couch behind Hardy, crosses his legs, and looks down at the book the boy's reading. For lack of anything better to say, he goes with, "So, what are you reading?"

Hardy looks up at Knight. He begins the arduous task of organizing any kind of response to the bland question. For a twelve-year-old kid from southern

California—Fullerton, to be precise—small talk from an older person is the worst kind of dull. Mind-numbing, inescapable, serious old person stuff. For this very reason, Hardy has successfully managed to avoid being trapped in a conversation with the Representative for most of the trip, which has not been easy inside the cramped—yet spacious—Winnebago.

Unlike most of the kids his age in Fullerton, it's only been in the last year that Hardy has developed a desire to show himself as a definite individual. He knows the trends. He sees his friends unloading tons of cash on Adidas and Nikes. It's not for him. He's not going to become a brand, and he's finding ways to show it, except for his bleached crew cut. Today, in the Winnebago, he's wearing a long-sleeved plaid shirt, unbuttoned over a t-shirt with a familiar, possibly symbolic graphic. Hardy has a comfortable way of being with people. He doesn't try too hard. He has intense interests, which he consumes for a more-or-less predictable amount of time and then abandons to move on. Currently, it's tropical fish.

He manages his response to the Representative, "It's a handbook for fish."

"It's a handbook for tropical fish? Is that what you're reading?" Knight tries again.

"Yes. It's for tropical fish," Hardy replies, with no apparent tone in his voice.

"Yes, sir!" Buddy calls back to his son from the driver's seat.

"Yes, Sir, it's a tropical fish handbook," he replies, obviously trapped. "It's for care and feeding. It's actually very specific. I have a thirty-gallon tank and a ten-gallon. Actually, the ten-gallon is empty. I'm cleaning that one. But I have breeding angelfish in the thirty. I've had eggs laid before, but I've never had them hatch. That's pretty hard. That's why I got the handbook. In order to get the eggs to hatch, there are a number of conditions you have to do."

"Well, isn't that something," Knight says to him as he diverts his attention away. "I would imagine watching fish in an aquarium is very relaxing."

"I guess."

"I also have the 'Field Guide To North American Birds' in case you want to..." Hardy begins to realize Mr. Knight's lack of interest. "In case you want to identify the 'never-mind.' They're actually common here."

Knight uncrosses one leg, then crosses the other.

Buddy, at the wheel, is making sure the Winnebago stays on schedule. The roads are decent, the weather's okay. This also pleases Alfred, or more precisely, keeps him in the back and out of the front seats, which pleases Buddy. Buddy came with the rented Winnebago; part of the package. He's the road trip facilitator, which means he's the navigator and the fix-it guy for everything in the Winnebago that could stop working properly, like the ice maker or the toilet flush. And like a typical long-distance driver, he's not much of a conversationalist. He'd prefer not to speak at all.

Hardy adopted his easy-going attitude from his father. Buddy is a heavyset man, meaning twenty pounds overweight, which doesn't concern him in the least. You could characterize Buddy as a loud-floral-patterned, short-sleeve-shirt wearer who is sometimes an Eagles fan, but that's a cliché, and Buddy isn't that. With a neatly trimmed beard and a decent pair of Ray Bans.

The Winnebago's route is not the obvious diagonal from southern California up to Washington, DC. When the route was being decided, Representative Knight wanted to stay south as far as possible before heading north. Something about the inclusion of southern flavor.

Ultimately, he convinced Alfred to agree to the trip by cobbling together some inspired lyrics about "Highway 101" and "Route 66." This being one of the rare occasions when Alfred conceded to one of Franklin's impulsive scenarios. The schedule had the time; not terribly disruptive.

Alfred is still thinking through the various probable press debacles at tomorrow's event. He shuffles through some printouts, then decides on the problematic topic of immigration rights. He's not obsessing; he's insistent. Walking toward Knight and the boy on the couch, he continues, "Okay, I know how you hate this, but we're doing this and we're doing this now. You've already been elected, but you can still be made the fool, and who knows, maybe they can kick you out."

Alfred channels the voice of a shrill suburban reporter. "Representative Knight, how are you? What are your current thoughts on registering illegal immigrants? Have you considered a different approach following the response you gave in Phoenix?"

Knight gives in to Alfred's insistence. He blows out a chest full of air, uncrosses his legs and leans forward on the couch, adopting his politician's composure. "Of course, I would like to thank everyone who came here today to add your voice to this symbolic trip to our Nation's capital. We recognize the imperative to include all those who have historically been left behind. Those who serve this great country and those who continue to serve this bounty of ideas; the greatest democracy in history. In the reality of this difficult time, there is not one person who should remain behind or be forced out of the national conversation. All people need to be brought into the fold and kept safe from the pounding on the door at midnight, the howling in the alleys, and safe from the wolves who stalk the perimeter of the fire."

"Are you kidding me?" Alfred barks at Knight. "Please, please don't do this, Franklin." Alfred takes a breath of composure. "Just tell me the requisite steps to get health care to unregistered immigrants living in the 29th District. How do we do that?"

"Amnesty." His one-word reply.

Knight stands and puts his arm around Alfred's shoulder. "I can do this. But, goddamn it, this is a road trip. It's a spiritual thing." Knight begins to pace. "There are histories out there, Alfred, histories of all kinds of immigrants finding their way, making it through, surviving, and succeeding. All those stories, and we're driving straight through it all. Blind to it all."

"Where on earth is this coming from, Franklin?" Alfred is clearly bewildered by this new storyline.

Representative Knight calls up to the driver's seat, "Hey Buddy, aren't we about to cross the Mississippi?" He turns to Hardy, still on the built-in, holding the handbook. "Let me ask you, Son, who were the settlers who came through this part of the country?" He's pointing out the window; trees whizzing by. "Where did they come from, and why did they come here?" Knight bends at the waist to face him head-on. "Here in Arkansas, the Mississippi River Valley? Do you know? Have you covered that in your history classes?"

It's difficult to sort through the thoughts buzzing through Knight's mind at this point. It might be the weight of it all, or it might be pure, unfocused frustration mixed with fatigue. Either way, he sits back down on the built-in. In that moment, Representative Knight stares into a deep, deep space. Uncharacteristically deep. Alfred can see it on his face.

Suddenly, like a prizefighter called back into the ring, the representative marches up to the passenger seat and whips the map off the seat to sit. "Yes,

Sir," Buddy tells him, "we're almost to the Mississippi, but we have to cross the Arkansas River first." Buddy reaches over and puts one finger on the map. "Right here, Sir. The bridge on 165. Right here we cross the Arkansas River. It's a major tributary. It's probably a grand ole river. Most likely muddy brown this time of year."

Knight scans the details of the map, the black lines of the highways crossing the fatter blue lines of the rivers.

"Here." Knight puts one finger on the map. "Right here. This looks like it could be a rest stop, right next to the river. County road 33, Buddy, just outside of Pendleton."

"That's where you want to go? Mr. Knight?" Buddy immediately considers this might be one of Knight's quickly passing interests. They pop up at fairly regular intervals, depending on the chatter. But the other truth of it is Buddy would love the chance to get off the highway for a break, smoke a cigarette, and stand out in the sun for twenty minutes.

"Yes, I do. You bet I do." Knight fires back. "Can we get the Winnebago down that county road?"

A semi-tractor that was recklessly changing lanes ahead of them not ten minutes ago makes another dive to the right. The sudden swerve kicks up some loose gravel, which peppers the Interstate, some of it hitting the Winnebago. Buddy steps hard on the brakes, everybody and everything not fastened down lurches forward.

"Jesus. This jackass is dangerous," Buddy calls out. He keeps the Winnebago at a steady 30mph to see what the moron's going to do.

"Sir," he tells Mr. Knight, "these county roads are two-lane. I can get us down that road, but I doubt it's going to be a decent walk down to see the river. I know you're wanting that. I don't believe you'll be satisfied just driving across the bridge. It is a spiritual thing. I agree with you there. But we have no idea what kind of people might be hanging around a river way out here. River people can be unpredictable."

"Well, let's give it a try." The spirited, upbeat swing in Knight's voice sounds convincing. "We can spend this entire trip driving from hotel to convention center, passing through it all, and never actually see any of it. How sad would that be? Interstate voyeurs not part of any of it. Sounds rather pathetic, does it not?"

"Yes, Sir, you got it. It's not too far." Buddy is genuinely grateful to give Mr. Knight his support and encouragement. It comes naturally to a man with a big heart. "Why don't you get yourself ready? Remember, it's a rest stop. It most likely won't be all that nice. My son will go with you to get your look at the river in case you need something. You can keep each other out of trouble."

Alfred listens to the two of them up front. He'll stay out of it. Based on experience, Franklin will get started on whatever path there might be, figure it might not be worth the mud on his shoes, and turn around and come back. Half an hour tops.

With the renewed vigor of a body overcome with purpose and a plan, Knight makes his way to the rear of the Winnebago, grabbing hold of anything to keep it graceful.

Still on the built-in, Hardy looks up to Mr. Knight, and with a remarkably complex and undeniably deadpan inflection, he tells him, "Actually, Sir, it's not amnesty; it's incentivize."

Alfred looks up from his iPhone.

Buddy was right; it doesn't take long to reach the rest stop on County Road 33. Representative Knight looks out the side window of the Winnebago. It's a beautiful, bright, sunny day with a lot of potential, nothing overtly foreboding. He looks around to study what might be the finer details, of which there are none. The Winnebago slides all the way into the remarkably small parking lot, and Buddy powers down the behemoth. Both Alfred and Hardy move to the other window to check it out.

"This should be good," Hardy's response.

"Half an hour, tops," Alfred's.

It turns out the rest stop is more of a dead-end turnaround than a quickie-mart gas station with restrooms. Although, there is a chunky cinder block hut painted National Park Brown, which must be the bathrooms. It doesn't really matter what the destination actually offers; Knight is determined to get outside and experience his great Pilgrim-Crossing Country. To stand on the bank of a great American river is the authentic truth he believes he needs, or read about. But, in all sincerity, he's determined to experience anything above the ordinary.

Knight opens the narrow, wood-grained panel door of the cramped little closet separating the driver's seat from the rear of the Winnebago. He reaches in and pulls out the Armani. The only jacket that could properly initiate the appropriately imaginative connection between who he is now, the Winnebago Representative, and what he's about to discover about himself if all goes well; the promise of the quest. How or why the Armani is appropriate, only the adventurer can know.

"So, you're actually going to walk down to the river? Is that your plan?" Alfred asks, subtly shaking his head side to side; no. "This is a rare occasion. I don't remember you doing anything like this. I didn't anticipate anything remotely like this. I would certainly love to join you on your quest. However, I have work to do here. So, I'll be staying here."

"Oh, Alfred. I completely understand." Knight turns to him and grabs both of his forearms, surprising him. The tone in his voice rings with an uncharacteristic sincerity. "Alfred, this is an important moment for me. I actually believe it's more than just my generation's nostalgic, spiritual journey bullshit. If there's too much mud, I'll just turn around and come back."

Buddy walks back to where Knight is preparing. "Sir, you're going to want to stay on any path they have there." Now that it's actually going to happen, Buddy has mixed feelings about the quickie adventure. "This is river country. There's bound to be a snake or two, probably water moccasin. Just stay on the path."

The word snake, gives Alfred a bit of concern. "Franklin, you listen to me. Buddy is going with you, and you're only going for a quick look-see." Alfred positions himself in front of Knight to better command his attention. "You stay on that path and when that path ends, which it will, you turn around and come straight back. Buddy, I respectfully demand you get him back here in one piece. One-half hour, not a minute more."

"Dear Lord, Albert, just relax, and Buddy, you're staying here."

Knight can't or doesn't say it, but he's thinking it. *This is that definitive moment. It's possible this entire trip could prove to have one singular occasion of honest integrity. Is that so much to ask? All the years of posturing and pandering? One moment, one authentic experience. I'm surprised I can even say it. What's the worst that could happen?* "This is something I'm doing on my own," Knight tells them. "It has to be that way."

"I respect that," Buddy calmly offers, which is his way. "How about this?

My son will go with you. He'll carry a bag or whatever you need, just to free up your arms, lighten the load. He won't say much." Buddy turns to Hardy, who's stood up to join the commotion. "Son, you'll go with Mr. Knight. And you'll be respectful of his spiritual walk. Keep the chit-chat to a minimum. Just follow along. If he needs something, you'll be there to help him. Take a thermos of water, and you'll be respectful of the representative's personal space and anything else he needs. You understand?"

"I do, Dad. I got it. I know respectful. I go to public school."

"And what about your heart?" The motherly Alfred chimes in. "Have you taken your medicine? You've been sitting in here for hours on end. It's not a good idea to jump up and go sprinting down some path in the woods."

In full disclosure, Knight has seen doctors about a heart condition that he and Alfred both thought might be serious enough to warrant attention. One blood test showed an above average cholesterol level. He was prescribed a low-dose statin. Another test showed a mild irregularity. Neither of them can remember how mildly irregular. Another prescription. The two of them refer to the heart condition whenever it might be persuasive in a conversation.

"Alright, Alfred, dear, relax." Now it's Knight's turn to do the mothering. "Honestly, it'll be fine, a quick look-see and back on the road to Memphis."

"Son, where's your windbreaker?" Buddy asks as he pokes around in one of the piles of stuff. He picks it up and tosses it to his son. "You might need it. And I'm telling you, Son, stay on that path. Don't be gone long, and don't get yourself into trouble, and don't talk to anyone."

"Affirmative, Dad." Thumbs up.

Knight considers the last time his heart gave him a bit of a scare. *That was a double flight of stairs a week ago.*

"Franklin, one last time, this is a short little walk to see whatever it is you plan on seeing. We do not have extra time budgeted for this."

"Dear friend, how can I explain to you a moment in time?"

Knight gives Hardy two quick pats on the shoulder. "Alright partner." He opens the Winnebago door and steps down the two metal steps onto the parking lot pavement. There are two cars parked in the lot, an Acura and a Honda Civic, both dirty silver, but no one is around, which seems strange. Knight looks around but not for anything in particular. The sun is bright and hot. Hardy steps down to join Mr. Knight. He looks around. Nothing in particular. They stand next to each other. Hardy seems taller outside. They both take one quick look at each other, then together they walk a short distance across the lot, halfway between the Winnebago and the far edge of the parking lot where the woods begin.

Alfred and Buddy step down onto the pavement. They both watch Knight standing in the middle of the parking lot. He will either turn around, and the whole thing will blow over. Or, walk to the edge of the lot and head off into the woods, with Hardy one respectful step behind.

Buddy is a big man standing next to Alfred. He gets his cigarette break. The bright sun is on their faces. Alfred holds his hand above his eyes to shade the sun.

"I don't like this," Alfred says to himself under his breath, "I don't trust this," a little louder. "This will end in disaster," he says to Buddy.

"Nah, they'll be all right. It's good for him to get off the bus for a bit. It'll clear his head. My boy knows what he's doing. He won't let anything happen."

In the next moment, apparently a moment of truth, Representative Knight, with Hardy respectfully one step behind him, walks over to the edge of the lot to the start of the path. *It's mostly gravel, so the county must have put some money into it. It looks as though it's had a good amount of foot traffic. It looks promising, inviting, and not much of a challenge.* "Exactly perfect," Knight says out loud.

Without hesitation and with only a tinge of trepidation, Knight considers— for the briefest of moments—to look back, but he doesn't. He steps onto the path and starts to walk straight into the woods at a decent pace. Hardy follows behind with just enough distance so Mr. Knight can feel like he's going it alone; his special quest.

After a few dozen feet, a thought crosses Knight's mind. *What kind of Holy Grail do you imagine you're going to find down there?*

Chapter Two

The thicket of trees and vines

As expected, as Knight imagined, the gravel path leads straight into the woods. The woodland mix is typical for this part of Arkansas and the Mississippi River Valley: oaks, maples, hickories, and here and there, a small grouping of pine. It doesn't seem like old growth, except for the occasional wise old trunk. The trees are spread enough to see short distances, twenty to thirty feet maximum. They are deep in every direction, except behind them, back to the parking lot. The tangled vines, summer grape, and Virginia creeper make the woods nearly impossible to walk through in any direction other than the path straight ahead. Representative Knight keeps a determined pace, but stops to look around about every fifty feet or so. The sunlight shoots down through the branches overhead in shafts of defined light. The warm sun on the ground fills the air with the smell of composting leaves. Immediately familiar. Knight watches the gravel, and the twigs, and the dead leaves at his feet as he maintains his pace. He also looks ahead to see how far the path looks cleared enough to keep going. The hot sun back in the parking lot radiating off the pavement is gone in here. A simple breeze.

"This is exactly what I thought it would be," Knight says to Hardy, ten feet or so behind him. "A path in the woods. Honestly, I don't know what all the drama was about."

"Yeah, this is great, Mr. Knight." A respectful response.

Knight feels the confidence of the path. He eases into the peacefulness of the quiet, occasionally punctuated with scripted thoughtfulness. *It truly is something very pleasant. A delightful path in the woods.*

Looking out through the woods, Knight realizes the thicket of twisting vines makes it foolhardy to venture off the path.

"You okay?" he asks Hardy, turning slightly to see for himself.

"Sure, this is normal." As Hardy keeps pace with Knight, he doesn't watch the ground. He looks through the trees for birds and anything else moving around. "I forgot to bring my Field Guide," he calls up to Mr. Knight. "I've already seen a Carolina chickadee and a tufted titmouse."

"Colorful names," Knight replies.

The two of them keep a decent and steady pace. Knight has no desire for a powerwalk. This isn't that. As they make progress, the woods stay thick and the path stays straight. *Someone has maintained this path. Or, it might be the years of people coming down to the river. The people Buddy talked about. I'm sure they're decent people.* The two of them walk a while longer without speaking.

The woods maintain their pronounced quiet, which is not lost on Knight. This is very much a part of the experience he'd forgotten to anticipate. *How long has it been?* Many years younger, Knight was drawn to the possibilities of an unexpected place in nature and exploring the idea of adventure. It's part of being young. You take risks on the off-road. Before the weight of responsibilities become managed limitations. Before the full impact of disillusionment hits its stride and paths through the woods become irresponsible. How far does that path stretch? The forest woods will offer a sense of purpose for those who seek it. Touch lightly on the soul. The empowering truth of the forest's promise is delivered by literature; the rambling through the woods and roaming the river valleys. Literature's quest for the heroic and earnest. Nature, the great facilitator, befriends the protagonist and defeats all others. Or, unfortunately, mercilessly abandons those not yet deserving salvation. Representative Knight may not recall Fenimore Cooper's last Mohican or Jack London's call, but they find him nonetheless. He may feel he is the initiator, but he is indeed another character on the author's path.

The most pronounced sound so far has been their feet shuffling the path. There is the occasional rustling in the dead leaves made by small birds. The sparrows and thrushes when you can see them. Above, there is a breeze, and when it catches the older trees, they groan. Ahead, the path makes a cave-like opening. The way forward appears to go up and over two or three short hills. It's hard to tell how many, but it looks promising.

"This looks very promising," Knight says to Hardy, thinking to give him confidence that their trek will be worth it. "The river is probably over one of these low hills. We're getting close; I can feel it," Knight says to himself aloud. He looks back again at Hardy. "You still okay?"

Hardy wants Mr. Knight to know that he doesn't need to be worried. "Sure. I'm okay. We had woods like this at camp. They were kind of like this. We didn't have a path, though. We'd just walk through. One kid would go off in some direction. I don't remember why, but we'd all follow him. Those woods were awesome. You okay?"

"You bet I am, Son." Knight's voice is definitely upbeat. "This is exactly what I thought it would be. You get these short little hills before you get the last one that takes you right down to the river's edge." He's become the expert. The trailblazer.

"Mr. Knight, do you hear that bird? Off there, off to the left of us? That is definitely a northern mockingbird. That bird will go on and on. They're a very tough bird. They'll chase anything out of their territory. That's probably why it's so loud right now. He doesn't like us being here."

"Well, that's his problem, right?"

"For sure it is, Sir."

The dirt and the twigs, and dead leaves of the path are being overtaken by vines and dead branches. The straight ahead has become the more challenging: up and over.

"Sir, you sure you want to keep going? It's gonna get muddy, or harder, probably." Hardy is mostly concerned about what his father is going to say if they're gone too long.

"This is a journey to the river's edge, Son," Knight tells him. He bends over to go under a larger fallen branch crossing over the path, then lifts one leg at a time over a clump of twisted vines, and turns sideways to work his way through a tangle of dead shrubs. "I know your generation has no respect for the essence, the poetry of a moment like this." Knight is getting a little winded. "It's not your fault, really. It's the fault of everyone… well, someone, the education system. What in God's name do they teach kids in school these days?"

"Sir, you wanna stop for a minute and catch your breath? That would certainly be part of the poetry of this moment. In my opinion," Hardy tells him, clever at reading the situation.

"I absolutely do not want to stop." Knight stops and puts his hands on his waist to take a few deep breaths. Hardy waits just behind as Knight decides what he wants to do.

After the decent pace to make it this far—on a path like this—taking a moment to catch your breath, to collect your thoughts, can let loose a particular type of indecision. Knight feels a creeping sense of unease. *Go forward or turn back?* Knight looks straight up into the tree branches. What can be seen of the sky is still the beautiful, clear blue of a perfect day. He knows from experience this is the time to take deep breaths. *This is not the time or place for any heart issues. Relax the body and take deep breaths.* "Do you know the secret to life, Son? Keep the heart beating."

Suddenly, there is a rustle in the leaves just to the left of them. It startles them both.

"Let's keep going."

Representative Knight and Hardy, his quest companion, continue on through the Arkansas woods. Knight is determined to stay the course, at least a little farther. "Stay the course! If it gets too thick, then we'll turn around, and that will be what the woods have told us to do this day."

Thorny vines are now part of the gauntlet, maybe poison ivy. They both notice the sound of the woods changing. The birds in this part of the woods are busy. Overhead, in the tree-tops, the birds are busier and louder. It's noisy.

Knight climbs over the next tree trunk and stops. Not too far ahead is the opening in the woods he spotted a while back. There's a hole of sunlight straight ahead of them. He raises his arm and points. "There!" Knight brushes off his jacket while he checks for snags or tears. He can't believe he wore the Armani into the woods, but actually, it makes perfect sense. Or, he trusts he'll know the sense of it when the time comes. "That has to be the river."

"I think you may be right, Sir." Hardy agrees, with more than a little relief, which he conceals from Mr. Knight.

They keep going, over the fallen branches and around the tangled vines. As they get closer to the opening, the glittering of sunlight reflecting off the river begins to show itself. It feels big. Powerful.

"I knew it." Knight swells with satisfaction, his prowess in the wilds of nature.

As it appears they've made it through, Knight carefully walks down the last ravine and up the other side. Hardy decides to run down the slope, too eager to get to the river. Halfway down, his foot catches a piece of the grapevine, and he sprawls headfirst to the bottom of the ravine. The thicket of trees and vines, and the length of his tumble isn't enough for a serious injury. But, a dagger of a broken vine—sticking out from the rest—catches his arm and tears a hole through his windbreaker and the plaid shirt underneath. It leaves a painful, but seemingly shallow scratch across his arm just above the elbow and just below the shoulder.

"Shit. That hurt."

In a few minutes, he's back up the slope and makes it to the top. Mr. Knight is only a few steps behind. They made it. They've come out of the woods, and they stand at the top of the last hill that leads directly down to the river's edge. The woods at their backs. The river stretches out forever in both directions. A moment of pride, exhaustion, relief, and a tinge of—what now? Honestly, for both, it's an overwhelming experience to be this close to such a marvel.

Mr. Knight and Hardy stand motionless for a long moment. They don't look at each other, and they don't speak. The river is a magnificent sight, especially having come straight out of the woods.

"Is it bad?" Mr. Knight asks him. "Your arm. Is it deep?"

"It's not too bad. I'll get a bandage when we get back. My dad will not be happy about it. This windbreaker is kind of new."

As the moments pass, they continue to stand dead still. Looking out across the width of it. The immensity of the river is a force, a power. This is how the river claims its territory, cutting through the woods. Its power is intimidation.

And now, the slow creeping fear that by doing nothing more than standing motionless, the river could do them harm. They walk a short way across the rocky-dirt top of the slope, and without speaking, they agree they've found a good spot to take in the breadth of it all. A good spot to sit.

Latte brown from the runoff of spring rains, the Arkansas River has come a long way across the continent to get to this place in front of them. The river starts high in the Sawatch Range of the Rocky Mountains and drops 10,000 feet before it meets the Mississippi. The river valley spreads across Arkansas, Illinois, Kentucky, Louisiana, Mississippi, Missouri, and Tennessee, impossible to imagine without a map. The Spanish called the river the "Napeste," and the French called it "Riviere des Ark." The Quapaw Tribe lived and hunted the banks. They named it "The Arkansas." It's a grand and immense river snaking through a giant chunk of the continent, surrendered to it by power of intimidation. Both Franklin and Hardy are humbled and intimidated.

For the moment, not prepared for any more adventure, Representative Knight looks back and forth, taking in the landscape. The river, with the woods lining both sides, stretches up and down for a few miles in each direction. A particularly rural stretch of the Arkansas; no buildings, no farms, no water towers hidden in the trees. Not one curve. Not one bend. Dead straight in both directions. The other side—too far to swim across—the trees are thick. The river itself is empty. Nothing except for one gnarled tree branch moving downriver, trapped in the river's pace. Above, circling turkey vultures ride the thermals coming off the river.

"I think maybe you're too young to see this river for what it truly represents." Knight's words quietly interrupt the silence. "I think it takes age to see this for what it is. I wonder."

Once you've arrived at a destination, when you're finally there, it changes things. It might change the reason you've set out in the first place. In the satisfying wonder of the moment, Representative Knight considers some kind of reassurance that he's here in some unique way. He does feel transformed by the immensity, perhaps. He feels changed, hopefully. But following the initial experience, the great power of the river, he senses the familiar, unwelcome enemy and friend slipping back into the perfect achievement of this moment. His arduously cultivated cynicism—perfected over years of practice—is invading the spectacle. It's the image of a river. A photo of himself standing at the edge of the great American river. It could be good. A small pamphlet, a press kit, prove once and for all…

"How old are you, Hardy? Sixteen? Seventeen?"

"I'm twelve, Sir."

"For hundreds of years, thousands of people struggling to survive crossed this river and headed west. Searching for a better life. Fighting the wilderness. You and I, we've lost touch, lost any connection to what this river truly is. This river…" Knight takes a deflated breath, realizing he has no real connection to the words falling out of his mouth. The metaphors materialize as if on their own, from a master list of narrative passages. The weight of this reckoning moves through his body. It was only moments ago, standing at the river's edge, he was the conqueror.

"Mr. Knight, lighten up. We walked all that way to get here. It wasn't that easy to get through those woods. Anybody would say that. And, we made it out here, and what a great view. We did it. You should be happy you got what you were looking for. That's what I think."

Knight's shoulders slump. His body is heavier now. The moment has clearly passed. He looks down to muddy shoes. Deflated by the familiar shallowness of his introspection. It doesn't come as a complete surprise.

Looking in the direction upriver, the dazzling, splintered sunlight patterns dance across the surface. This light show spectacle is mesmerizing. Knight squints his eyes to get the full effect. At this most perfect hour of the day, with this clear-sky sun at the perfect angle, the combination is an otherworldly opera of pulsing, patterned waves of light. Knight imagines the patterns are communicating something of a higher order, a metaphysical puzzle, or presence, or something. A distraction.

The sun's pure, harsh light and the silence of the air pass through him as he stands there. In truth, he feels weakened by the walk through the woods; knee strain, lower back pain, the slightest of chest pain.

He's also aware that the physical exhaustion is more than the walk through the woods. The deeper exhaustion from months of performing the role he's created for himself: the honest and diligent politician who's driven by moral integrity. The drudgery of the weeks of campaigning, the long drive in the Winnebago. The weight of it all has landed squarely on his sixty-year-old body.

"Maybe I should sit. I'll just sit here for a few minutes," he says to no one, maybe to Hardy beside him.

"That's probably a good idea, Sir." Hardy steps closer and comes around to face Mr. Knight. "Here, sit on this." He takes off his windbreaker, folds it into a sitting cushion, and puts it on the ground behind Mr. Knight. "Here, let me help you." He takes Mr. Knight's arm and helps him sit on the ground.

"This is a good place to be sitting." Knight's voice sounds weak. "Out in this fresh air, just a moment to rest." Knight tries to convince himself. He looks up at Hardy, who is standing in front of him. "You should sit down too. This is a good place to sit, especially with the snakes behind us." His tone is defeated. Knight is surrendering to the dialogue of uselessness; *what have I ever done?*

The back of his head and the tops of his shoulders feel the weight most deeply. "I don't feel well. Not well at all," Knight says slowly to himself. He bends his neck and shoulders back to look straight up to the sun. A painful straightening.

"This is not my age showing. That bullshit my opponents like to throw at me." He takes a shallow breath. Knight feels the tightness in his chest. The chest pain is more than a little familiar and alarming. *Should I do something?* He drops his face into his palms; his vision is becoming blurred. *This is the last thing I need right now.* "Did I eat lunch? Did I have breakfast?" he grumbles, just barely out loud.

Hardy puts his hands on his waist and takes short pacing steps back and forth, trying to think this through. "Sir, you're going to be fine. This will just last a few minutes, and then we'll head back." He stops his pacing and stands in front of Knight. "Mr. Knight"—he leans in—"maybe sit up straight and take deep breaths." Hardy can barely conceal his twelve-year-old's nervousness as he sees Mr. Knight sink deeper. "I'm going to get you some help. You sit here and breathe, and do not get up and start walking around."

Hardy feels the edge of panic creeping in. *Get help from where? There is absolutely nothing around here.* "Mr. Knight, do you think this might be a heart attack or something like that?" He immediately regrets asking it.

In a staccato voice, Knight fires back with obvious impatience: "I don't know what this is, but I don't like it, and frankly, I'm getting more than a little concerned, frankly annoyed. Let's get back up to the Winnebago. Help me back to the Winnebago," he manages, over his heavy breathing. "Alright, so this is the river. Enough, I've had enough. What a regrettable, frankly, what a tremendous..." Knight tries to stand, gets halfway up, then sits right back down. The weakness in his body is suddenly disturbing. "Maybe call someone. Give... what's his name? What is his name? Give him a call."

"Sir, we didn't bring the phone." Hardy knows the danger is real. The day has changed, they're in trouble. He surprises himself; he reaches over to Mr. Knight's shoulder and holds his hand there for a moment. Less sure; he begins to take short, slow steps in a tight circle in front of Mr. Knight. His thoughts are racing. He thinks of his dad, even hears his voice. He stops in place and looks out to the river. Mr. Knight's breathing is loud. He will have to do something.

What? Instinctively, looking around—as anyone would—he looks up and down the river. Out of the blue, there's a small boat. "Holy shit."

Hardy stares out at the river for a full minute. "Sir, there's a boat. It might be coming in our direction. Should I try to get their attention?"

Knight doesn't respond. Hardy has the momentary relief that he might actually get help. It seems far-fetched; a boat with strangers. He's now alternating between hovering over Mr. Knight and checking to see the progress of this little boat coming down the river toward them. *Stay calm. Stay calm,* he repeats like a mantra. Whatever this boat might be, it's giving him a sense of confidence. He'll figure this out. With no hesitation, he squats down directly in front of Mr. Knight, almost face-to-face. "Mr. Knight, what a great walk in the woods. You're a strong man. We'll sit here for a minute and let you rest." He keeps his face no more than a foot from Knight's for several long breaths.

Knight watches Hardy speak; he watches his expressions. But the boy's face is caught, centered in a bright halo of brilliant sunlight. Representative Knight and Hardy stay connected for several long breaths. "Son, I need to get you back," Knight says in a strangely mumbled tone.

Hardy hears these words. He stands up straight to check on the boat. He knows what needs to be done.

Chapter Three

It takes time to know a stranger

"Hello!" Hardy calls out to the boat on the river.

The boat's too far away. After a minute or two he waves his arms above his head, the universal gesture, hello, come, help. He waits for any kind of response. The thought crosses his mind to not act too crazy—maybe just one arm. Another minute and still no response. Not quite a mile, he can see what looks to be three people in the boat. It looks like it might come down the river this way. There's no sound of a motor, it might be drifting.

Not directly overhead, the intense sunlight is making blinding sparkles across the entire stretch up and beyond the boat. You can't look straight at it. The reflections make the little boat look like it's floating on a river of sparkling light. It's impossible to tell for sure how fast or slow it's coming or which direction it's actually pointed. Maybe it's coming this way.

Hardy turns to check on Mr. Knight. He's sitting with his knees up and his arms around his knees, with his head buried in his arms. He's resting, at least sitting still.

The little boat coming down the river toward them will take some time. Hardy looks around in every other direction for any sign of anything. There's nothing, an empty river in all directions except for the one small boat. Nothing along the sides and nothing in the sky except for the vultures up in the thermals.

After several long minutes, the boat has made considerable progress. The people in the boat must be able to see him on the shore. He tries the one arm waving again. They have to be able to see him.

More time passes, and it looks like the boat has shifted its direction. The waving worked. The little boat is coming directly toward him on the ridge. As it gets closer, Hardy can see two men. They're sitting, and they're rowing. They're pulling on wooden oars, and they're pulling them hard. A third man is standing straight up at the front, and he's holding one hand above his head, palm out—the universal gesture. We're coming as fast as possible.

Okay, this is going to work, Hardy thinks. What a relief! He walks partway down the slope to the river, a better spot for whatever might happen next when they get to the shore, right below him. "Oh shit, what have I done?" he says under his breath.

From about a hundred feet away, the man standing at the front of the boat yells out to Hardy, "You need help?"

"Yes, I believe we do need help," Hardy shouts back, trying not to appear panicked.

"Help? Is that what you need?"

"Yes, please help us."

"Yes, we're hurried. We'll catch ya."

With the shouting, Representative Knight lifts his head and looks back and forth between Hardy and the men in the approaching boat. *Strangers? At a time like this?* "This is not a good idea, not at all," he manages to say out loud. Hardy hears this but doesn't turn away from the man in the front of the boat.

With the boat now so close, Hardy feels a flush of panic.

Several more minutes, and the boat with the three strangers bumps into the shore. The man who was standing in front jumps out and pulls the boat a few feet up onto the bank. It's not very big, but it's heavy. As he turns back around to face Hardy, he says in a much more subdued tone, "Blessed be, Son. What's going on here? What seems to be the problem here, with the waving and such?" He shows only the slightest tinge of authentic concern.

Hardy stares, a little too long, a little too dumbfounded. It's the way they look... *What's the first thing to say?*

He's caught in the middle of an awkward situation. He can sense it; he knows it. *Strangers on a river, way out here in these backwoods, nobody else around for miles. In every single show, these characters are one or the other: the dirty, pervert murderer or the dirty, kind-hearted old guy with a fifth-grade education who wants to help but can't figure out how but eventually does.* He gives a quick glance back to Mr. Knight for some advice. *He doesn't look well, it's serious. He needs help, some kind of doctor. The Winnebago is way too far back through the woods. What would Mr. Knight expect? Just how much to say to these strangers? He is an important man. That's important. If we go back to the Winnebago, it'll be another hour or even more to get back to the nearest town. In Fullerton, people don't help people. That's the way it is. Policemen, firemen, maybe a bus driver—anyone else is weird. Look at this guy. This is it. Time's up. Say something. Maybe this guy can be trusted. This will probably work out.* "Well, Sir, this is an important man. Thank you for coming over here. We're having a health problem. We need to get to a doctor."

"An important man, you say? Well, this is a difficult situation, one way or the next, a hard time this."

The Stranger's voice doesn't feel right; it's not just the British accent.

"Let's take stock then, shall we?"

The Stranger stands, straightening himself and the long coat he's wearing. He's considering, assessing: "If we took the regular approaches, we'd certainly have to get him to a doctor, the closest one to be had." As the Stranger takes a few steps closer, he looks Hardy dead straight in the eye and then at Knight sitting on the ground, back and forth, back and forth. At about the third or fourth step, he offers a plan. "Come," he says in a peculiar, careful tone. "Help me get the gentleman into our sturdy, humble craft, and we will get him to a doctor as quickly as we can. It's my fortunate understanding there is a medicine facility just down the river, one mile or two by the crow."

The Stranger steps next to Hardy and speaks to him out of the corner of his mouth. "You're right to have caught our attention, Son," he says while he keeps his eye on the Representative who is watching and has decided not to speak. Hardy watches the man out of the corner of his eye.

Not a hundred percent sure about any of this, Hardy and the Stranger walk the rest of the way up the bank. When the Stranger reaches Knight, he stands for a short moment, then bends to lift Knight under one arm and gestures to Hardy to do the same under the other arm.

"Are you sure about this?" *It doesn't feel right.* Hardy takes another quick look at the two men in the boat and decides he'll give it one more minute. If he puts his hands under Mr. Knight's arm to lift him up, it'll be the commitment to whatever this is going to be. He will get in this boat on the river, with Mr. Knight and these three strangers and the man who is wearing a long coat. *Where would you even get a coat like that? It's dark gray. It looks heavy, hot. And it's fairly dirty, but it is a river, so things get dirty. The hat is the strangest part, like an old uniform. It's not a California hat; it's kind of dirty too. The pants seem normal enough, I guess, and the boots are weird but not too weird. He's maybe thirty. He definitely needs a shower and a shave. His face is okay. But I sure can't tell what he's thinking.* "Sir, do you honestly believe this is our best option?" Hardy asks the Stranger one last time in his best adult voice.

Right away, the stranger reaches over to shake Hardy's hand. "My name is William Morgan, Son. It's a daring stretch of river; undercurrents will grab you, take you under like a wicked wife. I've been up and down this river from time to time, and I know it well. I do believe we will find the medicine tents not too far off in that direction, down the river. I suggest we get going. By the looks of him, I'd say there's no time to be putting it off." Immediately a kind man. Hardy reaches out to shake William's hand, which they do with good, moderate enthusiasm. They both nod.

As they reach down to take hold under Knight's arms, he tries to stand up and shrug them off. "I don't know who you are. Soap is humanity's greatest invention. Where's my staff?"

Knight manages to stand, and he tries to turn around, to look around. Turning makes him dizzy, and his knees get wobbly. He collapses a bit but is caught under both arms by Hardy and William. The three of them walk slowly down to the boat. Hardy and William on either side of Knight, helping him down.

Representative Knight looks straight out at the river as they walk him down the slope. He is mumbling words that are somewhat disconnected, but his voice is oddly calm, convincing, and straightforward. "This damn river... more exercise than I've had in months, chapter by chapter... those poor souls. If you get me a decent place to sit, I can do my breathing exercises... I know where this is going, where this boat is headed…"

Hardy sees Knight's condition as worsening, worse than just ten minutes ago. He's lucky William came along when he did.

As he is helped into the boat, Knight becomes very quiet. He doesn't say a word. William, with Hardy's help, maneuvers Representative Knight into a sitting position in the front of the boat. He is definitely not happy about it, but he goes along with it nonetheless. He barely moves. Hardy sits next to him on a wooden seat at the front. He takes a quick glance at the two others in the boat. They watch him. The boat is wood; that's unusual.

With three wooden seats, the length of the little boat is maybe twenty feet long, head to toe. Hardy considers how it looks handmade. It's made by someone's skilled hand. Made of rough-cut wood, probably Northern cedar. Three seats: the middle for rowing, wide enough for two or three with the oarlocks on either side. The oars, about ten feet. The rear for steering with a wooden rudder, with enough of a pole to get a good hold, and the front seat for observing. The bottom of the little boat is as flat as flat gets.

"Have you seen a sturdy pint of a boat like this before?" William asks Hardy. "It's a typical flat-bottomed river boat, made for a river just as this. It's called a bateau."

There's no other way to put it; the bateau stinks. Dead fish, moldy rotting wood, and other unmentionables. The wood of the seats is rough; all the wood is rough, and the seats will provide splinters if not careful. Long, thick splinters. Painful.

It is definitely the crudest excuse for a boat I've ever seen, Hardy decides.

Knight is facing the woods. He stares deep into the trees with no expression on his face, resigned but observant.

William steps back out of the bateau and shoves it off into the river as he jumps back in. He walks to the back of the bateau, stepping over the middle seat between the two other men, and gets himself into position. He sits and takes the rudder pole to guide the bateau through the wicked wife's undercurrents, which the river is anxiously waiting to provide.

The minute the little boat breaks contact with the muddy shore, Hardy is flooded with doubt and a nervous stomach. Suddenly, a ticking clock. Only one more minute to change his mind. *Now or never. Thirty seconds.* There's a small sapling, an oak sapling—more of an upright twig—growing a little too far out from the shoreline. As the boat backs away from the shore, Hardy passes right next to it. He reaches out and lets his hand brush one of only half a dozen leaves. Stay in the boat.

Once Hardy has helped the Representative get as comfortable as he can, he turns around to get a good look at the two men sitting directly behind him holding the oars. They're also wearing dark coats, which are more than a little dirty. He doesn't want to stare, but these two men are an exceptional sight. For anyone.

"Good afternoon," one of the dark-coated men suggests, with zero enthusiasm and no offer of a handshake.

"Yes, good afternoon," the other dark-coated man offers. Their voices are unusual as well.

"We having a bit of a problem, are we?" one of them says.

"I'm Jack. And this... this, I'm afraid, is... well, this is also Jack. Yes, we're both named Jack."

The humor feels cold, which makes Hardy even more anxious about this entire situation. In this awkward moment, Hardy has no idea what is expected, so he waits for the next clue—anything. He senses they're not waiting for a reply from him, so he takes the chance to look more closely. They're all three about the same age, thirty-something. They don't look like they're related. They all need a bath.

"Alright, enough of the comedy," William tells the two Jacks with a bit of irritation. "You two powder monkeys get us back out there. Let out the true colors, gents, shall we? We have to get straight away downriver. We have an important gentleman here in need of some medical attention."

"Right away, Captain," the two Jacks answer in unison, followed by an under-the-breath chuckle from the more talkative Jack with brown hair. The other Jack has red hair.

Hardy hears the chuckle and thinks; *this better be right. This better be what it's supposed to be, or I'm in a lot of trouble.* "So, how long do you think before we get to this hospital? Do you think?" he asks William.

"Once round that bend,"—William's pointing—"and we'll most likely come up on it, all being equal. I don't want you bothered. There's nothing tricky or thorny. You're too young. Let me take charge here. You look after the old man."

Hearing the words "old man," Knight suddenly explodes. "You men are criminals! What happened to the Winnebago?" He is obviously struggling. "This may be right, but it isn't. In no way did I give my permission for this little boat trip on the river."

"We're going to take this boat." Hardy puts both hands on Mr. Knight's shoulders. "We're going straight to some sort of doctor's office," he tells him, trying to be encouraging enough for them both.

"Yes, Sir, we sure are," William offers, his voice not quite sincere. He looks away several times as he speaks. "We're in the fastest boat currently on the river. Fastest we've seen, anyway. A keelboat drags. They're heavy, really only good for dry goods and pelts and a boatload of misery, deadbeat sailors, Africans and English women with powder. And yes, we're headed straight for the medicine tents, just as your son says."

With Hardy's hands on his shoulders and a stiff neck and back, Knight does his best to turn to look back at William.

"Your son says you're an important man," William says, staring directly at Knight. "Isn't that a pickle?" prodding around for some kind of clue, "what kind of important man might you be, I wonder."

Hardy turns quickly to look at William. "I'm not his son."

In the event of encountering strangers on the river, everyone is at the same advantage of disadvantage. The safest protocol is to keep as guarded as one can without appearing to conceal something, which will be construed as competition or a threat. If you're not accustomed to this, you're immediately an outsider and untrustworthy, not to mention at risk. Knight and Hardy fall into this category. Representative Knight might have a bit of an advantage if the time comes. He'll default to his sophisticated District of Columbia skills: garble and obscure, or, if pressed, puzzle and mystify. If the point in question devolves into some version of a narrative, throw in the appropriate number of red herrings to bury it all in a clever confusion that leaves the opponent feeling as though the truth has been revealed, but much later they'll come up empty-handed and not even know it. On the river, it is never assumed that everyone is above board.

"I have connections." Fueled with a bit of anger, Knight gets the words out clearly. "That's how important I am. I'm an elected official of the people. And the three of you are in serious trouble if you think you can kidnap a United States Congressman. I can also tell you that by now there are people out here looking for me, most likely FBI."

"Sir, with all due respect," Hardy tells Mr. Knight as calmly as he can, "these three men are trying to help you. They are taking you to a hospital. Remember, you don't feel well, and this might be serious. It's not what you think." He's watching William's reaction as he's speaking.

"Criminals say one thing and immediately do the opposite; that is science," Knight says as forcefully as he can.

"Criminals?" William quickly spits back, revealing more emotion than he had planned. "What do you know about criminals? How much time have you spent in battle, getting your head shot off, spilling your brains for tomorrow's supper?"

"The battle metaphor, really? Is that where you want to take this?" Knight's skill is kicking in. "Let me tell you, Sir Long Coat, I am a member of the history intelligentsia. I carry with me an encyclopedia of history. I don't get the opportunity to draw upon it often, but when the occasion arises, I am not ill-prepared. And you, Sir, are hardly the soldier. That is immediately the character you present, if we're getting to know each other." Knight turns away to confirm his upper hand. "Use your metaphors wisely."

"Sir, you're not well," Hardy is now pleading. "Please, you gotta take it easy. Don't get worked up. It's going to be okay. We'll get to the hospital. They'll check your heart, and these men will go their separate ways. You don't remember how far from the Winnebago we walked. It was pretty far. It's too far to go back. We are pretty lucky these guys picked us up."

Until this point in the crosstalk, both Jack and Jack have stayed out of it, except for the occasional grumble. With the mention of the Winnebago, one of them—Jack, with the pronounced head of red hair—turns around to look at William.

"What exactly is going on here?" It's not a pleasant tone.

"Winnebago? Is that the name of your boat?" William asks. "Is that how you came this way up the river? I know you didn't come downriver. We came all the way down from the Osage Territory. That's quite a ways west."

Jack, with the brown hair, has stayed hunched over most of the time, squinting his eyes, suspicious of the entire exchange. He's obviously tired. The way he leans on his oar, one of his arms hangs down to his side, and he's losing patience with these two characters from... wherever they're from.

With each rejoinder, Knight is regaining his strength. Dialog is adrenaline. "A Winnebago is not a boat, you moron. It's a camper van. With amenities. For your information, we've come all the way from Southern California." Knight is now feeling his pounding heart. "Up river? I've been up every river there is. There will always be criminals like you up every river." Knight's rubbing his chest.

William is losing his patience as well. "Up river? So you're saying you have been farther up the Arkansas River. How far up river? As far as the Quapaw? The Kiowa? As far as the Osage? And by whose orders put you on the side of the river, waiting for a boat like this one to pass by? How far up, Gran'dad? This is an important question. Consider it well."

Familiar names, Native American names. Tribes. Representative Knight knows the names, maybe not with any amount of detail. William's listing the names of tribes in his British accent. Knight's lost his place in the bickering.

The questions and the accusations being tossed back and forth have finally drawn the other Jack—with brown hair—fully into the banter. Perhaps he's been waiting for the opportune moment, the height of the swordplay. He jumps in, offering a comical tone, "Oh yeah, he's a criminal. I'm a criminal, and Jack here, he's a criminal. No doubt about that. William's been a criminal for, well, let's say, two years, five months and seventeen days, give or take a hen's tooth. A boat full of criminals, a prize carnival."

"I don't think we need to be offering that information," red-haired Jack tells him. "It's far too soon. Relations are not yet established."

The bateau is no more than a few hundred yards from the spot on the shore where they pushed off. The rowing has been sporadic, to say the least.

"You may think I don't know what's going on here," Knight says, believing he's being crystal clear and consciously lowering the vitriol. "I don't know. Maybe I do know. The one thing you should know is to turn this boat around and get me back to the Winnebago."

Red-haired Jack pulls on his oar. Nothing more to add. He's finished with the squabbling. He'll stay out of it.

Brown-haired Jack can't help himself. "Old William here got himself nicked, back in Wales. Some regular drinkin' bout, ladies and other riffraff, no doubt. The dark side, you see. He got himself impressed. That's for sure the way it went. That's what they call it when you get yourself caught up with the authorities, you see. Impressed." He uses one hand to brush the hair out of his face. The other arm hangs oddly limp to his side. "They impress you right into the Navy, buttoned and brothered. So you see, Mr. Encyclopedia; crim - in - al!"

"Criminals don't belong anywhere. The Navy is a sacred occupation,"

Knight says as he drops his head to look away, looking at the bottom of the boat. "The Navy is a sacred occupation. Heroes are made in the Navy, not your common thief."

Knight never exactly served, or at best, his service is sketchy. At various points in his campaign, he's made vague claims of service, but they have never been distinct enough to warrant any type of confirmation. Garble and obscure.

Representative Knight associates himself with the ideals of the armed forces, the history of combat, and the righteous battles for territory and independence, self-determination, and freedom. The campaign for the higher ideals will forever remain the preamble of the greater American ideal. Representative Knight embraces it, maybe not directly, and avoids defining the particularly sticky points.

The bateau is not cooling down.

William feels he's forced to strategize his options, which means he has to reveal more than he'd like. "No doubt you've come upriver, and that's a shame. You've come up past the Spanish; they've let you pass."

"William is most definitely Navy press-gang," brown-haired Jack carries on. "Came across on the Prince George. Not much of a ship. Mostly dressed for battle, not so much for comfort. The old lady could do a hundred miles a day in full sail. I do confirm, Sir." Brown-haired Jack is speaking directly at Knight's back. "William is your common 'quota man.' In my mind, I do believe that makes him a criminal."

William ignores Jack's intrusions and attempts to stay on strategy. "I don't recognize your uniform, old man. What is this dark rope around your neck?" Obviously, referring to Knight's tie. "Some type of officer's ornament? I don't recognize it, but that's my weakness. And my weakness is no way a proof that you're not here, in this very boat, in the service of His Royal Highness."

At the beginning of the sparring match, Hardy turned back and forth between William and the two Jacks and Knight sitting next to him. None of it made much sense, but he felt it important to follow along. As the talk becomes more confrontational, he stares straight ahead, out at the river. He considers covering his ears with his hands, but it's a little too childish.

Representative Knight, master of duplicitous rhetoric, is forced to respond but wobbles a bit, "What highness you're referring to could only be…"

"That's right, old man, take a look!" William bolts upright and barks his order directly at Knight. "Stand up and take a look."

Knight accepts the challenge. He turns in his seat—managing to avoid splinters—and looks back to see what William is insisting.

William starts to unbutton his dirty, dark coat, twisting the tarnished top brass button slowly between two fingers, forcing it through the heavily stitched buttonhole. A quick moment of pause to secure Knight's attention, then button by button, the stagecraft of a veteran, one after the other, unbuttoned. In the finale, with both hands, he flings open the long coat to reveal a uniform of the British Navy. More than a little worse for the wear but there it is. "Royal British Navy," he snarls at Knight, "in the service of His Majesty."

Knight's speechless. Every retort he considers comes up short. The coat, the uniform… nothing.

William's uniform is standard issue for the rank of Midshipman, the Navy blue. It's a mid-length topcoat with gold embroidery running down both sides of the lapel. Large golden buttons run the length as well, on both sides. If it were clean and sharpened up, it would be an impressive sight. As it is now, its gritty realism makes it all the more baffling. Knight's dropped jaw and his stunned expression confirm what William has accomplished. The sheep are in the barn. Knight's beaten.

Hardy watches William's performance. His first impression—it's an amazing costume—quickly becomes confusing. It's an odd costume for out here in the middle of nowhere. He looks over to Mr. Knight for some idea of what's happening. The expression on Mr. Knight's face changes everything. Hardy realizes this isn't funny at all.

"This is the last uniform coat I have," William continues to indulge in the drama of his testimony, "given to me directly by King George himself. A bloody strong handshake to boot. Tea was served." But as soon as he says the words, his sarcastic pride turns petty with the thoughts he would just as soon like to forget. His posturing humor turns sour. Memories drift in, and they're difficult to dismiss. Faces covered with blackened dirt.

In a few short breaths, William is changed. The performance is over. His face turns saddened. The look on William's face is not lost on either of the Jacks; the memories are shared. They're fresh. The nightmare behind the sun's sunny day.

"This one issued to me on the docks at Portsmouth," William carries on, which is what a sailor will do. "I had one other, but it's long gone now. I was made to wear this dreadful coat all the way across the Atlantic." William is re-buttoning his coat. He's reconvening the purpose of the moment. "Six weeks aboard that rotten Prince George. I first put this uniform on in January. It might have been February of '79. Glad to have it. It was cold on that stinking ship. That's a long time for one coat, wouldn't you say? Old man?"

With the little energy he has left, Knight stands to face William directly. He's bewildered and confused. It shows in his tired eyes. "What on Earth is going on here?" His voice is raspy, and the words are choppy. "You can't be here with that. What is that thing? What are you supposed to be, and what in God's name are you talking about?"

"British Royal Navy." William answers with a robust but deflated pride.

Representative Knight shifts his weight, which gives the bateau a quick bit of rocking, sending ripples out from the sides. He looks down at the two Jacks on the middle seat. The two of them take their turn opening their dark and dirty topcoats. Brown-haired Jack uses only one hand to unbutton. They whip open the coats, showing Knight their Royal Navy uniforms, but with only an understudy's effort, they don't bother to stand.

The ill-at-ease, the confusion, and edgy distrust is thick. There is nothing of any clarity to say; there's nothing to do that will untangle this puzzle. Equal mistrust all around. The river holds them all captive in the bewildering twist of plot.

When the round has settled and the air sits quiet for a moment, brown-haired Jack feels the need to stir it one more round, one more time for effect, "Midshipman Jack..." He gestures. On cue, they both pull open one side of their top coats to reveal—stashed into the inside coat pockets—impressively sizeable knives. Scottish Highlander knives, they're not standard issue, but among the regiments, they're common. About ten inches long with decorative patterns carved in the bone handle. The blades are clearly sharp. They're maintained, and they are definitely threatening, especially to Knight, to whom they're directed.

Knight turns to Hardy, looking for any type of explanation, completely unhinged. "Did you know about this? Are you part of this?"

"Sir, I'm just a kid." Hardy tries not to show his eyes tearing up. "Sir, I can't tell what anyone is talking about. Jesus, Mr. Knight, I'm only a kid." He looks out to the river. There's nothing there.

"I can tell you what we're talking about, Son." William takes control of the moment to summarize the various proposals for crosstalk and threats. He has no further interest in or need to conceal any part of his identity from the elected official. "We're talking about the British Navy, who are assembling their fleet down at the mouth of the Mississippi, which is exactly where we're headed—not far from here, not far at all. I can tell the two of you." William is aggressively jutting his head forward at Knight. "You're not going back the way you came."

Knight hears William's words. His mind is picking through what makes sense; any amount of sense. He can't quite come up with anything coherent. No words for a response.

Hardy hears William's declaration, and he sits up straight on his seat. He cocks his head slightly, just enough for William's benefit. He waits one more second for his part to play. "You don't know anything about us," he tells William with the conviction of a young man's determination.

Without hesitation, William's reply is softened ever-so-slightly for Hardy, "That is accurate young man, but I can't have your old man here, who you say is not your father, speaking to his officers about the three men you came across one day on the Arkansas; that won't go well for us."

"Not well at all," both Jacks say in unison.

Chapter Four

The scars left behind

The air is hot until the sun passes behind the clouds rolling in. In this part of the country, they're called thunderheads—more drama from overhead. The bateau is finally making decent progress, keeping a steady pace. In spite of the cramped quarters and the heated episodes of frustration, the threats and counterthreats, sometimes tempered with restraint, some progress is being made. In a small boat on a river this size, it's prudent to confirm your alliances. They might save you from what lies ahead. The river, however, maintains its prolonged and overwhelming disinterest. Unperturbed and moving as one massive continental flow. The swirls and the patterns that form and reform across the surface might have something to add, but for now they go unnoticed.

The thought crosses William's mind that he might have played his cards a little too soon. The British Navy can be very inventive when planting its spies and infiltrators. They can put on a decent act. He recalls a memory of a situation not too long ago in the company of another strangely proper gentleman out in the countryside where he didn't belong; his language was more than a little peculiar. He played the scenario well; no one the wiser.

Admittedly, this old man riles him. He might have let his temper push him into revealing his true purpose on the river. It's too late. He's committed himself and his traveling partners to carry the weight of these two strangers on the river, as far as need be.

Knight collapses back onto the wooden seat. He drops his head into his arms, which he's folded on his knees. He speaks down into his body. The others in the boat can barely hear the nearly complete resignation in his voice. "What Navy is going back... The Navy taking me back to the Winnebago?"

Hardy draws his head closer to Knight. He wants to comfort him somehow. He keeps one eye on William. With the layers of suspicion piled up in the boat, he has realized the confusion is not any more or any less troubling for him than it is for the others. And truth be told, Mr. Knight's back-and-forth emotions are probably kind of regular for him. Hardy can see his place in this now, and it's not the role of the child.

Whatever's been said, it's in the past. There's an urgent matter at hand. William's voice flattens to an all-business sincerity. "If the British have come all the way up the Mississippi, to the mouth, and moved up west into the Arkansas, not all that far from where we sit, then we have big troubles. Our paths will cross, and we're most likely lost." William parses his words carefully. "Our one chance is to get to the mouth of the Mississippi first and get downriver, as far south as possible, and no one has words for no one."

William and the two Jacks sit with the idea for a minute or two, running through the river logistics. William is looking at Hardy, wondering if he can appreciate the predicament. Time means everything now.

"This Arkansas is wide; we can slip by them and take it in the night," brown-haired Jack adds.

"Not wide enough, Jack," William tells him.

"True, they'll have to contend with the current." Jack's thoughts rush out of him, piecing together the picture of it. "Depending on how twisted the river is, we could get around them to the outside, but we're nothing to them. They'll be in full flotilla, looking for agitators. They'll have every gun on us. Across the width of this river, it's a sure shot turkey shoot, and we're finished. On the Mississippi, we'd disappear."

Red-haired Jack takes in the logistics; he's had many similar predicaments. He reveals his position on the subject clearly and precisely; he spits over the side.

"They're a ragtag group. That is to our advantage," William continues. "A bunch of Americans and a few French. He's got a dozen or so free slaves joined with him too. To be sure, they can hold their own, load, and reload as fast as the others. It is my sincere belief that Captain James Colbert's been put in charge. It's their best option. He's been around these valley rivers most of his life. He knows the Indians well too, intimately. He's got Chickasaw sons, and more than just a few." William is speaking to everyone in the bateau, but he's directed this particular delivery to both Jacks, and he's looking straight at them. "Colbert is known to go after deserters; that is a fact." William watches their faces register the words. "I'm sure you two gentlemen understand the situation. The British Navy does not treat deserters with much respect. Especially not second-timers."

"We got it, William, one hundred lashes, maybe more. We all three of us know they hang deserters."

"We'll get hanged," red-haired Jack finishes it.

The three of them look at each other's faces, puzzled by their thoughts. Once again, the river turns dark. Without speaking, the reality of their predicament realigns their energies. The two Jacks grab the oars and set to the rhythm of pulling hard. William keeps the bateau in the best, strongest current, avoiding eddies or any other cunning river undercurrents. He watches the shore to measure their progress. He also watches the gaps in the trees and brush for any British or Indian scouts poking out here or there. Mostly, he's looking for any sign that someone has passed through, discarded regiment debris washed up on the mud or torn off pieces of uniform stuck in the branches.

Hardy watches the way William holds his face, his tight, rigid jaw as he studies the shore. His eyes don't relax. They stay concerned, wary of some threat. He has a simple, kind face that he won't show as kind. His brown hair drops to the line of his jaw. And the hat, the strange museum hat that hides a part of his face, makes him seem intent on spotting the next thing to come along. William is not a tall man. His shoulders are broad. His arms are strong. He's been on the river for a good amount of time. It shows in his body and in his face. He can surely lose his temper, which is odd for such an otherwise kind voice. William is two people. One who is forced to confront the threats that the river is fond of throwing up in his face and one who has been the witness to more than his share. If the river would let him, he'd be on his way home.

The break in the cross talk momentarily relieves Knight's struggle, his stupor, and his anxiety. All is not right with these three con men. His expertise is telling him it's a situation of poorly conceived criminal activity. All signs indicate kidnappers. He's had many encounters with the dubious hypocrites of Washington. He's gone toe-to-toe with pathological liars in his law practice. He considers himself gifted at reading the poker player's tell. But his trustworthy gift of catching any overlooked detail is failing him. He's off his game. Now that he has the moment to recompose himself, he's not so much trying to piece together the inconsistencies as he is trying to reassemble his ability to read the situation. They've gone to great effort to concoct this scheme; the uniforms and the ludicrous stories of armies of ships coming and going up and down the river. *What is it they want? Who in God's name would pay a ransom? Alfred?* He looks up and out at the river, avoiding any eye contact.

"If this Captain Colbert's headed up the Arkansas, his orders will put him at the post on the river, Fort Arkansas. We've been through there." Brown-haired Jack returns to the strategy conversation. There's little time to piece together the possibilities. "They'll be bloody set on beating out the Spanish at the fort." He speaks with a serious sailor's conviction, turning his head side to side, making sure his mates catch the brevity of their predicament.

"The Spanish played their hand and took over the fort. They're calling it Fort Carlos the Third," red-haired Jack adds on, with a nastiness he hasn't shown before. "So that's the way it is, and one thing is for certain: Colbert may have his orders, but the man's pride will certainly not give three deserters some pleasure time to rest up and drink what's left over."

"We're not going back." William quietly rests his case.

"Not going back?" Representative Knight has heard his reentry point. "I would strongly encourage that position. Indeed, going back would be a waste of all of our time. Indeed, let's head straight for the rendezvous point. Let's get the exchange over, so we can all get back to regular business. I'm sure they'll pay whatever you're demanding. We won't haggle about that detail of money."

"Silence is preferred," red-haired Jack slurs back at Knight.

It takes considerable effort for William to ignore, yet again, the busy Mr. Knight. He looks to Hardy in the front of the boat and shows him the briefest of a smile, the whispered wink of recognition and sympathy. Kindness. William says to him, "And thus the fear of danger is ten thousand times more terrifying than danger itself." Hardy feels the connection. To be honest, the quote is not at all familiar, but it's a nice feeling.

"No more quotes. In the name of all that is holy," brown-haired Jack wails to the sky above.

"Let's pick it up Gentlemen." William's voice is once again a relief. "Pick up the pace."

With the steady pace, the woods pass quickly. In the moments of quiet,

Hardy sits sideways on his seat to face the woods and picks out the calls of one or two different birds. From this distance only the loudest can be heard: grackles and blackbirds. And sometimes, without staring directly, he watches brown-haired Jack pull his oar. He only uses one hand, one arm. The other sleeve of his coat hangs to his side. The two Jacks have to adjust the strength of their pulling to keep the bateau moving straight. Brown-haired Jack sometimes pulls twice to keep pace with red-haired Jack. In a moment of quiet, Hardy lets his twelve-year-old curiosity slip out. He's been wanting to ask, "What happened there? What happened to your arm?"

"What do you think happened, Son?" brown-haired Jack snaps at Hardy. "What always happens? Musket lead, that's what happened."

He takes two more one-handed pulls with the oar.

"What you got to understand, the musket lead is a dirty whore, the best of the worst. All she wants is to make love with a man's body, find her favorite special place, and tear it open and leave you helpless."

Hardy winces, sorry he asked. Embarrassed, he looks down.

Brown-haired Jack watches Hardy's face for several minutes. His thoughts soften, and he sees only the face of a young boy. That's all he is, just a kid. Jack hears the outright bitter meanness of his words and his voice. It's not who he is. He feels ashamed. In this young boy's face, he sees the faces of the young boys, elbow to elbow, below deck, out of the sunlight, covered with grit, their white eyes in shock from the deafening noise of the cannon fire and the stink of it.

The deadness of shame he feels of himself bleeds through his thoughts. *What business is this for a child? How is it grown men let this happen to these children? When did this world change so much for the worse? Is this British game worth all of that young blood? The grand old gentlemen let this happen; the putrid ideals of the few let this happen, and I'm a part of it.*

Jack takes several more pulls on his oar.

"What I said, Son," he says to Hardy, "I can't apologize cause I'm not the man who said those words. You see, I can't be that man. It's a horrible thought to be that man. I am sorry for what he has said to you. You don't deserve words like that."

Jack stops pulling the oar and lets it hang in the oarlock.

"A young boy should be at home with his mother, playing nine pins or tending chores, not blown apart by thirty-six pounders blasting through the ship's hull. Stuck all full of splinters, bleeding to death off in a dark corner while the rest of them made to carry on or they'd wind up the same. Running gunpowder from the magazines up to the gun deck. Forced or not, they got themselves enlisted, no more than fourteen years old like you."

Jack turns away from Hardy. Face down, he watches his boots. "The history of men is the history of conquering," his voice is beaten. "Taking from the other for the betterment of your own. You don't want to be in the British game, dear brother? Then you put on the turncoat and you wind up on this river, lucky to come across others who carry the shame. The one bit of good fortune is this river will take anybody."

"Both the deserters and the determined, brother," red-haired Jack adds.

"Dictates of Tyrants," William says just under his breath.

Brown-haired Jack takes to the oar. Downriver is their option. He keeps to the rhythm and watches the oar push against the water. He can sense Hardy is watching him. He has that right. The young boy will be troubled to find the right words they can share. Hardy studies the lines in Jack's forehead. It's not much of a struggle to imagine what Jack has said: a ship, with cannons and gunpowder, young boys in the dark smoke, and the loud danger. It surprises him how easily he sees their faces. His heart swells up inside of him. He's not felt this way before. This is a dreadful pain that's very close. He feels the impact of it all. It's not far from here. The effect of Jack's words has changed the way he looks at the three of them. What surprises him is the quickness with which he understands the terrible images Jack's words have put in his mind.

"The gunshots were too deep in your arm," Hardy says to Jack. "Your arm was in bad shape, so they had to take your arm off to save your life. That's what happened. I believe I understand."

"That's pretty much the whole of it, Son. More than you can know, more than I would ever want you to know. I'll tell you what, Son, you call me Jack Lank-Sleeve. How about that? And you call this miserable Molly, you call him Jack Red-Hair. Obvious reasons. How about that? That work for you?"

"Yes, Sir. And I'm sorry for what happened to you. Thank you for telling me your story." Hardy reaches over to Jack Lank-Sleeve's dangling cuff and shakes it like he's shaking his hand. Jack Lank-Sleeve's face opens up with a smile, grateful for any forgiveness.

Representative Knight has been shaking his head back and forth while looking at the wet bottom of the bateau. Back and forth for minutes. The little bit of water in the bottom of the boat swirls around his shoes. He's done his best to keep them out of the mud and out of the water. Now it seems rather pointless. Now that he's been kidnapped.

"Mr. Knight, have you been listening to Jack Lank-Sleeve?" Hardy has faith that Knight will suddenly understand the honesty of Jack and William. It's become his job to find the right words for Mr. Knight to recognize that it's not his fantasy or their fantasy. It's plainly a situation they are all in together, all of them, however they got there and wherever this is.

"Mr. Knight, who do you think William or Jack Lank-Sleeve would contact to arrange this idea of a kidnap?" Hardy takes a chance. "Think about it. It's a crazy idea. How would they talk to them from out here on a river?"

Knight looks up. "Son, you can't know what these criminals are capable of. You're too young. I need you to stay out of this until I ask for your participation. And I need to know if I'm being heard."

"Mr. Knight, honestly, I don't think that's what is going on."

"Petty criminals. It's what I said. I know it. I know the mind of a criminal. The lesser mind is always predictable."

"They're not criminals. I know they're not. How about this? I'll ask William to go to the shore and drop us off." Hardy moves in much closer to Knight. He's speaking in a hushed tone. "They don't need to take care of us. We're in their way. They need to get down this river as soon as they can."

"Son," William tells Hardy, "I wish I could do that, but when the British find you, and they will, they'll have awful ways to make you talk about this trip we're having on the river today. I'm sorry, we'll have to continue on together until we all get a break."

"There it is!" Knight jumps in. "You see, no plan to release the hostage." Knight stands to complete his tirade. "A child would underestimate the criminal mind, but not an adult, not an elected official."

"Son, do your best to keep him quiet," Jack Lank-Sleeve tells Hardy. "Old William's gonna get mean. He just can't help it. With all his time with the authorities, that's where he's learned it. We're going to want to keep him facing the sunny side."

William's temper might well have come from his drunken behavior in years past, confronting the constables in Wales. He is an educated man, but his frustrations and his anger will swell up. How can anyone know why? Months and months up and down the Mississippi and the Arkansas and the Ohio rivers, searching for other kindreds to get overland to Newport. Or find a way down to New Orleans to get on a return ship to England; may be a wild fantasy. The direction of his life now is to make it downriver to get home, take care of his ailing mother. His patience with Knight has gone to the dogs.

"Sir." Hardy is desperate. "They don't know anything about an elected official. They're not from that part of the country. They're from a place, far from this place. They're in the British Navy, but they're way out here on their own. Can't you see that? They're deserters."

"They're not deserters!" Knight yells out. He throws both arms up into the air. "Deserters, my ass. Who would believe that story? Someone in Hollywood, that's who. They're criminals."

William hits his breaking point. His body is full of agitation, which he can barely contain. He stands. He turns to face out to the river, and he kicks the wooden back of the bateau several times. He turns back around and climbs over the middle seat, shoving both Jacks aside. They tried to stay out of his way but weren't quick enough. Thinking he'd heard a comment from Jack Red-Hair, he turns back and shoves him harder a second time. William forces his way directly in front of Knight. He stands for less than the briefest of moments and grabs Knight by both of his upper arms and deadlifts him straight up from where he stands. William looks directly up into Knight's face. With the same force, he slams Knight back into a standing position directly in front of him.

"I've had enough out of you. You understand that, old man? Enough."

William grabs the corner of his hat and yanks it off, throwing it into the back of the boat. And there, on his forehead, is the letter 'D' burned into his skin with a hot iron. The scar it left behind.

"Deserter! Old man. I'm not going back and neither are you."

In a burst of energy, probably more shock, Knight immediately jerks away from William. He pushes William, who falls backward onto Jack. Without thinking, in a sudden impulse, Knight jumps out of the bateau. He doesn't quite make it. His foot catches on the side, and he falls face first into the river and goes right under.

"Mr. Knight!" Hardy yells, getting to the side of the bateau.

When Knight bobs back up, he tries to go directly for the shore, fifty feet away. Knight's attempt at swimming is too out of control to make any real progress. He flaps the water with his arms, trying to get closer. A terrible swimmer. The jacket—his prized Armani—doesn't make it any easier. His shoes make it difficult as well. Hysterical. Between gulps of river water, he is saying, in the same disturbing tone, over and over, "Who do they think I am?"

Hardy yells out to Knight. "Mr. Knight, this river is too strong! You can't make it to the shore. There's no way to get on that shore." Turning to William in a simple and sincere voice, concealing any panic, he asks, "William, can you please help me get him back? I don't think he can swim."

Even with the burst of energy and his impulsive determination to leave them all behind—somehow prove himself—Knight doesn't have the strength required to make progress through the water.

"This is going to slow us down," Jack Red-Hair says to anyone.

"We're going to have to do something," Jack Lank-Sleeve follows.

Knight continues to splash his way, making loud and slow progress, until he reaches the scrub brush lining the river. Which is a miracle.

The river along this piece of shore is deep, and the brush is thick along the edge. Best guess would be red buckeye, sweetshrub, and buttonbush. No thorns, but thick. There's no way to get through this shrub to get to the actual dirt of the shore and out of the river. Knight grabs the branches jutting out several feet and uses them to pull himself along, one branch at a time, making slow progress in his hysterical attempt to find a break in the shrubs. Adding to the chaotic intensity, he can't stop talking. He's repeating, "… British Navy, my ass, deserters, my ass…"

Hardy considers jumping out and going after Knight. He knows he's a decent swimmer. It's not that far. But he waits to see what William will do.

Everyone in the bateau has a different interest in Knight's attempt at escape. With an unsympathetic, casual indifference, William maneuvers the bateau closer to Knight, no more than twenty feet away, following along at the same pace with no real attempt at a rescue.

As Knight is moving from branch to branch, his head bobs periodically—only halfway above the surface—his eyes at the level of the river. Knight is pulling himself along. Each piece of branch takes him only a couple of feet farther downriver, sometimes almost disappearing under the dense overhang of shrub.

Hardy is leaning as far over the side of the bateau as his grip on the raw wood permits. "Mr. Knight. Sir, please! Please come back this way."

Jack Red-Hair's having a great time with Knight's desperation in the audience of the best circus in town. "Pull out the trombones! This show needs a bit more fanfare." He stands and applauds, clapping into the air. He has an obviously foul look on his face. Hardy sees this and recognizes the cruelty.

"We need a drum roll here. He's about to go under."

Both Jacks and William know very well that on this river, the hand of death will reach out and pull you under. Jack's jumping up and down is making the bateau rock wildly from side to side. Only those who have been in the thick of it can have this irreverence for a human life. William widens his stance to stay balanced.

"Mr. Knight, you're going to drown," Hardy yells.

"Let the old man take the deep dive," William says with cold sincerity. "It's better for us."

"William," Jack Lank-Sleeve shouts at him, "you're not as far gone as you're playing it. We both know it. Get over there and get the old man back in the boat. For the sake of the boy, if nothing else."

Hardy has to act; he has to do something. He quickly grabs one oar and tries a few different ways to hold it as far out into the water as possible. It's heavier than it looks.

William says to Hardy, who doesn't hear him, "Let him go, Hardy. You're too young to know the future of it."

Knight's head is bobbing up and down at the water level as he is gasping for breath and spitting out the water he's taken in. He can only see less than a foot in front of him when his eyes are above water. The branches are thick around him, but when he pulls himself up, the river current pulls him down.

With one difficult breath, as his eyes come up—inches above the water line—he is suddenly face-to-face with the rotting head of a dead deer, trapped in the same thick branches. It's only a few inches from his face and covered with maggots.

Knight is paralyzed with sudden shock. His breathing stops. He doesn't move one muscle; the top of his body hangs from the shrub branch, and the river pulls at the rest of him. He stares at the deer head, sickened by it, captured by it. The sight of it, the stink of it. He holds the last breath as his ears pump the sound of his racing heartbeats.

For the first time in this cacophony, there is complete silence in the bateau. Even Jack Red-Hair has suddenly suspended his commotion.

In the pumping sound of his heartbeat, Knight hears the faint sound of Hardy's voice. It becomes more pronounced, more clear. He hears Hardy's words pleading with him. "Mr. Knight, please don't leave me here."

Those words. Knight pulls away from the deer head, he turns toward the boat and sees Hardy reaching over the side with the oar. He moves his body in that direction. The shock is behind him. His body in the water is no longer the hysterical flailing. His body glides toward the bateau as his arms pull him smoothly through the water. The fabric of the Armani helps give him power through the current.

Once Hardy sees that Mr. Knight will save himself, it's a tremendous relief. "Here, Sir, grab the oar. I'll pull you over."

The moment Knight turns back toward the boat, the clarity of his thinking returns to him. He sees his thoughts and the flashes of decisions he's made or tried to make. Everything before the smack of the water is an old man's confusion. His perspective on the entirety of this situation is higher and broader. He's as much at the center of this Jules Verne odyssey as any of the rest of them. All together. All in it together.

He makes it to the side of the boat and grabs Hardy's oar. He says quietly, so only Hardy can hear, "Let's get down this river."

Holding onto the oar at the side of the bateau, Knight looks over to William. "Alright, William the Deserter, help me up." Knight's voice is sincere but not surrendered.

"Get him back in the boat," William says flatly to both Jacks. He's giving them an order.

"Commendable decision," Jack Red-Hair says as they both grab Knight's arms and haul him over the side, back into the bateau.

"Don't do that again, Sir, could you promise us?" Jack Lank-Sleeve says quietly to Knight. "You don't know what you have done to the boy. If you did, you wouldn't have done it." He reaches over with his one hand and scrubs back and forth across the top of Hardy's head. "You see, you've turned his hair whiter than it was already."

Hardy takes off his plaid shirt and uses it to dry off Knight's face. The graphics on Hardy's t-shirt are the "dream catcher" symbol, the hoop with the hawk feathers. Mr. Knight's clothes are soaked. When Hardy reaches over to take the jacket off, Mr. Knight pushes his hand away. The jacket will stay on. "It'll dry better on."

They look at each other. Knight reaches over to Hardy, puts his palm on Hardy's head, and holds it there for a moment, just long enough.

Once Knight is back in the bateau, William sees that his own perspective on their situation is not as sturdy as he had thought. Why should it be? Is Knight really that much of a threat? Who or what has put this man here? Who's decided on this arrangement? These thoughts trouble him now.

William steps back to his place in the back of the bateau. He sits and takes hold of the rudder. *Why would I have considered this Mr. Knight's drowning as something profitable? He's as much a part of this as any of the rest. And the boy, who is not his son, why would he have come along? What kind of fool was I to see these two as spies? That is the nonsense the man Knight was protesting. I have to see this more clearly, have to figure my role in this if this is going to work, any of this. These two are not at all like any of the fellows we've taken up with and seen off. The key is to get down this river. That has to be what all of this is about. For all of us.*

"Alright, well, here we are," Knight says out loud. He pulls and brushes his pants and jacket so they'll dry as straight as possible; they actually feel a cool respite from the sun, and Knight would never concede the responsibility of appearing presentable.

"Shall we proceed?"

"We head down to the Mississippi. That's what we're to do," William says, with a more subtle confidence and a little more respect for what is being shared here in the bateau, on the Arkansas. "And we pray to the good Lord to let us beat the rascal Colbert and his band. That's what we do." He puts one finger to the air. "Thus we never see the true state of our condition till it is illustrated to us by its contraries, nor know how to value what we require but by the want of it."

"Dear Lord, blessed be thy name," Jack Lank-Sleeve begs, "the last of the quotes Dear William, save our souls."

William ignores him, like the dozens of times before. "We row our boat hard. There's not much of a day left for it. Night will be along and slow us, but we'll not get ourselves hanged." Facing both Jacks, he tells them, "Let's get it going, Gentlemen, to the Mississippi or to the noose."

The river is dead flat. Moving as one giant body. Still, no interest in the bateau. Night is coming fast. It could be that a slight breeze has picked up from behind.

Chapter Five

Off to better worlds

The early morning light. Finally, the dawn battles back and fills the airy space with cool whiteness. One more time, with determination rewarded, the night's monotony is in retreat. Up and down the river, all souls share the mixed blessing of relief that they've made it through one more night. And the anxiety for what the river will bring in the light of the new day. The river surface is painted by the sureness of the morning sky until the first oar breaks through and the dark spreads out underneath.

First to let their presence known, the crows bark in the trees, a flash of black here and there. Be it known, intruders, you are being watched, a harsh morning's alarm for those in the bateau letting go of sleep. But, certainly a reprieve from a long night of uncomfortable sitting and persistent worry. All on board are chilled to the bone. William guides the bateau from the back. He's hunched over, buried in his coat to keep himself warm. He's exhausted. Of the group, his night was the longest.

William lets Jack Red-Hair know it's his turn at the rudder. They both stand and painfully straighten the night from their spines and then switch seats, careful to keep balance.

"I'm thirty-three," Jack Red-Hair says to William, obviously humbled by the long night. "A body stiff from a night without a good mattress and bed is not a welcome day. I feel as old as the old man."

"It's no easier for me, Jack. I'd surely take leaves on the ground," William tells him. "We could pull up and sleep one or two nights on the ground, but the time lost could cost us more than an old man's back."

Jack Lank-Sleeve has given his coat to Representative Knight and Hardy. They huddle underneath it like a tent, the musty, damp wool preferable to the night's chill. Knight is awake, but he lets Hardy stay asleep at his side. William sits down next to Hardy and looks to Jack Lank-Sleeve up front; a transfer of the watch. He buries his head into his knees with a mighty exhale.

As Jack Red-Hair steers and rows from the back, Knight asks him, in an early morning hush and nearly all animosity gone from his voice, "I don't really know how long you might have been on this river. Why would I even ask, but what do you three eat?"

"Maybe you noticed we don't have muskets. No deer. No squirrel." Jack Red-Hair leans in. His intense mistrust is now a weary bitterness. "With a little luck, all over this valley you'll find Americans dug in here and there. Some places, they've made villages. Not so much villages, more like a few houses strung together in a hole they've managed to cut out of the woods. Those who haven't run off to join militia stay behind with their families and have to barter with anyone passing through. One day it's the Chickasaw and the next the Quapaw, depending how close to the river. Sometimes even a few Osage will make it down this far. Guard the children." He lets a pause sit in the morning air, but not too long.

"The Americans in the Valley are very good at performing relations, and they'll be on the sure side of anybody passing through, lessons learned through tremendous sacrifice and great hardship. Those performances have to be razor sharp. You could call it the true best theater. They'll pull out the drums and fifes when the Brits pass through. The arrogance of the British will demand everything, or burn it black to the ground."

From the front of the bateau, Jack Lank-Sleeve pulls a sliver of dried, hard meat from his inside coat pocket and hands it to Knight. "Salted pork. You can thank the Americans, those who find true favor in men like the three of us. And they're generous too. It's mostly dried meat, but sometimes cooked roots and maybe a meaty stew. Some out here can get flour that's come up river. Time to time there will be some baked donations, which is a very fine day. These folk know who they can trust. We only have a home-bound agenda. And we're not the only ones, Sir. There are packs of deserters running through these woods and up and down these valley rivers."

Generally speaking, people are most easily talkative in the early morning and just at the start of the night. Representative Knight feels the toughness and the weight of the hard meat. It has sharp edges.

"It's jerky. That's what it is, Seven Eleven jerky."

"I have only a small portion left," Jack Lank-Sleeve adds, "give some to the boy. You'll have to wait for a more generous piece until we get down to the Mississippi. It has the saltpeter. We rubbed down the pork with a bit of gunpowder when we had it. It should still be good. He needs it more than you."

"You know," Jack Red-Hair wants to keep it going, "I miss the good old days of firecake." A welcomed but utterly tasteless mix of flour and water cooked over open fires. "Anybody else?"

"Firecake was better than starving." Jack Lank-Sleeve is genuinely fond of early morning chit chat.

"The good old days," Jack Red-Hair adds, "back when your brain started shrinking from the starving. Correct me, it might have been on the ship coming over. Either way, you've had a shrinking brain for quite some time."

"The good old days, out of food, out of luck," Jack Lank-Sleeve adds on.

With this particular sunrise, William is very much aware that the primary business is to get downriver to the mouth of the Mississippi and beat the odds. If rumors prove correct, they'll need to accomplish this distance before they meet Captain James Colbert and his makeshift regiment coming up river, most likely to the Arkansas Fort, which would be unfortunate. If they can get past Colbert at the fort and get out on the Mississippi, they'll need to disappear into the rest of the traffic moving up and downriver and conceal themselves from any British, or Spanish, or anyone favoring war over commerce. It's not a small amount of business.

Of the three, William—despite his temper—is the given leader. But what he doesn't know is the true gauntlet of the Mississippi's challenge.

Every trader on the river must stop at each of the many posts and present proper passports and pay the duties. If you try to run it or are unable to present papers, the cargo is confiscated, and your crew is either imprisoned or sent back, on foot, through the woods, which is not a good reward.

No matter how impenetrable this gauntlet, as always on the river, those clever enough will succeed. While some commerce is a lost cause, there is a good deal of smuggling, and some smugglers get downriver like thieves in the night. With a good plan and steady nerve, you can make it all the way to New Orleans. William can certainly rise to the Mississippi's challenge. He's sensed it coming. The first order of business is to get down the Arkansas to the mouth.

It's not a small amount of business.

With full morning light squarely on the bateau, Hardy drops the heavy coat and stretches his arms out to meet the day.

"Good morning, Son." Other versions of good morning come from everyone.

"Hey, good morning." Hardy gives a big smile all around. "That was a long night. I could hear you guys." Hardy stands to stretch his legs and look around. He looks down the river. It's still so far. Then rubs his hand along the shoulder of Mr. Knight's jacket. "It's getting there. I think crows just don't like people." Hardy turns around to look back up the river. "I guess we've come pretty far, right? When I was first waking up, I wasn't sure, you know…"

"Sure about what, Son?" Knight looks up at him.

"You know, sure we'd still be here. On the river, in this trip."

"Well, Son, we don't know…"

"It's okay, Mr. Knight. I'm kinda glad we're still on the river. It's better than Fullerton. Nothing happens there. And where else are you gonna share a crappy wooden boat with a one-armed sailor?"

"Alright, take it easy on me, you dog." Jack Lank-Sleeve takes a fake swipe at Hardy's head. "Now take a seat. We're serving dried pork for breakfast, and you're right on time."

Knight hands Hardy the last piece. "The trick is to clamp down with your teeth on only a small portion and pull hard to wrestle off a bite."

"Thank you, Sir, Jack Lank-Sleeve. I was going to ask. Well, anyway, thanks for the jerky." Like Mr. Knight, he's had the Seven Eleven jerky.

"I just wish I could let my dad know I'm okay. I know he's really worried about me, probably really scared for me."

Jack Lank-Sleeve puts his one hand up to his face, almost putting it inside his mouth. "Just eat."

With the sun up and the day upon them, William can't let himself rest for more than half an hour. Time on the river is far riskier than time camped in the woods. His rest is over. He straightens his shoulders to regain his priorities. "I fear we won't beat Colbert to the Mississippi. Without one portion of God damn luck, we won't have our chance on the Mississippi. This morning will become afternoon before we know it. Mercy for the moral is a fool's estimation."

"Then we'll keep a steady pace. We'll keep the focus and make it all the way," Jack Lank-Sleeve tells him.

William steps over and reaches under the seat where Jack Red-Hair is working the rudder. He pulls out a haversack. The three of them have each managed to keep one small bag throughout their time on the river. William's haversack is fairly filthy by now, but the small gray canvas bag, waxed to waterproof it, contains all of his personal pieces and the last of his keepsakes. William digs through and pulls out a small book. The leather cover is beat-to-death, and the pages barely hold together. He thumbs through it and quickly finds what he's looking for. He's done this many times before.

"Here it comes, dear God deliver us." Jack Lank-Sleeve is once again poking a little lighthearted fun at William and his book. By now, William's book has become a rally point for their shared humor. At other times, the sobered voice encourages them to continue on, which is, of course, William's intention. William believes in the power of the quote—a voice outside his own. He holds the book far enough away from his face to read the small type. "It is very rare that the providence of God casts us into any condition of life so low, or any misery so great, but we may see something or other to be thankful for. The pleasure of your company, Gentlemen, no greater gift than that." He looks up to judge the reception by the looks on their faces. This time is better than some of the others. Given the circumstances, probably to be expected.

"So you see," he tells them, "we keep our thoughts to the task and never mind the obstacles, and the river will be ours. A little luck can bring fortune, even to the sinners who don't deserve it, like the three of us. I suppose. Maybe with the young boy, we'll get our piece of her luck."

Satisfied, he slips the book back into the haversack and pushes it back under the seat.

"Well, look at that," Knight tells them. "We're traveling with a Harvard man. Keep you ears open, Son, and you'll learn something. Thank you for that, William, a very pleasant good morning thought for the day. What's the book?"

"We'll need to get on the big river," William tells him.

Jack Red-Hair begins to row only a little harder. "You're giving away our food. That right there might be the end of us, luck or no luck."

Hardy moves over on his seat to lean over the side of the bateau while he chews. It was a long night. He watches the reflection of his face twist and warp in the ripple trail of the boat. It could easily be somebody else. "I like the taste of gunpowder. Never would have guessed that." Looking across to William, he asks, "How far do you suppose we need to get by this afternoon to beat the Captain, in miles?"

"That, Son, we cannot know for sure. But we can stay steady. That we do know for sure."

"All right, I was wrong. You're not petty thieves, and surely you're not cowards. I'm man enough to admit it," Knight announces as he looks back and forth between William and Jack Lank-Sleeve.

"You're out here for your personal reasons. I believe I might understand the morality of the conscientious objector. I'm familiar with the creed. The Vietnam War? Right? I'm certainly of the age." Knight takes a moment, a short breath to try again. "But why are you out here at all? Here in America? Nobody forced you to enlist, or was it the sort of 'go with the rest of your chaps, off to enlist, to fight the good fight' sort of thing?"

William looks across to Knight. "Sir, I could tell you how ignorant a statement that might be, but what would be the good in it? We are here for very different reasons. I don't know why you are here or even who you are. I don't recognize the militia clothes—the black cotton of your pants—but I respect that you're caught up in this like the rest of us. I assume you're Ohio, maybe the Illinois."

"William, I believe at this point in this story, I can call you William," Knight asserts. "And now that we're past the friction and reached some amount of civility, I can tell you that I also do not know why myself and the boy are here in this boat on the Arkansas river at dawn. And I don't mean the existential dawn." Knight speaks more to himself than to William. "But tell me this, where have you been before this coming together, on this boat? From where did you desert? What was your turning point? That's what interests me."

"Sir, you said it right there. We all have different stories." William turns to look upriver. "Some ready to tell; most waiting to be written, wouldn't you agree?"

Telling your own story to others is not something men do on the river. Some do. Most don't. It's a vanity to indulge in it. If you're on the river, you've been brought there by the decisions you've made or haven't made, and you're stuck with the one and only challenge: how to get off it. When you're on the river, you're traveling to a place to make something more of your life, and when you're not on the river, you need to get on it, to get to the same better life.

"Every sailor in this bloody mess has a different story," Jack Lank-Sleeve quietly adds. "And the story is always the same. You hope for one thing and settle for the other. A turning point is a grand idea." He stands for a quick moment, to rearrange the fit of his coat. "A flash of powder in the sky. Sure enough, I woke up one morning, lower deck, and thought to myself, in between eighteen-pounders blasting through the hull, Jack, you're just not suited for this. I held my time until we were close to shore. Then I says to the Quarter Master, 'I'm off to better worlds, goodbye and good luck,' and, I'm over the side."

Hardy is captivated. He's leaning as far forward as he can.

"I was raised a Catholic from my mother. That's my civil side. My father taught me about fighting and the crown and the glory. But I'm not Navy for what I believed in. That's why I am here with you, on this mucky brown American river. I know now what it is I do believe in, and the Navy is not part of it."

Jack Lank-Sleeve looks straight downriver. "A few of us came down the Ohio river, looking for others like us. What else could we do? Try to find others and make a place? Wait it out, and if we could muster any kind of luck, make our way to the British docks on the eastern coast. Keep a dream to make it back home. We all have different plans. William is still willing to believe he'll find a wife and make a home here. I suppose it's not too far-fetched. Colbert did it. Course William's better dream is to make it all the way back home to his sick mother. Jack, your Jack Red-Hair, he doesn't think about one day to the next."

"We all come from different places," William breaks in, "but we'll all end up with the same rope if we don't beat Colbert to the mouth of the Mississippi."

After a long night of respectful quiet, any decent morning will bring out the talk. Voices put to their stories will finally put an end to the night. But for the moment, the morning is quiet again. High cirrus clouds move in over the direct morning sun. The river finds itself another hue.

"This Colbert," Knight respectfully takes it up again, "you've now mentioned this name more than a few times. A man that we are apparently desperately avoiding is lurking just around a bend ahead. This may sound strange to you, William, but I feel I need to speak with Colbert. In our story, it's Hardy and I who are trying to desert."

"You really are a simple man who still cannot see clearly this world." William sighs, knowing the banter will not get them any farther downriver. "You see what is right in front of you and you turn away to think it something else."

"Alright, that may be true," Knight offers.

Frustrated by the slow progress, William pulls his oar hard and begins a loud, rhythmic exhale with each pull.

"Then again, maybe we are the same. You, sitting on the river bank, the way you were, right out in the open. You're either poorly advised militia or a damn fool. Maybe I'm the one turned away from the face of who you are. What I'm telling you, Sir is that there is a face on this river that neither of us can turn away from. James Colbert is the captain of a flotilla headed this way. A face of a man we do not want to see looking back. The man has lived with the Chickasaw Indians, and he knows this river better than any."

"A British Navy Captain raised by Indians. Why not? Good twist."

William pulls hard. His exhales break his words into parcels. "It doesn't matter one bit… what you think of me… not one bit… the river… will win this thing… if we do not make it downriver… this very morning… paddle hard with me… and I'll tell you what I know."

"The man has a violent temper," Jack Lank-Sleeve tells them. "And we'll be in no position to discuss terms."

"We're deserters," Jack Red-Hair adds, "let's go down the list: it could be tarred and feathered or tied to a rope and swung overboard, ducked or keel-hauled, maybe dragged round the underneath of the ship. A simple flogging is never enough. Most likely, your standard 'cat-o'-nine-tails' hanged from the yardarm. Colbert hangs deserters, you fool old man. The moment a man enters the service, he waives the rights and privileges he might be entitled to as an English man. The language of The Mutiny Act is well known by every soldier and sailor serving the Crown. The British—the exemplars of just and fair morality—maintain no tolerance for desertion."

Chewing jerky to get it to soften up takes several minutes for each bite you manage to tear off.

"The British moved against Fort Jefferson," William tells Knight between pulls. "We thought the Chickasaw were with us one hundred percent. The Spanish held the fort with some American militia. We attacked from the western side of the Mississippi, several miles below the mouth of the Ohio, where it joins up with the Mississippi." William lets the oar drag a moment to catch his breath. "Captain Colbert was wounded in the arm, right above his elbow. Not that bad. We'd all seen worse. Much worse. The Chickasaw could see something else. A white captain, wounded in battle, was not a show of strength. It was pretty quick they figured it was no longer their fight. They knew how the standoff would go, so they left the fort and went off back to the river. The Chickasaw had enough experience with the British command to know they'd debate the situation for days. Which they did. So there we stayed, dug in along the Mississippi for days. Days and long days after days. We starved. All of us starved. Waiting days for them to decide if we were to take that fort in full."

William moves closer to Knight on the bateau middle seat. "Let me ask you, old man. Do you stay put with the officer's orders, a man you do not know, or care to know, most probably you despise. Do you starve to where you cannot even lift your musket? Do you have any idea how many men have gone that way out here on these fitful rivers and all across these black woods? Starving to death is not a metaphor for the historian's chronicle. Or do you smarten up and listen to God's voice of reason and put the bloody heel to it, like we did, to survive this miserable account?"

"The three of us found each other up in the woods," Jack Lank-Sleeve tells Knight. A good memory. "It took the three of us to outsmart the Indians we avoided when we came southwest through those woods."

"Except for the one particularly spooky-looking devil," Jack Red-Hair adds. "But he wasn't interested in us. We'll never get to the bottom of that one."

"He had lost his mind," William tells them.

"Mostly, they weren't looking for us, and we were smart enough to not leave a trail all the way through Osage territory to find this river, the Arkansas river. And lucky to come across this boat, left behind by some others going somewhere else. God bless their souls. She's now our mistress of choice."

"Amen," from Jack Red-Hair.

"What is truly extraordinary," Jack Lank-Sleeve continues, "from my account is how every place on this Earth is so different, one from the next.

Along with the black bear, what you'll find in these valley woods will change a man. Just look at the three of us."

William gives him the knowing, slightly impatient smile of a brother's smile, then switches to his oratory responsibility. "…thus we never see the true state of our condition till it is illustrated to us by its contraries." He waits for any response. "And that right there, gentlemen, is the best of them."

"Alright, ladies, a round of applause," Jack Red-Hair adds while he watches the river intently. There's more to review. "The Captain is about sixty years old. He's possessed of good health and a strong constitution. He's a particularly active man, I'll tell you that, despite his years. It's true he had lived among the Chickasaw for forty years and boasted that he was owner of a fine house and some hundred and fifty negros. He was fond of saying he had several sons by Chickasaw women. I will tell you this, and this is all you need to know. The man has a violent streak when he's crossed. You do not want any part of this. And this last part… Are you listening, Sir? You're sitting in a bateau with three of his deserters."

Representative Knight thinks for a moment. "Jesus, that tells it." He gives it another minute. "I want to thank you for that, William, and Jack. I honestly do. It gives me a better sense of things."

In an interminably long career of people aggressively elbowing for one position over another, never has he been in the company of men like these three. What is it about them? What exactly is this integrity, if that's what it is? For Representative Knight, sincerity is the awkward space between two points of strategy in play.

"You may not see this in me, not directly," Knight concocts his oration, "but as an elected official, I merely need to know the essence of what I am addressing. My well-honed intuition is a compass I have trusted for the length of my career. Many has been the occasion when an adversary believed me to be tricked into responding favorably to some cockamamie proposition which had no relation to the truth of the situation." Knight can taste the drivel accumulating in his mouth like paste.

"Sir, there are boats," Hardy says matter-of-factly.

"Boats. Okay, yes, boats; it's part of the scheme of it."

"No Sir, boats." This time pointing.

"He's right." William's voice is a knowing and toneless confirmation. "There are boats coming up behind us."

Chapter Six

A true puzzler's paradise

"Canoe." William closes his eyes in disbelief, one very deep breath and a very long exhale. "They're Indian, and they're coming up on us fast."

"I believe you're right, William, looks to be four." Jack Lank-Sleeve rubs his forehead, unable to conceal his bit of panic. "Why, Lord, have you forsaken us and put us here? I knew the storm of this would catch up to us." He looks to Jack Red-Hair. "We're lost to the Mississippi now."

"What, in God's name, do you mean canoes and storms?" Knight spins back and forth between them.

"Nothing here is written, Jack," William bursts back. "Grab hold of it."

"Grab hold, your captain's arse," Jack Red-Hair snaps back. "There's no outrunning them. We pull to shore and get out and sit on the bank, show we're not a threat."

For a Catholic boy like Jack Red-Hair, raised outside of London, his first encounter with a tribal American left a lasting impression. Most British deserters in the Mississippi Valley have had consequential encounters with one or more of the tribes. It's nearly impossible to be roaming through the woods and rivers and escape a confrontation. There is never a certainty as to how these meetings will turn. For the loyalists and the American militias, those occasions are more measured. The encounters are predetermined by commanding officers and tribal chiefs. For Jack Red-Hair, a terrifying image of a figure in the woods is not easily dismissed.

"How do we know they're a threat? Pull over and let them pass? Is that the idea?" Knight muddles out loud.

"We know they're a threat," Hardy says. When Jack Red-Hair suggests they pull the boat to the river bank, Hardy immediately accepts the job. His body stiffens to focus his attention, looking for the place to do it. There are only a couple of spots that are not thick with brush and branches. In one of those, he sees what might be a piece of clothing stuck on a branch, dragging in the current. "They're a threat because everything on this river is a fucking threat." Hardy looks to William for further instructions.

William squints through the blinding, sparkling sunlight on the surface. "Looks to be a good count, five boats. Four canoe and one pirogue being towed behind. Two Indians in each canoe, except the one in the lead, and one man, English or American, in the towed pirogue. He's wearing a coat."

William's first assessment proves to be accurate. The canoes are approaching fast. They're lighter and faster than the broad, heavy bateau. They're made from stitched cottonwood bark, and they're efficient. The pirogue is roughly the size of a canoe but made from the same rough-cut pine as the bateau. Tough to paddle, it drags in the water. Up and down the Mississippi Valley rivers, pirogues and bateaus are loaded with trade. Upriver to the river tribes: blankets, guns, ammunition, and alcohol. Downriver to New Orleans' ships to Europe: fur. The bateau is versatile but not well suited to outrun a canoe.

"If these Indians prove to be Quapaw or Chickasaw," William tells them, "then our play will be to act very carefully, word by word. Thinking before speaking is well advised." If there was any amount of frivolity in the morning's chinwag, it's finished now. Everything's changed. Both Jacks and William start to recount every experience, every encounter they've had with Valley Indians, details being an imperative. "Those two tribes are in treaty, or they were last we knew. How they take to British is less certain. They'll want to know how we're aligned. Caddo or Kiowa, then we'll do okay; no quick moves. We have nothing to give them. They'll see that in the bateau. If they're Osage, then we're put in a tough situation. Our fate will be with the almighty. Why he's put us here, we'll soon find out. Do we see what's coming?"

"Yes, Sir, we do," both Jacks say simultaneously.

"We'll hold tight." Jack Red-Hair stays steady on the rudder. "We've done alright with these savages so far. There's nothing here much different."

"So we're in serious trouble?" Hardy looks to William. He can feel a panic building in his chest, the waiting to see what he can't imagine.

"Son, all these tribes in this valley are tricky, not one more so than the rest. The British Command didn't honestly prepare sailors like myself and these two here for anything like what this valley can bring upon you. But the time we've spent in these woods and on these rivers, we've got a fair foot. I promise you that." The vigor of William's indisputable confidence is reassuring. The anxiety of the approaching canoes feels lighter.

"This river has been red with blood from every Indian nation," William lowers his voice to speak directly with Hardy. "Every tribe at war with the other for a long time, long before us. Whichever tribe is on its way to meet us, however savage they may be, I promise to do my best to not let anything happen to you." William takes a deep breath. "At the same time, there is no steady truth to anything on this river. Relations can turn around one day to the next. These Indians may be very grateful to see us out here."

"We both know that to be fiction," says Jack Lank-Sleeve, "if they take us for trade and not kill us straight out, we might have a chance."

William turns back to check the progress. "Two by two by two, with one more and one more trailing behind. That's eight of them. That's a sour kettle of fish."

"Damn son of a bitch." Jack Lank-Sleeve throws his hat to the boat's bottom.

"You're saying we're about to be taken prisoner," Knight announces, throwing his arms out in exasperation, "by a group of American Indians who have suddenly come upon us from God knows where. Words can't define how impossible that sounds, honestly."

"Native Americans," Hardy says, looking in their direction.

The canoes are now within two hundred feet from the bateau. Jack Lank-Sleeve has moved to the middle seat, with Representative Knight in between. Jack and William stay hard to the oars. Hardy's up front. The crows in the trees break the tense air—not welcome.

Suddenly, from one canoe, "Howa!" Then from another farther back, "Howa, howa."

In the bateau, the words are heard clearly, but they're not recognized. It could be a simple greeting, hopefully a simple hello greeting.

The Indians start to shout and howl and call out a barrage of squawks and screeches and yelps, animal yelps. They're clearly excited. William sees it as far too much commotion, a bad beginning.

Jack Red-Hair swallows hard.

"Dear God," from Knight.

A sincere "wow" from Hardy.

Jack Lank-Sleeve shakes his head.

One hundred feet now, and it's clear that two of the Indians are waving dark-colored poles in the air.

"Rifles," William says, calculating the situation.

Out of nowhere, the crack of a rifle shot tears open the scene.

Every body in the bateau jerks from the shock of it.

The whooping and the yowling in the canoes immediately doubles.

The powder blast is a cloud of white smoke that is left behind, as the canoes are now at fifty feet.

Several more shots suddenly crack the air, each one surprising, unnerving.

William and the two Jacks stay steady. Knight and Hardy instinctively flinch and drop as low as they can.

William watches intently as the canoes close the gap, keeping his shoulders straight and a simple no expression on his face. He's close enough now to study the figures, pick up clues.

As the group of canoes paddle closer—no more than twenty feet from the bateau—the canoe with only one Indian paddles to the front, demonstrating he will speak first. The loud hoopla and the rifles fired were clearly coming from two of the canoes behind, each with two Indians, who are now standing with their rifles held vertically by the long barrel of the gun. And they are clearly in good spirits; jokes are being tossed back and forth with plenty the outbursts of laughter. Pushing, punching, and shoving to the extent a canoe will take without dumping them over.

The standing figure in the lead canoe reveals a great deal. The successful deserters in the Mississippi Valley depend to a great extent on the skill of cataloging the subtle differences in the markings on the skin, the crop of the hair, the symbols and designs on the bags and breech cloth. Differences between a passing cordiality or a hostile come across. Any sudden appearance of Indians on the river is an absolute threat until relations are established.

The figure stands erect, and, in obvious command, he reeks of it. William recognizes the familiar red-spiked hair stretching from the Indian's forehead to the back of his neck, only an inch or so wide but stiff, spiking straight up and dramatic. The rest of his head is shaved. He is a warrior of high rank, perhaps thirty-five, not much more. He wears two feathers tied to the back of his head with strips of thin leather. Around his neck are a dozen ropes of beads made of colored bone, an inordinate amount of beads. From the waist, he wears a wide tie-belt of whitened deer skin, which holds a wide and draping blanket down to his knees. Deer skin moccasins reach up just below the knee, and they are wrapped with straps dyed green. The warrior is close now. William can see the rough life of the river in his face.

For several minutes, William studies his appearance. He reads the graphic marks and symbols on the warrior's chest and arms like words in a book, periodically diverting his attention to the others paddling closer—still rowdy and obviously much younger. The most revealing symbols painted across the man's body are the white figures painted large across his chest. These resemble thick and swirling question marks pointing out in every direction, dreams perhaps. Up and down his arms are painted short waves in green and red. William believes these to represent claw marks from a grizzly attack that show he was the skilled victor. The beauty of the man's markings indicates they have been applied with great care and sophistication. This leaves no doubt. William takes a deep breath and looks at the others in the bateau. The worst of all possibilities.

"Osage," he says under his breath, better not to be heard. "They're Osage."

Both Jacks immediately understand the implications. No eye contact and head down might be their only chance of delaying any violence that could suddenly erupt. Violence is not unfamiliar, and typically with the Osage it's staged with a particularly pointless cruelty. There will be no real sense to any skirmish, and only with a little bit of luck will they be allowed to move on and put the encounter in the past.

William turns to Knight; they look each other square in the face—a penetrating exchange, fast and hard. Knight understands right away that there is finesse to be shown. William needs to quickly school Knight about what is happening in this initial moment and the probability of what will happen next, which will not be in their favor. There's much to be avoided and plenty to conceal. It's a dangerous game. William has the hint that Knight can play it well if he has the proper briefing. It'll have to be quick.

He leans into Knight and, in a quietly tempered voice, "A tribe that dominates all up and down the Arkansas River and much of the Mississippi Valley. Very smart, very clever, with territory broad across the Valley and beyond. They've deceived the Spanish, attacked the French furtraders, tricked the Chickasaw, and fooled the Quapaw. Their treaties are much desired but never trusted. They barter alliances until conditions change, then allies become adversaries. These shifting relations are squarely about who controls the rivers. Osage are known for their particular style of brutality, which is unforgiving and not of God's world."

Representative Knight sees a clever contender in William, worldly and knowledgeable. His intelligence will prove a show of strength. He feels a sudden flush of envy but quickly lets it go. Those are larger issues and deeper disappointments. A remarkable man. These Osage may have met their match.

The Osage have developed the most extensive trading networks in North America, which is fact well known. They inflict their dominance to brandish elaborate modes of leverage over Valley Tribes as well as the Europeans, who are in constant battle for the same territory. Osage took military risks to gain advantages over the French trading empire. When the Spanish took over Louisiana from the French, the Osage outplayed the best of the European strategies to retain their dominance, thwarting Spain's attempts to establish its own dominant rule.

The Spanish in the Mississippi River Valley are plagued with the possibility that the Osage will ally with the English against them for better trade. The Spanish will engage in the barter of all manner of goods to accommodate the Osage temperament, however immoral the exchange. The young warriors and scouts traveling up and down the rivers express the ability of the Osage to out-navigate the competing claims of sovereignty from both the British and Spanish. Anyone on the rivers not Osage are essentially intruders. The young warriors are primed with invincibility. Their thoughtless sport can turn deadly, and often it does. The other dominant tribe on the river, the Quapaw, trade with the French and patronize the Spanish.

"There's still a great deal of Indian slave trade up and down these rivers." William keeps his voice low, rushing to get it all in. "The young Osage like to test their elders. They'll take up a raid, and they're exceptionally skilled at the hunt. They'll trade whatever they get their hands on to whoever will trade back. In this stretch of the river, they will have their intention set to the Chickasaw scattered throughout these woods, and they'll head straight for the Spanish to make the trade."

In Osage skirmishes and raids, the young men have the opportunity to prove themselves as skilled warriors. This is a rite of passage for them. It gives them influence and prestige. A young man's urge to attain glory as a warrior and to be noticed and honored can mean inflicting violence. They rarely give up these opportunities.

Knight is beginning to feel indebted to William. This world is so much greater than what he brings to it. It's a sinking feeling. But he's quickly brought back to the moment at hand. They're in quite the untenable situation, and he's ill prepared.

William stays on Knight for a moment longer. He sees Knight calculating the relationships: the players, the sensitivity, even the diplomacy. He sees it in Knight's eyes. "Mr. Knight, these are a complicated set of circumstances, a true puzzler's paradise. We've had months and months and just as many encounters to work these relations out to satisfaction. You are a smart man. What you do is watch and pay attention. What you don't do is offer your suggestions or try to make this less than what it is. It'll turn against you." Satisfied, he turns back to the canoes.

The four rowdy Osage are relentless in their unruly shouting and shoving. Every few minutes, a loud yelp, then the same from the other three. There are momentary lulls, then, with another joke—more of a wisecrack—they explode again with the noise of foolishness that carries across the entire river. The crows dare not speak, dare not move. They're every bit on edge as all the rest.

The Osage warrior, who stands erect and motionless in the front canoe, is not distracted by the young hooligans. He keeps his attention, without the slightest expression, directly on William. Their exchange will determine a great deal.

Most concerning to William are the rifles. Each of the four young troublemakers are holding a "Brown Bess," a French flintlock musket, the most common on the river. A muzzle-loading, smooth-bore musket. With these particular rifles, William knows these Indians have traded heavily with the Spanish, probably a good many times. Where these trades have taken place is a serious concern. What the Indians traded for their muskets, if not fur, is too much a disturbing thought for the moment.

William commits to the long, cold stare of the contest. He's not new to this; he's every bit as skilled. He stays bound to the confrontation but must subtly recalibrate his focus to look farther back, to the fourth canoe and the pirogue behind it. The two Indians in the far canoe don't appear to be Osage and are only barely tolerating the situation. One sits with his arms crossed, his eyes closed, clearly waiting for the nonsense to come to an end.

In the pirogue—which is tied to the canoe—is another sailor sitting alone in the middle of the boat. He wears a British uniform and is tied with rope around the upper arms, all the way around his body, keeping his arms tight to his sides. Clearly, if he were to jump out of the pirogue, he would immediately go under.

The Osage in front still doesn't move a muscle. He knows this is understood as a threat, a show of strength. At his height in the canoe, he looks down at William, his superiority confirmed. He considers the two other British are not a threat, their presence here a waste of his time.

The Osage shifts his attention to the strange man and the boy. This puzzles him. They do not belong with the British. In the bateau, none are held captive. The British uniforms are filthy. They are in desertion of their war. The American and his boy are not from the Valley. There has been business here that has not included his tribe. This business will not be tolerated.

Hardy, with not one single blink, his jaw drops, he cannot look away. The sight of this tall, standing Indian, this magnificent painted man, and all the rest of them, along with the canoes, is as astonishing as it is thrilling. Some amount of panic is undoubtedly a component of thrill.

Knight, after conferring with William, decides he will look in the direction of the standing warrior, but he will squint his eyes, giving him opportunities to observe without offending with a prolonged stare.

As the anxious minutes tick by, William and both Jacks—without words or eye contact exchanged—simultaneously acknowledge the conspicuous reality of the encounter; they have no rifles.

The four warrior rowdies feel the shift of the moment now as well; their voices lowered and the physical pushing and taunting lessened. Suddenly, they're waiting.

In these tense, frozen minutes, the constellation of canoes—with the bateau and the pirogue—floats in unison down the Arkansas, a flotilla tethered by trepidation, a drifting ensemble of intimidating characters.

Like the diplomat that he believes he is, Knight inserts himself to take advantage of the temporary lull. This will be his turn to establish his role in the contest. He decides the mediator's position might work best. It has in the past.

He'll break the ice. "It seems we're all moving in the same direction…"

"Let them speak first," the captive in the pirogue at the rear tries to interrupt, "let them tell what they wish to do here." But he's not quite quick enough.

"Perhaps we could give each other a hand…" Knight waits for any response from anyone.

William spins to Knight, and with both hands makes a quick gesture of no. "Too late," he mutters.

Knight takes the awkward moment and adds, "What a magnificent bunch you are. Where might you be headed?" Another long silence. "We're all on the river today. We're all headed somewhere." Still nothing. Knight re-calibrates to his no-nonsense courtroom voice and barks, "What is it you want? Who are you? We demand to know your intentions." He clears his throat. "Are you here to share your food? Because that would be very much appreciated."

One of the young warriors takes his turn at diplomacy. He's had his patience tested. He grabs his rifle in the middle of the barrel, pushes it up over his head, and shouts out as loud as his voice will let it. "Osage will say."

"This certainly constitutes an unfortunate turn of events." Jack Lank-Sleeve and Jack Red-Hair, grumbling across the bateau.

"I'll bet they're not here to share food," Hardy says while looking down at the wooden bottom of the bateau.

The older warrior relaxes his stance, and he turns his stare away from William. Posturing for dominance is becoming less necessary the more the intruders speak.

A primary rule in diplomacy is to maintain relentless pursuit but know when to quit. Foolishly, Knight believes that with a touch more antagonism he can put them in a little better position. "Unless you tell us your intentions, we'll continue."

"Don't do it," William interrupts.

Never to relent in a war of words, "We'll continue our journey. We must reach the Mississippi River as soon as possible. We have several appointments. Perhaps you could help us get there a little sooner. We only have the two oars." When Knight's finished, the entire group of the Osage are rightfully stymied by the arrogance of the American—not sure what he is promoting. Not well understood, and clearly, he has underestimated their threat.

From the canoe farthest back, there is a call out from one of the two Indians who, apparently, are not of the Osage Tribe. He calls across the flotilla, "Osage, do not dig graves."

Another young Osage warrior, with the same gesture of the rifle overhead, cries out, "More to the Spanish to trade. This day still full."

A third young warrior drops his musket to the bottom of the canoe. He lifts a small wooden barrel, a pony keg, a three-pounder. He forces open a cork, holds it to his face with both hands, and takes one long, sloppy swig from the small barrel. Then he too yelps at the top of his lungs, "Not full."

"I tried to say it," from the captive in the pirogue.

"Over before it began," Jack Lank-Sleeve says to the rest in the bateau.

The fourth of the young Osage warriors switches his grip on his musket to flip the muzzle straight up into the sky. His thumb pulls back the dogshead, and with a finger to the trigger he fires a shot to the air, screaming, "Nikka Osage."

Both Knight and Hardy jerk downward, deeper into the bateau. William merely looks away.

"I am Niwashake." (Knee-wa-shock-a) Finally, first words from the tall Osage warrior who has dominated. They're delivered in the most impressive, deep and clear voice and in an immaculately impassive tone.

"This day I am the leader of the Osage hunters. You will come with the Osage."

"As I expected," William reports to the others, "this will be a challenge."

Still standing at the front of his canoe, Niwashake back paddles with his oar, pulling his canoe back away from the bateau.

The four young Osage rowdies paddle their two canoes toward the bateau. This only takes minutes. The reason for their erratic and disturbing behavior and increasing threat is now crystal clear to William and the rest. They've been at the pony-keg probably most of the day, skunks on rum.

The "Fiery Double Distilled Rum" is actually high-proof wine diluted with water. It's traveled up the Mississippi from the African enslaved-labor sugar plantations in the south. An item of very frequent trade. For the younger of a tribe, the wine is more diluted with water. For the experienced, the wine is of a higher quality and is less diluted. The trade in high-proof alcohol is one of the important factors that undermines peaceful Spanish-Osage relations. To young Osage warriors on the river for a hunting party, this is of no concern. More hoots and hollers.

Quickly, the two canoes pull alongside the bateau, both on the same side. One of the young Osage, still holding his musket over his head, steps into the bateau. He staggers, almost losing his balance when he steps in. This sways the bateau side to side for a moment. With his balance back under his feet, he takes two short steps to put himself in front of Representative Knight.

William, Hardy, and the Jacks hold their breath waiting to see. Suddenly, the young Osage juts his head down at Knight's face. He holds it there, twelve inches between them, face-to-face. When Knight tries to divert his eyes away, the Osage makes another quick jolt to Knight's face. After several long breaths, it's the Osage warrior who turns his head slightly away; his balance unsteady. He suddenly turns back and blows a quick puff of breath into Knight's face. Poof.

This brings a new wave of hooting and hollering. Rifles waving overhead, and the pony keg is passed around.

The Osage in the bateau becomes keenly interested in Hardy's t-shirt. He steps over to Hardy, reaches out, and pulls aggressively on the shirt. He rubs his hand across the silkscreened graphics on the front—the hoop with hawk feathers—as he does this, he says, in a very deep voice, "Indian."

Hardy understands the strange complexity of the moment. He knows the word "metaphysics." He's heard it. Something about alternative universes, some part science and mostly fiction. He's twelve. He also knows to keep quiet. His t-shirt has changed the atmosphere of the confrontation, at least for the Osage. Moments ago, the warriors were in high spirits, making mock threats and careless gestures. Their faces are now genuinely serious and impatient. Their glares are unsettling and threatening. The inexplicable about-face that alcohol does so well.

Chapter Seven

The one true thing

The four Osage—the oldest, not more than eighteen—were raised to become skilled hunters and eventually proficient warriors. Hunting, scouting, trading, and hostile conflicts are the coming of age and a measure of stature. This collective investment culminates in tribal dominance over broad stretches of territorial and not-so-territorial lands. The Osage train their young boys well.

This is not their first hunting party, but the pony-keg rum is a recent addition to the new generation's rite of passage. Boyhood friends in their village who become young men together give them the added value of invincibility that anyone older can easily recognize.

Their hunting party has come down the Arkansas River from farther west, near the territorial borders of the Kiowa. Each of them wears the same loose-fitting deerskin leggings that are tied with strips of leather at the waist and wrapped from the calf to their ankles. Their torsos are strong, except for one, and they're bare except for the pouches for powder and musket lead strapped across their chests. Around their necks, the same impressive number of beads. Their black hair is pulled tight to the top and tied with strips. Each of them has several feathers tied to their hair. One of the Osage has a pronounced scar on his cheekbone. It's not an ugly mark. Not as formidable as their elder, but absolutely impressive. Each proud of the way he has dressed for their hunting, which gives each one of them an inordinate amount of reckless teenage confidence. Fearlessness is dangerous. They share the thrilling anticipation of unpredictability.

Despite the risk, William takes the opportunity and leans in to whisper to Jack Red-Hair in front of him. "This could work in our favor if they're headed for the mouth."

Without turning around, Jack responds, "If not, then we are done."

The four Osage have shown their dominance, and the foolhardy high spirits have become aggressive and nasty. Niwashake decides he has no desire to contribute further to the business of the day. The young warriors of his tribe may conduct their sport without him. He considers these four tiresome and no longer worthy of his attention. He's finished with the game. For the moment, he sits and waits. His canoe barely keeps pace with the rest. Occasionally, he looks up to feel the warmth of the sun on his face.

The pony keg is still being passed between the Osage. They reach across the canoes. Their talk is blunt and quick, their muskets still held in position. The warrior in the bateau takes two steps forward. He stands for a moment, then grabs Jack Lank-Sleeve by the shoulder and forces him off the seat, onto the bottom planks of the bateau. Jack Lank-Sleeve stays low and keeps his eyes diverted from the Osage.

Representative Knight is crouched low with Hardy at his side. It's much more of an insult for him than Hardy. *How insulting to treat an elected official with this amount of physical threat, but must it be disrespectful as well? There has to be some wisp of civility in these felons, whatever costuming they've prepared.*

Being held captive on a river presents a much clearer set of circumstances for those in desertion. The one and only option is to overpower those in charge. William and the two Jacks have seen the closeness of battle, so this situation doesn't seem impossible. When captors rearrange themselves physically in small boats, different options are presented. Also, contrary to the way it appears, the greatest opportunity here—and William and the others know it—is to bide their time until the alcohol runs its course. In this hot sun, it's predictable to within thirty minutes' time. They share this recognition without saying it, so they wait for it.

With the flotilla making steady progress downriver and the initial round of antagonism spent, the two Indians who have kept pace in the rear canoe take advantage of the momentary lull and quietly paddle forward. They pull their canoe—tethered to the pirogue—alongside the rear of the bateau on the opposite side of the two Osage canoes. One of the Indians grabs the side of the bateau to hold the boats together. He has words for William, and he feels no need to conceal his voice.

"We will not interfere with the danger you are in," the Indian tells William.

"For that, I am sorry."

"I can see you are Quapaw," William tells the Indian.

"You have knowledge of the valley." He speaks with William in a steady and regular tone, like strangers exchanging directions on the open road. "Quapaw cannot risk trouble with the Osage. Our loss will be too great. The British have come too far into the rivers. The peace between our tribes is fragile. British are outside of this; they don't particularly matter. Osage trade very well with the Spanish, but that can be broken quickly. Quapaw have trade with the Osage, and that too can be broken." With an odd gentility, he smiles at William.

William is patient, a valuable moment of exchange. He holds himself still.

"The Spanish will trade with Osage because they need Osage to accomplish their goals on these rivers. Quapaw, Chickasaw, Caddo, and the Osage all know the Spanish are fools to believe they will take this valley land. But we use their foolishness to our advantage."

"Why are you here with us?" William's voice turns the Osage warriors in his direction. He lowers his voice. "If the Quapaw are hands off the British in the Valley, if we here in this bateau mean nothing to you, then why are you sitting here, speaking with me?"

The Osage in the front of the bateau turns back from watching downriver. He looks directly at the Quapaw who is speaking and says, "Your business here is small. You should turn back. Go back to your village." He throws his arm out and points back upriver.

The Quapaw speaking with William cups his hand around his ear as if to listen. "Your rum calls you, your dog is barking for you, don't make him get angry."

The Osage warrior quickly whips his musket into position, aiming directly at the Quapaw. The other Osage join in to taunt. "Quapaw dogs are under our feet." The Osage warrior pulls back the hammer of the musket, with the loud click, it's ready for the shot.

William quickly looks to Hardy. "Stay down, Son."

"Jesus Christ, does this ever end?" Knight calls to William as he covers Hardy with his arms.

Jack Lank-Sleeve covers his head with his arm.

Jack Red-Hair lowers his head slightly but continues to paddle.

The Quapaw, with the rifle pointed at his chest, slowly leans back.

"The rifle will not fire on Quapaw, not on this day," Niwashake calls out to the Osage warrior, his canoe much farther behind. "Put the rifle down."

The elder Niwashake has decided to intervene. What has changed his mind is a complicated topic, one of the many intangibles shared among elders on the river.

William can see now that relations have become even more volatile. In all likelihood, the young warrior will feel he must test his elder, show his strength and indifference.

The air is brittle with tension. But their confrontation passes quickly. William overestimated the teenager's resolve. He will tolerate the elder, at least for the moment. The young Osage drops his rifle to his side and calls for his turn with the pony keg.

In the bateau, everyone takes a breath.

William, with little to lose, takes advantage of the pause in the posturing and power play. "Where are you coming from?" He calls across to the bound British sailor in the pirogue, not more than twenty feet back.

"Upriver, same as you, headed downriver straight into this purgatory, same as you."

Since this first exchange didn't prompt any hostility from either of the two Quapaw or any of the young Osage, William continues, "What's your name?" He keeps his tone as deadpan as possible, showing no urgency.

"Fredrick Udolph, from Württemberg." The sailor also maintains the expressionless exchange.

William immediately realizes the additional complication of their situation.

"A Hessian. That puts you in a different category than the rest of us."

"I'm a dead man like the rest of you," Fredrick replies. His tone of resignation says it all.

"Bought and paid for by George III," William says to Fredrick.

German soldiers, the Hessians, are brought into the war to add numbers to the British ranks. The supreme show of power. They've sold themselves to the British endeavor for no other reason than to feed their children. True for many British regulars and American patriots and loyalists.

"Here for the wages," Fredrick tells William.

A year's wage can make the difference back home. Food for the table.

But Hessians are several strides separated from the ideals of patriotism or just cause. Oddly, in the war, but not part of the war. Thirty thousand Hessians serve across the continent for the British.

William knows this opportunity may not come up twice. He's keenly interested in news about the British on the river. He's willing to risk a violent response from the Quapaw next to him. Any information about the river campaigns might provide some semblance of a plan for their escape. As predicted, the four Osage appear to be rapidly slumping into the slurs, giggles, and recklessness of rum on this sunny afternoon.

"Like I said, we came down the Arkansas, but I started my run much farther north, up on the Ohio." Fredrick wisely understands this new opportunity to partner with William and his collaborators might be his best chance, but his exhaustion hinders the breath he uses to speak.

"Well, friend, there were a few of us attempting the run. We had ended up with the British Rangers under Captain William Caldwell. This was up on the Mad River in Ohio Country. Caldwell pulled together an enormous mixed-bag: Shawnees, Delawares, Mingos, Wyandots, Miamis, Ottawas, more than a thousand. I'd never seen that. None of us had. The Indians were being supervised by the Pennsylvania loyalists, so they looked as though they had some level of commitment. Their purpose for being there was for the sake of their own territories. They wanted the Americans routed as much as any of those British. A strange assortment of desires. Not one picture at all."

"But the attack never came," Jack Lank-Sleeve adds, deceptively looking away. "We've heard this, William."

"We were set to move into the Ohio Country, but they turned us around, and we returned to the Mad River to face off with Clark. But the attack never came." Fredrick continues, "Your man is correct; never came at us. After that, most of the Indians picked up and left. They had nothing to gain by staying. Sie geben auf."

"So, you quit as well, picked up, and left." William's eyes go soft, his poker's tell. He's let Fredrick know that he's among friends. "I don't judge that against you, friend. I surely don't. We're in the same boat here. I'd say that's a joke only deserters can appreciate."

Fredrick tries to give William what he can. "Clark had a large keelboat; this one could have been fifty foot long. It carried forty some sailors, and, Sir, it was truly fully fitted, enough weapon to do us all in. Since their plans were temporarily suspended, he had nothing better to do than patrol the river."

Fredrick's voice drops considerably softer, feeling his way through his words. "What he was looking for were the deserters he knew had broken off."

"I'm sorry to hear that," William offers. "I consider you brave to make it as far as you did."

"I believe I may affirm that truth as well," Jack Lank-Sleeve tells Fredrick. "Danke."

William and Fredrick give a quick look to check on the status of the Osage and the Quapaw.

"We thought for sure we had broken clear off," Fredrick continues. "I was with two others who had come to the same conclusion. We had come as far as we could but had to cross the Ohio River to make it any farther. We knew it was a risk to come out of the woods. We had no choice. We waited until a good half-light and took the risk. We swam halfway across, to the point where we could see them at the same point they could spot our crossing. It was at a bend in the river. The river's pure meanness—that was our mistake. I made it across and up into the woods. I was the only one made it to shore. I was the better swimmer."

Fredrick looks across to the trees, then turns to the trees on the opposite side. "The river cuts through the forest while the sun does nothing to stop it. I came a long way south to get to this river, to meet our friends here, to be traded like deer meat." Fredrick bends his neck to the side to scratch his cheek on his shoulder. "So, now I truly give up. I believe I may, with great truth, affirm that no man ever participated in more unfavorable a set of circumstances than I have done."

"Fredrick Udolph, I can't tell you the amount of sorrow I have for you," William tells him. "It is truly unfortunate."

"Do not speak now," the Quapaw says flatly. He has no need to threaten.

Mr. Knight and Hardy have been able to relax themselves as the circumstances have temporarily cooled down. They sit on the wooden planks of the bateau bottom, an unjust insult for a gentleman of his age. They watch what they can without making eye contact.

Again, for the moment, all is quiet.

Four river crows begin their flyover across the width of the river, a long crossing. When they pass overhead, they have nothing to add.

Niwashake has tried to maintain his passive indifference to the trivial transactions of the four young Osage. His voice is spoken softly, but his words are of consequence. "I will leave this part of the river now. My business here no longer has purpose. The young Osage will prove themselves to be skilled in the hunt, or they will be shamed for what they have done on the river."

Before any more can be said, William speaks loudly to all gathered, "If the Osage trade the British to the Spanish, they will be seen as petty Indians who cannot comprehend the strategies of war."

As he back paddles away from the canoes, the bateau and the pirogue, Niwashake calls to William, "British captives to trade with the Spanish makes life much more simple. The Spanish are very close. The Fort Arkansas is just downriver, very easy for the Osage."

Paddling his canoe backward—while all the other boats move swiftly forward with the current—Niwashake will soon be gone. His last words to the others must be called out loudly to be heard: "A true warrior will do what is best for his tribe. The old man and the young boy must be taken far downriver."

In minutes, he is gone from sight.

William thinks for a moment; *strange words from an elder, 'far downriver,'* then loudly clears his throat. The two Jacks, Fredrick, Knight, and Hardy look directly at him. William knows he has their full attention. "Dangerous waters. Watch carefully, our chances have diminished."

"These savages will murder the lot of us if it suits them. Any provocation will do," Jack Red-Hair adds before he turns away.

Knight offers, "A tired drunk could be easier to wrestle."

Hardy listens to the others speak their minds. He waits and watches William. At that moment, William turns to Hardy. They share the connection's assurance. Men of age can surely find direction in the expressions of the young as readily as youth are guided by those of age. "I will wait for any sign," Hardy says out loud.

William calculates one last chance. He moves closer to the side of the bateau to show his connection to the two Quapaw, who look to be preparing to leave the flotilla as well. It shows in their faces.

"Quapaw are known for their intelligence," he tells them. "Surely much greater than the Osage." He gives the two Quapaw a chance to consider his words. "Surely they can see that if harm will come to British, the Quapaw will have to answer to their chief, who will be forced to make concessions with the local authorities. They will be held accountable. You must take us back to the Quapaw village, Togadimma."

They appear to be considering William's words. Their expressions are not hostile, but neither of them are sufficiently convinced to take action. One of Quapaw speaks directly to William with a surprising amount of sincerity. "The four Osage troublemakers coming downriver passed by our village, Togadimma. They wanted to pass by without being noticed, but they were very loud and foolish. Chief Angaska knows the British Captain Colbert is on the Arkansas, so the river is troubled. The Quapaw must be smart. Four young Osage with rum cannot end well for any tribe on the river. This is why Chief Angaska sent us to follow the Osage. If harm comes to any Indian on the river, there will be vengeance, and treaties are always delicate."

William leans as far forward as he can. "But you must see that rogue Osage Indians cannot bring good to the Quapaw River."

The Osage warrior, sitting in the bateau only a few feet from William and the Quapaw, pulls his body forward and says, "We will take the British to the Spanish at their fort and see what we can get. Osage will not listen to Quapaw's words. What is taken from the river, the river must give freely. The Arkansas belongs to the Osage."

The Quapaw now leans closer to speak with William. "Crazy Osage are trouble, but the Quapaw know of such things. The four warriors are disrespectful to their tribe, and treaties will be challenged. It is better for Quapaw if these four ignorant fools cause trouble between the British and the Spanish. Better for us. You will be on your own. If treaties are broken this day on the river, Quapaw will not be part of it. This is the way the world is now, and for this, I am sorry."

The two Quapaw speak. They keep their voices low, but they are not concerned by the Osage. They untie the pirogue as Fredrick watches intently, then tie it to the bateau.

"The foreign British will go with you now."

With that, the Quapaw back paddle their canoe from the bateau, then turn to head back upriver. They disappear more quickly than Niwashake. The circumstances of the day have changed considerably.

"You will bring more rum, which is good for our thinking, and more guns, which is good for our hunting. Captives are the best prize for our hunt." The young Osage are now unrestrained, and it can be felt by everyone. The two canoes, the bateau, and the pirogue move swiftly downriver.

Hardy turns to Mr. Knight. "Sir, are you understanding what is happening now? We're going to be traded like slaves when we get to a fort not too far from here. It's pretty clear that the five of us are caught in between. I don't think William has a plan, not yet. I'll bet he'll have a way out of this, soon probably. I can't believe this is really happening. People actually treat other people really awful and cruel. I never thought I would be in the middle of it. I guess everyone thinks that."

"This form of cruelty never seems real." His thoughts are racing every which way. "Even now, in the middle of it, it's not real, not to me. I'm not that gullible. Son, I'm just not. I don't believe any of this is going to happen; the trading and the selling. A psychologist will tell you when you're trapped in some type of terror dream—they have specific names for them—you cannot actually be harmed. They don't work that way. There's a terrible threat. It's called impending doom. But it's not an actual physical threat. We cannot be physically hurt, certainly not killed. I expect to be in my kitchen making French toast at any point. You should too. Or your bowl of shredded wheat or health food cereal. We should raise our heads above this, and I don't mean with arrogance. The Aldous Huxleys of this world did not make their sacrifices in vain. We'll look above this psychic plane and sort of see ourselves from above, sort of thing. But I will tell you this, Son." Knight grabs hold of Hardy's shoulder. He's practically shouting, "If the opportunity arises, I won't be the one to hesitate. That oar, that oar could make a sturdy weapon. We'll see what trading can happen with a few broken ribs and fluids gushing into a rapidly collapsing lung."

"Mr. Knight. Sir," William yells across to him, "you have got to keep your voice down. You don't know these characters. They'll turn on us for no reason but the one you're giving."

"I will allow that directive from you, William, for no reason other than you seem to know what you're doing here with these delinquents."

With the unpredictability of a wild dog, one of the Osage in the canoe lifts his musket and takes aim at the bateau, five feet away. His rifle swaying far from steady, he fires the gun. The suddenness of it surprises everyone on the river. Even the other Osage flinch at the crack in the air. The musket lead seems to have gone nowhere.

William takes a quick look around. No one is struck. He looks at Jack Lank-Sleeve the longest. Jack Lank-Sleeve looks over to William, and the two of them know the futility of the situation. He looks at red-haired Jack as well. They can sense the impossibility of reasoning with the Osage; they share it. It's not a surprise, not unexpected. There will be no reasoning.

"You two," Jack Lank-Sleeve says to William and Jack, his voice the lowest point of surrender, "you're sparrows trying to outrun a hurricane. God can barely see you out of the corner of his eye, if he's even looking at all."

Jack Lank-Sleeve leans as close to Hardy as he can without drawing too much attention from the Osage in front. His empty shirt sleeve dangles at his side as he speaks in a trembling voice, the color of pain and far too much sorrow. Hardy feels the immediacy of this moment in his voice. He is speaking only to Hardy, taking care not to be heard by the others.

"Listen to me, Son. You do your best, and you will make it through. I promise you that. There's always a way; trust your instincts. Brutality can never succeed. Listen carefully now. You must get yourself and your partner downriver as far as you can get. You will live long, and there is much for you to do. Both of you will work together, protect each other. William will do what he can, but on the river, people part ways before they expect to. There's no time to talk this through."

As he is finishing his words to Hardy, he leans sideways, inching to the side of the bateau. "I'm finished, but you will make it through."

In an instant, Jack Lank-Sleeve drops his body over the side of the bateau. There's barely a splash.

Hardy scrambles over and throws his arm out, reaching to grab Jack. But when Jack first moves his arm through the water to swim, Hardy realizes the decision he's made. He doesn't want to be rescued or called to for any type of help. It's his decision.

William and Knight lunge forward. They see what he has done, but they don't throw out their arms to stop him. It could be they heard what Jack was saying to Hardy. The echo of the splash washes over them.

Jack Red-Hair will not look up from his paddling. He knows exactly what has happened and why Jack has made his decision. He prefers not to watch it.

He might have done the same. Perhaps he yet may.

None of them call to Jack. It's the respect that they show.

The Osage watch the foolish British sailor. They'll wait and see. If anything, it's an inconvenience. The Osage warrior in the bateau mumbles swear words. He's clearly frustrated by the deserter's action.

Once he is a few feet from the canoes, Jack Lank-Sleeve swims smoothly, even with only one arm. He's done it before, trained himself for the adjustment. He swims in the direction of the river bank. He's a solid swimmer. He doesn't look back.

Hardy sees Jack is not swimming madly to get away and wishes he would swim much harder, much faster.

The Osage remain in their positions, their breathing unchanged. They are waiting to see how far Jack gets.

Jack swims steady—for several minutes—to get within twenty yards of the bank. When he reaches a point too close to the river bank, the young Osage warriors simultaneously exchange a few grunts. Maybe they've slurred a decision. The Osage, who is by himself in his canoe, begins to paddle and quickly maneuvers his canoe over to Jack, who is still making progress. He will make it to the bank and get up the side in only a few more minutes. He's a darn good swimmer. Hardy clenches his fists, and his body goes rigid. His face is twisted with grimace. Representative Knight grabs Hardy's forearm, squeezing too tightly.

The young Osage paddles his canoe within a few feet of where Jack continues to swim. Jack hears the slap of the water on the side of the cottonwood canoe, but he doesn't look back. The others in the bateau and Fredrick in the pirogue breathe heavy, helpless breaths. They quickly consider turning away, but they don't. The canoe pulls closer to Jack and turns sideways between him and all the other boats. Hardy watches Jack disappear behind the canoe.

In one horrific turn, the Osage lowers his rifle, not bothering to take aim. Barely looking down, he points the rifle to where Jack must be swimming. The loud crack of the rifle shot stings out across the river. Only Knight and Hardy are startled. Their bodies jerk with the shot. Hardy stares at the canoe. He is paralyzed, not one breath.

William and Jack Red-Hair now turn away. They look down. They will not give the Osage the satisfaction of letting him witness the shock on their faces.

In the measured time of only a few heartbeats, pumping hard in Hardy's chest, the body of a man floats out from behind the canoe, held tight by the current, moving faster than the rest.

Jack Lank-Sleeve is face down in the river. He is finished.

"Osage hunters are good with the musket," the Osage who has killed Jack calls to the others. All four howl to the sky. They have done well.

In a fixed stare, looking only straight ahead to the open river, Mr. Knight says quietly to Hardy, "Whatever that man told you, you must honor."

The canoes and the bateau with the pirogue reform their positions and return to a quickened pace downriver. Osage make good time on the river. In very little time, Jack Lank-Sleeve is gone from sight. As the boats round a bend in the river, the crows reconvene overhead, this time making their opinions known. There's a definite rudeness in their cadence. It's the same count, more than likely the same crows have decided the boats are of particular interest. Who can know why? The current moves quicker here. The eddies are more frequent along each side of the river's edge.

The bateau leads the way downriver. The Osage in the front stands to better scout the river for any sign of others who might be out on it or recently passed through. He's also looking for any signs of the Arkansas Fort. The two Osage canoes follow close behind, still in high spirits.

William, Jack, Knight, and Hardy don't speak. Their racing thoughts fill the raw and sickened space. Unappeasable urges to take revenge, *vile and unholy savages. Take the Indian's body. Revenge. Beat it. Tear him open with bloody ugly revenge. Wash our hands with his blood.*

Soon enough, these thoughts and pulsing desires are washed away, washed with the warmth of Jack Lank-Sleeve. Better than all the rest of them, a decent man, a good friend.

Fredrick drops his head. Exhaustion from a life lived too long. William looks over to check on him. Through the brows of his eyes, Fredrick connects with William just ahead in the bateau. William needs Fredrick to know their connection in this place. They share that connection for as long as they can. A silent shared exchange is an archive of pain's suffering. The agonizing frustration of one more good man whose life has been cut and finished. *When will the rest of them, all of them, across this miserable Mississippi Valley realize it's the river who snickers at death? The river drowns all dreams.* The slightest wisp of a weary smile is their recognition. Fredrick drops his head to his knees.

William looks up into the sky. *Is there anything there, anyone at all?*

He turns to Jack for their moment of connection; the stories they have written, miles of passage through forests and woods, dreams and hopes with them all the way. Every mile of the river a trial, made all the better by their Jack's dear company. The best of any companion. In the end, he chose the better place. A good soul. How proud we are of him. William and Jack can see it in each other's eyes. They will bide their time. A bloody revenge will not make this right, but how little they care for morality's guidance.

Jack Red-Hair looks away from William to see Mr. Knight's face. He keeps the strength of conviction to pass to Knight. Representative Knight must know this too, as he looks over to Jack Red-Hair to share the suffering of this wanton disrespect for human life. The pain of a man's death. The shot of a gun takes everything. It lasts forever. But he is also separate from the rest of them. The poor man's murder is the reflection of his confusion, a puzzle he cannot piece together. The river has taken the confidence that has allowed him to maintain the person he has been for so long. *What am I now? Sitting across from the Jack with red hair, a troubled man in a boat on a river. In a place and in a time. Without the experience to know where and how to belong. Who am I now?* But there is a clarity in their connection. Jack with red hair gives Knight the exceptional clarity that comes with rage. Knight takes it. He feels the pulse of the added adrenaline that comes with sudden determination. But it catches his thoughts in mid-stride. What to do with this new precision? How does it all fit together? The rush becomes a sickening mistrust, feeble and of no use to any of it. He's tired. His shoulders and his back slump down from the weight of it, the agonizing moment. He drops his head like the others, and there are the shoes and the mud.

Knight shifts his weight and looks over at Hardy, who is sitting next to him on the middle seat. Knight realizes there is one true thing in this tormented, storied nightmare. It's the boy. He reaches over and takes Hardy's chin in his hand, raising his head to look into his eyes. He wants to show Hardy strength and give him that strength. On Knight's face, a wince becomes almost a smile, but the smile quickly fades into the same strained blankness of the powerless resignation they all feel.

"Dear Boy, we're in the middle of a situation neither of us has the ability to comprehend. I cannot, I can't…" Knight can't find the words. He pats the top of Hardy's head and turns away. The unspoken they share.

In that moment, Hardy feels Mr. Knight's desire to gather the strength to protect him. In spite of all that has happened, he has a sympathetic trust in the man. There is a trust in knowing enough about him, a man who lives with his own limitations. He's a man who wants to accomplish more than he will probably ever be able to do. This will get worse, maybe never better. His thoughts turn to what his father might do, in this place, in the boat, here with these terrible men. What could he do? *He was my friend. How could this world let that happen? Fairness is such a stupid idea. He was a good person; he was kind.* Hardy looks out into the long distance ahead. The river stretches straight and flat for miles.

"Chickasaw."

The Osage in the bateau—who has become the leader—calls out, suddenly, out of the blue. He points downriver several hundred yards to three canoes that are pulled up onto the riverbank. The canoes are empty. He knows the tribe from the painted symbols on the canoes. These symbols are childish, unsophisticated offerings to the river.

The other Osage let loose a quick series of hoots and yelps. The lead Osage quickly waves his hands. Quiet! The other Osage immediately understand the opportunity.

The Osage leader in the bateau's front suddenly turns to face William and the others. He appears very proud of himself and excited. "I am Po-hi. You are now part of Osage hunt."

William closes his eyes in pronounced and utterly fatigued disbelief.

Jack Red-Hair stops paddling and lets his oar hang in the oarlock. "Let lightning strike me dead."

Representative Knight and Hardy look at each other. Of course, it will get worse.

Fredrick, with this news, sits up, looks up and says, "Fellas, this might be our opportunity."

Chapter Eight

The world is this way

The river is rushing, pulling hard to get the boats downriver.

Po-hi, the self-appointed leader, turns to the other young Osage, and with a foul sense of glee, he asks them, "Wa-ka-ka-xe shko ki-de te shko-ta—do you want to go to the show?"

The raiders begin their preparations without the slightest amount of wasted effort. The two canoes turn to go back upriver, the bateau with the pirogue reverse their direction as well. Po-hi raises his musket to Knight but speaks to the others in the bateau and Fredrick in the pirogue, his face an ugly snarl, "Speak now and you will bed with your British in the river."

The Osage sit low in the canoes; they've wrapped the oars with leather, and they paddle hard. The only sound is the muffled oars stroking the water. Po-hi's musket ensures that the bateau's oars keep up with the canoes. The boats are as close to the shore as possible. From the woods, they cannot be seen.

William and Jack assume there will be another bloody scene in the woods. These tribes are a violent combination. Who knows what to expect? If the Chickasaw in the woods are level-headed, they could outsmart these butchers and avoid serious trouble. Being taken with the raiders into the woods would be the worst scenario; very risky, a good chance you will not be coming back out. The woods give their own permission.

Po-hi points to a spot on the river bank. The Osage have positioned themselves far enough upriver to enter the woods and come back around to surround the Chickasaw without being discovered. Slave raid strategy.

The Osage spring into action, still without a sound. They step out of the canoes into the shallow water and the mud and pull the boats far enough up the slope of the bank to make them secure. Po-hi steps over to Knight, takes his arm, and pulls him up from his seat. He puts his hand across Knight's mouth for a quick moment. Knight understands the gesture and nods his head. As Po-hi is dragging Knight to step out of the boat, Knight reaches for Hardy and pulls him up out of his seat. He will not let them be separated. Stepping out of the bateau, the thought of his shoes in the mud gives Knight a quick challenge. The two of them are brought up to a spot on the river bank, where they wait for what comes next. They look at each other. The fear of it has not yet become panic. They just don't know what to expect and look away to see what is happening with the others.

One of the Osage brings a rope over to Knight and ties the rope loosely around his neck, then pulls it tight. It's heavy and bristled. It's a shock and confusing. He realizes he has no option but can't imagine what plan would include him.

"Dear God, is this really necessary?"

The rope is long, but the Osage keeps Knight close. Every few steps, he gives it a jerk as they walk over to the others assembling on the river bank. Knight keeps one hand on the rope to lessen the pull on his neck.

"Dear God, is this really happening?"

The decisions about who will go into the woods and who will stay behind are quick. Hardy is brought over to stand next to Mr. Knight. The youngest of the Osage raiders—no more than sixteen—motions for William and Jack to step out of the bateau and into the pirogue.

Fredrick, William, and Jack sit where they can. The pirogue is full. The young Osage stands on the bank next to the pirogue with his musket at attention. William and Jack nod to each other. It seems there might be a little luck left to be had with a sixteen-year-old. At this point in the preparations, Fredrick assumes he'll be left behind. Staying with the boat is the best chance to survive this new trial. If William could give enough of a distraction to the Osage guarding them, Jack could get at the knot of the rope. Then he could do the rest. William, whispering under his breath, "Hold tight, there might be an opportunity not to be missed." The Osage guard watches their every move. William fully appreciates that any quick move would trigger a sudden violent reaction. The guard is a teenager, and more than likely, this is a new position in a slave raid. He'll want to prove himself.

Po-hi and the two other raiders stand shoulder to shoulder; they face straight ahead to the woods, their backs to the river. With focused attention, they're waiting for just the right moment—some subtle signal from the woods or pulse of adrenaline. Muskets are primed and ready. Knight and Hardy stand with them, making an extraordinarily odd mix on so many levels.

Representative Knight looks down at Hardy and cocks his head. "We'll see what happens now."

Hardy nods. "I guess."

The tension in the air—everyone but the Osage can feel it—is that the dangerous arrogance of these teenagers will shove them into a violent confrontation none of them actually intended, and they'll not have any amount of intelligence to stop it before it becomes a bloody, useless waste of lives. Anyone shot? anyone killed, for any reason, at any point?

It appears as though the raid is ready to begin.

Po-hi motions for the hunter on his left to enter the woods to the far left. He will enter straight ahead, and the young raider holding Knight's rope will follow him. That Hardy is untied and given only the simple command to follow close behind is as strange to Hardy as anything else happening around him. It appears to be a strategic decision made by Po-hi. More than likely, it's assumed that if the young American were to run off and make it back to the boats, he'd be shot dead there or he'd not make it through the night, anyway. But it doesn't feel right.

With the raid for slaves about to begin, the Osage know they will show little concern for the relations between tribes in the valley. They will eagerly jeopardize the peace and trade treaties shared by many neighboring tribes. They will do as they choose. They are Osage.

After European goods entered the economic system of tribal trade nets, the role of the captive changed. The desire for guns, metal, and ornamental trinkets placed valley tribes in a buyer's market. In these evolving circumstances, readily available furs are not the only items considered valuable to European colonists. Indian captives destined for European enterprise are of high value and make good barter. Slave raiding appeals to the warring nature of regional cultures, a connection to the territory wars of the past. A proud history. These young Osage warriors will not be told the ways of their world. Whatever their intentions, the Osage raiders are aware of treaties that have been delicately assembled by those who have suffered the most. Why they would jeopardize so much can only be speculation. Young Osage, like many young warriors, are capable of instigating foolhardy adventures, often with disastrous repercussions. Young people rarely appreciate the difficulties and histories of hardship accrued to achieve a more prosperous way of life.

With no announcement, Po-hi takes two deliberate steps, then quickly moves straight forward, disappearing into the woods. The other young raider, along with Knight and Hardy, follow quickly behind. The young raider on the left enters the woods at an angle, which allows the Osage to cover the greatest amount of ground as they move deeper into the woods. It also gives him the strategic opportunity to surround the Chickasaw. The Osage raid begins on the river. The river, on occasion, will deliberately appear tolerant of foolish behavior, like a caregiver or a nurturing parent. The river will wait patiently for reckless oversights and errors, like a trap for the blind. It will spring and strike. Deadly consequences for the uninitiated. The young Osage accept the river's challenge; they flirt with it.

The river's woods are a different field of play. From all sides, above and below, physical threats lie in wait; desperately wanting to taunt the opponent. Figures and beings lurk everywhere. The young Osage have been trained for the stealth of the hunt. This quickly dominates their every move and strategy. When the young raiders step into the woods, what remains of the drunken rum quickly sobers. The woods are ready to pounce. Across the valley, the best stories include a chapter of how the woods snatched those unaware of the shades and tones throughout, never to be seen again, disappearing into the spirit of the woods, sucked up and now part of its skin.

Po-hi, in the lead position, moves with silent confidence. His moccasin'd feet take rapid steps on the small branches and leaves of the forest floor that cannot be heard. He bends at the waist, eyes intensely forward and his ears tuned to the slightest interruption of the forest's routine. He covers ground quickly.

The young raider to the far left of Po-hi moves with equal silence. He has smartly broadened the area of their raid's approach. As they cover ground, the two raiders keep just enough distance to see each other through the fallen trees and thick brush.

Every few minutes, Po-hi stops still, and he drops to one knee. He uses the silence of the woods to catch any clue. He waits for only a minute to hear anything the woods may offer. If there is no conversation, he continues on. The raider in the rear intuitively follows the same path as Po-hi. He brings Knight and Hardy along with him, but they keep a safe distance. They stay out of sight. Not a sound.

Po-hi reads the density of the undergrowth in the woods. If it is too thick, a Chickasaw would pass around. He smells the air and listens intently to the birds. If the birds continue their cross-talk in the thick of the woods, he will keep steady. If he hears disturbed calls or the broken chatter of the birds in the short distance ahead, there are Indians in the woods. So far, there's only the banter of everyday business.

"I'll need to rest," Knight tells the young raider who holds his rope. "Can we stop for just one short minute. A minute or two?" He makes every effort to speak with a hushed voice, but he is out of breath and can't manage the whisper. His knees are the weak point. That pain will only get worse.

The Osage spins around to look at Knight directly. "This is not adventure."

"Please, I am not fit for this. My knees are not what they used to be. Do the words 'chronic pain' mean anything? 'Osteoarthritis?'" Knight bends at the waist, keeping one eye on Hardy. "Perhaps I could just wait for you here. Tie the rope around a tree. I'll be patient as a saint, quiet as a church mouse. Let me think, what would be the equivalent?"

The young raider, with as much drama as the momentary break will allow, steps closer to Knight, making sure the old man can watch his eyes move slowly down the length of Knight's body and legs. "Feet will move." A particularly unpleasant tone.

Representative Knight nods his head, and the three of them continue forward with the raid.

Hardy keeps the momentum through the obstacles, only slightly off pace behind. He watches Mr. Knight's ordeal, but he doesn't say a word. Several times he thinks, *why not just turn and take off, get back to William and Jack at the river?* Each time, he realizes he can't leave Mr. Knight alone in this. So he keeps going. He doesn't want to think about what lies ahead or how much worse this could become. *Keep up, just keep going.*

Po-hi carries his rifles straight up and down as he makes his way through the woods. But the obstacles of the path require that he periodically stop to tamp down the powder, cloth, and musket ball to keep his rifle ready.

He keeps the raid at a quick pace. The farther he moves into the woods, the keener his focus on the smell in the air and the sound of the birds. He has chosen his path well. He has let the woods show him the way.

The birds farther ahead are noisy and busy with their alerts. Their business has changed. Indians have come into their territory. Their distress leads Po-hi in their direction.

Po-hi slows and scans the woods, panning his head in every direction; there are only the trees and vines. He softens his breathing, better to listen, then returns his focus to what is directly ahead. There is a darkness that does not belong. Immediately, Po-hi drops to one knee, his eyes fixed on the shape. It is not the shape of the forest. It is a figure.

He waits for any movement. The figure doesn't move.

Po-hi won't be constrained by a lengthy wait-and-see. He's impatient. Careful steps, and he will close in on the figure to force whatever action is necessary. An Indian without wounds will be best for trade. He moves forward ten feet. Closer still, another ten feet. The figure is strange to not move forward or turn and run. Ten more. The figure is clearly an Indian. He has no rifle—an Indian in the woods with no rifle.

With the limited instinct of a young man, Po-hi rushes. As he sprints the distance over a tree trunk and around a prickly shrub, the Indian still does not move. He is close enough; he stops. Po-hi is suddenly stunned, confused. The face is not a Chickasaw. It is his elder, Niwashake, standing in front of him.

"Why are you here?" Po-hi's muffled bark. He encourages the disrespect in his voice. "You are not needed here."

Niwashake patiently waits for the young raider to catch his breath before taking one step forward. His voice is calm, almost still in Po-hi's ears. "You are in these woods; you are on this hunt." One long and patient breath. "I am not here for these matters. I am here for reasons you cannot see."

Po-hi takes one step back away from Niwashake. It's all he can do.

"What the young and foolish Osage do in these woods with the Chickasaw will have serious consequences which you will know. But these are also not my concern."

"These woods are Osage woods." Po-hi's arrogance is challenged. "They will give us what we hunt."

"It is clear that Po-hi is a brave and eager warrior. If the day will come when you will be in this world with the respect for which you truly hunt, you must choose a different path. This day in the woods will not take you down a path of respect and knowledge. The scars of this day will not be like the scar on your face; that is a scar of pride, the mark of a young man learning his way. The scar of this day will be a scar of shame."

Po-hi takes several steps back from Niwashake. "Po-hi will walk fine without your words."

Niwashake waits for their words to be carried off by the breeze into the woods. He lets the moment pass.

With a powerful serenity, he speaks again: "The young white boy will go down the river, down to the source of its ending. This is not part of your world. I am finished talking." These words drift deeper into the woods; they bounce from tree to tree, leaving echoes as they disappear.

Po-hi turns away from Niwashake. He feels defeated by the Elder. His path in the woods is confused. He walks away. The purpose of his path are now too many. He changes direction several times. Too many paths to follow.

Suddenly, in the distance, the snap of a twig on the forest floor brings him back to his place in the woods. He crouches low to wait for a following sound. The Indian stands tall in a position of guard. There will be others in his party. A warrior standing watch here in the woods means they are a food gathering party. The others will be digging the ground for wild potato. This is what the woods should offer here—this dirt, this sunlight. He slows to a crawl.

Po-hi sees the other young Osage raider far to the left and signals to go deeper back, come around the party. He knows the Indian guard in the woods will be listening for the sound of moccasin on the ground. He would do the same.

The Chickasaw warrior—who stands guard in the woods—listens to the sounds of the day and keeps watch through the thick woods for any motion that doesn't belong. The Indian keeps his guard, but he is also untroubled by the pleasant day and the time of the late afternoon sunlight. There is no danger here. His rifle is easy in his hands as he enjoys the voices of the women behind him, who talk among themselves as they dig the shallow ground for roots.

To his ear, there is the occasional giggle and even a laugh out loud coming from the three Chickasaw women. They wear long dresses made from both deer pelt and the cloth of blankets. Tied at the waist with strips of hide, their jackets and shirts are made from thin cloth, and they wear around their necks several beaded necklaces. One of the women keeps an infant by her side as she digs the dirt. The child is wrapped in deer hide. Spread around the women are several baskets. Some of these are already full. They talk about their men and their children; they talk about the sky and the problems back in the longhouse of their village. Mostly, they made jokes about their warrior guard, whose name is Piominko, and his short legs.

The moment has come. Po-hi raises his rifle and moves one quick step at a time to a position of attack. He has positioned himself well. His quickness has brought him close to the Chickasaw guard, and he's been undetected. More quick moments pass. The advance on the Chickasaw must be now.

Suddenly, in the trees, the clamor of birds goes silent. The woods are silent.

The Chickasaw guard reads the sudden quiet, and his body stiffens. Without hesitation, his rifle is raised, and it listens intently to find its target. His feet hold tight to the ground. The leather grabs the dirt. In the back of his mouth, Piominko feels the dryness of his tongue. He must swallow. The three women see his body and his rifle change position. In that same moment, they move into a tight group, crouching as low to the ground as they can. They, too, are quiet. The infant's soft noises are now the only sounds heard in the woods. Far too quiet.

Piominko is breathing very low, each breath long and slow. His body cannot make sound for the ears. His rifle pans slowly across. It cannot disrupt the current of air. Sunlight shooting down through two branches overhead, striking a dead brown leaf resting lightly on the ground, flickers through his attention. A beetle walks across the bark of a dead tree. And then there it is. He catches the sound of one moccasin ever so slightly touching the ground. This gives the entirety of his senses a direction through the trees. With one more silent step, in one beat of the heart, the confirmation brings him to full defense.

Po-hi realizes his mistake and instantly charges forward, his rifle up at aim, into a position thirty feet from the Chickasaw Piominko. There he stops abruptly, his position fixed. Musket aimed.

"Osage," Piominko cries out. The woods are broken.

"Chickasaw," Po-hi says in a very ordinary tone.

A fragile peace between the two Valley Tribes has become a standoff in the woods. A picturesque but dangerous image.

The Chickasaw mother of the infant quickly moves to put her child out of sight behind a fallen tree trunk nearby. She wants to believe her baby will be safe there. She quickly returns to the circle, with the two other Chickasaw women huddled together.

Po-hi's eye stares down the black iron length of the musket's barrel while taking slow, short, deliberate steps toward the Chickasaw—one after the other after the other.

Piominko feels the weight of his rifle as though it is his arm. There is not one point in the constellation of his awareness that remains unconsidered, down the length of his musket's barrel.

Both weapons aim true, and each will let loose its purpose at any flinch of weakness, any quiver of opportunity.

Po-hi began his hunting with other boys of his Osage Tribe. He was the youngest of them to go behind to surround the Chickasaw. When he was much younger, his first shot of the musket was a misfire that burned his face with the powder flash. The scar he carries gives him pride in his early ambition. The scar is also useful for intimidating strangers on the river—the tools of a skilled actor.

The Chickasaw Piominko is named by his tribe to mean "war prophet and leader." As a very young boy, he was trained by the Elders with sticks and toy tomahawks to defeat other boys, who were draped in bear hides, charging into the village from the forest. A young warrior must learn to show strength, to not back away from large, frightening enemies in the woods or threats from the river.

Piominko's dramatic change from a guard standing at peace with the forest day into a threatening adversary is not lost on Po-hi. Piominko is truly a threat.

Both young men believe, with the conviction of a tested warrior, that they are reading the situation to perfection. They see it from every angle. With no doubt, each is the more skilled in the hunt. Each believe their strength and their cunning will give them the victory of first shot. There is nothing more they need.

Po-hi takes one more half-step forward. His vision crawls down the barrel, inch by inch, framing the Chickasaw's chest with the rifle's tip. Piominko tilts his head ever-so-slightly to show his tightening aim on the Osage, one more small bit of his superior skill.

The entire forest is frozen in the moment.

One solid block of everything. Time has stopped. It holds itself in place.

The two proud heroes no longer feel the metal of the gun; their bodies have fallen away; there is only the long iron rifle with a small ball of lead.

The sharp crack of a musket shot splits time in two.

Both bodies flinch. In an instant, their grips loosen, and their muskets return the weight to their arms. Both guns drop slightly from their target's sure-shot, but their eyes stay locked to each other's stare. Cunning and skill are past. A flash of confusion sweeps over them both. Time is suspended, and now it's empty. The sudden scream of the Chickasaw mother is heard distant and muffled, the sound of it swallowed by the forest.

Piominko's rifle wavers; the weight of it is heavy.

Po-hi looks up slightly, shifting his focus to behind his opponent. There is a small cloud of white smoke just at the edge of the woods. Po-hi has lost his chance to prove his bluff and take the Chickasaw without injury. He stands stunned, watching the white smoke break apart into swirling waves, each bound by its own determination to go in its own direction of purpose.

The front end of Piominko's rifle, far too heavy, begins to drop. He is shot. The musket ball from behind has struck his thigh and torn a hole. He can no longer stand erect. Fiercely defiant, Piominko is forced to drop to one knee. He cannot defend the others of his tribe.

The barrel end of Piominko's rifle is now resting on the ground, and his body is giving in to the collapse of his weight. He stays his fixed stare at the Osage, a show of strength.

The Chickasaw women tighten their circle, their heads buried in the heap of their three bodies.

From behind Piominko, the young Osage who had circled behind walks forward to show himself to Po-hi and divides what remains of the gunpowder smoke. It is his rifle that fired the shot, and he is afraid to hear the reaction from his leader. He walks with the shame of his mistake, the premature shot.

Into the confusion, the third Osage raider, holding the rope to Knight, walks into the scene. Knight—at the rope—walks in with Hardy still a few steps behind.

Both of them are shocked and bewildered by what has taken place. Another episode of useless violence. They stop and wait for something to make sense. Let the Osage sort this one out.

In the next moment, no less surprising, Niwashake walks out of the woods to join this circle of misfortune. He doesn't offer words, and he doesn't look at the Osage or the Chickasaw. Surprisingly, he walks deliberately over to Hardy, takes hold of his shoulder, and pulls him to his side. They will stand there and wait patiently for the rest of what must happen.

On cue, Po-hi walks straight across to the Osage who mistakenly fired the shot. He stands in front of him; the exasperation in his voice is unmistakable. He tells him bluntly that he has lost the value of their raid to capture the Chickasaw for trade. More than once his anger shoves the young Osage, nearly pushing him to the ground. "The Chickasaw warrior is of no value. He cannot be traded. His body is worthless." Whatever is left to trade from this raid, he will not have his share.

At the river, William and the others heard the shot. They move closer together to speak. There is now an urgency. They feel it, but what can they do? The frustration of the moment either clouds their thinking or clarifies a desperate plan of action.

"A sacrifice may be the only way. I'm willing to say it," Jack tells them. He's no longer concerned with the whispering or disguising his tone. "I know you're both thinking it."

The Osage, standing five feet away, hears the words. He's not sure about the meaning of "sacrifice." He uses his rifle to show he's still very much in control.

William makes a mighty exhale. His thoughts wrestle their way back. He decides on a quote. His haversack, with his book inside, is over in the bateau. He'll have to best recall what he can. "In the course of our lives, the evil which in itself we seek most to shun, and which, when we are fallen into, is the most dreadful to us, is oftentimes the very means or door of our deliverance, by which alone we can be raised again from the affliction we are fallen into." Whatever the circumstances, William's book-quotation voice remains consistent. It's as if he has decided that the words serve their purpose best if they float above the uneasiness of that moment.

"William," Jack must contribute. "You are a dear soul and a terrific companion, but how in the good graces of heaven is one of your quotes going to get us out of this predicament?"

"A level head, Jack, and surely a trust in our abilities. We've been in worse; nothing has changed; we're still at the mercy of one single opportunity."

Fredrick knows it too. "All we need is the one."

Chapter Nine

The deer at the spring

The woods begin to fill again with the birds' chatter. Representative Knight and the Osage holding the rope to his neck are now the farthest outside the assembled group. He calls forward to Hardy, standing immediately next to Niwashake. "Hold on," he tells him. "This is probably about over. I believe they have what they came for, and most likely, we'll be set free, or, God knows." Knight waits for a minute to see if he has been heard and understood. "How are you? Are you seeing the other side of this? Are you thinking clearly?"

Hardy hears Knight's words, and he thinks, *what a strange thing to ask at this point.* "I don't know, I guess, I'm okay. What happens now? Should we try to run out of here? I don't have any money."

Little of what is happening here in the woods makes sense to Hardy. The violence is hard to accept, but it's obvious. He acknowledges that he's being given some kind of special treatment—no rope. The Elder appears to want to protect him, but he's not really a threat to anyone. These thoughts only make the confusion worse.… *what does Niwashake think I am? What am I supposed to be to him? It's too much to look at him. The Osage are not that much older. How do they have guns and they're treated like grown men.*

Piominko cannot stand. The commands he gives to his body to stand are quickly rejected. His leg will not respond. The pain is of little consequence. He cannot defend the women of his tribe. He'll stay kneeling on the ground and do what is necessary.

Po-hi walks toward him and bends to pick up the rifle lying on the ground. When he is close, Piominko swings one arm at the Indian, trying to strike a blow. It's of no use. The frustration of a young Chickasaw warrior who has lost all chances swells up inside of him. He shouts, "Go from here! Take your pride and leave us in peace!"

Po-hi steps back to him and puts the butt end of his musket to Piominko's chest and delivers two quick jabs. Piominko grabs the rifle. They both confront the thoughts of the other. With one last shove, Po-hi yanks the rifle away and steps back to walk away.

"We must leave this place quickly," Po-hi says to the other Osage raiders. "Chickasaw may be in the woods, and we have a clumsy hunter who cannot keep his rifle quiet. That is our disadvantage. We will take the Chickasaw women. It is still a raid."

Knight understands the hand gestures of the Osage as they are preparing to leave this spot. He sees the women being made to begin the walk back through the woods to the boats. "And what do you imagine you would like to do with myself and the boy?" he loudly asks to anyone, spinning around and flailing his arms. He then looks to the Elder Niwashake, who he hopes has some kind of command over the teenagers. "You can't possibly expect us to continue on this misery campaign. We are not from here. This is most definitely criminal behavior, as defined by the entire civilized world. Take this rope off of me and let myself and the boy walk back to our boat. We'll have nothing to do with your vicious cruelty. You can do what you want, but we're not part of this history circus. Do you hear me?"

Not understanding the meaning of every word but clearly sensing the demanding tone, Po-hi walks straight over to Knight. "You will hang after the Chickasaw is finished with the rope. You have come through our woods and come up our river. Not worth the trade. We are done with you."

Knight leans forward, his hands on his hips. He bends at the waist, "Hang?"

With the rope around his neck pulled tight to keep him back, Knight tugs to take steps toward Po-hi. "Hang?" He pivots to Hardy. "What cineplex theater do you suppose this is?" He spins back to Po-hi. "You can't possibly hang an elected Representative to the United States House of Representatives." Knight's shouting. "Do the words civility, judicial process, illegal, immoral! Do they mean anything to you?" His heart is pumping hard in his chest.

"Mr. Knight, you gotta back down," Hardy calls across.

Po-hi steps up to Knight. With both hands, he shoves him backward. "Militia has a big mouth."

Niwashake watches the nastiness and the posturing escalate. He stands without expression. He's put his hand on Hardy's shoulder and will wait to see how far the young Osage will go to earn his shame. Hardy won't go up to the Osage Po-hi and confront him. It won't do any good. *It can't possibly become a real hanging, that's just not possible, and why doesn't Niwashake at least try to stop them.*

The Osage know the situation must end quickly. It's too loud and too much extra business. One of them steps forward and unties Knight's rope, then throws it over the good branch of the tree immediately outside of the gathered circle. Once the rope is over the branch, there is enough to fit the noose around the wounded Chickasaw, who has been brought next to the tree. The noose is slipped around Piominko's ankle. Several of the Valley Tribes hang the discarded upside down by one leg to die.

His rifle at Knight, Po-hi keeps close watch on the quickness of the preparation.

"This is barbaric and entirely unacceptable." Knight is gripping his chest.

Po-hi has finished his patience for Knight's chatter. He steps over and puts his face inches to Knight's face and holds it there for several intense moments. With the ferocity of quietly mouthed rage, he spits his words at Knight. "Barbaric is a not white man's word. Osage know barbaric well. We are chief of barbaric." He waits for any words Knight might have to return.

Niwashake keeps to his place. He can now see he will not out-think or out-smart Po-hi's dangerous strength. The reckless actions of the young warrior will forever be misdirected until age can make them right.

Hardy cannot imagine what to do next.

The three Chickasaw women make themselves appear to be helpless and vulnerable. For now, they try to move away from the rifle pointed at them, but with each step, they are forced back into their tight group. The mother of the infant can barely walk. She shuffles her feet as her companions help her along.

Defiant throughout the unfolding ordeal, despite the pain of his wound and the indignation of being outsmarted, Piominko will not give them the satisfaction of showing weakness. His strength will not leave him; it will embrace him when the rope is tight. He knows he will die from the Osage hanging. He has seen others of his tribe hanging in the woods. If he had the chance, he would do the same. If he had heard the young raider's steps on the forest floor before the shot, he would hold the rope.

When the violence and the aggression slip into a momentary pause, Niwashake sees his moment is now upon him. His purpose must be made. He walks Hardy over to the brave and bleeding Chickasaw, kneeling on the ground, the rope tight to his ankle. For a short minute, Niwashake looks down at Hardy and feels the anger and confusion racing through the young boy. How painful this must be. The boy belongs so far from this place. He will know the generosity of his strength when the time will come for it.

Without a word, or any preparation, Niwashake takes hold of Hardy's wrist. Hardy feels the grip and tries to pull away but only wrestles for a moment. There's no real reason to resist. Gently and with no hesitation, Niwashake places Hardy's hand directly on the bloody open wound on the Chickasaw warrior's thigh. It's immediately astonishing and awful. He looks up at the Elder. There is nothing to know from his face. His palm is pressed to the warm blood of the open wound.

Hardy doesn't want to look. He can hear Mr. Knight's shouting. The Elder's grip is firm, but he can't look. Why is this happening? I'm twelve. I'm just a kid. A twelve-year-old's tears begin to blur his vision, then Hardy looks at his hand on the Indian's wound. The feeling of it is somehow more than the sight of it. The red of the blood between his fingers begins to cover the top of his hand, now a hand in a blur of warm red. His hand stays on the wound, and now he can't look away, won't try to wipe the tears off his face.

There is more than the warm wetness in his hand. He can feel the rhythmic pulse in the blurry red. The Indian's heartbeat is there in the blurry field of red. A clouded sky of red. The strength of the Indian's heart gives an ever-so-slight beat to the red sky. It's hardly there, but it stays. It feels natural and right. A regular pulsing rhythm in the sky—like the pulsing red of an ambulance—is always a sign; harm will be over soon. Knowing there's safe passage, Hardy looks down from the sky to the front of his canoe. They're making good progress against the current, which is a moment of pride. He didn't think he actually had that much strength in his arms.

It's definitely good he has the strength because there's not a lot of extra time to get upriver to the stream where he needs to go. The stream connects to the river about a mile or so up ahead. Arms can tire out quickly paddling upriver.

It will be tricky not knowing which stream. There are several along this stretch. They're all wide enough for the canoe, but from the river, they look much the same.

Not sure which stream would be right, he looks around for any clues. Looking behind him, Hardy sees the reason he's making such good progress. A man sits behind him in the canoe, and he's doing most of the work.

"Hello," the man says, "I was waiting for you to turn around. Good to see you. I know you're wondering which one of these streams to turn up on to get to the spring you're looking for. I think I can help with that."

"Wow, so sorry, I didn't see you there. Sorry. Thanks for any help. By the way, I'm Hardy. You can call me Hardy. Everybody does."

"Then that's what I'll call you. Seems like a good enough name to me. Over there it is. You see it? I'm Jack, you can call me Jack, and you're pulling more than your weight, Hardy. I couldn't get there without your help."

"Oh, thank you, Sir. I see it. I think you're right. It has to be the one. It's got the right shape to it. Can I ask you how long?"

"How long for what, Hardy? Let me guess, how long did it take to grow my beard? Is that it?"

"How'd you know that, Jack? Just a good guess?"

"Hardy, of all the conversations I've had on this river, over all these years, most definitely the one I've had the most is how long to grow my beard. When I started out, it was black as coal. Now as you can see, white as snow."

Jack's beard is every bit more than a foot, and thick.

"The answer is—and I'm sure you'd agree, riddles are a poor excuse in a conversation—but the answer is: I didn't grow the beard. The beard grew me. What say we head up that stream over there? It'd be best if you'd paddle on the left."

"I'm on it, and I disagree. I think a good riddle is better than a conversation about the weather."

The two of them make a good team. They make a good swift turn into the tributary, not too fast, and they manage to not lose too much of their steam going in.

The stream is not more than fifteen feet wide. It's deep enough to not be a problem. The canoe sits high on the water, one of its many attributes. In no time at all, the two of them have made it up the stream a little more than a mile. The woods are dense, as usual, but at this point, the bottom of the stream is clearly visible, the dead leaves and tree branches clear as day.

"We'd make better progress," Jack knows the woods like the back of his hand, "I believe if we get out here and you walk the rest of the way up to it, that would be the better idea. It can't be that far. The water is already running clear. If I had to guess, I'd say less than half a mile."

They pull the canoe up. It's secure, not going anywhere.

"I'll stay with the boat. You'd be better to go this part on your own."

"But you're a tracker. You know the path better than I do."

"Well, you're not wrong about that. I know my way through these woods and across these rivers. You'll be perfectly fine. You just follow the creek and it'll take you right to the pool at the spring."

"But what if I…"

"Son, there ain't a chance in the world you'd miss the spring. It'll be right where it's supposed to be, and you'll walk right up to it just like you're supposed to, I just know it. Mind your Ps & Qs, and you'll be fine, better than fine."

"My dad would not agree with you, not at all. That you can count on. But, okay, I guess I can trust you, bearded Jack. I'll go it alone."

There doesn't seem to be many birds throughout this part of the woods. Is that a good sign? Who can remember which way it goes?

The two of them say their temporary goodbyes and be carefuls, and Hardy takes a big breath, and that's it. All the preparation he needs. All the confidence in the world. He heads up the creek. The spring will be up there somewhere.

Jack was right. Walk along the creek. It couldn't be easier. The sun shines through here more than other places. The branches up top are thinner. That makes it all the more pleasant. *Whatever happened to my windbreaker? Oh well, don't need it in here.*

Up ahead, not too far, there are a couple of large boulders. "That must be it." One is actually huge.

Hardy walks straight to the boulders. They've made a small pool. The water is exceptionally clear, like water in a bathtub. "This is actually nice." Looking around, there's not much more than more trees. The woods go off in every direction. "I'm actually thirsty. I don't think that water, that water can't be polluted—way too clear. I'm not sure why I'm talking out loud…"

Out of the blue, an Indian walks straight out of the woods and right up to the pool. "That water is exceptionally good water. For Osage, the water of the spring is medicine. A gift to the Indian people from the Spirit of the spring."

"Hello there." Hardy tries his best to not act startled, but of course, he is. The Osage is a striking, impressive figure of a man. Like the others he now knows. The presence of this Osage is, more than anything, his strength and confidence. A powerful man with the friendliness and ease of a child. "You should drink the water if you are thirsty," he tells Hardy. "All tribes share this medicine water. You are welcome here."

"Maybe in a minute, but thank you."

Everything unexpected should be expected. On the opposite side of the spring, another Indian walks out of the woods and straight to the pool of the spring. The Osage is correct; all tribes are welcome here. Chickasaw councils are held here at the spring in the woods.

The Chickasaw is carrying an incredibly large and fat deer over his shoulders. When he gets several feet from the pool, he turns his body to drop the dead deer to the ground. The deer isn't as bloody as you would think. Another incredible thing to witness at the spring.

"The Chickasaw has been successful with hunt. That is good for him," the Osage says to the Chickasaw on the opposite side, maybe the slightest edge to his voice.

"Why would the Osage be jealous? One day the hunt is good. The next day there is nothing to show. The empty hands of every hunter are a good joke to the crow. The Osage knows this well."

The Chickasaw kneels at the edge of the spring. The water will quench his thirst. He cups his hands and reaches into the pool, then pours the water out on the ground as an offering of respect and refreshment to the Spirit of the spring. He bends at the waist and puts his lips to the water to drink.

"Why does the Chickasaw drink the water where his illegitimate children may drink?" The edge in the Osage's voice has turned ugly. "I am proud, and I drink at the headwaters."

"Chickasaw and Osage are brothers. Let them drink together," the Chickasaw kindly tells him. A really pleasant man.

"No. The Chickasaw pays tribute to the tribes that led our nations to war."

Standing next to the spring, the Osage squares himself; he straightens his shoulders and he stands a little taller.

"The Osage lies. His tongue is like the snake's. His heart is black. When the Great Spirit made his children, he said not to one, drink here, and to another, drink there, but gave water that all might drink." He looks up, still kneeling at the edge.

The Osage doesn't respond, but as the Chickasaw leans over again, toward the bubbling surface to take a drink. The Osage walks casually, deceptively behind him, and in one sudden instant, the Osage throws his heavy body at the Chickasaw. He lands on top of him, the advantage is with his weight.

"Shit." Is all Hardy can say, didn't see it coming.

Too much the advantage, the Osage can easily hold the poor Chickasaw's head under the water. The Chickasaw flails his arms, trying to grab hold and pull the Osage from his back, but he can't get the hold. His arms splash wildly in the pool. For a brief second, Hardy thinks it looks rehearsed. The Chickasaw stops fighting back, and his body is limp. In no time at all, he's drowned.

In that moment, Hardy feels his presence, his place between the two Indians in the pool of the spring. This is not something you easily put into words, this feeling in the two men. He feels the strength of their will and the strength of submission. They share it equally.

Hardy stands, waiting for what might come next. It happens fairly quick; the Osage steps out of the pool and gives a quick look to Hardy and then to the deer on the ground. The Chickasaw floats face down. Somehow, it doesn't feel like he's drowned dead. But the understanding is that Hardy should walk to the deer and put his hand on its body. Is there life in the deer that lingers? So, this is what he does. Hardy kneels next to the deer. Its body seems larger than it should. There is the musket's shot. A hole torn in the deer's shoulder just above its front leg. There's very little blood, not hardly enough. He notices the Osage walk back into the woods.

Hardy reaches forward and puts his palm onto the deer's wound. It feels familiar and important. He'll keep it there. Seconds fly by. The deer is truly an impressive body; the weight of it, the warmth. Being this close is a privilege. It's hard to put into words. There is life in the deer. Hardy can feel it. It's not surprising that there's a sudden quiver in its body, an ever-so-slight trembling in his palm, almost a pulse. Hardy feels the grip on his wrist. It seems to tighten, then loosen. In an instant, the hand holding Hardy's hand on the open wound lets go. There's only his hand on the torn open flesh. In the time of one breath, it feels enough. He pulls his hand off of the wound on the Chickasaw's thigh and looks up to Niwashake standing next to him.

Niwashake quietly tells Hardy, "You will go downriver."

Hardy, in his waking, simply nods his head yes to the tall, impressive Indian.

As he is getting back on his feet, it's Mr. Knight's voice that is the startling return to the terrible situation in the woods. Knight's overwhelmed by Niwashake's unacceptable and perverse treatment of the young boy. He is calling out to everyone assembled, over and over. "This is impossibly wrong. There are laws, so unimaginably unacceptable, animals, raised by animals."

It's Niwashake's words that sit in Hardy's mind. The excited adrenaline slows in his body. He stands still and feels his way through it. There should be panic, but there isn't. The simple words are more than what they are. He feels the deeper pull of the something he will understand when the time for it comes. There's no name for it, no good way to describe it, and that's not important. *There's a deeper something… the blood and weight of how it feels are part of it, but not like being told something. They're not dreams, and they're not something easy to know. They're between here and there. You don't have to figure them out. There's not some hard confusion to figure out or something scary or shocking. It's all kind of simple, actually.*

Niwashake sees it. Of course he knows it. The other Osage see it. They understand it less. Representative Knight can see it now, and he doesn't understand any part of it. Hardy is calmly standing still in the swirling commotion. He's clearly untroubled by what should be a trauma for a young boy. He looks around to see how the others are watching him, but not much of that seems to matter too much, so he waits for what will happen next.

For Piominko, the pain becomes more than even the bravest can bear. He looks straight to the sky above, and from the depth of his body comes a howling cry of agony that echoes through the woods.

After an eternal moment, he turns to Niwashake. They exchange their shared knowing, a connection between two Indians in the woods. Two men who have come this far to be in their lives. They share the knowledge of a survival that must always end. Piominko knows his understanding of life's end is not at all the same as the Elder's.

To Knight, this last bit of cruelty is too much to bear. He walks in quick, tight circles, the shock of a witness. There is no reason for this human savagery. No one else here can see this criminal behavior for what it is: human weakness and the corruption of decency. The fullest expression of all that is immoral.

Niwashake has given Piominko his chance to be weak before his God. He can now accept the return to his beginning. But, Piominko is not ready to return.

The time for Piominko's reckoning has passed; the time of this place must finish. One of the Osage grabs Knight's shoulder, and with a tug, he shows Knight they will leave. Representative Knight—with Hardy next to him—walk out of the clearing and into the woods. They pass Piominko, the rope noose at his ankle. They will make their way back to the river. Po-hi calls to Knight, "Maybe you will swim with the other British in the river."

Another Osage gathers the three women, who do not resist. The Chickasaw women know their time of escape may still come if they are fortunate. As they pass Po-hi, who is holding the other end of the rope, they call him "filthy dog." When the mother of the infant passes, she calls him "filthy maggot of the dead Osage dog."

All have passed into the woods except Niwashake and Po-hi. Piominko is on one knee. His thoughts and his feelings are only for him to know.

Niwashake steps forward to Po-hi. His voice resonates much deeper. "You will leave this place. Your business here is finished now. You will not fight my words. A young warrior will respect the Elder. You must see the path and walk that path if you want the respect of others." His voice is both sympathy and wisdom.

Po-hi considers the words of the Elder. He watches the Elder's face and can see the path to walk away from the foolish young warrior that he is, standing inside his body and his thoughts. But for no reason he cares to understand, he turns the other way. "I will walk out of these woods, but the Chickasaw women, the militia, and the British are my property to trade. You will not follow."

With one sudden and decisive move, Po-hi hands the rope to Niwashake. He gives the Elder his best scowling expression, turns away, and walks into the woods back down to the river.

Niwashake waits, without motion, for several long minutes. He welcomes deeper consideration, returning to his thoughts of what has taken place here in the woods. So much of it is the expression of an ignorance between men that will forever be a useless fall from a higher place. The boy, he believes, has been the purpose of all that has been exchanged in the woods. He believes he has completed his purpose, which gives him a quiet peace.

There is still the sound of agonizing pain that comes from the tortured Indian kneeling on the ground. Niwashake walks over to Piominko and unties the noose around his ankle. The two Indians share another moment. In the silence of this exchange, they recognize the woods of the river will always give another opportunity for those ready to receive it.

Niwashake reaches under Piominko's arm. He pulls him up, helping him to stand. The pressure from Hardy's hand has slowed the bleeding. "You will continue for many years and with many children. Your canoe will wait for you. Your village will be happy to see your face. Your children will make you crazy, like all before you."

Niwashake walks away from this place. He walks deeper into the woods, away from the river.

Piominko will wait for his strength to return and then walk to the river and his canoe.

There is little discussion at the river bank. The Osage know without speaking who will sit in the canoes, the bateau and the pirogue. The sun is getting late, and the young Osage want to get back out on the river and make quick progress.

The three Chickasaw women are put together in the pirogue. They stay in a tight huddle and sit quietly. They will not anger their captors. Now is not the time. The Chickasaw mother sits in quiet agony. She has not given up, not yet. One of the young Osage will take the rear of the pirogue.

Po-hi sits in the rear of the lead canoe, heading downriver. Representative Knight and Hardy will be in this canoe. Po-hi has little trust in Hardy. Niwashake's words still bother him. He will keep Hardy close. Po-hi will paddle the canoe. He can see they will make slow progress if the old man is made to paddle.

Fredrick, William, and Jack Red-Hair are back in the bateau. The third young Osage unties and unwraps the rope around Fredrick. When the rope is off, Fredrick slowly lifts his arms straight up. The pain of it won't last long. He has a renewed optimism for an opportunity that he imagines will come soon. Such a great amount of optimism. The Osage takes position in the bateau's front to keep watch on the river with his rifle in his hand.

As the fourth young Osage stands next to his canoe, he makes the announcement. "The roots dug by the Chickasaw women are left behind. It's food the Osage will want." Po-hi tells him, "Go quickly into the woods for the potato and you will catch up with our boats farther down."

The young Osage darts into the woods.

Hardy sits at the front of Po-hi's canoe. When the boats are moving downriver, his position will be the farthest front. For now, he sits with his elbow on his knee and his chin in his hand, waiting for all the others to get themselves ready for what will come next. All the violence that took place in the woods, thinking it through, it seems to grow distant. For now, he watches the water.

The Osage have finished the raid of this place in these woods and will move downriver with as much speed as the canoes will give.

As they make progress downriver, the boats stay close to the shore. There may yet be Chickasaw in the woods. As the boats were loaded, William kept an eye on Hardy. He saw the trauma in his face. He expected it. To involve the young boy makes little sense for a hunt-to-capture raid. He will watch for the answers to his questions. William knows there is more here than Osage brutality, but how was it handled? How much is left to be done? *Is there something more the Elder wants from the boy?*

Fredrick leans in to William and Jack. "What are we a part of? Some idea about that would be very helpful right now. Shall we consider what's to be done at the Fort?"

"Whatever we're a part of, it won't matter much," Jack Red-Hair offers. "We got to ride this out and look for our chances."

Fredrick listens. He hears Jack's frustration. He sits up straight, unconcerned about the Osage with the rifle in the bateau's front. "The Indian mind and the Indian spirit is to believe the world belongs to them," he says quietly to his fellows. "They invade, they take, and they kill those who cross their path, who are only defending their own way of life. The Indian mind respects this as the way of the world. Only their world is the correct world."

"What people on Earth don't believe the same?" William says.

Willing to give the dark tone its due, William gives it a moment. But his experience tells him to keep their thinking clear. "When the Spanish had complete control, they named the old fort William Carlos the Third. It's the Quapaw and the Chickasaw who call it Fort Arkansas. We're going to need a strategy, at least some idea of a plan."

"This may work out to our benefit." Jack sits up to get into the conversation. "If the Spaniards take us as a show of good faith, they may have no use for us when the Osage slavers leave the Fort. Think positive men."

"Think positive? Who is this man?" William gives Jack a quick shove. "I don't recognize him."

"Alright, I deserve that, I do. Maybe I'm thinking now that I'd rather swim through the water than stay stuck in the mud."

"That doesn't make much sense, but I like it."

Now that the boats are moving at a steady pace down the river, Fredrick watches the Osage in the canoes and the Chickasaw women in the pirogue. He's looking for some sign of what might come next. The three women have remained quiet from the time they came out of the woods. They've shown no resistance, no real struggle with the Osage. Why are they not more aggressive, knowing what is ahead for them at the Fort, with the Spanish?

Fredrick watches one woman as she holds the hand of the woman next to her. Her hand becomes tighter and tighter, becoming a tight grip. She trembles and puts her head in the woman's lap. The other woman brushes her hair with comforting strokes.

The young Osage returns to the spot in the woods where the Chickasaw women were digging for potatoes. He's out of breath but gathers the baskets. He will only carry one full basket back to the canoe.

The Chickasaw mother in the canoe has both of her hands tightly gripping the hand of the other woman. In only a few short breaths, her body shakes with unbearable agony. The two other women wrap their arms around her, holding her tight. Their faces share the connection.

The young Osage has finished putting the potatoes into the one basket he will carry. As he stops for a moment, he hears the faint sound of an infant's soft murmurs coming from behind a nearby fallen tree. He knows the sound but can barely recognize his thoughts of what to do.

The Chickasaw mother begins to cry, at first the weeping of a mother's despair. In the next breath, she cries out, the full howl of outrage and of helplessness. In the next moment, she subdues herself to weeping into the arms of her friend. She will not let the Osage see her pain.

The young Osage stands over the infant wrapped in deerskin. The child is staring up into the treetops, watching the wind blow the spring leaves. At just that moment, he is suddenly distracted by a pouncing in the leaves. He looks up to see the tail of a gray wolf disappearing behind a tree. The wolf comes near when he is hungry. The young Osage turns and quickly takes the basket of potatoes and darts back into the woods. He leaves the Chickasaw infant behind.

The mother in the canoe knows why she left her child. She made the choice to trust her infant to the woods rather than the Osage. She has seen how the Osage would treat a Chickasaw child. Savage cruelty is not uncommon on the river.

Po-hi surveys the river. He turns back and sees the canoe of the Osage, which will soon join with the rest.

He watches downriver for several miles, looking for any sign of the fort. He is also looking for any other boats on the river at this time of the late afternoon. He calls to the other Osage to make quick time to the Fort. He will want to do the trading quickly and return to their village back up the river, before there is trouble.

The sky has clouded over with a muted sunlight on the murky water. Knight sits quiet and exhausted. How does this all come together? How can any of this be acceptable? Hardy watches the wind blow patterns on the surface.

The patterns appear erratic and unpredictable.

Chapter Ten

Dark Corners

The late evening sky, muted with a stratus-clouded sun, is dropping behind the trees on the far side of the river, creating patches of deeper shade still bound to the chill. The two canoes, the bateau and the piroque move downriver in a precision-straight line.

Po-hi stands tall, his focus forward. The Arkansas River at this stretch twists and turns back on itself. The horseshoe bends can hide other travelers until both parties are unexpectedly engaged, for better or worse.

As the procession rounds a bend, a large mule deer with a full rack of antlers is hurriedly making the crossing.

One of the Osage raises his rifle for the kill. Po-hi makes a particular grunt. The rifle is lowered, not the time for deer. As he drops the rifle back down to his side, the Osage momentarily pauses the swing of the rifle to take aim at Hardy. Hardy turns back from the impressive sight of the deer to catch the gesture, more arrogance than a threat, but still, there is something to it. He doesn't flinch.

Representative Knight watches the quick threat of the rifle. "I wouldn't worry about that. I believe that particular form of violence might be finished for the moment. Certainly more is to come."

"I'm not worried about it," Hardy responds. "The dude's a punk."

"Well, there you go. I would say that's about accurate. I like the word thug, although that's probably a little too urban."

"You're right, Sir, 'thug' sounds like a Netflix blurb. I'll go with 'fucking asshole.'"

"Well, I don't disagree. But what would your father say about that language, although I believe we've had that discussion."

"You have no idea what my dad would do right now. For sure I do not want to think about that. One word: ballistic."

"I haven't known Buddy that long, but I would guess he'd probably not be calling for help."

"No, Sir. I don't think that would be part of it. It's more like the long shaft of that rifle being shoved up some part of his anatomy."

"Not all together unpleasant."

"Are we shoving rifles?" Jack Red-Hair can't resist. "I believe I'm in the mood for some rifle shoving. I wouldn't be opposed to it."

"So it's shoving rifles now?" William, absolutely primed, "I have some experience with that, to demonstrate for any first-timers."

"I'm not exactly a first-timer," adds Jack, "as you know from personal experience."

"I believe I do recall that you're very fond of that part of the anatomy, Jack."

"On the contrary, William, where is your memory? It's you who were not satisfied with the length of the musket, if I recall."

"By golly, you're right, Jack. I also quite remember that you and our dear departed Jack would have nothing to do with the steel of the rifle. I believe you both preferred the more human appendage."

"All right," Knight breaks in. "I do believe the sailors have arrived at the bar."

"No, don't cut them off, Sir," Hardy pleads. "I'm really learning something."

The three Chickasaw women have their own conversation. They speak in half-words and phrases. A touch of humor can ease the anguish of a painful predicament. One of the women makes small-talk about how bad a cook she is. The dogs won't eat her food. The mother still buries her head in the lap of her friend.

The sun has now fully set, and the half-light of evening begins its setted stage for the flotilla. When Po-hi spots the dock protruding out into the river, he gestures to the other young Osage to make their way toward it. They have arrived at Fort Arkansas.

Along the shore—below the ten-foot high, mud-red bluff—there are a series of vertical pine poles secured in the river mud. Tied to the poles are a variety of river boats. The largest of the boats, a keelboat, which could carry more than twenty men, and the smallest, another pirogue. The Osage recognize several cottonwood-bark canoes that belong to Quapaw, already at the Fort conducting business with the Spanish.

William recognizes the Quapaw canoes as well. The painted spiral symbols on their canoes are immediately familiar. He's had some experience with the tribe. They're by far more accommodating than the Osage.

The Quapaw had a long, prosperous relationship with the French until the British claimed the Louisiana territory east of the Mississippi. Then the Spanish, who were unknown to the Quapaw, occupied New Orleans and claimed all of Louisiana west of the Mississippi, which included the Quapaw territory. Wisely, the Quapaw avoided any entanglements that obligated them to choose one European power over another.

After more than half a century of unrelenting hostility, the Quapaw allied their tribe with their adversaries, the Chickasaw. These treaties allowed both tribes to avoid exclusive ties to either the British or the Spanish while establishing good trade with both. The Quapaw and the Chickasaw have formed a strong alliance. They see the Spanish and the British as their pawns.

Jutting out from the river bank—about twenty feet into the river—is a make-shift floating dock made from rough-cut timber lashed together with rope. Across the dock and up the shore is a ten-foot-wide set of log stairs dug in and anchored in the red dirt.

Po-hi brings his canoe to the river bank ahead of the others and steps out onto the sandy mud of the river's edge. He thought to keep his moccasins dry but quickly diverts his attention to Hardy and Knight as they stand in the canoe. He supervises the others paddling their boats in with gestures and very little speaking. Po-hi is arranging how the boats are hauled up the river bank. The Osage will not tie their boats. Po-hi expects a quick departure.

Within the Nation of the Great and the Little Osage, a young warrior like Po-hi is far too young to embrace the current, complex relations with the Spanish. The history of Osage relations with the Spanish in the Mississippi Valley is overwhelmingly a history of small altercations preceding great violence. Confrontations, small skirmishes, horse theft, quickly escalate and very often become the brutal murder of men, women, and children. The Osage use violence as a territorial expression. The Spanish—to their credit—have determined that reason can not persuade the Osage, not by any they've employed so far.

The balance of power turns on the actions of individuals. The longevity of the Tribal Nation and the great European powers depends on how men conduct their business with other men. Alliances can quickly sour. The Osage cannot be trusted at Fort Arkansas, but it is also a great opportunity for the Spanish to demonstrate cooperation. Po-hi is too young to appreciate the precarious position in which he's placed both the Osage and the Spanish. Arrogance, with the Spanish at the Fort, is risky business. And with no lesser degree, there's the British.

Gathered on the river bank, the decisions are made. The deserters, William, Jack, and Fredrick, are tied at the hands and a rope around their necks will connect them. The three Chickasaw, the most promising of their trade, will be tied only at the wrists.

"The boy with the man will not be tied with rope."

Representative Knight and Hardy, standing next to each other on the river's shore, share the same thought. *What on earth are we doing here?*

"So what happens now?" Hardy throws out to anyone.

"Keep your head down," William tells him. "That's what happens now."

By the time the entire group reaches the top of the bluff and walks out onto the field of the village—adjacent to the Fort's stockade—evening is night.

The first structures, about one hundred feet from the river bluff, are two visitor houses. One is a longhouse, the other a small square-shaped house. Both of the houses are made from rough-cut timber and are remarkably crude.

The two houses are for travelers doing business with the Fort. High-ranking Spanish, conducting official military business, are brought into the homes of the villagers nearby.

Across the rise of the field, the village can be seen only by the lights in several houses; candle lanterns, oil pots, kerosene lanterns. Torches, out in the open, are scattered here and there for a few hundred feet. Hidden in the farther distance of the night is the Fort's stockade.

The four Osage—with their captive bounty—make their way to the longhouse. The longhouse is the better of the visitor houses for the Osage tonight. It is the largest, and the entire group will be inside.

Although Osage are not frequent to the Fort, they know the Fort is a place where many types of people may come. River tribes and loyalist militias pass the Fort going up and down the Arkansas, not all overt enemies, but not friendly either.

The Osage assume there are Quapaw at the stockade, possibly inside the longhouse. It will be scouted before they go inside. The Osage will keep their bounty close and concealed for their trade with the Spanish in the morning, their muskets loaded and close by.

Po-hi anticipates the Chickasaw women put the Osage in a precarious situation until the trade is done. He will move undetected in the night, and he will move carefully in the morning. When the Spanish engage with the barter, it will be to show their alliance with the Osage. When the deal is done, the threat of Chickasaw revenge will turn on the Spanish. The hubris of a young Osage. Complicated relations. Ever shifting.

Po-hi pulls open the heavy front door and cautiously steps inside the longhouse for a quick first inspection. Inside, there are several kerosene lamps that give spots of light down the length of the dark interior. The lamps sit on short shelves fixed to the wall, giving just enough light to each part of the room except the far corners opposite the entrance. The corners are strangely too dark, given the spacing of the lanterns. But, there are many things to consider. The four small vertical windows along one side of the house reveal a moonless night. The blackness of the night sky adds to the darkness of the room. There is not one piece of furniture inside the longhouse. The house is empty. No Americans. No Quapaw. Po-hi is suddenly puzzled. Who has lited the lamps?

Gathered just outside, each wait their turn to enter the house, out of the chill. The Osage keep one long musket at William, Jack, and Fredrick and one at the three Chickasaw women. At this point in the evening, Knight and Hardy don't warrant a musket's threat. With a simple gesture from Po-hi, they pass through the doorway into the house. Po-hi is the first to claim where he will sit for the night, closer to the rear than the front. Across from him, the windows and the night.

The captives are grouped in the middle of the room and are made to sit back-to-back in a tight clump. This is the first time the deserters have been this close to the Chickasaw women. It's awkward for everyone. The Chickasaw find the close company of the deserters to be very unpleasant. To the Chickasaw, the men are dirty and their smell is especially foul.

The three other Osage take places along the same long wall as Po-hi, closer to the front and the door, close to the captives. Each of the young men is grateful to welcome the respite the longhouse offers for the night. The timber wall of the house makes a fine back rest. Each one of the long muskets is propped against the wall next to the sitting Osage, upright down the length of it.

Representative Knight and Hardy stand inside, next to the door after it's closed. Knight figures better to wait than be barked at minutes later. Hardy is too tired to do anything but follow along. He can barely hold his head up. It's more than enough for one day. Knight keeps a keen eye out for anything else unexpected.

William takes the opportunity—in a whisper, "I don't believe we've been here before, Gentlemen. A whore in the night, this fort. Currently, it's the Spanish, which means the British, most likely Colbert, are probably on the river, just off from the docks, lurking around in the dark with his troop."

"One eye out," adds Jack. "It's all we can do now."

"The children will get sloppy," adds Fredrick. "It won't be long."

Po-hi walks over and takes Knight's arm to move him to his place for the night. Hardy follows. The three of them walk past the deserters and the Chickasaw women. The women have settled in and hold each other for comfort. As Hardy crosses in front of him, William puts one leg out to stop him. He looks up at Hardy and motions for him to come closer. "I don't believe this elder in the corner might be who he says he is," a little closer, "it's more than just a feeling, and it's becoming more clear to me the longer I sit here in this stinking place. I can't yet think it through. I only have the pieces of it, but I know you're part of it, Son. Are you hearing me?"

"Yes, Sir, I hear you," Hardy tells William respectfully, "but I don't see anyone over there."

"Sit and don't say a word. I'll watch out for you, and we'll deal with this in the morning."

"Yes, Sir."

Po-hi puts them in the back of the room, farthest from the only door, almost unseen in the dark corner.

Knight sits before Hardy, and he immediately lets out a fairly dramatic sigh of relief. "The floor will have to do, given the circumstances."

Once he gets down and tries to get comfortable, he's presented with the less than agreeable, hard, splintered wall. Accepting that he doesn't have the backrest of choice, he gives in to the temptation and lies flat on his back. He could use the jacket, roll it up for a pillow.

Hardy sees that Representative Knight has been able to get a little comfortable, so he sits down, cross-legged, to start.

"You know what, Son." He wriggles to get comfortable. "I think I could sleep on solid stone just to get off that river, out of that miserable boat." Knots in the pine floor.

"Yeah."

"I know you're tired, Son. I think we're okay for the night. Will you be able to fall asleep, do you think?"

"Yeah."

"Have you ever been to the Hyatt? Did your father ever take you there? Let me tell you, those pillows… Egyptian cotton cases. I believe there's a memory foam, maybe mixed with goose down. They're a remarkable achievement. See if you can sleep. Once you close your eyes, you'll be out, I guarantee it."

Po-hi walks over to his spot and sits. He uses the comfort of the wall to its best advantage.

"I was hoping for a decent plate of something stewed up." William's beginning to relax. "Just once, out in this godforsaken wilderness, I'd like a plate of something from back home served up for supper. Is that too much?"

"BillyBoy, if I could do that for you, I surely would," Jack tells him.

"Jagerschnitzel, pickled herring, spaetzle, and we'll finish with a healthy portion of the Alsatian apple cake." Fredrick looks up to the dark inside of the roof, dreaming with his eyes closed.

"And you, Dear JackieBoy, what would be your pleasure on this most disagreeable of nights?"

"Well, Sir, I will have one large portion of severed Osage head, roasted to well done, peppered with a good quality port and served with a sprig of parsley to the side. That will be all. And glasses for my two best barn animals if it's not a trouble. This has got to be tough on you, William," Jack adds, "Not having your book at hand to read us a goodnight quote. Terribly sorry about that."

"Not to worry, I'll make up for it. I'll make a philosopher out of you yet, you uncouth imbecile."

"You Brits cash in," Fredrick tells his partners. "I'll take first watch."

When the ill-tempered group stepped into the longhouse, there was the impressive stench of kerosene and rotting wood, and the dark chill with no warmth of fire. Do the Spanish treat all their guests this way? Now that the Osage, and all the rest of the weary, are finally positioned and ready for the retreat of night, the chatter winds down and exhaustion blankets them all.

Hardy watches the room settle in for the night. He realizes this is the first time he has seen the younger Osage Indians sitting this still, the first time with no drunken threats, hunting, or shooting and killing. As the Osage are softening into the sleep of their night, he takes long looks at their faces. Teenagers sitting next to each other, each with a long rifle at their side. One guy must spend a lot of time keeping his hair just the way he wants it, with the dark red band he wears around his forehead. And the way his hair is parted, perfectly down the middle, with the feather tied to the back. *It must take a lot of work to keep it that way. Their faces are older than their bodies.* Their backs resting against the timbered-wall, they're awake when they're asleep. They know what is happening in the room with their eyes closed.

The three Osage know they can catch sleep if they can but also know they are on guard against any intruders who may come through that door: Chickasaw. They will guard the door and hear the night outside, but after this day, they cannot help but think of their warm beds back in the village.

Po-hi looks across the room and feels proud he has brought the captives to trade and the deserters to offer the Spanish. He also knows the morning with the Spanish will be full of complications. Rest may come for the body, maybe not the mind.

Hardy sinks into his spot for the night. His back to the wall, he drops his head to his knees, giving in to the weight of the day.

In the dark quiet, pieces of the day flicker in his mind's eye. They won't sleep. He can't wrestle them into a sequence that makes any more sense than a parade of pieces. Behind the half-light, there is a figure. It's enough to know that it's there. It's not a troubling puzzle to be solved. The memory of his hand pressed into the blood, the rocky surface of the boulders, too hard to put into any sensible order, patterns on the river, an Indian's arms thrashing at the clear water. The warm wetness of his hand stays with him, but slowly all of the day washes together into a rhythm of fuzzy thoughts that becomes the sound of breathing, and then the parade trails off. The choir of soft and slow breathing in the dark room is soothing. The fluttering kerosene flame of the last of the lamps punctuates the rhythm. Now come the first images brought from night's side, night's dreams, and with these there is another's breathing where it hadn't been moments before. It comes from the corner close to him. He doesn't need to lift his head. The breathing has a slight rasp, the breath of an old man.

"You have come to this place, but you do not know why you are here," the voice feels deep and yet more faint than the slightest of a whisper. It barely brushes Hardy's face.

Hardy lifts his head from his knees but doesn't look to the corner.

"A young boy must be tired from this day. What you have experienced would make an old man like me very tired. You are right to turn to the dreams you wish to see. I will not keep you from them long."

"I'm not sure I understand." Hardy's thoughts might also be words spoken.

"Of course you don't. I am a stranger in a dark corner of a room in a house in a place you do not know. Think of this as humor you're not meant to understand."

"Well, yeah, it's been enough of a day for me. I can't really say what all that was about. I mean, some of it."

"No, you cannot say." The old man's voice takes a good amount of delight in the exchange. "Because you've only just come to this place."

"Sir, I don't mean to be disrespectful, but I'm not really understanding what you're telling me, and I don't see who you are."

"You are a young man in this place, and you are here with the other young men who have brought you here. They cannot see the world in which they live, just as you cannot see this place where you believe you do not belong. All the young men in this room have many things in common."

"Okay, I guess that's right, but it seems like the wrong way to put it."

"The young Osage warriors believe what they see inside this wooden house is what they have done." The old man quietly takes his time, aware of Hardy's tired attention. "They believe to do well on the river will bring wealth to themselves and their tribe."

"It's kind of terrible though," Hardy offers.

"This is an accurate assessment."

Hardy can hear the old man smile at this.

"These are terrible things. An Elder may not always control the light that brightens him to the others in his tribe. I have brought you the story from the past so it may find you and bring you close to understanding the way people live in this world."

The Chickasaw man is floating face down in the pool at the spring.

"Can you see what took place between the two tribes at the spring? Can you see that now?"

"Yes Sir, I'm awake, and it feels important to you."

"It is fitting that I am the stranger this night, here in the Fort of the Spanish who have come upon this land. Stolen what they can. So it is fitting that I am the stranger, and you are also a stranger here, so the two of us may speak."

"Yes, Sir."

"You know the Chickasaw is drowned. His troubles are gone."

"Yes, Sir."

"As the Osage pulled his body from the water, it became agitated. From the bubbles rose a vapor that slowly became the form of a venerable Indian with long white hair. The murderer recognized the face of The Great Elder, the Father of the Chickasaw and Osage nations, and a man whose heroism and goodness made his name revered in both these tribes.

"The face of the patriarch was dark with wrath, and he cried, in terrible tones: accursed of my race! This day, thou hast severed the mightiest nation in the world, were the Elder's words. The blood of the brave Chickasaw appealed for vengeance. May the water of the Osage be rank and bitter in their throats.

"Then, whirling into the shape of an elk-horn club, the Father of the two nations brought the club full on the head of the wretched Osage, who cringed before him. The murderer's head burst open, and he tumbled lifelessly into the forest creek, that to this day, is most foul.

"Then, to perpetuate the memory of the Chickasaw, the Father smote a neighboring rock, and from it gushed a fountain of delicious water. The bodies were found, and the tribes of both the hunters began on that day a long and destructive warfare, in which other tribes became involved until forest peoples were arrayed against river peoples through all that region."

The Elder rests his coarse voice and waits to see if Hardy has heard his words. At this time of the night, after this day, a simple pause can seem very long.

"Can you know this legend?" he asks Hardy.

"Thank you, Sir, for the story, and I think I understand it. I don't know if you know where I'm from, but I... People have a hard time admitting they're wrong. It's a sin to be stubborn that way. That's what I believe your story is saying. I'm close anyway."

"Maybe the young warrior from California," the Elder is charmed by the sound of his own voice, "maybe he can see this world after all."

"I don't know if that's true."

"These two Indians come to the spring to tempt their place in the world and create an opponent, each in the other. They believe, like eager young warriors will often believe, a warrior must have an opponent. They believe there is more to be gained by taking from an opponent, but do they see what is lost by making an enemy?" He strokes his long, white hair as he contemplates the ending.

Hardy is trying his best to stay attentive to the old man. He's a very tired twelve-year-old.

"Do we believe these old Indian legends have a place in the world of daylight? Is the story of the young boy on the river only for him to know? Maybe the young Osage believe their story will be greater if they act with such disregard. And maybe still, the young Osage believe the young boy from California will have a greater story to tell with the disrespect they show him. They believe, in the boy's story, that his people will need more than what they first see. And the Elder must slip the legend into this story to make the greater story."

The Elder sits quietly stroking his hair.

"The boy warrior will go down the river to see what needs to be seen."

"Okay, Sir."

"The boy warrior will sleep."

Hardy puts his head back on his knees, more comfortable than before.

One last flicker and the kerosene lamp is finished.

The busy chapters of twilight sleep can have many twists and turns. Po-hi walks through such a place and hears whispers from far away. The whispers come closer, and they become louder. The whispers he hears come from just outside the longhouse. Expecting the voices to disappear into the rest of the night, he waits.

The silence of the night returns only for a moment. Other faint sounds and barely discernible voices come from the distance. Po-hi sits straight and takes quick looks at the young Osage in the room.

Slowly rising from his sitting sleep, he stands erect in his spot, his musket in his grip. He walks slowly to the door, stepping around the Chickasaw women and the deserters who have relaxed into mounds of sleeping bodies. He won't wake the warriors until he has some awareness of who or what is moving and speaking in the night's distance. Po-hi walks to the door and puts his ear to the wood. Across the room, the black windows offer no clue. He waits. Po-hi forces his patience to hear what might be outside.

Slowly opening the door, the hinge of the door speaks loudly, so he presses his body through the opening and steps outside.

His moccasins feel the cool dirt, and the air of the black night is still. Po-hi keeps his focus on the torches in the distance. At this time of the night, any show of disturbance will surely pass under those torches. After several minutes, the torch light has no intruders or villagers who might busy themselves at this hour. He stands for several minutes, waiting for the quiet of the night to be confirmed.

Under a torchlight, a figure darts across, the figure of a man. The man is wearing the jacket and pants of an American, not Indian. This single figure isn't an alarm. People in the night run to their houses. Then, just as suddenly, another figure runs through the light. Instinctively, Po-hi raises his musket, but he has no target.

Po-hi transforms himself into a warrior, ready for a skirmish. His muscles tighten, his musket raised. He listens intently and looks to see where the running men are coming from and who they are running from in the black of night. When two more running villagers pass through the light, Po-hi takes aim. His back is to the door, his aim straight ahead.

Po-hi keeps his focus straight down the barrel of his musket to the torchlight across the way. In the corner of his eye appears a figure coming around the corner of the wooden house only a few feet from him. An Indian has suddenly appeared out of the night and caught him off guard.

Po-hi's body immediately spins to face the painted white marks on the Indian's chest. His rifle swings to take target, and he calls to his tribe inside. "Chickasaw!"

Shocked by the suddenness of it, he stands frozen for an instant. Po-hi's luck has turned. At just that moment, another Chickasaw has come around the opposite corner from behind. The Chickasaw's musket is aimed squarely at Po-hi's back. The shot is fired. The loud crack of the gunpowder blast is the first to pierce the village night. The musket ball tears open a hole the size of an apple in Po-hi's back. The violent punch to his body fires his musket into the night sky. His ruptured back seizes its position. His legs stick to the ground. His rifle drops to the dirt. The Chickasaw who faces Po-hi lunges and with great speed pulls a knife from his waist, then swipes it across Po-hi's neck. His body drops backward to hit the ground. On his back, he feels the warm, wet dirt. He looks into the night sky, searching for a moon. The two Chickasaw stand facing each other, the shock of sudden blood. Po-hi is finished.

Chapter Eleven

The bloody rush is let loose

Before the first musket shot splits the night, Fort Arkansas and the Spanish occupants are already under attack. The British Captain, James Colbert, and his partisan regiment have pulled their flotilla—oars muffled with leather—into the north bank of the Arkansas River at the bluff. Only a short distance from a dozen square village houses and the visitors' longhouse where the captives and the young Osage have secured for the night, but not yet the shot of a rifle.

On the fields above the river, Captain Colbert set out for the fort and brought his regiment—in silence—through the village, house to house, taking prisoners. There were voices, muffled by the British, barely heard across the night,

Colbert's force, numbering eleven mixed-blood Chickasaw, many of them his sons and nephews; five enslaved Africans, owned by Colbert; one Frenchman; and sixty-four British Navy and American loyalists.

The loyalists' rationale for aligning with the British is for each a different story. There is little in their lives and the subsistence of their living that they have in common. The moral righteousness of the war carries little weight for these men. Truly a mixed bag of disparate sorts brought together by the one leader who could manage the task.

Captain Colbert is a Scot. Many believe the man landed in Savannah, Georgia, in January 1736 on the ship "Prince of Wales." James Colbert made his way west to the Mississippi Valley, and adopting the ways of the indigenous, settled among the Chickasaw, who for many years had aligned their interests with the British. The valley found Colbert's favor. Colbert married into the tribe. His first two wives were full-blooded Chickasaw. A testament to the enlightened times, the Chickasaw accepted the British Captain into the tribe, not as an act of strategy, but rather they could see in Colbert an honest soul.

In less than half an hour, Colbert's raiders have moved from house to house.

In the middle of their raid, they approach one particular house in the village and bust open the door. It is the house of the Spanish Lieutenant Don Luis de Villars and his wife Doña Marie Luisa de Villars. Villars and his wife heard the first musket shot. Inside, they wait anxiously to see who will come through their door. Entirely unexpected, it is Captain Colbert himself.

Lieutenant de Villars is immediately taken by the complicated presence of James Colbert. Forceful and aggressive, yet respectful and gentle. He smiles throughout their contest but without a trace of vindictive dishonesty or malice. His teeth are fairly rotten, brown like the river. Colbert and de Villars are courteous. They are both high-ranking, so there is no real threat. It is mostly the protocol of military. Lieutenant de Villars and his wife are taken prisoner.

A quarter of a mile across the field, in the direction of downriver, is the stockade of the Fort. The stockade is red oak timber—thirteen feet high—each with diameters of ten to sixteen inches split in two. The vertical timber is then reinforced in the interior by similar stakes six feet high. On top of these interior six-foot stakes is a banquette—two feet wide around the inside perimeter—the place to take position and defend.

Fort Arkansas is commanded by the Spanish Captain, Jacobo Dubreuil, with his Lieutenant, Luis de Villars. The Spanish Captain and his lieutenant command thirty-three Spanish Americans of the Louisiana Regiment, four Quapaw, and three French Americans.

With the attack begun, only the light of the torches can show adversaries to allies. Hearing the shot at the village, the Quapaw inside the stockade quickly paint themselves with vermilion to initiate their participation. The face and body paint is made from iron-bearing minerals mixed with grease.

The Chickasaw move quickly and without the slightest sound. The British and the Americans make easier targets. They can't sufficiently deaden the sounds of clanking metal weapons and what not, tied and strapped to their uniforms and bodies.

Musket fire can be heard across the village. The bloody rush on Fort Arkansas is let loose.

Outside the longhouse, the two Chickasaw stand shoulder to shoulder just outside the door. Po-hi's body is on the ground in front of them. The Chickasaw who fired the shot bends over the body, looking into Po-hi's eyes, wanting the recognition of his kill. With the sense of pride now pulsing through his body, he slowly stands. As he raises his head, a young Osage darts into the doorway from inside and stops, his musket raised, he fires. The Chickasaw is blown ten feet out into the dark, his body torn apart. The other Chickasaw immediately swings his rifle toward the figure standing in the door and pulls his finger on the trigger of his musket. Inches from his face, the flint merely clicks, and the powder fails to spark. His rifle is misfired. He looks up in astonishment and quickly flips the rifle to use the butt end to bash the Osage in the face. In that instant, another of the young Osage breaks through the doorway and fires his musket. The Chickasaw is blown back and hits the ground. He's caught the lead in his shoulder. The bullet strike is far from fatal.

The last Osage pushes past the other two and sees the Chickasaw on the ground, struggling with his wound. His body writhes with pain, his hand squeezes his shoulder, and he cries out, furious with rage. The Osage takes several well-ordered steps to the writhing body, positioning himself directly over the Chickasaw, his feet on either side. He pushes the muzzle of his musket into the Chickasaw's chest and fires. The spray of blood shoots straight up several feet.

Two Chickasaw are shot dead. The three Osage stand outside the door of the longhouse, shoulder to shoulder in defense. Breathing heavily, they aim their rifles into the night. A pounding heart makes the steady aim of the long and heavy rifle all the more difficult.

The efficiency of the British raid proves Colbert's military prowess. The raid is a surprise attack. Residents and visitors are caught off guard in the middle of the night. Colbert's regiments are now moving throughout the entire village.

Word has spread there are Osage at the longhouse. It becomes a target.

Hardy and Representative Knight—like the other captives in the room— are jerked awake by the blast of the first shot that killed Po-hi. They spring to their feet and stand in suspense. In the quickening threat of confusion, Knight quickly pushes up the sleeves of his prized Armani jacket. His eyes are wide with the intensity of an impulsive response. Often, the sudden and unfamiliar will elicit a peculiar reaction.

Knight quickly swings one arm wide and pushes Hardy behind him. He slides into position, spreading his legs and bending at the knees. Squaring off his shoulders, he gives a couple of quick jerks of his head to loosen his neck. His preparation is a pronounced sequence; short, fast-paced jogging in place, fast and forced heavy breathing, and some swiveling body moves. He's primed. He's an athlete composed and ready. Looking straight ahead, eyes to the door, squinting, a furrowed brow. More than merely eager, he takes a few mock punches at his opponent in the empty air. He's become a prizefighter, a street fighter. Not a clue, but he believes he stands ready.

William, Jack, and Fredrick, and the three Chickasaw women, have turned away from the bloody skirmish outside the door. Knight's performance is too much. The women actually step back. The old man American has been possessed. Hardy is stunned as he watches. William doesn't think to close his wide-open mouth. Jack walks straight over to Knight. With one quick slap to the face, he tells him, "Get a hold of yourself. This isn't theater."

Hardy's dismay lasts only a moment longer. He reaches up and grabs Mr. Knight by the shoulders and shakes him, once hard and once harder.

"Stop!" he yells in his face.

Knight is stunned by this, and his body slows. His arms drop back down to his sides. Hardy pulls the sleeves of the jacket back down to their proper place and tugs at the lapels to straighten his jacket and brushes him off. Knight looks around. He's not in the least puzzled by his odd show. In fact, he's left with a bit of confidence but doesn't say a word.

"Get back down," William barks at them all. "Get your bodies low to the ground."

"Will we be killed? Will we be shot?" Hardy calls out toward William.

"We're under attack, Son. It's too soon to tell," Jack Red-Hair tells him, "one thing though, that savage Indian got what he deserved. God rest Jack's soul."

"William's right," Fredrick tells them. "Stay low. For certain, someone's coming through that door."

For the moment, the shots just outside the longhouse have stopped. But in the distance, the rifle fire continues. The Chickasaw women sit back down close to each other, anxious anticipation hanging in the air.

William, Jack, and Fredrick exchange quick looks. They'll wait for the initial thrust of the skirmish to take its natural pause. That's how these meetings work. None of this is unfamiliar. With the Osage gone from the room, they quickly untie, break their ropes, and think through how to execute the options they've only partially discussed. They keep an eye on the door and the three Osage just outside.

"No time for the windows," Jack's voice a loud whisper, "they'd hear the glass out front."

"Let's just see about that," William offers. He quickly gets to the door and, as he closes it slowly from behind, he confirms their position. "No good. We'll have to wait to see if they move off."

"We'll give it a little more time," Fredrick tells them as he digs through the Osage bags and satchels for any kind of weapon.

The three Chickasaw women watch the deserters rush about the room and listen to their frantic words. The women speak to each other in whispers as they methodically untie their ropes and stand, seemingly unconcerned. They brush off their clothes and fix each other's hair. The women walk as though they are one body. At the wall, near the door, they stand and wait quietly. They watch William and Jack, who are still pacing about. The Chickasaw mother only watches the floor.

William takes notice of their confidence and wonders how that can be, despite all that is taking place. He then considers what might be the obvious: the village is filling with Chickasaw.

Knight and Hardy lie on the floor, facing each other. The room is tense but quiet for the moment.

"We can't fight whoever is coming through that door." Hardy searches for the right tone. He's frustrated that Knight has taken so long to realize this new danger. "Mr. Knight, we're not from here. Anybody coming through that door will see that. They won't know what to do with us. There will be elders or commanders called in to tell the soldiers what to do with us. Our best option is to look weak and not very smart and show we surrender. Let William and the others fight their way out of this."

A little ashamed and more than a little surprised by the boy's maturity, Knight tells him, "You're right. You're absolutely right."

"He is absolutely right, Sir," William says to them both. "Do what the boy says, play out the surrender, and you'll most likely be taken along to whatever's next. The Chickasaw have a definite way of dealing with strangers, not like the Osage, a very different tribe."

William takes a deep breath and lowers his head. "This here is a true battle. As big as the rest of the big ones. There is a fort at stake with this. This is no small skirmish. The river's our only way out of this mess. The Chickasaw are not here for their women. There's bound to be British outside that door, and the British are here for the Spanish."

Jack is looking at Hardy. "You two are in a category all your own. The three of us, we're not with you. Understand that. We're deserters, and the British will not hesitate with us like they will with you."

"We will have to run for it," Fredrick calmly adds, "if we get the chance, and that will be coming, trust that."

Before Fredrick can finish, two rapid-fire rifle shots are heard just outside the closed door.

William and Jack take backward steps, waiting for what will come next. Will the Osage rush back inside?

Jack turns to Fredrick. "Not one single weapon in those bags?"

The door bursts open, nearly torn from the hinges. Three Chickasaw warriors bolt inside, their rifles aimed high. Just as quickly, they stop in position. They know the women of their tribe, but each of them looks past the deserters and into the dark corner.

Representative Knight and Hardy lie still. After the shock of the door, they keep their breathing low.

Barely moving his head, Hardy looks up at the three Chickasaw standing in the shaft of torch light spilling through the doorway from outside. Despite the chaos of the moment, Hardy feels the touch of pride. He recognizes this tribe. The next moment turns anxious. He feels the Chickasaw Piominko and the blood on his hand. It feels like a long time ago.

Near the open door, the Chickasaw mother speaks to the warriors. "We will leave this place quickly." Her hushed tone is heard by all as a contradiction to the frenetic activity all around. Her voice shifts deeper into her body. "For my child in the forest, I will not show them pity."

The Chickasaw warrior assures her he will make this happen as he gently takes her arm to walk with her, his head bowed in respect. Before they pass through the door, the Chickasaw mother turns to give William a look of acknowledgment, perhaps appreciation. It's an exchange only the two of them could put into words. They pass through the door. Her two companions follow behind.

The two Chickasaw warriors are joined from behind by two silhouetted figures, framed in the door's torchlight. "Step aside," one of them instructs the Chickasaw.

Both of the warriors lower their rifles to their sides. They relax their bodies. Each steps aside to let the British soldiers easily enter the room. The Chickasaw are not taking orders from the British, but they accept the chain of command.

The two figures walk into the room, British soldiers with a deliberately casual pace. For these two soldiers, there is no emergency, no urgency to what will take place next in this night of sobering contests.

"Well, my word, isn't this a peculiar sight to be revealed on this night of nights. What exactly do we have here, Benjamin?" One soldier teases to his British colleague. "I don't believe either of us wa was expecting this." He appears to have a slight stammer. "How pleasant. Looks like deserters to me, wh-what about you? What do you suppose the Captain would want us to d-do about this? Especially in the middle of his raid." The stammer and the posture are immediately repugnant.

The soldier raises his rifle toward William, Jack, and Fredrick.

"Perhaps we e-end this business right now so we can j-join the rest at the st-stockade." He cocks his musket's trigger while the stutter stays in the air too long. It gives the night's air an additional putrid taste.

"Not to be hasty, Benedict. We don't have orders for that," the colleague, Benjamin, tells his cocky mate. His voice feels far less confident, the patronizing sidekick, perhaps.

William lets out a long, impatient sigh. "Nothing new here."

Benedict, with several quick steps toward William, thrusts his rifle inches from his face. "Ready to get on with things? Is that what we are?"

In one long, deep breath, William's thoughts return to a place he fights hard to resolve. *Why is it I am never reaching it, always pulled back into the world of these small minds that grab hold of a wicked past and refuse the future for us all? How much farther must I go? All this wasted time dodging the river rats that crisscross this valley. How much farther until I'm past them all?*

The only way to end these dark thoughts is to recite quotes to his colleagues from his book. Sometimes they're held in his memory. At this moment, they're not.

"Take off that hat!" Benedict snarls at William, and with the fat of his belly, he rolls out the words. "Let me see it."

"That would be my pleasure." William takes hold of the corner of his hat and, with a whimsical flair, he flings it at the soldier, Benedict, hitting him in the chest.

"D." Benedict growls, blubber in his cheeks. "As I expected, filthy deserter. Traitor to the r-rest of us."

Benedict lowers his rifle to William's chest and points it at his heart. "Why is it you can't find it in yourself," he jabs William's chest several times with the rifle, "to honor King George with a pr-profound se-sense of duty to our Great Britain and to our God above who watches as we conduct the business of this world? Why is that, deserter? Is it because your whole s-sorry life in the streets and taverns you pissed away all good intention with your black-hearted campaigns to defile the Empire with treason?" His thick stubby thumb pulls back the flint cock, 'click.' "Why don't we fix your problem right here and now, make the world a better place of it."

"Drop the rifle," Benjamin calls out. "How is it your mother raised such a hot-headed sausage?" He steps over and places his hand on the barrel, pushing it down.

In quick succession, one of Colbert's African slaves enters through the shaft of light, with heavy deliberate steps. A tall man wearing a dark cotton suit.

"That's correct, only take them prisoners. That means don't shoot them, soldier," he says to everyone, looking back and forth across the room, then stopping to fix his glare at the porky Benedict.

"Now step aside, if you would," the authority in his voice is delivered with a deep resonance, "I have other business in here and it comes directly from your

Captain."

The African walks over to where Knight and Hardy are still flat out on the floor, watching with their heads up.

Knight mumbles, "Yet another twist. Will this night ever end?"

The African looks down at them. "I have orders for you two. The captain seems to think you may have some value in the area of information. The captain also wonders if you might know something more about the comings and goings on this river, more than even he is aware." The tall man leans forward. "If you're wondering how the captain has word of you, let me tell you this, rumors spread quickly on a night like this."

The African turns to Benjamin and Benedict. His words roll out with quick efficiency. "But first, you two, please escort these three soldiers, deserters perhaps—I can assure you I don't care—to make certain they go with the rest of the soldiers up to the stockade. They will be needed. It will begin soon."

"No, I most certainly will not," the cocky Benedict counters. "They will not go up to a battle with the Spaniards, not these three. These three are prisoners of the King, and they will be escorted to the house with the re—rest of the prisoners of this raid, which, I too, realize is c—currently in progress."

"All right, I'm sure your captain would agree. I am certainly not willing to have a confrontation at this point." The African tacitly agrees with Benedict. He has other business.

It becomes apparent to William, Fredrick, and Jack, as well as Knight and Hardy, that this African has a special relationship with the Captain Colbert. He clearly has some arrangement, and the other British soldiers are duty-bound to respect it. The ever-diligent British chain of command. When Jack and William turn to read each other's faces, like the brothers they are, this night gets even stranger. Our chances are on the upswing, are the thoughts they exchange.

Both Benjamin and Benedict raise their rifles and step behind the deserters. They form a tight group standing a few feet from the open door.

"When we get outside," Benjamin moves closer to William, "we'll need to move quickly and keep low." The closeness of his body and the tone in his voice feel of genuine concern. He motions with his rifle to move closer to the door.

"Stay l—low indeed," Benedict stammers. "Both His Majesty and the hangman want you in one piece."

William looks down at Benedict's uniform jacket. The poor buttons can barely pull it together.

"You must realize this is far from over," Fredrick tells Jack in a low voice.

"Most certainly not over," Jack says through a smile. "Between here and this hangman's noose is a long path of anything-could-happen."

Fredrick steps first through the open door and passes into the night. Jack pauses for a moment, framed in the shaft of torchlight. He turns his head back to Hardy. Jack gives Hardy a warm smile. He wants to assure him that through all of this night's waste, this is how companions become close friends, a bond forever shared. Jack Lank-Sleeve would want this to be shared. Jack Red-Hair turns back and walks through the door out into the Arkansas night.

"You go ahead," the African quickly tells Benedict. "You should be with the other two outside before they run off. The captain would not appreciate that."

With his rifle pivoting, Benedict scans the room one last time. "What His Majesty wants with these b—barn animals, I cannot guess." Unexpectedly, one quick glaring stare at Hardy, then he turns, rifle up, and walks out the door.

Hardy cringes from the cold look. "That man is a fat nothing."

Knight clears his throat. "A bit player, hardly that."

Hardy sits up, cross-legged, and watches Benjamin and William stand facing each other, still several feet from the open door. He strains to listen to what can barely be heard. William and Benjamin exchange words for a few more minutes. The African appears to give them their private space.

"You think you've made choices." Benjamin confides to William in a very low and somber voice. "You may even believe in those choices. Truth is, and you know this better than most, no one knows why we're here."

Benjamin drops his head. The confidence in his voice is slipping. "Follow orders and survive this bloody campaign." In the next moment, he quickly looks up and puts his face to William. "Desertion won't get you back home."

Without hesitation, William speaks. He feels the intimacy in their exchange. "You will never get back to your family with that thinking. I can feel you know this. You have to be smarter than the rest." He puts a hand on Benjamin's shoulder and pulls him closer to speak directly into his ear. "Align your actions with what you know is true. There's only one way out of this,

Benjamin, friend." William steps back.

Benjamin stands for a moment. He takes a deep breath and then tells William, "You're an honest man. I'll give you that." He motions to William to move to the door. "We'll need to get going now. This night is far from over."

The African has not intruded into the shared moment between the two soldiers, but he now tells Benjamin, "You should go ahead. I have words for the deserter. I'll send him out to you straight away."

"Are you sure that is what you want? This man is more clever than you might first think."

"Do go ahead, only one minute. I'll send him out."

Benjamin passes through the torchlight of the doorway and into the night.

William and the African step closer to the open door. As they both turn to stand face to face, they become silhouettes in the torchlight. Mr. Knight is mesmerized by the picture. Hardy knows, at this point, he won't hear the words exchanged, but he understands what is being spoken between the two of them in the light.

In an exchange of silence, William speaks first. "I have gone about as far as I can with the story, with the boy. I trust the two of you will come together. He still has a fair way to go. I may be needed again, but at this point, I have no clear sign of it, but good luck to you. I can tell you're a decent man. The river will provide most of the direction."

They both extend their right arms and place a hand on each other's shoulder for the briefest of moments.

William turns and takes two precious steps toward Hardy, points to the dark corner of the room, shrugs his shoulders, and raises his arms. 'Who knows?' Then comes the smile.

He looks proudly at the young man sitting cross-legged in the dark, barren room. "Stay together. No matter what happens, stay together," he says to Hardy in the warmest way. "We'll make company again. I'll just bet we will."

William turns around, and he too, passes through the torchlight and out into the night.

In the first instant, Hardy is stunned. "Was that goodbye?" Then he quickly remembers that William knows more than all the others. They will meet again.

The African turns back from the doorway and walks over to Hardy and

Knight. The last three in the room.

"I am Barbury. I'll get to know you," he tells them politely, "I believe you can see there is coming and going in this night." He crouches down to be closer to the two of them and says very matter-of-factually, "But now, I will take you to meet with Captain Colbert. He seems to think you might have knowledge. Knowledge he can use. So now it comes to the time for you two to meet."

Barbury carries a musket, a Brown Bess, like the rest of the British soldiers. A large man, an older man. He keeps his appearance as clean and as well-attended as he can, given the circumstances.

An African, obviously enslaved, carrying a rifle? The contradiction is not lost on Knight. The deeper this goes, the more unbelievable it gets. Where is the precision of history when you need it? Any number of cavalier thoughts race through his mind, none worth mentioning.

"We should go quickly," Barbury tells them, standing up, favoring one knee over the other. "It will be more difficult to cross the open field to the stockade if we straggle."

"May God give me the lines to read," Knight says to them both. He steps toward Barbury and tells him directly, "The relations in this room, nearly as complicated as the D.C. cocktail circuit, I'll give you that."

Barbury gives him a slight chuckle. "Sir, only you would know what that might possibly mean. And, dear God in a lightning bolt, it's always best to keep a sense of humor."

The three of them take short steps to the doorway. Hardy is two or three steps behind them. Barbury has his rifle lowered and follows Knight through the door and out of the longhouse.

It's strange that they left me to be the last one to walk out of this place. A handful of thoughts cross Hardy's mind. *Maybe they feel that after all we've been through, I can take care of myself. I guess I can.* The room suddenly feels as empty as it is. Hardy looks back to the corner where the Elder sits quietly, as he expected. He can sense how the Elder is not connected to the rushing conflicts of this place and this night. The two exchange a nod of respect as they look toward each other. The soft intensity of their connection. He hears the Elder's voice, yet his face is only the slightest of a smile, a contended old man. "See past the actions of what is sudden in this place."

Hardy turns to the open door. He shrugs his shoulders. "Why not?" With one deep breath, he crosses the shaft of torchlight and walks out into the night.

Outside, the air is much cooler and the scattered sounds of conflict—the shouting and the rifle fire—are heard more clearly, sharply. The room of the longhouse was much more of a refuge than Hardy had considered. The night is still so dark. Hardy joins Barbury and Mr. Knight, who are walking toward a Chickasaw who stands facing the only Osage warrior who can be seen in the darkness. He holds his musket squarely aimed at the Osage, who does not move. Not sure what to expect from the night's additional conflict, Knight and Hardy walk forward slowly. Knight stumbles on the body of Po-hi. Quickly, Barbury grabs his arm, and they take a few more steps. Hardy looks over, and in the darkness, he sees the bodies of two of the Osage warriors. The bodies have been pulled together, lying next to each other. Things change so fast, they're suddenly forever.

"We will see what this is and then we'll make our way to the stockade," Barbury tells Hardy and Knight. "Captain Colbert is probably already there."

"What anyone can do in this darkness? No one can see a thing." Knight exhales in frustration. "For the life of me, I don't know why I don't just walk away from this."

"What is taking place here?" Barbury patiently calls out to the Chickasaw. He hears quiet chatter coming from nearby and turns to see the three Chickasaw women standing close. Their bodies are rigid, eager to take some kind of action.

Barbury can see one woman holding something in her hands. In the dark, it's easy for the other two women to conceal it from him. Let's get this over with is his impatient concern.

The Chickasaw mother walks over to the young Osage, the last to stand alive. He will not move. Defiant. She stands still and then turns her head to look up into the night sky. In that moment, the clarity of the black sky becomes her resolve. It fills her.

"My child's name is Itawamba. You will say his name."

The Osage does not speak.

"My name is Tanawa, and you will say my name."

The young Osage finds the words he chooses to say to the mother. They come easily. "I am Ogapa-hi. My tribe are the Downstream People, and I will only speak my name."

Tanawa walks deliberately back to the other two women from her tribe. She is handed the tomahawk. The women give Tanawa a quick embrace. She then turns and walks back to the Osage, Ogapa-hi.

Each of her steps a methodical contemplation. She walks around him and stands at the warrior's back. She can see the young man is breathing heavily. His skin stretches tightly across his back until the exhale.

Two rapid steps, and Tanawa gives one short cry out into a moonless black night. Ogapa-hi joins the dark, his eyes close. With one strong and steady hand, she fiercely swings the tomahawk, plunging the sharpened metal deep into the warrior's spine. The only sound is his loud exhale. He will not cry out from the pain. The young Osage warrior drops to the ground. Ogapa-hi is finished.

Tanawa doesn't show any of the others any sense of satisfaction for her brutality. This is not revenge. She has done what is just. *I move slowly and I walk steadily. I keep my head to the ground with my thoughts to the above. I have returned what has been taken.* Among the Mississippi Valley Tribes, there may be shared moral protocol for fair justice or the return-in-kind tolerance for the transaction of murder. These understandings may be spoken, written, and may evolve with time. But it is forever a failed effort to presume to understand the actions taken by a mother whose child has been mortally threatened.

She believes she has completed the exchange with the Osage warrior. His death is the natural way. The way of the river and the forest.

Tanawa walks back to the other two women. They speak between themselves and for no one else.

"I can't think of anything to say," Hardy says quietly out loud, for Mr. Knight. He knows Mr. Knight is thinking the same thing.

"Why are we part of this?"

Knight quietly shakes his head. He can't find the words.

Out in the darkness of the village, the scattered sounds of the conflict continue. Tanawa walks back to the Chickasaw warrior who held the Osage captive. She faces him with her back to all the others. The young man keeps his head down. A mother of his tribe has been through too much. She does not need the bother of another Indian pressing on her thoughts. He will take the canoe, and the two of them will go back upriver to the place where she was forced to surrender her infant to the forest. Only a few words and the understanding is done. Tanawa and the young warrior walk quickly away from all the others. They will make their way down to the river and the canoe. The tomahawk is left with the Osage.

"Everybody's at war with everybody else." Hardy's voice sounds louder than it is. Knight turns to face him, never more at a loss for words.

"Let's not even try to understand any of this." He's now lecturing loudly, "From now on, it's forbidden. I won't allow it. We'll stay out of it. We'll keep moving forward until it all comes to an end, and we're not discussing the options."

"That's just not possible, Sir!" Hardy shouts into the night, "What they do is forever! That's what this is! Forever."

Representative Knight gives it a minute. "Look where we are right now. That's what is foremost here. Out here in the middle of the night. I am the adult. I take that responsibility, but look at me. I'm an old man. Do you want me to throw my body at an Indian and try to change the course of this? What the hell do you expect of this? We're stuck here. We're doing the best we can. I've already said it dozens of times. It's not our business."

Hardy keeps his head down and slowly lets out his thoughts. "This will always be our business. And I'm glad she killed him."

Barbury steps forward to join them. He clears his throat and studies the young boy. He considers what must be said. "What that Chickasaw woman has done with that young Osage is between the two of them. Whatever that might mean to the two of you, I can assure you that is the world that never ends. And right now, for the three of us, this night's business is just beginning. Dear God in a lightning bolt, this night will be long."

The three stand, looking away from each other. Hardy wipes the wetness out of his eyes. Only a short time passes. It feels much longer. Sudden rifle blasts, not far off, and all three duck from the shots. The Chickasaw walk off into the night.

"All right, so we keep it low," Barbury says, bending at the waist. The three exchange looks, and then quickly, it begins. Out into the night, almost sprinting, except for Representative Knight, they head out in the stockade's direction. The rifle fire has intensified over there.

Chapter Twelve

A burning building

A dozen flickering torches are spread across the night. Sporadic cracks of musket fire, the white flashes and the stink of gunpowder smoke mix with the chilled air. Uniformed men, groups of two or three, or by themselves run in every direction, calling out orders and directions. "Go this way!" "Over here!" "Over there!" A startled woman screams, a child's crying is muffled by a parent's hand, in the otherwise still and dark moonless night.

The outlines of small houses are drawn by torchlight.

"That house right up ahead there, straight ahead." Barbury calls to Hardy and Knight, trying to pass through the open field unscathed, and clearly winded in the sprint. "Almost there."

Hardy stays close behind Barbury, keeping up. Representative Knight is doing the best he can. He's not far behind. All of them running, bent over at the waist to stay low. The rifle fire is much closer, much louder, and the three of them are closing the gap on a group of small houses near the edge of the village, closer to the stockade.

"All right, I see the house," Knight's winded from the run, "but I don't understand. We're going to that house? Captain Colbert's in that house? We're meeting him at that house?"

"Let's get out of the open, and I'll explain."

Captain Colbert's first wave of the British attack on Fort Arkansas, the stealth of a silent, seamless capture of the Fort's habitant village, has progressed. At this point, there's a minimal amount of chaos until the soldiers can reconvene, deal with the prisoners, and regroup for the focused attack on the Spanish military over at the stockade.

As Representative Knight is running and limping, his first sight of the small house surprises him. It actually is a house. Even in the dark light, he sees the small structure is covered with wooden shingles. It has two windows and a door. There's a chimney, an actual chimney. Foolishly, his first thought is of a hot shower.

The house sits in a row of maybe half a dozen others, on each side of what could be considered a street, although it's only dirt. A historical recreation for some kind of vacation history adventure crosses his mind. As the three make their last sprint through the open, there appears to be a British soldier standing at the door, maybe there to receive them. Knight thinks food, refreshments. When the three finally make it to the house and get cover from the rifle fire, they see the soldier at the door is Benedict. All three, catching their breath, exchange looks of pronounced disappointment.

Barbury stays bent over with his hands on his knees. Knight's hand is on his chest. Both trying to catch their breath. Hardy is ready for more bad news.

"You three were lucky. I wasn't sure you'd make it," Benedict snickers at them.

Unphased by the run, Hardy walks straight up to the soldier and brazenly asks the prickly Benedict, "Are the prisoners inside?" He puts his hands on his waist and juts his head forward. "Tell me, do you have the deserters inside there?"

"Step back, Son." Benedict straightens up and squares his shoulders. His sarcastic greeting becomes a soldier's threat. "Look here, Blackbird," Benedict tells Barbury, "I suggest you keep your militia boy in line or the t-two of us…"

"One moment, one moment." Barbury cuts in. "We're just out of breath, not quite the right words just yet."

"Let's find the words, shall we?" Benedict snipes back.

Barbury takes Hardy by the shoulder and pulls him back. He turns him away from Benedict, so he can speak more directly. "Son, we're out here in the open now. This is very different than back inside the longhouse. You hear that rifle fire? Men are being shot and killed around us. That makes the situation very unpredictable. Watch what you do and mind what you say. You're not wearing a uniform."

Hardy looks into Barbury's face. He holds his head still for one long moment, then gives a quick and subtle nod to let him know he understands.

Barbury turns to Benedict. "We'll be passing inside now. I believe you know the Captain's business here, and I speak for the Captain."

"Sure, I know your business," Benedict tells him. He turns away and looks to the ground.

Barbury steps over to Knight, who is still catching his breath and watching Hardy, more than a little surprised and pleased by his exchange with the British guard.

"Captain Colbert thought this might be a productive introduction," Barbury tells Knight. "I have no idea what he is planning, but he's heard from others, and he believes you to be an educated man. Again, rumors."

"Well Sir, all right, that I am," Knight says to Barbury, finally standing up straight. "I like this man already." Knight turns to Hardy. "We need a turn of events, do we not?"

Representative Knight brushes any dirt there might be from his jacket sleeves. "What are we discussing here? You're about to make an introduction? Is that what this is? Urban sophisticated meets cultured worldliness? Is that the occasion?" Knight's increasing interest is spurred by the idea of ending this middle-of-the-night, drudging through the mud. "With someone inside, a prisoner, I assume?"

"One hundred percent correct," Barbury says.

"Well then, let's get to it. Not exactly my formal training but certainly not too far afield from my Washington duties." Knight is standing up quite straight and brushes any dirt from his hands. "Diplomacy, Ha! Liars, traitors, and thieves, my favorite audience."

"The British…" Barbury corrects himself. "I mean 'we' are holding the Spanish Lieutenant inside. Captain Colbert believes you might do well to speak with the Lieutenant. Possibly devise or otherwise concoct some type of plan to exchange the Spanish prisoners." Barbury is interrupted by musket blasts, much closer than the others. "I beg your pardon," he tries to continue, "you must certainly realize, a man as much as yourself, I'm not given, I don't really have the disparate details, but we should get inside."

Hardy can't help but think Mr. Knight has finally met someone with whom he can have the kind of conversation he enjoys—way too many words to say something fairly simple—you can see it in his face.

Barbury steps over to the door and, as he reaches for the doorknob, Benedict beats him to it and grabs the knob first. Benedict, looking at Knight, says to the three of them, "They're prisoners. Make no mistake, the Spaniards are g-gifted in their deception."

"No match for the British," Barbury tells him as he places his hand on top of Benedict's and turns the knob and opens the door. "Dear God in a lightning bolt, no match for the British." Barbury, Knight, and Hardy step inside. An immediate and overpowering smell of moldy wood and malodorous perfume.

"What manner is this?" The first exchange comes from Lieutenant de Villars, in his broken English. "This is not the appropriate company for this." His voice is loud and predictably irritated; he's being held prisoner. The look on de Villars's face is utter confusion. The appearance of the three supremely irregular persons, who have just entered the room, is as inappropriate as it is peculiar. "What is this? This is an outrage."

De Villars's wife, a large woman, sitting alone at the one table in the room, says to them, most pointedly to Knight, "You cannot speak with us. Go and send someone else." Her heavy Spanish accent, is even heavier than her husband's.

Compared to the brutality of the first of the night's events, Knight is immediately pleased by the challenge. A battle of wits is the perfect antidote to the verbal contests between testy soldiers and the well-meaning but lesser educated. In the blink of an eye, Representative Knight calculates his response to the Spaniards. His mind outpaces his thoughts; lists of lists scroll past. After decades of honing the art of power diplomacy, his options are reduced to three. One: performed admirably in a court case years ago, necessitates a concerted and focused disinterest. Two: an amazing dodge, leave the irritable opponent with an uplifted renewal of spirit. And three—he'll go with three: the positioning play of the introduction. "Perhaps I could get a small drink of water? Rum, if you have it, a dry Port, even better." Immediately Knight feels he finally has a leading role in this otherwise plodding debacle in which he's been consistently miscast. "It may be early morning to some, but it's been a long night for the three of us; why not make the most of it, I always say."

Lieutenant de Villars and his wife Doña Marie Luisa de Villars have no option, under the circumstances, but to tolerate, perhaps entertain, the elderly gentleman in the oddly attractive jacket. They clearly don't have a snappy response.

In the room with the Lieutenant and his wife are their two servants, who are sitting cross-legged in the corner of the room. They have been instructed to sit quietly, which they do. There is only one British guard in the room, and he stands at casual attention near the one door, barely awake. It has been a long night for him as well. The poor man.

Lieutenant de Villars's officer's uniform—the dress regulations of military Spain, issued by the Louisiana Regiment—is a white coat with blue collar, cuffs, vest, lining, and breeches, and white metal buttons. De Villars's hair is parted straight down the middle and turned up on each side with a simple curl, powdered, gathered, and tied into a pigtail with thin black patent leather strips. Letting no opportunity go to waste, de Villars wears white canvas leggings held up by black leather straps. His shoes are black cordovan, exceedingly well polished.

The wilds of the American continent and the close to the Earth necessities of the Mississippi Valley should offer the opportunity to relax the high maintenance dress of the Europeans. But to the contrary, the wilderness of the river's forests enhances Lieutenant de Villars's desire to separate himself from the rest of the river mud.

Hardy has come into the room with little expectation. *We'll see what this is. Let Mr. Knight do his thing. The adults will figure out what they'll need to make sense of it. Maybe they'll have something decent to eat.* He's exhausted, but every new situation is impressive, every new place is curious. He considers how the Spanish Lieutenant's appearance looks like it's straight out of the same illustrated history book he's thought of several times already. All of it looks so authentic. It's a strangely intriguing proposition, but he's too tired to think it through any further.

Having heard Knight's first effort, Barbury steps back and looks around the room for an empty chair.

Pleased with his initial effort, Knight marvels at the Lieutenant's uniform. The coat and the details of it all, and he's kept it so clean.

Doña Marie is sitting, but Knight can see that she is wearing a long, full gown made from a type of silk he hasn't seen before. In the kerosene lamplight, the rose color of the gown is a good choice.

Knight takes the initiative—for no other reason than to test himself—he takes hold of the ladder-back chair, pulls it out, and takes his seat at the table to join Doña Marie. She is indeed a very large woman.

"Nothing about this is ideal," he offers the Spaniards. "I believe we would all agree." His follow up. "And perhaps," he pauses strategically, "perhaps this is where we begin." Both husband and wife simultaneously turn away in the same direction.

Barbury walks to the other side of the room, where there is an empty chair. He stands for the introduction. "Lieutenant Don Luis de Villars from the Louisiana Regiment, up from the New Orleans," Barbury announces with forced but sufficient pleasantry, "I make pleased to introduce you to the Mr. Knight, American from the Mississippi Valley, perhaps affiliated with the..." Barbury stops and tries again.

"Mr. Knight is a prominent with the Loyalists here in the river Valley. He has pledged his loyalty to the Crown, and like the rest of the fellows, he shares the concern that chaos, corruption, and mob rule are all that will come from this so-called revolution. Mr. Knight is devoted to the Loyalists' cause with no patience at all for the Spanish intrusion, and he has announced, on several occasions, his devotion to what is morally correct, and he will go to his grave defending it."

Barbury takes an exhausted, deep breath. He has no intention of participating in this particular side show any further. Confident he's done his job, he sits. Captain Colbert could find no fault with his performance. Hardy walks across the room, a little attitude, and stands next to Barbury.

Knight rolls his eyes and clears his throat. A confusing but interesting list of attributes, more than he's used to, a loaded charade. De Villars steps over to take his place at the table and, as he is sitting, he painfully considers his options to respond. "Pardon?" is all he can manage.

Knight quickly intercedes. "Lieutenant, I am Representative Franklin Knight from the great State of California, 29th Congressional District, San Fernando, and I am extremely pleased, dare I say perplexed, to make your acquaintance."

"Quien es este burro?" the Lieutenant counters. "This is not making sense."

"Nothing more than pirates in this theater," the Señora tells them. Her voice is so filled with tempered anger that when she speaks, a bit of her saliva runs down her overly powdered chin. "Speak to my husband with respect or not at all."

I've seen this before. Hardy is thinking it through. *I can't remember where it's from.*

"Señora, Señor," Knight methodically lowers his voice, fine-tuning his approach, "my apologies. I believe the difficulty here is that we all come from such different backgrounds, very different places. We're all struggling to appreciate the significance of this meeting and to be mindful of the respect each of us should show and each of us should expect to receive."

"The burro is eating its own mouth," the Lieutenant says to his wife.

Doña Marie blurts out a tiny, delicate giggle with a little more saliva. No one in the room can say a word. The slowly dripping saliva has brought everyone to the edge of their proverbial seats. Not one breath. Finally, she takes a little white embroidered linen handkerchief from the lace cuff of her blouse and delicately daubs her chin. There is a simultaneous exhale across the room.

"All right, impulse control is an issue for most Europeans," Knight's brilliant rejoinder, "we understand this. Perhaps it might work if we explained a little of ourselves."

"A British Loyalist can expertly explain the double side of the back—of his backside," the Lieutenant stutters back at Knight.

"I don't think that means what you think it means, Sir, but regardless, please tell us where you are from and how you came to be here, Lieutenant de Villars. Por favor."

"As you wish, Loyalist. As an officer in the Spanish military, and since I am momentarily detained, I can spare you five minutes of polite conversation, if that is what you require." De Villars strokes his short, black beard, which accentuates his reasonably attractive face.

"As you can see, I have reached the station, the rank of Lieutenant. I have come up your fat and filthy Mississippi river to serve the honor of King Carlos III. I am of high rank."

In the field outside, a series of musket shots interrupts the Lieutenant. Everyone assembled at the table waits to see if there will be more.

"I don't see how this is going to work," Hardy says to Knight from across the small room. "I don't think you really get how serious this is." Turning to look at Barbury, sitting in a chair beside him, he asks, "Do the British really hang their prisoners? Barbury?"

"That is exactly what we are here to decide, I mean, discuss," Knight tells Hardy in a subdued tone. "I don't want you to be concerned about this. I know what I am doing. Don't forget I'm Washingtonian."

Lieutenant de Villars waits for the interruptions to subside to regain his audience. "I served in the great battles against Portugal, fought the Apache in Mexico, and was wounded in our country's failed invasion of Algiers. I am one of the many soldiers of the Lisbon Regiment, volunteered to transfer to the Louisiana battalion, dispatched to New Orleans." De Villars pauses with several long sighs of fatigue, which he conceals with his hand. "I don't know if this is what you want to hear. I'll tell you about my childhood out of respect.

"The oldest part of Sevilla, you may have been there, but I would guess you have not, La parte vieja de la ciudad. The old section is on the left bank of the Guadalquivir river. This is where I spent my time as a boy. In the mazes and narrow twisting calles, and the small village squares. There is a somewhat more spacious layout in the central district near the Cathedral of Santa Maria, but my family would not go there.

"Since the British had blockaded East Coast ports for a few years while the Americans worked hard to make us their semi-secret ally, we brought the flour and the cotton fabrics and the weaponry up the Mississippi.

"I wasn't navigating the Mississippi for the Americans out of sympathy for their cause. We sided with the American patriots because it furthered the interests of our King, England's enemy for as long as I care to say. Our rival, you must see, Mr. Knight, sitting at this table. We are part of a great power conflict.

"I was among many Sergeants First Class who rose to officer rank over the years. Although Spanish society is estratificado, stratified, is that correct?" De Villars looks across the table at his wife. "More than one talented sergeant failed to rise because of his unacceptable wife. Officers' wives socialize, you see, and women of peasant background, without education or genteel manners, such as my wife, were deemed uncouth and inadequate. No advancement. This, of course, could never be my circumstance."

De Villars reaches across to hold Doña Marie's hands. She quickly daubs her chin again, then reaches across the table to Don Luis. Her portly upper arms and shoulders and her hefty bosoms make it difficult for her to reach her husband's hands, even though the table is not very large.

"My husband and I are here at Fuerte Carlos, on this dirty river, at the discretion of his majesty, King Carlos," Doña Marie tells them. "If you intend to take us prisoner, I will need several more servants. As you see, I have only the two. I assume this is why you have brought me this houseboy." Doña Marie looks over at Hardy.

Hardy cracks a smile. It's getting good.

"And what am I to do with only the two negroes?" She looks straight at her husband's face, letting him know she could have a temper fit at the circumstance.

"Only two is insufficient."

"Madame, Señora." Knight lurches forward in his chair. "I can assure you, you're getting fuck all out of this deal." Knight belts it out and then quickly recovers his negotiator's demeanor.

"Privateers," de Villars says, looking about the room at nothing in particular, "speaking for the British Royal Crown, an offense to be expected."

"Barbury, I would appreciate it if you would bring your chair over here and join us at the table," Knight asks him, pretending or actually losing patience with maintaining his diplomatic character. "If these vulgar Spaniards are going to continue with their insults, I would prefer they know who they are insulting."

"Mr. Knight," Barbury says, trying to be accommodating to Knight's situation. "Honestly, if you think my storytelling will in any way assist your business here, dear God in a lightning bolt, I recommend you try an alternative strategy." Barbury drags the ladder-back chair over to the table.

Another rifle shot, much louder, nearby.

Barbury waits to see if there will be more. He sits.

The Spaniards drop their heads in unison.

"Everyone at this table, right here in this house," Barbury's voice is measured and convincing, "is witness to the fact that Mr. Knight, the appointed in charge, has demanded I sit at this table. That should be obvious and remembered if this affair goes the other way."

"Thank you, I appreciate it. Tell us why you're here." Knight recalibrates the tone of his voice to "kind and clear." Civil diplomacy, or he just wants to know Barbury's story.

An African, enslaved sitting at the table of a Spanish Lieutenant, should be enough to end any amount of ceremony in the small house. In any other situation more normal to the day, Barbury would be put to severe punishment for his transgression, no matter who is responsible. Whipping, shackling, hanging, beating, burning, mutilation, branding, or simply imprisonment. Disobedience infractions, like sitting at this table, could require knives, or guns, or field tools. The whip is by far the most favored, it's the quickest and least likely to soil the correctional officer's uniform.

The slave courts are fond of ritualistic punishment that both dramatizes and sustains power relations. Punishment can be inventive, even creative. The horror of brutality is extremely convincing.

Representative Knight is oblivious to any of this. These details make few rounds within the intelligentsia of history. Plus, he's focused on the game.

"Why am I at this table? I could tell you that. " Barbury begins deadpan and quick; he's concerned with the activity outside the door. He sits, hands folded in his lap. "I could paint that picture, but I can assure you it is a world so far different from this one here that you would never be able to see it the way it is. At this table sit four people who cannot see any more of the picture than just faces at a table. None comes from here and none of us belongs here. What we share is the shot of a rifle. I am a slave, and I don't think any of you have actually met Captain Colbert. He's the owner of me. I belong to him, his property from a ways back, long about the time he took up with the British. What you don't see is why I do his bidding. I could run off. Many have. Africans here in this valley have about as many reasons to be here as they have reasons to run off. What you can't see is there's only one path to get free, and no two Africans see it the same way either. I got sold to Colbert, but now I can see that being with the British is my path. The rebels and the revolutionaries don't give away freedom, no they don't. Some Africans think colonists' promises are better than the British promise. All of us believing siding with someone will get us our future. I choose to not run off. You see, it's my choice. That would give me a short-term freedom, but consequences would come up on me. So I choose to stay with Colbert, do his bidding. Africans don't have any big idea about country and crown. We see that cause from the Spanish as the same with the British, the same all around. Take what don't belong to you and call it victory. With this war over, I am promised a freedom to sit in a fine old chair like this one and do absolutely nothing. No bidding for anyone at all."

There is a momentary silence, with the exception of the pronounced, heaving breaths from Doña Marie.

"My, what colorful language," Doña Marie says to the table, "but before you continue, I would like you to bring some food. Go quickly now, hoecakes, and three bowls of porridge, perhaps cornmeal pudding. Then we can hear the rest of your wonderful story."

"Yes ma'am, I will go see about your midnight meal straight away," Barbury tells her, looking straight at Knight.

"You see, Sir, Mr. Knight, I see freedom coming for me by being right here at this table."

"Haven't you had enough to eat?" Hardy lets fly to the room. "Looked in a mirror lately?"

"That's enough, Hardy," Knight tells him. "What would your father say about that language?"

"Trading insults?" Doña Marie says to Knight. "Spaniards will take these people and force them to become civil, to dress and act with civility. That's what will come of this Mississippi Valley." She struggles for a few quick breaths, then continues her declaration, purposely looking away. "How do you suppose my husband and I judge your civility? You have no place speaking to us about surrender or any such matter. Your peasant garments have no place at this table. I expect you have insufficient imagination to entertain how repellent we find the way you dress, that coat."

"My jacket? My Armani jacket?"

"Oh brother." Hardy sees it coming.

Knight pushes his chair back from the table and stands. "I believe this conference, or whatever we are calling this, is concluded." Knight clears his throat, then collecting his diplomacy, "if given the opportunity, I believe I have a clear idea of the nature, the personal intentions of the determined Spanish Officer and his charming, if not perennially peckish wife, for whom the phrase, 'I could eat a horse,' clearly has a certain resonance. I've enough of a description to devise a coherent plan of surrender with Captain Colbert. I have my recommendation."

"Make your recommendations, Sir," Lieutenant de Villars tells Knight, "the Spanish will maintain this fort. That is my recommendation."

Representative Knight takes the few steps over to Hardy and pulls him by the collar of his Native American t-shirt. Hardy is ready to leave as well.

"Mr. Knight," Hardy brushes off Knight's hand, "you're great at this. I would vote for you."

"This negotiation has gone exceedingly well," Knight says to the room, "and I believe we are ready now to confer with the man in charge. So, let's make our way in that direction and conclude this business while it's still fresh in our minds. Shall we?"

"Mr. Knight, with respect, I wish most ardently to convince you otherwise." Barbury's voice is concerned. "Inside here is much safer than crossing that field out there. Chickens scattered by a fox. You hear that musket fire? There is no shame in puttin' off the inevitable. These battles often wind down to a skirmish. Could end up a fistfight between two base hirelings in no time at all."

"There is no doubt the engagement out there in that field could downplay itself and become just as you say. However, I am not in the position the, the emotional conviction to continue with this." Knight rubs his chest.

"Consider this," Barbury says, standing and putting the broad palms of his hands on each of Knight's shoulders. "Look around here. Take one more moment. You see a spare, nearly empty room, nothin'. Except at this table here, you have one arrogant son of a bitch's teat Spanish Lieutenant who is currently sitting disconnected from his ability to maintain a defense of this fort. And let's place the honor where it fits, his pot-bellied, miserable wife, who cannot for the life of her let one pleasant expression drip from that fat mouth."

De Villars and Doña Marie mutter comments to each other in Spanish. No one else in the room can hear.

"There's no shame in stayin' until the daylight, see what's developed," Barbury tells Knight, an earnest plea.

"I do most certainly respect that opinion, and, yes, the rifle fire, and yes, better safe than eager. However, one more minute trapped in this nothing room with these foul Spaniards is more that I can reasonably be asked to endure. I'm quite certain your Capitan would agree."

"I have an opinion about running around out there." Hardy steps over to Barbury and Knight. "Bad idea."

"Son, this is an adult decision," Knight tells him.

"Let me also say to you, Mr. Knight," Barbury says, looking directly at Hardy, "you will most certainly find a kinship with the Captain, guaranteed. A kinship can prove valuable in a profoundly complicated situation like this." He turns to look at Knight, "not unlike yourself, and no disrespect, he's a fool for rushing into a battle, which is where we are headed directly."

Doña Marie lifts a small ivory, silk embroidered reticule, her makeup bag that she's kept on her lap. She picks out the small painted tin container, opens it, and reapplies even more white powder, which is made from lead. Her face is a pasted confectioner's cake.

The three of them walk to the door.

Barbury turns to the Lieutenant and his wife, incapable of suppressing a final bark. "Keep your seats."

Representative Knight, also incapable, "what a pleasure."

Hardy, "McDonalds delivers."

Barbury ushers Knight and Hardy out the door and into a position immediately outside the small house. He shifts his attention to the field. The inside banter is over. He realizes leaving the house to the open field is a dangerous move. The Captain would not expect him to bring the two Americans straight away, but it might as well be done now as later. The rifle play up at the stockade will not be ending soon.

Benedict, still positioned at the door, says quietly to Barbury, "I would weigh your options c-carefully from this advantage. Colbert's with a good portion of the regiment, and they've held a position out in that field far too long. You know how he conducts himself. He's bound to make a hasty move before t-too long."

Barbury stands, his back to the wall, and squints as he listens intently to the rifle fire exchanged across the field.

Soldiers, and even regular civilians preparing to charge onto a field of battle where musket lead is the currency, will quickly put aside their petty squabbles and committed differences. When a man's true adversary is having his own head blown clean off, other trivialities are an afterthought.

Chapter Thirteen

With the morning light

On the river, Tanawa and the young Chickasaw make good progress against the current of the wide, night-black river. The young man is strong, and Tanawa keeps him at a good pace, a good rhythm.

"What do you see in the stars of this night?" he asks her. Simple and untroubled talk is good. The young Osage can feel the anguish coming from the mother in his tribe. It brushes his skin and mixes with the chill.

His own mother is a close companion to the mother Tanawa. He has known the mother his full life. For a young man, this is a very long time. Tonight, his strength with the canoe's paddle is the frustration he feels in the struggle to understand why this has happened to the mother. He wrestles with thoughts he's too young to control. His rage attacks the river. His own mother, like a sister to Tanawa, was not with the others gathering roots. This blessing of relief is also a thin blanket of shame. His own family is safe.

"The sky is clear, and the stars are bright." Tanawa's voice is slow. "Their light is enough to guide us down this river tonight." With the sound of her own voice, she realizes she is grateful the young man has spoken of easy things. There is already too much weight in the canoe.

"The Chickasaw mother is heavy with the fear for her child." He realizes immediately he has wrongly returned her thinking to the child. "You are wise for your hatred of the Osage." Hoping to hide his clumsy words, he paddles hard. He will try again to keep Tanawa in lifted spirit. "The great father watches you and guides you down this river tonight; giving us the stars and their light."

"The young man should watch the river, not the stars," she tells him. "The river will have branches that are much stronger than the bark of the canoe."

A smile crosses his face. He pulls harder on the paddle.

Tanawa sits in the canoe's front and watches straight ahead. She is confident the son of her close friend will take them quickly to their destination. He is a good young man and a smart young man. The good-natured one in the group of boys whose daily business was to invent very creative ways of causing trouble, but this one's feet are on the ground when he walks.

"Keep the front of the canoe pointed at the darkest spot on the horizon. Stay to the spot," Tanawa tells him. Her voice is a forceful voice. "The river at night, for no reason at all, will invent ways to give trouble to those who watch the sky."

"The middle of the river will keep us away from the sandbars and the trees," the young man tells her with pride. "I have been on this river many times at night. You should think of small things."

"You are right, young man. I should not let my thoughts join the fox and the others who hunt the woods at night."

"Whoever hunts the woods this night is no match for the two of us," he tells her with two feet on the ground.

Tanawa turns back to the young man for the briefest of a moment. "Your mother has made a smart and brave young man, but our contest is not with who hunts the woods. It is with the time that we have been given. The stars may give us light, but they are not generous with time."

She looks out ahead to the spot where the stars are dim, to the horizon where the river reaches out to the night sky. "To hear why the stars care for us, or turn away from us, are the many stories spoken by the Indian. If you are clever, you can understand why the Indian has written these stories. And when you must take care to other matters in your life, other troubles which are part of the forest and the river, then these stories will wait for you. It is the stories that watch and wait to be known."

Tanawa knows with her heart that to continue in the conversation gives the young Osage a good sense of purpose. She will continue. "All children have dreams of the stars in the night sky. When the stars speak, it makes them happy. They understand their place in the forest and on the river. They can see how their people belong in the world."

"The great father gives the stars purpose tonight, that much is certain," the young Osage says to her. He feels his place in their speaking. "They are his stars that will take us to the place of your child."

Barbury looks out across the field. Any bit of evidence seen in the darkness is important. "Captain Colbert is hunkered down somewhere in that field, dug in with the rest of the British regiment." He calculates the distance to the Spanish at the stockade by the sound of muskets firing from the banquette along the top.

Representative Knight sees Barbury assessing the logistics of the open field. Impressed, he moves closer to him. Knight senses the challenge. The stockade sits in the middle of it, all sides wide open. The fields must be composed of low rising mounds, none with sufficient height to give cover, but it's a dark night.

There is a quick series of musket shots to the left of the stockade. Barbury quickly points to them. "There! Colbert has to be in there somewhere. There must be a ravine in there, hidden from us standing here."

"That makes it interesting," Knight says, putting his hands on his waist and bending forward. He wants to believe he sees the ravine. He also wants to believe he has some type of military experience.

"You and I have shared words, African."

Barbury drops his arm, hearing the voice from behind.

"Some of them profane," Benedict tells Barbury, his voice low and genuine. "I would say to you again, weigh your options. You've had frequent opportunity to stand witness to those fellows who embraced the encouragement of their orders. In the hot sun, their bodies bloat up like bags of potatoes. You've seen their orders. I know you have."

"I weigh your words, soldier. We go by the grace of God."

Barbury takes several steps out, away from the cover of the house. The more exposed he becomes, the lower he crouches as he walks.

"What do you see?" asks Knight. "What are you thinking?"

"As I said earlier, Mr. Knight, and I insist you keep this forward in your considerations. My one order, currently, is to place you in the company of the Captain, and that is what I plan to do. There are other considerations. I accept the weight of those, but only the one is the direction we'll take."

"Out there? Put the two of us together out there?" Knight walks out next to him. "Why not find another secure house? There are plenty to choose from, and hold there until your captain can come speak with me there. We're not soldiers, and what about the boy? We can't take him out there. You're the only one of us with a weapon."

Hardy steps forward to join them. "Out there? You can't be serious. How can running out into the middle of that gunfire get us anywhere except shot dead? What is out there for us?"

Barbury is patient. "I'm following the orders."

"We both know you received that particular order from Captain Colbert well before his raid turned into a full attack," Knight advises him. "We've been through a long night, each one of us, but it's fairly obvious the killing out there is just getting started."

Barbury steps back to the side of the house and brings them into a tight group. There are several more rifle shots from the stockade.

"I'm saying to you," Barbury's voice becomes belligerent, "the two of you will do exactly what I am telling you to do." His rifle, still pointed at the ground, he switches hands with it. "This out there, that's nothing to what I have been through. Nothing. The worst that could happen out there is you getting shot and killed. There's much worse."

"Barbury," Hardy says, turning to look at the ground. He takes several deep breaths, and when he looks up at Barbury, he carries the voice of a young man. "We understand you're following the orders from your Captain. You're a slave, and you trust that by following those orders you'll be in a better position to get out of here, where you don't belong, when your time comes. It may be just hope, but we get that. I understand it." Hardy takes hold of Barbury's forearm, which surprises him. "I'm asking you how Mr. Knight and I get out of here when our time comes. What is it we have to do? It's not doing whatever that Captain says. He doesn't know who we are, and you know what I am saying. I know you do."

Barbury squats to Hardy's level. "Son, dear God in a lightning bolt, there might be a bigger plan and there might not be. I can see clearly the two of you are not from this place, not even this valley. To know the bigger plan, you have to keep moving forward. That's what I know. Moving forward through all this." He points to the stockade.

Knight waits for the moment to subside. "I might be the only true skeptic among the three of us," Knight tells them, his voice course and much louder. "I know for a fact that the boy and I have no business being here. We've both known that since William came along. But if you're telling me to run out into that burning building in order to find our deliverance, then I can't be part of this."

Knight bends over at the waist, his face grimacing with a sudden pain. He begins to rub the Armani jacket over his chest as he continues. "In the sequence of all these terrible things that Hardy and I have been put through, this one takes the cake. It's a shitty idea."

"Sir?" Hardy tries to look him in the face. "Is it your heart?"

For a moment, Knight stays bent over in a succession of deep breaths. He slowly stands up straight, looking at Barbury. "I won't let you take the boy out there. I owe his father that much."

"God damn it, we're going out into that field."

A series of rifle shots crisscross the field out near the stockade. Barbury stands motionless for a moment. He raises his arm and, with two fingers, he rubs his bottom lip. "I don't know of any plan," his voice much more subdued, "or the broad sketch of some kind of departure from this mess of a situation. I swear on the grave of my family, I don't know it." He drops his hand to his side. "I'm taking the two of you out into that field to find the ravine, to find Captain Colbert, because I believe it will connect us to where we are headed. And by that, I mean get us all, all three of us, back over to the river and headed down south. That has to be the course of this."

Hardy takes a couple of steps away from Barbury and Mr. Knight, then turns back to look at them. "If we go out into that field, there will be something for us we can't know by staying here. Something will happen, some kind of agreement or something," he feels a flush of honest confidence, "some idea will come up that we can't think of standing here." He looks to Mr. Knight. "Maybe it's this captain, who knows."

"All right, Son, there you see," Barbury's voice turns a little more upbeat, "there is a plan. And I trust you as much as you'll be trusting me. Shall we agree on that?"

"Yes, Sir, we can agree."

Knight raises his hand, palm flat, to signal stop. He holds it here for several moments. "I don't know what the two of you believe you're agreeing to." Knight lowers his hand and brushes some dirt off his jacket. "What can I add? Let's see; it can't be worse than what we've already been through. But for sure it will be." Knight takes a couple of steps out from the safety of the house. He turns to them both. "And not to be callous, but who are you? You've suddenly been dropped into our predicament, and now what? Follow you out into some gunfight in the middle of the night so you can buy your freedom from a British, Chickasaw Indian Captain, slave owner? Are you bartering us, exchanging us for passage on some steamer? Headed where? Africa?"

"He doesn't have a choice, Mr. Knight." Hardy takes another step away from the small house. "It's not more complicated than that."

"Sad bunch, the lot of us," Barbury says in long drawn-out words, then switches his demeanor. He readies himself. "Stay low, stay right behind me. There's a ravine out there, and I will get us there in quick order. Trust me."

All three turn to face the stockade across the field.

"Mr. Knight, you have my word I will let nothin' happen to this boy, dear God in a lightning bolt, now let's get going!"

Knight grabs Barbury by the lapels of his jacket and pulls him to his face. "I will hold you accountable mister, whatever your circumstances, believe it."

One, two, three, they're off into the black night field, shots are fired here and there.

The young Chickasaw feels his arms and shoulders becoming tired. The canoe is heavy. The black night sky behind all parts east is beginning its flirtation with dawn's light. When the night prepares to leave and you've not been with your bed, the weakness of the body is that much greater. Tanawa can sense the young man's arms are losing the strength she needs them to keep. She will continue. "Between night and day, there are wonderful stories of the spirits who take their places in the early morning light. They watch over the change from dreams of the night to dreams of the day. These dreams of the day can be very difficult for a young man, an older woman, too."

"Is there a story you would tell me now?" His resolve to keep his strength to the paddle will not let the canoe slow to the current against it. Her stories are most welcome.

"When the sun reaches for the day, it leaves the night behind." Tanawa keeps her voice low, just between the two of them. "When a young man reaches for the day, he leaves behind his childhood dreams to become a young man, like you. It was the same for me. Like every young girl, I was never away from my mother or my father. Never more than an arm can reach. But in that world of a young girl, my thoughts were always with my dolls. Together, we had many friends. Most of them would never allow themselves to be seen, not in the day. All of our time together was the making and the telling of our stories. The people and the animals we would meet and some we would invite into our adventure. We would go down the river to find others who would want to come with us. A young girl explores the river with the friends she shares with her dolls many years before the canoe.

"As I grew older, my dolls and my adventures were not as good for me as the adventures I shared with others in our tribe. In truth, I don't remember saying goodbye to my dolls. I don't remember when they were gone or where they might have gone. They became lost in all the other things that a family collects and, in time, no longer needs. I'm sure I must have said goodbye. It is very sad to imagine I never said goodbye. The adventures I had with my friends in the tribes became the stories I tell. The stories of those adventures make the memories new again. The stories are a new adventure each time they are told. These stories are much more difficult to leave behind. These stories try much harder to stay near you than a doll who wishes to be left to her own. Would you like me to continue?"

"I would like that. But I believe you will want to make the story short. With the morning light will come our destination."

"You are a smart young man. That is not a story. You will come to know that the days you have in the brightest of sunny days will be the memories you will chase down many rivers, and when you are even older than you are now, they will be the stories you will tell."

The canoe stays steady against the current of the river. The story won't tell that the current was pushing hard against the canoe.

At the half-way point, catching their breath, the three of them have stayed low and kept a steady pace. Suddenly, there are several more shots—much closer than before—and this time they're followed by hoots and yelling.

The night sky invites the morning's light. Fort Arkansas is revealing its stockade, and it appears abandoned. The row of vertical timber—the front side of the fort—is impressive. In the middle of the front row of timber is the wide entryway. The gate into the fort is framed by timber, several feet higher than the rest. A handsome effort indeed.

Too exposed, the three of them push forward. Running just ahead of Knight and Hardy, Barbury sets the pace. He turns his head slightly. "This is not the worst of it."

"Right into the burning building," Knight says in a winded voice.

From this point—as they keep to the sprint across the field—the smoke from the musket powder can be seen in the dim light, but there is still no clear sight of any soldiers along a British line. The smell of the powder out here mixes with the dirt, a different stink to the air.

"We most definitely have to pick up this pace." Barbury is practically shouting in his winded voice. "We're out in the open here, totally exposed. Up there," he says as he's pointing, "right outside the front of the gate. Do you see them there?"

"I see them," Hardy calls out.

"I don't see a thing." Knight can barely answer back. "I'm watching the ground."

"There's four or five Spanish front guard up there. They're staying low, and they're hard to get at. We do not want to be spotted by…"

Two or three musket balls split the dirt right near Barbury's feet as he's running. "C'mon, let's go," he shouts back at them. "This is the run for it!"

The three of them immediately abandon the idea that staying low helps hide them from the Spanish rifles. It's now a crazed sprint to a point in the field they haven't quite spotted. Up and over several mounds, the rifle fire is almost constant. Musket balls whizzing through the air and suddenly, there it is, the ravine. The line of British soldiers, all lying belly-down on the cover-side of the ditch, their rifles peering over the top edge, all down the line, all firing at the stockade.

Barbury, Knight, and Hardy immediately lunge into the dirt of the ravine and quickly flip onto their backs, three in a row. The cold dirt. The pink sky. Without turning their heads, they look at each other, not a word. Their heavy breathing barely catches a breath.

Not a moment passes and the soldier next to Knight, flat out on his stomach, fires his musket. The explosive crack, a shock. "Jesus." Knight winces.

"We're in it now," Barbury cries over to him. He turns his head to Hardy. "You alright, Son?"

Just above Hardy's head, the strike of musket lead spits dirt across his face. With one hand, he brushes the dirt away from his eyes. With the other, he gives Barbury a thumbs up. Remarkable bravery.

Barbury watches the exposed side of the ravine's top edge, maybe ten feet opposite. "Alright, there's no way better. Let's get this done," he says out loud as he lifts his head and looks down the row of soldiers' bodies, all flat against the side of the ravine. Why so few? The thought suddenly strikes him, where are the rest? He does a quick count, down the line, about a dozen British soldiers, maybe a dozen more Americans from Louisiana, two or three Chickasaw, and two or three of Colbert's other African slaves. He doesn't know them well. At the far end, Colbert is looking straight at him. The two of them connect, and they immediately reestablish their agreement. They nod and the Captain quickly looks away.

Barbury turns to Knight. "All right, Sir, I know you have some idea why we're here in this ditch, but let me explain the details right here and now."

"Explain all you want, Sir, but let me tell you, I'm not moving, not just yet."

"Well, that's just it." Barbury moves into a crouched position, staying as low as possible. "You are!" Grabbing the shoulder of Knight's jacket, Barbury pulls at Knight to get him into the same crouched position.

"Hang on, just give me one goddamn minute, and for Christ's sake, take it easy on the jacket."

Knight lifts himself up and moves closer to Barbury. He ducks his head even lower. "I understand the objective here. We have to get all the way across these soldiers, down to the far side, without getting shot in the head. Is that it?"

"That's it precisely, Sir. Shall we?" Barbury takes Knight's arm, and together they start out, half crouch-walking and half hands-and-knees crawling, figuring out as they move how they will physically maneuver across the row of bodies without getting shot.

The first two or three soldiers don't much mind the African and the odd-looking American crawling over their lower legs. They're focused on the stockade. Fighting in a ditch is close quarters. Several bodies farther along, the soldier rolls onto his back, reloading his musket. "Well, Lord above all creation. Whatta ya know. What the hell are you doing out here, Blackbird? We thought you'd taken off."

"No, Sir, James, not that smart, never that lucky. How you hold'n up? You ain't shot yet? You getting the job done?"

"Colbert's got us stuck in this ditch. How do you think we're holding up? The man needs some kind of plan."

"Well, Jimmy, you are in luck; that's what I've got right here," Barbury tells him as he moves Knight a little farther, "and Son, for once in your sorry life, keep your head down."

"Tell the Captain we're looking for the big idea here," the soldier tells Barbury as he rolls back over. "Will you do that for me?" Then his musket fires, a blast of powder flash, inches from his face.

Barbury and Knight inch forward, body over body, until they reach two Chickasaw warriors, lying on their backs, knees up. All four exchange looks. Could there be a more peculiar configuration of souls? One warrior gives Barbury a mock soldier's salute.

The rifle shots continue from several directions while the four of them stay put. Knight stares. He's mesmerized. Barbury and the Chickasaw wait. They study each other's faces, but their focus is measuring the incoming shots.

Suddenly, the other warrior flips on to his stomach, inches up the side of the ravine, and takes aim toward the Spanish guard and fires his musket. He shouts out a battle cry. It sounds like crows. He flips back over and slides back down to face Barbury and Knight. Then he salutes.

The two Chickasaw have no serious concern for the chaos in the ravine. One of them hands the other a small piece of dried deer meat from the pouch at his waist. They both stare at Barbury as they chew. It's unclear if they are familiar.

Representative Knight looks back in the direction they have come and sees Hardy making his way across the British and American soldiers to catch up. Each soldier quickly turns, surprised by the boy, then just as quickly turns back to the business of the fort's stockade.

"I thought we said stay put," Knight calls across to Hardy.

"Well, I didn't hear that, and you didn't say that," Hardy calls back as he quickly moves in, squatting next to Barbury.

The soldier closest to the three of them, an American Loyalist, keeps his rifle aimed at the stockade as he turns his head sideways to Barbury. "Blackbird, you need to keep those two up against this side of the ravine. If the Spanish up there move across the banquette in our direction, they'll have a clean shot straight down into the bottom of this ditch."

Before Barbury can answer, a soldier—a dozen bodies in the direction he's just come—is struck with musket lead at the top of his shoulder. The poor soldier cries out the shock of the pain, and his body spins into an upright position. His recoil has made him more exposed, and as he grabs at his shoulder a second musket ball strikes the back of his neck. His body flies to the mud at the bottom of the ravine. The soldiers nearby see this. One of them calls out his name and slides down to hold his head up out of the mud. They all duck their heads lower. Not much care can be made of it. The soldiers continue their fire against the stockade and toward the front gate, where the Spanish guard are dug in.

Barbury turns away from the shock of the wounded soldier and immediately grabs Hardy at the shoulders, picks him up, and slams him backside into the side of the ravine. "Now I am telling you. You stay put right here. Do not lift your back off the dirt. Not even one little finger. I know you can hear me cause I'm saying it right in your face."

Hardy receives the blows from Barbury's voice, and all he can muster is a simple nod. Overwhelmed by the shock of the soldier being so violently killed and so close by, he can't move anyway.

Barbury gingerly brushes some dirt off Hardy's forehead, and then quickly turns to Knight. "You and I are making our way down this ravine where I shall deposit you and your impressive diplomacy in the presence of Captain James Logan Colbert. At which point, the two of you can diplome your way through whatever it is he thinks you're going to offer him. And dear God in a lightning bolt, I am coming back to right here and I'm staying with this boy until... well, until the next miserable part of this comes along."

With one quick look at Hardy, Knight lets him know they're together in this hopeless mess.

Barbury pulls at the jacket. "Let's go."

The two of them crouch and crawl to make their way across the many bodies until finally they reach the company of the Captain.

Barbury can barely get it out. "Sir, may I introduce..."

Colbert cuts him off and in a surprisingly casual voice asks Knight, "Come up here, will ya, take a look up here."

Duty done, Barbury turns back toward Hardy. Knight watches him crawl across a few soldiers and then realizes his own position, stuck in between the retreating Barbury and this new project. One more goddamn challenge.

"Our musket fire barely penetrates the evergreen oak. We'll need a better plan. This ravine is 'pistol shot' from the stockade, to our advantage, there is no doubt but..." The Captain scratches his head and turns to look down at the Representative.

Colbert reaches out and grabs under Knight's arm, pulling him up the last bit of the way to the top of the ravine's edge.

"There's only a few Spanish patrol guards positioned out in front of that gate, their front line, thin though it may be. They're crouched in low, some mysterious cover. Back behind them, behind some circus curtain, they have an African loading their rifles. They could be in there all day."

Knight is simultaneously shocked and surely impressed. He's speechless. The Captain's insane to be so cavalier out here in this seriously dangerous position, surrounded by all manner of... and yet the man conducts himself as if he were at a conference room table in the middle of a board meeting. In no time at all, Knight feels an increasing compulsion to side with the man and get to the bottom of the challenge. The reality of it all be damned.

Colbert looks out to the stockade, but he continues the casual conversation. "Both 'The Western Spy' and 'Hamilton Gazette' out of Cincinnati wrote that I've come down from some far heaven to solve battlefield propositions like this one. Can you believe that? Well, those accounts actually chronicled my move against Fort Jefferson, the post on the east side of the Mississippi, several miles below the mouth of the Ohio. No contest for the modest Captain James Colbert. Ha! The truth of it right now is that we can't get at those Spaniards dug in there. And they've already delivered several of my men. So, let's hear it. What's your plan to it? Take a minute or two."

Knight is too stunned to answer back. He stares at his hands and forces himself to regain some amount of presence, alongside the notorious Captain, who has been the subject of almost every conversation this entire time. Well, a good amount of them, for sure.

He'll have to ease himself into this rapport while stuck in the vortex of it. It's a miracle he can conduct one clean thought. Start with what you know. Start with what is obvious. Look around. *There's the Captain's boots. Alright, the polished black leather is wrapped with strips of animal hide, a remarkably odd mix. He's wearing the British half pants, the bottom cuff is just below the man's knees, and they're Navy blue and fairly dirty. The white stockings are also fairly dirty.* Captain Colbert wears a shirt which should be considered typical officer attire, the bright red, quality cotton, with a tight row of polished brass buttons down the front. But inexplicably he wears several deer hide straps crossing his torso from both shoulders to his waist. Each of the straps has an apparent purpose. He has pouches, and powder horns, pistols and blades, and a beaded, fringed leather bag. Around his neck, Colbert wears a kind of neck ornament of forged silver in an extended oval, with symbolic engravings. It's tied on each side with a leather strap that's tied in the back. He doesn't wear an officer's hat. Instead Colbert has his long brown hair, which reaches to the middle of his back, tied in the back with a beaded strap of dark leather. One couldn't name a more intriguing appearance.

With the air whizzing with musket lead, Knight recalls being told that Colbert had spent a good portion of his life with the Chickasaw, which explains this costume.

Knight scooches his way up to the Captain's face; the two of them, face to face, exchange their examinations and then wait for the other to speak. Musket lead pings the dirt around them.

Colbert is easily sixty years old, but the lines of his face are those of an athlete, not a sedentary old man who has collected his years in idle. And not a bit of gray to his hair. His eyes spark with the excitement of this current puzzle. Captain Colbert is clearly in his element. The battle for Fort Arkansas. The Captain is redolent with gritty determination.

On the river, the young Osage has done well. The young man has brought the canoe up the river with clever efficiency. It is Tanawa's stories that have defeated the strength of the river, and now she can see the spot on the river bank where hours and hours earlier the canoes were pulled onto the shore. And where, with the others of her tribe, the Chickasaw mother went into the woods for potatoes. Her heart is beating fast. She's already moved to the very front of the canoe. The moment the small boat touches river mud, she leaps over the side. The young Osage knows he is to wait behind. This is the business of the mother of his tribe, who will enter the woods on her own to find her child.

"Look here man, I'm educated. You're educated. Your thoughts on this are welcome here." Colbert blurts out at Knight with a big smile on his face.

Knight can't believe teeth that rotten can still be in his mouth.

The rifle fire sings out, and it would be easy enough to speak in a normal tone and be heard. Nevertheless, the two men half-shout at each other.

"I'll bet we have a lot in common." Knight finds a few words. "Certainly our education, wouldn't you say?"

"I'm told you play some role in the government," Colbert fires back. "I can't say you don't look the part. It doesn't matter; the Loyalists won't be as necessary with all the incoming British. You'll soon be an old issue, wouldn't you say?"

"Old, I would suppose…" Knight can't get it out before Colbert cuts him off.

"I've heard down the line they call you Representative Knight, so that's what I will call you. Representative Knight, you can call me Captain Colbert."

Colbert is momentarily distracted by activity taking place up near the stockade gate. "Representative Knight, what we have in common is we're both caught in this ravine and we both need to untangle a way out. I don't imagine you're that devoted to the loyal cause, just looking at you. One only dirties one's fingers by meddling with it. So I will assume we can put our minds together here and solve this riddle. Forge a consciousness, impress our intelligence upon them. How about that? Might be what we have in common, wouldn't you say?"

In an instant, two of the Spanish patrol guard standing at the front of the stockade gate are shot. The reloading African is also shot and killed. The British hooray so much that several of the soldiers fire their rifles into the sky.

"Captain Colbert," Knight lets loose in a fast-paced response to the shooting, "though my education for this type of situation is probably limited compared to yours, I have yet to bring down a fort. I would say this might be the time for a rally? Wouldn't you say?"

"Representative Knight," Colbert throws Knight a big smile, "I would say your education is fine. A damn fine idea!"

Knight cringes at the toothy smile.

"Don't stop to think," Knight fires back. He wipes his forehead. The prize fighter has returned, and he scrambles up the two feet to get a better look at the stockade gate. A challenge. A goddamned real challenge is what this is.

Thoughts racing, Knight can feel the adrenaline shooting back at him from the stockade. He's charged with the excitement by the challenge of it all. This might be the something he's waited for, for a very long time. A seriously thrilling moment. He can barely calm himself enough to get the words out, his officer's orders, goddamn it.

"Send six men straight up and over," Knight spins back to confront the Captain, "tell them to run up there in a zig-zagging pattern and shoot to kill." Knight's in commanding form, his voice is loud, steady, and strong. "And everyone left in the ravine will put out a barrage of cover fire. Get their asses up that ridge and give them cover fire. We need that front guard gone! We need that gate. And goddamn it, we need some creative energy up there. Do I have to stand up and wave a baton?"

Colbert stares at Knight, surprised and delighted. His jaw drops. He immediately springs up, standing erect, pointing and yelling down the line. "You there, you six," he shouts as he's pointing at the men, and then with one arm, back and forth over his head, over and over yelling out, "get to the gate, to the gate, go, go, go."

With Colbert's cry still hanging in the air, the 'picked-six' scramble up and over and run straight at the stockade gate. Here and there—mostly mid-way— several stop, take aim, and shoot. Then the others do the same and continue the charge. As the Spanish front guard stand to take their defense, they're shot down. It's clear now their numbers are less than expected. The charge on the Spaniards is indeed a strategic success.

On top, along the banquette of the stockade, the rifle fire doubles. When the front guard are eliminated, Colbert's six men turn and sprint back to the ravine. Once they make it, they dive headfirst out of harm's way. The open field is by no means a victory. The Fort remains firmly with the Spanish.

"Now we'll see what they've got," Colbert sheepishly suggests to Knight.

"Didn't really clear a way up to the gate, did it?" Knight replies, half turning away. "Alright then, we know the charge by force only got us so far. Act Two, we'll need a chorus call, a surprise twist, catch the audience off guard."

Chapter Fourteen

The Garroted Man

Inside the fort, up on the banquette, the face of a young boy, tucked tightly into the corner, has witnessed the Spanish front guard meet their bloody demise. The ragged efficiency of a musket ball from a Brown Bess, at even medium range, will tear a wide open hole. When the last unfortunate soldier down below smacks the ground, the boy turns away and scurries across the banquette to the stairs and quickly down to the stockade dirt. A young, twelve-year-old Quapaw, the same age as Hardy, sprints across the open court and abruptly stops, directly in the company of one Captain Dubreuil, Commandant of Fort Carlos III, Fort Arkansas.

"They're all killed, Sir, everyone, including the negro," the boy tells the Commandant, in decent enough English, the only language they share.

"Esta bien, esa parte esta terminada, let me think for a minute," speaking quietly to himself as he looks up into the gray blue morning sky. Captain Dubreuil has pulled an ornate chair out into the open air where he sits as his soldiers—up on the banquette—keep the British pinned down. Even after the front guard have been killed, "Let me think, let me think."

"I could bring you more of your special coffee, great commander. Would that suit you?" the young Quapaw asks him in his most respectable tone.

"That indeed would give this next decision to be made a much more clinical approach. Yes, let's do that." Dubreuil extends his hand, holding the empty Sévres porcelain cup and saucer to the Quapaw boy. The gold paisleys on the cup flatter the silver lace just beneath the blue cotton of his jacket's cuff. Dubreuil's officer uniform, Louisiana Regiment, consists of a white jacket with blue collar, cuffs, vest, lining, and breeches. All the buttons are enameled white. His white canvas leggings are held up by black leather straps. In the Western Hemisphere, the regimental blue collar and cuffs are detachable when the white uniform is laundered. Dubreuil keeps his immaculate. For a large bear of a man, he wears the uniform with an obvious comfort. Jacobo Dubreuil Saint-Cyr takes great pleasure in the finer things.

On the rivers throughout the Mississippi Valley, fort after fort have changed occupancy, between the Spanish and the British, for more than a decade. Shipping passage on the Mississippi River has been critical to both efforts. Captain Dubreuil came down to the Arkansas River from the Ilinueses, the upper Louisiana Territory, one of the administrative and political subdivisions of French Louisiana at the time of New France. Fort Arkansas is considered of minor importance. It's the farthest west the war has reached, but it must be held, which is why Dubreuil was dispatched.

Not long after Dubreuil arrived, he ordered the fort to be reinforced and an expansion of the Commandant's small house inside the stockade. Dubreuil's dispatch—to the less than spectacular Arkansas River—he considered an insult. The expansion to his house included a small room, a more private chamber, to escape from the dull, repetitive business of the military. Dubreuil is as adept at multi-tasking as he is at retreating from his duties.

Commandant Dubreuil hands the cup and saucer to the young Quapaw, who takes it carefully and walks briskly to disappear into another small building. Dubreuil stands to signal a lesser officer to come to his side. Even during a battle, he will not present himself as the uncultivate who bellows across the stockade. The officer rushes to stand at attention. "Send ten more from the Louisiana Regiment up to that banquette and keep those forest rats away from my gate. Tell them to conserve their powder. And ask them if they'd prefer the British come through our front door to wrap them in medical rags soaked in their own blood."

The officer salutes the Commandant, then he disappears around the back of the house, off to the storehouse where the remainder of the Spanish troops are waiting.

This will provide me time. Dubreuil strolls as he is considering, speaking low to his own consultation. "Social station cannot be tested. It is a physical guide of the universe. Any patrician in such circumstances is required to take repose. Brilliance cannot be conceived with the snap of a finger. It takes many the effort," Dubreuil says, comforting himself, censoring any embarrassment for the loss of the front guard.

A familiar consideration once again becomes the solution of choice for Dubreuil. He walks straight away to a door on the side of the Commandant's house, his chamber, which is securely pad-locked. With two fingers in the lower pocket of his vest, he feels for the right key. Once again, the familiar friend, he pulls the key from the pocket and gently slides it into the slaymaker lock, an ornate polished brass with two opposing dragons on either side of the keyhole. "A gentleman's repose," as he opens the door, passes inside, and closes the door behind him.

The room inside is dark, but just enough of the gray morning comes through the gaps in the timber walls to give him sufficient light. The rifle fire outside is pleasantly muffled. Rushed but not in haste, Dubreuil picks a wooden match from the drawer of a small decorative table in the middle of the tiny room, which is maybe ten feet square. One by one, he lights the various ornamental brass lamps that are placed on short shelves at regular intervals around the perimeter. The lamps, when they are lighted, give the room ceremony. Pleased with the appropriate timing and order of his process, Dubreuil finds the second key in his vest pocket, unlocks it and pulls open the doors of a small wooden cabinet. The opposing doors of the pink cabinet are painted with idyllic pastorals of the Spanish countryside, each with a large grouse.

From a shelf in the cabinet, Dubreuil pulls a small, round enameled tin and a short roll of black patent leather tied up with a single strap. He places them both on the table and pulls up a ladder-back chair painted with butterflies to sit comfortably in his sanctuary. In ordered succession, he unties and unrolls the leather and picks out the thin glass laboratory tube, which is exactly ten inches long. He opens the round enameled tin, placing the lid on the table eight inches to the left. Dubreuil puts his hands in his lap and looks around the room to breathe in his privacy.

With the timbre of the room near perfection, Dubreuil puts one end of the glass tube into his right nostril and bends at the waist to put the other end of the tube into the light brown powder in the tin. With one noisy and quick snort, he takes a good amount of the powder into his nose. The powder is yopo, a magic-religious, psychoactive snuff.

South American shamans describe the yopo experience as an opening of the third eye to perceive into the light of the non-physical, spiritual dimensions. Dubreuil sits quietly with his eyes closed for several minutes, waiting for the spiritual dimension to kick in.

Yopo powder makes a long journey to get to Commandant Dubreuil. The powder is made from crushed seeds grown in the Orinoquía plains of South America. It travels north to the Viceroyalty of New Granada by ship to Cuba, then New Orleans and up the Mississippi where Dubreuil first traded for it. It could be that he was looking for something a little more stimulating than Spanish Port. The wilderness of this continent demands more innovation than European experience can provide.

As Dubreuil's ceremonial snuff takes effect, he continues with the sequence of his private experience. He stands up from the table and walks over to a piece of draped, dark blue velvet pinned to the wall, framed on both sides by kerosene lamps. The fabric is twenty inches square. With a pronounced sense of anticipation and awe, he unpins the fabric. As it floats to the floor, it reveals a sheet of paper, a vertical rectangle, which he has secured to the wall behind a pane of glass. On the paper is a printed image, an etching in dark indigo ink. The etching is by the Spanish artist Francisco José de Goya y Lucientes. The title of the etching, which Dubreuil knows very well is 'Garroted Man.'

Garroted Man depicts a bearded and unkempt man being killed by a garrote, the standard civilian method of execution in Spain. The man is a prisoner, sitting on a stool with his back to the post, wrists bound and a hinged iron collar closed around his neck, the garrote. On the prisoner's right there is a single, long beeswax candle with brightly burning flame. Dubreuil pulls his chair back around to sit directly in front of the Garroted Man.

Barbury felt the urgency to get back to Hardy as quickly as possible. He waited long enough to see if Colbert actually wanted the company of Mr. Knight, or if it was another of his whims. They appeared to be consulting, so he turned and headed back to Hardy. His large frame is tough to keep as low as he would like. The long rifle doesn't make it easier. As he crosses through the ravine, he stumbles more than once on the legs of soldiers who continue their fire, the load and reload campaign against the stockade.

"Get down, Blackbird," a solider calls to him, as Barbury steps over. "You'll draw fire."

"Keep your head down, soldier, and you'll be ready for supper." Barbury's voice is winded by his gauntlet.

The blasts of persistent musket fire dominate everything.

Barbury sprints the final dozen yards, agile, as if he were twenty years younger. As he reaches Hardy, he slides in next to him and flips onto his back, his jacket flat against the grassy dirt. Both Barbury and Hardy, on their backs, are halfway down the side of the ravine, the safest place.

Hardy watches Barbury catch up with his breath. He seems better fit than Mr. Knight. He's waiting for some word, anything from Barbury, about a plan or why they need to be stuck here, in this ravine, in the middle of this battle. Something in all of this is supposed to start making sense. It's what they talked about.

"All right," a few more deep breaths. Barbury has to talk loudly in between the musket blasts. "Alright, I put the two of them together. That part's done."

"Good. And you stayed low." Hardy doesn't feel it's necessary to shout. "And you made it back over here. And thanks for coming back over here."

"I don't believe you saw it, not from where you're lying," Barbury continues in between the musket fire. "The Captain took out the Spanish soldiers up at the front of the gate. I believe they thought it might be to our advantage to clear the path up to the gate. It should have been. It backfired; it only made it worse for us. We're stuck down here worse than we were before."

After Barbury speaks, the two of them lie still on their backs and say nothing for a long several minutes. The gunpowder smoke mixed with the wet uniforms stinks.

Barbury looks up at the clouds that seem to fill up the sky as they move across. He realizes his thoughts are flying through his mind all on their own, in any direction they choose. *This might be one of those moments to just give up and let them fly. This Mr. Knight, and bringing him to the Captain... what an odd combination. They don't fit. And for what purpose? They've never met, and for sure, they have not one thing in common. Maybe men like the two of them are just always in common. They already know a partnership. If Colbert can get through that front gate and get into that fort, what then? Take them all prisoners, and put them on the river? To go where? New Orleans?*

How is it I got so connected to this man doing all this bidding? How is it I have to struggle so hard to see my path now? It was always in my pocket. This British thing, poor fools lost in this parade. These good souls running to the cliff. Is it the boy? Has this boy made my path more difficult to see? Am I running to the same cliff? When do I turn off and go off on my own? When the last battle is done? Macbeth? When Colbert shakes my hand and tells me goodbye. Free to go where I please?

"How long?" Barbury says out loud.

"What's that, Sir?" Hardy can see Barbury is lost in his thoughts. He waits patiently. In this chaos, how can a man sit and be in his own mind, think things through? That can't be easy. I'd like a bigger picture at this point, how to get out of this place. How to get all the way out of here. I wish I had never gone down to the river in the first place. Maybe just take off, go it alone.

"The bigger plan, remember?" Barbury moves a little closer to Hardy, so he doesn't have to speak so loud. "We'll think about the bigger plan, that's what's next. Stay alive, that's what it is."

"Okay. I respect that. I guess."

Only a few feet to Hardy's side, a musket blast shocks him. His body jerks. Hardy inches closer to Barbury; their heads are close enough that they both speak in an almost hushed tone.

"Stay alive," Hardy tells him, "is what everybody's been saying since we first got into the boat. It doesn't mean that much anymore."

"Alright, Son, but let me say this, the bigger plan is always there, dear God in a lightning bolt. It's your heart keeping you moving forward. But staying alive is part of it too. Otherwise, well, getting yourself killed along the way is just not productive."

Both Barbury and Hardy consider being stuck in this ditch will go on for some time. Barbury doesn't consider his rifle would make much of a difference. He lets it lie.

"Barbury," Hardy says slowly, "I keep thinking that something is going to come along, someone is going to tell me something that will be more important, something that will actually work. I mean, clearly, I'm stuck here. We're both stuck in this ravine, but I'm stuck in this whole place. Everything coming down the river has kept me stuck. And it just keeps going, from one place to the next. I can't come up with any idea how to get home."

"I'm sorry you're stuck in this ravine, Son. It makes no sense for you to be here. None that I can see. I wish it were different."

"Me too," Hardy says, "I wish it was different for both of us."

"You know, some fool's always saying this. 'Maybe you're not looking in the right direction.'" Barbury tilts his head slightly. "Life's but a walking shadow, a poor player, that struts and frets his hour upon the stage, and then is heard no more; it is a tale told by an idiot, full of sound and fury, signifying nothing."

"That's a good one," Hardy tells him. "I'm gonna guess Shakespeare."

"Learn by listening. My plan, Son, my plan started long before Colbert came directly into it. The truth of it is, I'd already been bought and sold a few times. Times change and times come along. We knew the British were moving into the Western territories; that was the talk. I made my decision, siding with the British is better for Africans. We believe the British can get down to New Orleans. I'll be taken along. I can't honestly confirm why New Orleans might be the best of all this, but I have to believe that. It's a modern place. It's full of intelligent people schooled by the French and then, well, a number of people, so it has to be smarter than Natchez. Down the Mississippi, all roads lead to New Orleans.

"I knew there was a British Captain at my last auction. And I knew that if he was to be my owner and if I were to get myself into a better situation, then I'd have to make that happen for myself. When the other bidders came around doing their inspection, I'd make myself look sickly and weak. I'd bend over and make my back look almost broke. I'd heard about this Captain Colbert, but to see him was quite something. That long brown hair and the tanned hides he wrapped around himself. The man was a sight. When that man stood in front of me, I stood up strong as a bull. A bit of a wink in my eye, I believe I made him determined to have me. The odd thing of it, I think right there and then he made me stronger. There's a plan here, Son. Maybe I can help you find it. I believe I'm determined."

"The soldiers in your British regiment, your team, seem to leave you alone. You're 'hand's off' to them. I don't understand it. How could I? But I can see it." Hardy tilts his head slightly away from Barbury. "But Sir, there are things you don't know about your British side, really, really important things…"

"Of course there are, Hardy."

"No, you don't understand. What I could tell you would change your entire plan and your faith that siding with the British will pay off for you once this war ends. It's not a good idea for you."

"I think we're starting to trust. I mean look at us, one old African slave lying here in this miserable dirty ditch alongside a young American boy who doesn't know his right from his left, but he knows he wants to be a man. What else could this be but trust?"

"There's a bigger world to this, Barbury, and you don't know it."

"I believe that's true for both of us, Son."

A syncopated rhythm of musket shots cut across the space between the ravine and the stockade.

"A lot of musket shot," Barbury says. "Tell me this, Boy, I'm sorry you don't know how to get there, but where is there? Where are you living? You're not from down in the Louisiana and for sure not from up in the Illinois. Maybe farther east? Tennessee?"

"It's called California, but I think we should just skip over that. Why don't you tell me where you're from? I know you're a slave. You told me, and I've read about them."

"That's right, Son. I am a slave. But I wasn't born into this. And that is a very long story and not one I am going to part with right here in this ravine. I got stolen and taken to a ship and down below tied up and nearly starved. Some did. Their bodies would stink and rot. Tell me about your California."

"After hearing that, I can't really talk about where I'm from and how I grew up. Well, anyway, it wasn't that bad. My parents are good people, and my dad is a great man. He's very good at seeing the right side in people. That's what he's tried to teach me. It's actually a good way to look at people. Especially kids my age in Fullerton. They don't have that much going on. There's not much to do, which is why a lot of kids like to get into trouble, I guess. Fullerton isn't that bad. I could say I was different, and kids treated me bad because I was different, but it's not true. I was just about identical to everybody else."

Hardy takes a long pause. "I think that's what I see now. I just keep going along, like everybody else. When I had the chance, I didn't figure it out. And now, being here, I know I have to figure this out. They've told me to keep going down the river, people I believe and trust in this place. So, I'm going down the river. That's what I'm going to do."

"That sounds like a good way to put it."

Representative Knight finally has words for Colbert. "That might not have been the best plan. We'll need another one."

Colbert looks at Knight with a keen sense of 'we did the wrong thing.' "All we did was give them reason to send more rifles up top. We're more pinned down than before. You should have thought up something maybe a little more creative. You played the rook and now you put us in check."

"Captain, they're brave men, and they did what they were told. A damn fine job of a rush. Let's not forget that." Knight brushes off his jacket.

"It makes the front approach through that gate a decisively more complicated affair." Colbert moves his body up the ravine wall a little farther to make his face-to-face with Knight more persuasive. "And you designed it."

"All right, let's consider what we have gained in the broader plan. When the chess pieces are rearranged, different opportunities present themselves. That's what we have now: a better opportunity. Okay, I'm going to say that sounds like bullshit? In my defense, I am the politician here. I alone am skilled at turning the phrase back on itself. Do you have that word yet? Have you invented the term bullshit? Keep it in mind, it's very handy."

"All right, genius politician, how can we maneuver around to a different approach?" a raised eyebrow and a hand to his chin. Colbert's getting the rapport he had hoped for.

"With this limited manpower?" Knight defaults to one of his better skills, deflect then improvise. "That thing up there is a box, four sides. You have to get in through one of those sides. We don't have a hovercraft to drop in from above. This isn't a rupture in time or a science fiction scenario. I retract that. The front gate is our only option at play here, Colbert. It's the front gate or nothing."

"A junior lieutenant's strategy," Colbert's retort. He performs a quick flail of his arms into the air, then a well-crafted exhale of exasperation.

"I will not disagree with that," Knight's retort, "and very convincing, by the way."

"And it was more your plan than mine." Colbert attempts the final word.

Knight lets the final word hang in the air for a minute. He's the first to turn away.

The rifle fire is steady from both the ravine and the stockade's banquette. Musket lead continues to strike the dirt around both men.

Immediately following the killing of the Spanish front guard, the entire

British regiment, except for the Chickasaw, thrashed about with reckless caution. Now there's little movement.

Typically, in an attack on a stockade directly following an incremental success—like the killing of a division of the opposing regiment—there is a furious reprisal from their fellow soldiers, fearless abandon. Following that, there is the return fire, a show of committed strength and power. Following that, there is a lull when a soldier's aim becomes fatigued and, after the adrenaline, little lead connects with a target. This period typically becomes a concern for a captain, a waste of resources, particularly powder.

In this typical moment, Representative Knight sits watching the dirt, methodically counting the musket ball strikes. His right leg nervously, rapidly pulses up and down. The attack on the fort has become less an urgent calculation for lives and deaths and more a bewildering contest, a game from which he can't secede.

"What the hell am I supposed to be here?" Knight is aggressively mumbling to the dirt. "Is this… what this is? What the hell is this?" His voice is getting louder. "Is this supposed to make sense? A strategy buried in a nightmare game plan, some kind of anxiety dream?" Knight sits up and suddenly slaps his own face, once, then twice. "I've come all this way to do what? Play the part of a military leader, a battlefield impresario?" Knight stops and looks out to the stockade. "Wake up," he whispers.

Knight turns to look down the row of bodies prone against the ravine, made even more impressive by the row of rifles. He spots Hardy and takes a moment to watch him huddle in the ravine. He seems to be safe where he is. After a few moments and another quick brush of the jacket, "Okay, well, so be it," he says, much louder than moments ago. "History goes with the mindful, or some shit like that. I would have thought I was a little old for the part, but this fort must be taken. It's a pure strategy issue."

"A what?" Colbert replies.

"There just might be a legitimate reason I'm here in this ravine, Captain. Being the outsider, I should have the objectivity to get this story straight."

"That's certainly good news," Colbert tells Knight. "You're definitely an undefined, loyalist, militia, undeclared. And here I am, conferring with such a sort as yourself, in the middle of this attack, which the British Army delivered to my charge. My position here is certainly not incidental to this conversation.

I'm going to need you to put your mind to this, and I don't mean a temporary maneuver that puts us back where we started."

"Mr. Knight," Colbert, now realigned with the sobering truth of the situation, "they have guns up there. I want you to take a look up there." Colbert points to the top corner of the stockade. "Those two covered up windows, up there on the far right, and the other one just around that corner. You see those?"

"I do," Knight replies.

"Those, Sir, fall into an altogether different category. They're not some pretty sitting spot for an officer's wife to gather her thoughts while contemplating the mysteries of the forest and beyond."

"Okay…"

"Those tricky embrasures are bullet proof, and when those Spaniards slide them open, you and I are looking at a couple of smooth-bore, muzzle-loading cannons. And no doubt, they're mounted to swivel, which means we are extraordinarily vulnerable. When they put flame on the goose-quill, they'll pound this ravine like peppered pork. We have a problem."

"We have a problem to solve, dear colleague."

The two men slide down the ravine wall to the bottom in unison. They sit upright at the same time, staring across to the opposite side of the ravine.

Colbert tells Knight in a simple tone, without a streak of emotion, "My record is a good record. You can check with the British command. I have had six successful routs up on this Arkansas and farther down on the Mississippi. I have out-maneuvered, and I have proved smarter than the Spanish at every one of our conventions. I am not about to get beat back here on this little slip of a horseshoe bend on this river, so far west that it makes no sense to be here. I've already lost too many who have come with me. Souls cast down by my broken promise. I need a plan here, and I mean right now, a plan more clever than the devil himself could conjure, and I don't believe it has much to do with 'charge the Fort' and see who has the greater number at the end."

"Captain, we're in agreement. The third act is certainly ours to steal."

Commandant Jacobo Dubreuil inches his chair a little closer to his Goya etching. Two of the kerosene lamps across the room have burned out, and he can't be bothered at this moment to refill them. More precisely, Dubreuil knows from experience, a room ever so slightly more in the darkness will allow his guest to speak more freely.

In one continuous motion, Dubreuil crosses his legs, straightens the lace of his cuff, and cocks his head to the right, stroking his goatee.

"Once again, I must apologize. I know what I have promised. I know that I have gone back on my word." He slowly drops his hand to his lap, where he intertwines his fingers. "When last we spoke, you gave me the consultation I requested, and I have not yet delivered my promise to release you to your own private sanctuary." Dubreuil cocks his head to the left. "Your place with your God in your heaven."

He waits for a moment, inching his head forward, peering deeper into the etching, waiting for the garroted prisoner to speak.

"You may take your time, that I understand. A man in such a state as yourself has only his time with which to bargain. With that I am familiar." The studied cadence in his voice gives Dubreuil great pleasure, which fuels the intoxication.

"I've told you my stories, as you have told me yours. It occurs to me only now, the paradox you present to me, the magnificent irony. Your heaven is eternal life, or so you have claimed on several occasions, and yet you are in such a hurry for me to bring you there. It waits. You rush."

Across the small room, one more kerosene lamp burns itself out, the darkness one more increment increased. "There, you see," Dubreuil lets loose a full-bellied laugh. "Time is not a leverage, it's not to your advantage after all, dear friend. It will run away from you like the others have."

A man alienated from that place where the invention of his person, inhabiting a character so well crafted, that it confirms to all peers a champion above the rest, each performance an ovation. A man yanked out of that place, a home, and dropped into the valley of the dirty Mississippi cannot pass without some kind of psychological repercussion. Fair to say.

"You know what I ask of you," Dubreuil inches forward, "one mere, one last… Am I not perfection? Am I not?" Dubreuil listens intently, trying to conceal his eager attention to receive the inspired strategy from the garroted man.

"Thank you. Thank you for saying that, but deceit is not your strength."

He waits.

"The British and their infamous Captain? Am I not the only officer in the entire Spanish soldiery with the vision to bring this tedious contest back to the orchard? How is it you feel you can challenge me? Of the two of us, it is you who are clearly garroted. You're the prisoner. How dare you suggest otherwise?"

Dubreuil abruptly stands. He takes a few paces, circling the space in front of the etching, suddenly kicking the chair across the small, dark room. It crashes against the wall.

"Why can't I do well for myself? You're the one who promised I would be unshackled. That was your promise, and I have done all that you've asked of me. Your arrogance is unacceptable."

Dubreuil can't contain himself. He begins a slight whimper of a cry. "I will find that way, with or without your permission. The direction of my chapter will not be concealed from me much longer. You will rot in your miserable station until I give my permission, and I will not have these vulgar British stand in my way."

Dubreuil goes to the front door, and opens it to find the young Quapaw is standing there patiently waiting with the coffee. Dubreuil completely recomposes himself. "You are so kind," he tells the young Quapaw boy, as he takes the cup and saucer. "Now go to the embrasure, there up on the banquette. He points. And tell the gun officer I need to speak with him. I need this done quickly."

As the young Quapaw runs across the stockade to the ladder and climbs to the banquette, Dubreuil is repeating over and over, in Spanish, then Latin, "Los que no tienen paciencia seguramente triunfarán, utique qui pro patientia." Those with no patience will surely succeed.

The Quapaw boy reaches the north bastion of the stockade where the six-foot cannon—one of three—is mounted on its carriage with four-foot diameter wheels. He speaks with the several Spanish soldiers positioned around the six-foot gun. When Dubreuil sees the Quapaw has transferred his order, he walks out to a more central location in the stockade, careful to leave the door of his private quarters slightly open, exactly three inches.

The gun officer makes his way down to Commandant Dubreuil.

"Your name is Agustin. That's correct, isn't it?" Dubreuil asks the soldier. The young man stands at attention. "And where are you from, soldier? To where do you hope to return once the British abandon their effort here?"

"I am from Armisgroten, the small village above Seviloe, Sir." He purposely keeps his response to the Commandant short.

"And how old are you, soldier?" Dubreuil straightens his cuff.

"I am eighteen years, Sir."

"And what happened to the sleeve of your jacket, soldier?"

"It was torn by wood splinters, Sir."

"And what happened to your arm, soldier?"

"It was torn open by the same wood splinters, Sir."

"You'll need to get that wrapped in cotton from the storehouse as soon as we finish this next order of business." Dubreuil takes a deep breath and holds it for several moments. As he exhales slowly, he asks the attentive officer, "Tell me, Agustin, do you believe, would you admit, if you were under a tremendous amount of pressure, would you agree, we are mortals, every one of us, prisoners of our flesh?"

"Sir?"

"Fire your cannon, soldier, and have not one serving of mercy. Take off the top of the ridge to expose their bodies and let the muskets take their turn. Take them on the field and save the business of conducting prisoners for other fools."

Dubreuil reconfigures his composure yet again, now with the attention to the details of his military position. "Ram well the wad put over the powder," he tells the officer. "Before you charge the piece, sponge it well, to clean it of all dirt and filth within-side. Precision, officer. That is my order."

"That's our regular business, Sir."

Dubreuil stands stationary to watch the gun officer, Agustin, go all the way up and across the banquette to the gun embrasure. British rifle fire continues to pepper the outside of the stockade. The officer gives his orders, and the two gunners set to the business. They prepare the proper weight of gunpowder—taking care that the powder isn't bruised in the ramming, which weakens its effect. In the muzzle end of the iron cannon, they use the long ramrod to ram down the cloth cartridge containing the gunpowder, followed by a wad of hay, and then they throw in the ball, a hefty four-pounder.

Commandant Dubreuil walks back across the stockade to the private house. He doesn't feel the need to conduct any further business, not for the moment.

The two gunners stand next to the cannon, ready with the portfire—a paper tube with quickmatch inside, held in a wooden handle. When lit by the linstock, the portfire will burn for several minutes. The portfire will set a gun off in the rain. Upon orders, the gunners will use the portfire to light the goose-quill tube containing gunpowder, forced into a vent hole in the back of the iron gun. They finish their preparation, and they stand at attention for the order to fire.

Dubreuil signals the young Quapaw to come collect the cup and saucer.

"For the Commandant." Agustin orders the fire.

The portfire softly touches the top of the goose quill tube, and the spark of the salt peter speeds down through the rigid quill, through the inside of the vent hole. The last spark in the quill leaps out to gently touch the cloth cartridge, which by now has familiarized itself with the gunpowder. The powder inside the cloth finds itself in an inevitable situation. It must explode. Its force is trapped to only one exit; it must go through the four-pound lead ball pressed firmly against it. The ball has no choice. It's forced out through the six-foot-long narrow channel and out into the wilderness.

The recoil from the ball and the blast throws the heavy cannon backward several feet. The gunners will wrestle it back into position and make it ready again for the next.

The older British soldiers in the ravine knew the blast was imminent by the activity up at the embrasure. The younger, new to Colbert's regiment, are caught off guard. The explosive blast is a shock to everyone in the entire arena, those inside on top along the banquette, those inside the stockade conducting other business. And those outside of the stockade, the British, spread across the ravine. The blast brings everything to a stop. The ball tears through the air. Only the quick can see the streak of it. The violence of the strike is thirty feet past the ravine. The explosion of earth, dirt, wood, and rock, shoots up high into the air, then rains back down, scattered.

Captain Colbert watches the dirt fall and the thunder of it hitting the ground, then immediately swings back to Knight. "We may be too far wide at this angle," Colbert yells at Knight, who is very close to him. "That might buy us time. They won't know to swing the cannon mount this far until they get a little more accuracy. They have to reconfigure their embrasure."

Representative Knight quickly shakes it off. "The cannon fire will tear us apart. We won't last long."

"The Chickasaw will turn and head back down to the river," Colbert tells him.

The two of them crouch back into conference mode. Even though Colbert expected it, the cannon blast is a serious addition and merits reevaluation. But it also fuels a sparkle of delight in their strategizing energy.

"It's not a might versus might battle. Clearly, they have the big guns." Knight uses dialog recalled from somewhere.

"We're back to the clever strategy, friend." Colbert works to contain himself.

"Rout these bastards out of that fort. You can't beat them at their own game," another hazy mix from Knight.

As Representative Knight thinks through the revised predicament, he surprises himself with his knack for recalling bits of seventies front page news. "We have to pull from history."

Knight is fired up. "This is exactly the same configuration as Hill 937." He's using his hands in small contained gestures. "They called it that because it was 937 feet above sea level. It was a neck-to-neck battle that went on for a disastrous ten days. It depleted the resources of the North Vietnamese, and the US did little better. May of '69."

Colbert leans in and takes hold of Knight's hands, trying to stop the gesturing.

"Part of Operation Apache Snow, which had the objective of clearing the North Vietnamese out of the South. That hill had to be taken, just like your Fort." Knight leans in, pulls his hands away, and now covers Colbert's hands, holding them still. "That hill had no strategic significance, none. Sound familiar? The US commanders took a bull-headed approach to capturing that hill. And they paid for it, unnecessarily heavy casualties. They called it 'Hamburger Hill' because it chewed up the fighting men."

Knight tightens his grip. "If Hamburger Hill tells us anything, it's that the bum rush is foolhardy, plus they have the advantage and we don't have the count. We have no idea how many men they have in there. In battle, you prepare for the worst-case scenario." He releases his grip on Colbert's hands and sits up to straighten his back to look directly at Colbert, and he holds that position, waiting for the response.

"I sure enjoy your company," the Captain tells Knight. "Not familiar with the details, but I sure get the gist of it. Your Hamburger Hill is a place... we'll call it a kind of strategy short note."

"Exactly, it is a place, well, more of a famous turning point."

"You're talking like a man a little too friendly with the New Orleans rum. But I remember my first time. You can't forget it. The cannons do that to a man." Colbert sits up, straight and sober. "But with a full amount of respect right here, between you and me, we're going to have to get a lot more productive in our thinking."

"I'm aware of that. We've established that. We're definitely out-gunned. Captain, I believe I have a plan!"

Chapter Fifteen

Hooligans from Hades

Barbury tries to put himself in a better position to see where the cannon strike hit. "If Colbert didn't expect the Spaniards to pull out those cannons, then he does now."

"That's the loudest thing I've ever heard." Hardy is practically shouting. "I've never heard a real bomb before."

The musket lead starts again to ping the dirt around the two of them. Barbury slides back into the safer position.

"Maybe with our trust," Hardy tells Barbury, returning to his hushed tone, "Maybe we should be honest and say out loud, we're probably not going to make it home."

"Son, the cannon doesn't change a thing. We'll make it out of this. We still have a way to go."

Barbury looks up. He watches the clouds roll along one more time. Maybe something from his past, the clouds, will give him permission.

"Let me tell you a bit more history on this subject of a plan." Barbury's steady tone. "When General Cornwallis, maybe you've not heard of this history, well, when he and the rest of his British army entered the Virginia, most of those soldiers were wearing cowhide tied on their feet for shoes. This man was determined to attack Lafayette and his French at Richmond. Understand, the man had seven thousand soldiers to feed. The man had thousands of black followers of the flag. So every one of Cornwallis's soldiers had his negro carrying all his provisions, and the officers three or four. Cornwallis's army was called a wandering Arabian Tartar horde. And every place this horde passed through was eaten clean, like an acre invaded by a swarm of locusts.

"These British placed a lot of trust in these Africans. They were essential to Cornwallis in order to supply his army. They did the foraging for the hungry forces, driving livestock and stripping the fields and storage cellars. At this point in the story, stop to ask yourself: were the Africans slaving for the British because they were slaves? Or were there bigger plans at work? Remember our bigger plan, Son?"

"Of course I remember," Hardy tells him. "I know what you're trying to tell me with your story. I can see you believe it."

"Well, there's more. Cornwallis has sent a thousand Africans, maybe more, out to roam around and take or steal what they find, and there is not one British soldier looking over them. The British were forced to trust, or they gambled their trust. Either way, we slaves had the bigger plan."

Barbury turns back and looks at Hardy. "Word was that the British fed good, and they paid good. A thousand more Africans found their way to Cornwallis, nothing like slaves had seen before. He paid runaways to do all sorts of labor. The bigger plan, Son? Africans had a plan to latch onto. That's what all that suffering was for. It's we Africans who are using the British to reach our goal. You wonder why I'm down here in this ditch. It's because I'm watching this story unfold and, dear God in a lightning bolt, I'm going that direction."

"I can see you believe in an idea that is bigger than what others see. It's your bigger plan, Barbury. I can hear it in your voice, the way you talk about it. You believe you're on your way away from all this, a way to get back to where you feel you belong. What I'm telling you, Sir, is that you need to see a way that's going to get us out of this ditch. Pretty darn soon, forget about freedom."

Barbury raises his head and straightens his shoulders. "Freedom means everything."

Hardy lowers his head. "You won't see it."

The gunners prepare the cannon for the second shot. The cannon is charged, sponged and loaded. "For the Commandant," gun officer Agustin orders to light. The spark in the quill jumps to the gunpowder's cloth cartridge. The cannon explodes.

The second cannon ball strikes the top ridge of the ravine about thirty feet farther down the ravine from where Barbury and Hardy are hunkered down. Representative Knight and Captain Colbert are farther up the ravine.

The shot is more accurate. Its strike destroys the top edge of the ravine, immediately shredding the bodies of two unfortunate British soldiers. With the ravine exposed, before the hailstorm of dirt can finish, the Spanish take advantage. They've prepared, and their rapid musket fire peppers the jackets of two more British, killed while the soldiers on either side of the blast take new cover.

Colbert sees his regiment being torn apart as the Spanish have intensified their effort. The advantage of the ravine has become a trap, and to turn and run back out would put easy targets on their backs. Captain Colbert, being fond of parading his military prowess and cultivating his notoriety—he's definitely stumped. Slaughter is imminent.

Colbert turns to look at the muddy bottom of the ravine. "I will not be dishonest to these soldiers," he says, mostly to himself.

He slides down the side of the ravine and crouches at the bottom, both hands cupped to his mouth to yell down the length of the ditch. "Keep fire on the embrasures! Show them our strength! Conserve your powder! There'll be no reinforcements. We'll have this fort!" He drops his head, staring into the mud.

As soon as Colbert finishes the call out, two Chickasaw scramble up the opposite side of the ravine and take off running toward the forest perimeter. They're skilled at navigating rifle fire.

Colbert shakes his head. He shakes his whole body like a dog shaking off lake water. He pushes his body back up the side of the ravine, close to Knight. "Let me be honest, I don't see the future here with this one. I think my vision has left me. The Chickasaw call it—the search for the proper place at the end will consume those who cannot surrender to it." He juts his head forward next to Knight's. "Do you hear what I'm saying to you, Sir? I fear I have broken with my promise. These souls will never get back to their true life and be with their families."

With the shock of the second blast subsided, Knight uncurls himself from the ball he has made of himself. He talks straight at Captain Colbert, just loud enough for only Colbert to hear. "You may call me crazy, but I believe I've got it. On the future grave of Bill Clinton, I believe I've got it: one good old-fashioned bluff." Knight is now reeling. "We'll need to play to their sympathy, reinforce their masculine drive. You know the term 'macho morale?' I may have just made that up, but it doesn't matter. We'll lead them to believe they have made the correct decision. We need to engage their sense of heroism. We need them to want to be the moral victor. They're Spanish, for Christ's sake."

"Mr. Knight, this is hardly a game, but I can see you have what you believe to be the solution to this misjudgment I have made, and I do think you're an educated man," Colbert replies, regaining a bit of faith.

"They want this fort, Captain, but they don't need it. They will let it go. They will walk away to prove to their Royal Highness that they have chosen God's will and indulged his higher ground. The moral victory." Knight stops to let Colbert take it in. "It's so simple; that's why it's so perfect."

"I'll need two good-shot soldiers to go with me, fast ones. We'll need a diversion to make it back across the field to the village. I'm going back to the prisoner's house, where you have Lieutenant de Villars and his robust wife. Now, you're going to trust me. Is that clear?"

Without hesitation, Captain Colbert raises his body just enough to wave at two soldiers, signaling them to come to him to take orders. They all stay low. "Take this man to the prisoner's quarters straightaway. Cut back and forth across the field. Don't make yourselves an easy target. And don't let this man be killed. He has the plan for the way out of this ditch. Am I clear?"

"As the stink of a dead body leads to the horses."

"As the shot at the moon lowers your chances."

"Gentlemen, you are colorful. I will give you that," Knight's response.

The two soldiers grab Knight's arms to help him stand, and the three of them get their bodies in position, ready to dart up the side of the ravine and sprint across the field.

Knight turns back to Colbert one last time. "I want you to put trust in this, Colbert. It's going to work. Trust me. I'll be back, half an hour, tops."

Colbert grabs the lapels of Knight's Armani jacket and pulls him closer. "What's the plan?"

"We'll force a surrender! We'll force them to barter for the lives of the officers you hold prisoner, including Lieutenant de Villars and his wife. The one gamble is if the Fort's Commandant, stuck in that stockade, finds that cow as miserable as everyone else. It's a gamble."

"That's a brave idea for an American."

"Are you ready, Boys?" Knight's at the absolute apex of exhilaration. The two British soldiers exchange doubtful glances. Knight looks down the length of the ravine. He sees Hardy with Barbury. Hardy doesn't see him.

"On the count of three… forget it, let's go." Knight and his two soldiers dart up and over the side of the ravine.

The recoil from the second cannon shot has been more extreme than the first. It throws the entire carriage of the gun far enough out of position that the third shot will again be mostly for fine-tuning the accuracy.

The blast of the third shot has the same effect as the first two. Bodies across the banquette and the ravine jerk in reaction. The strike explodes the ground ten feet in front of the ravine, almost directly in front of Hardy and Barbury. No one is killed; the reset wasn't accurate.

Hardy is shaken and covered in dirt. He opens his eyes. "I don't think the next one will miss." He spits out dirt on the ground. "They're getting better with their aim."

Barbury is nervous and agitated. He rubs his head. "That may be true, but if we were to jump up and run back, they'd shoot us right dead. They're ready for the clean shot."

Barbury slides his jacket off without raising up his body. He starts to put it over Hardy, tries to cover him.

"Don't do that, Barbury. Put your jacket back on. You're going to need it. This is the time, before they can reload that cannon, you have to decide." Hardy forces the jacket back into Barbury's hands. "Before they can blow us up, we're going to get Mr. Knight, and we're going to make a run for it, back into the woods."

"And you think that by running off, I will get my freedom out in the woods?"

"No, Sir, not your freedom, but the rest of your life."

Barbury looks to the top of the stockade.

"We're ready, and we're gonna wait for it." Hardy looks across the field and back at the stockade. "There will be a sign. It's gonna happen."

Commandant Dubreuil, startled by the third cannon blast, has shaken it off and walks slowly back to the slightly ajar door of his private quarter. As he gets closer to the door, he begins to giggle under his breath in response to suggestions made by his garroted prisoner.

"Oh my, listen to these profundities. Are we concocting a plan in exchange for your freedom? Is that what you'll have me believe?" He reaches the door and opens it just enough to slip inside, and he gently closes the door behind him. Once inside, he hurriedly walks to the etching on the wall, glancing at the yopo tin and the glass tube on the table. "You are more clever than the devil himself. Could it be that I have measured you lower than your creativity warrants?"

Dubreuil bends at the waist and puts his hands on his knees, looking down at the wooden floor as he continues his squeaky laughter. "How divinely silly. How wonderful a persuasive anecdote. And may I add, why not? Are we not together in sharing our fatigue with this stalemate? Both as bored with our own considerations as any of the prisoners we've had before?"

He picks up the piece of dark blue fabric and pins it back on the wall to cover the garroted prisoner. "Now, now, I will not forget your brilliance. When I return, we will discuss the terms of your release. We are both gentlemen, and we both understand quite well the theater of this world."

As the final pin covers the etching, "Shush, shush, I am not a madman. I will keep my word."

Once the etching is covered, Dubreuil makes his way back out of his room, locking the door. Barely able to stop himself from rushing, he walks to the middle of the stockade and abruptly stops. He quickly calls and gestures for several of his regiment, including several Quapaw warriors, to line up in front of him.

Dubreuil walks back and forth in front of the assembled men. He politely pushes a man back or pulls a man gently forward. He needs to have these men in a straight, shoulder-to-shoulder line. None of them has the slightest idea of what the Commandant is thinking, and the perversely gleeful expression on his face doesn't help.

He calls over to the young Quapaw boy who earlier had brought him coffee, and he prepares to give orders. Dubreuil takes several steps back away from his rag-tag row. There are eight assembled; tall, short, one quite heavy, and two Quapaw with very intense expressions of disapproval. Pleased with what he has, he begins his list to the boy. "I will want face paint, the red and the vermilion. I will want many feathers, a basket full. And strips of colored cloth. If you have not enough, then tear up the officer's uniforms. Rope and twines to drag behind them." He looks to see if the young Quapaw has understood the extent of his requests, and, satisfied, he waves the boy to go.

Dubreuil turns to his sortie party in order to educate them. "I now understand why they have brought my temperament to this holy forsaken stretch of this river valley."

The Spanish soldiers say, in unison, "Sí, Señor!" The Quapaw mumble at the dirt.

Captain Colbert pivots between watching his regiment respond to the pelting from the banquette's fire and looking back across the open field to see when Knight will emerge. It's fitting that Colbert should see it first, the piece of white cloth—tied to a wooden pole—being walked onto the field.

Astonishing and unexpected as it surely is, Colbert now knows Knight's plan, at least the first part of it.

The Spaniards across the top of the banquette spot the white flag as well and, almost in unison, stop their musket fire and stand to get a better look.

Commandant Dubreuil hears the cease in the musket fire and moves to a small ground-level window. He pulls the sliding wooden panel to the side to look out at what is happening across the field.

With the Spanish guns quiet, the British cease their fire as well and stand and turn to see the flag, now midway in the field.

Not a single musket shot or cannon blast. Not even a single word spoken. The entire battlefield is silent in awe and seriously baffled by what is happening.

At the exact same time, Captain Colbert and Commandant Dubreuil utter the same confounding name. "Doña Marie?"

Doña Marie, spectacle that she is, is in fact walking in front of the pole with the white flag. She is walking cautiously and slowly. Very close behind her is a short British soldier who carries the pole. He is petrified, his steps are clumsy, and he appears as though at any given moment he'll turn around and dash back for cover.

The two of them are making their way across the field. Doña Marie uses one hand to lift her long dress, and in the other, she carries a sealed envelope. Against her nature, she doesn't say a word. The woman is supremely irritated. It shows on her face, but she's also triumphant at being the center of attention. She's not one bit frightened by any of it.

At the midway distance between the village houses and the stockade, Doña

Marie stops, the flag with her.

An astonishing sight to the soldiers on both sides of the fort's attack, Doña Marie stands in the open field, her huge, rose-colored satin dress billowing in the breeze, her robust body tightly filling the gown. Her black hair piled on top of her head, and everywhere, on her dress and in her hair, are tight little ribbons and cloth-starched flowers. Doña Marie's face is powdered white as snow, and her lips drawn red as blood, the lipstick made from beeswax and red stain containing copious amounts of mercury. There she stands waiting for a response, her thoughts composed. *Finally, they see what I bring to this warren of primitives, wallowing in their own excrement.*

Captain Colbert is dumbstruck and waits to see what action he should take, unprepared for any. Commandant Dubreuil prepares to send one of his soldiers out to test the ceasefire and to retrieve the envelope Doña Marie holds in her hand. At the last moment, he changes his mind and sends the young Quapaw boy, who has proven so diligent to his needs.

Slowly, the young Quapaw emerges from a side door on the stockade. He wasn't given the time to paint his body, so he is as embarrassed by his appearance as he is terrified by being exposed in the open. He walks toward the large woman in the field; he takes his steps carefully.

When the boy reaches the spot directly in front of Doña Marie, he stops to wait for her response. He wouldn't dare reach for it. Doña Marie grabs the young boy's hand and slaps the envelope on his palm.

Suddenly, and brazenly unexpected, Doña Marie throws her hands up in the air in disgust. Her gesture is made for the entire collection of soldiers and attending officers. She is well rehearsed in the theatrical flair of commanding attention.

Dubreuil sees her gesture. He's seen it before, and realizes the unfortunate circumstance that will require him to walk out to join the painted corpulent princess on center stage to retrieve the envelope himself. He walks over to the side door and walks out onto the field. Most of the way, he walks with his head down, the rest with his head straight up, looking at the clouds in the sky. He will not appear cowered or perturbed. Another bit of dreary business in this otherwise futile effort from the British to take his command of Fort Arkansas.

Dubreuil reaches Doña Marie and the young Quapaw holding the envelope. It is the protocol for the commanding officer to take the orders of surrender, typically delivered by the commanding officer of the opposition, but these are a mixed bag of circumstances. He holds out his hand, and the boy gives him the envelope. Doña Marie glares at Dubreuil while asking, "Shall we expect a luncheon?"

The Quapaw boy skedaddles back to the stockade.

Clouds passing over momentarily steal her spotlight.

Tanawa covers a good amount of distance, keeping a steady pace. She doesn't speak. Not a sound. The heavy breathing of a runner passing through the woods' gauntlet, not a sound. When exhaustion from the vines and branches begins to control her body, she puts it out of mind. As Tanawa keeps to her race, the heaviness of her lungs separates her body from her thoughts. They move now as competitors. Tanawa's tears stream across her face to gather in her hair.

Deeper into the woods, her crying out is unleashed as she leaps over yet another fallen branch, an uncontrollable wail at the forest, rhythm'd by her runner's breath.

She knows what will be next. There is a light, a different quality of forest light ahead. It will be an opening in the trees.

It is the duty of the forest to contribute now. The forest must see that she has given her fullest spirit. For the first time, Tanawa slows her running to a fast-paced walk. She approaches the edge of the brighter sun on the forest floor, a cautious step-by-step.

Tanawa has finally returned to the place of the wild potatoes. She stops. She stands stationary, not one muscle moves. Across from her, on the opposite side of the ring of sunlight, the gray wolf stands, staring back at Tanawa.

The she wolf emits an almost imperceptible growl without shifting her focus. Her lip curls and quivers. Tanawa stands fearless.

Captain Colbert climbs out of the trench he has occupied for hours and hours and takes a few steps in the direction of Dubreuil and Doña Marie. With nothing to add, at this point in the robust theatrics of the morning, he stops to wait for what happens next.

Barbury and Hardy have also climbed out of the ravine, as have many of the British soldiers. Everyone is waiting for Dubreuil to make a definitive move. What is the envelope?

"Let's go, this is it, our chance, Barbury." Hardy is lightly tugging at Barbury's sleeve. The older and wiser knows it's not an opportunity. It's far from over.

Representative Knight finally emerges from the rear of the village house and walks out toward the Spaniards in the middle of the field, but he also stops short to see what will develop. He looks across the field to Colbert. The two of them connect and exchange looks of trepidation mixed with a good amount of surprise; the sum of it: anxiety.

From the edge of the sunlight's ring on the forest floor, Tanawa takes one single step forward toward the wolf. Not the slightest movement from the wolf. The entire forest blurs, then falls away. There is only the intensity exchanged between them. There is no other thought. Tanawa steps forward again. The wolf lowers her head ever so slightly. Their shared focus is unwavering. The guttural growl of her one trembling lip can be heard now across the stage of their standoff. Tanawa understands the growl as a challenge and so she takes it. She takes a fearless two steps forward. Receiving the boldness of the dare, the wolf gives the impression of a sudden lunge without actually stepping forward. A bluff.

Commandant Dubreuil breaks the wax seal and opens the envelope. He flutters the paper to straighten it. Next, he pulls out his wig spectacles from a vest pocket, puts them on, careful not to disturb his wig, and he reads as Doña Marie pulls at her wig to straighten it. "Can we move this along?"

From the distance, Knight can see that Dubreuil has started to read the surrender letter. He mouths the words while Dubreuil reads.

"Le Capitane Colbert has been sent by his superiors to take the post of the Arkansas, and, by this power, Sir, he demands that you capitulate. It is his plan to take, with all his forces, the Lieutenant Luis de Villars and his family. The fate of Doña Marie Luisa de Villars, together with the other women and inhabitants of the village, rests in your hands."

Doña Marie relaxes one shoulder and lets her head drop the smallest possible amount, almost imperceptibly. Commandant Dubreuil suddenly lifts one arm into the air. He holds it there one full minute.

Tanawa stands still, poised. The she wolf has made her intentions clear, both their intentions have been made clear. Their purpose has not been diminished by the threats from the other. Tanawa breathes one last breath. She feels across her back and her shoulders that the forest has favored her, not the mother wolf. At this moment, there will be no other consideration. She exhales and starts the walk across the sunlight. She turns her head down to the ground. She has broken her focus with the wolf. Her purpose is now greater than only herself. Her fear of the she wolf has vanished, taken by the forest. She walks slowly and deliberately, with a knowing humility. There will be no surprise.

With the Commandant's hand raised high, and not one distraction throughout the entire arena. The Arkansas Fort, and with it the river, will go to the British or stay with the Spanish. Another of history's decisive moments. Not one distraction could be possible. And yet, there is one; the finale.

The large metal hinges of the stockade's front gate eke out a considerable rusty squeak, to the absolute astonishment of the British in the ravine and everyone outside of the stockade. All heads turn. Both sides of the stockade's front gates swing open. Every single British soldier leans forward, their jaws dropping in unison.

Inch by inch, the gate opens: two feet wide, six feet wide, ten feet wide. Colbert and the entire British regiment stand transfixed. In one of those impossibly rare, Earth stands still, frozen in time moments, there, in front of the world and the British, stands a collection of devils, demons, and hooligans from Hades. Terrifying painted faces, clothes from the underworld, pots and pans tied about them, weapons tied to their legs. They stand in a row, expecting their audience to drop dead from fright. With no warning, the hooligan devils start screaming. The loudest their voices can scream and cry out and hoot and holler and yell out Indian war whoops, words no living human has ever heard. Then, just as suddenly, they leap through the open gate and bolt toward the British in the ravine, screaming and hooting as they come. A fright beyond all belief.

Capitan Colbert somehow manages to turn away, and he looks directly at Knight. The two of them stare intently at each other, their mouths open. They both shake their heads 'no' in disbelief.

Colbert breaks the stare. He looks down the ravine. Half of his soldiers have already run up the side in retreat and are sprinting toward the village. He raises both arms and shouts to his men. "Let's go! Let's go! The devils are upon us."

In their attempt to get up and out of the ravine, some soldiers drop their rifles to better scramble. In no time at all, the entire British regiment is running back across the field to the village houses. They don't say much. Soldiers in shock don't cry out.

Some of the devil hooligans make it as far as the ravine, some not even that far. They all slow their running and eventually stop. No need to continue.

Commandant Dubreuil offers his arm to Doña Marie. The smugness of a victor courses through his veins. She takes his arm and, together, they walk casually back to the stockade. Dubreuil listens patiently to her new dietary demands as they walk. He is more than a little disappointed that the drama of his actors passed so quickly. He considers how painfully ironic that his enemy has escaped while he still feels the prisoner.

Hardy and Barbury watch as the British run back across the field. Neither of them saw the masqueraders as enough of a threat for a retreat, but they understand what happened.

"We missed our chance, probably," Hardy resigns.

They walk at a normal pace back toward the village and to the river.

"Much worse. I've seen much worse than that," Barbury says.

"Not even close to Army of the Dead." Hardy's final comment.

Tanawa walks unwavering through the sunlight on the forest floor. Slow steps, true steps. When she is ten feet from the wolf, nothing but forest air between them, suddenly the wolf turns her head to the trees. She smells the air and quickly darts off, disappearing into the woods.

Tanawa knows the fallen log, and she rushes to it. There she sees her infant daughter sleeping quietly, wrapped in the deer hide, dappled sunlight on its little face. Before she takes her baby into her arms, Tanawa howls the wail of her tribe into the sky, to the trees, and to the forest. She picks up her baby and holds the infant tightly to her. The baby opens her eyes to see her mother's face and the trees above her. Tanawa cannot contain her joy and gratitude for the forest's generosity. The tip of a wispy cloud moves in front of the sun. The light in the forest turns. Tanawa's thoughts turn back to the tomahawk and the Osage warrior. What she feels for the young Indian is not for anyone else to know. She hugs the infant tightly and speaks quietly to her child before she turns to go back to the river.

Chapter Sixteen

The business of this world

By the time the British soldiers make it to the houses of the village, they have slowed their running retreat. They've seen their pursuers stop at the ravine, with little interest in crossing it.

Most of the British soldiers are walking slowly, burdened with the weight of fatigue from more than half a day in the ravine. Some of them stumble from their injuries and are helped along by othe rs. Their dirt-soaked uniforms are spotted here and there with blood. There will be some amount of medicine and bandages at the keelboat when they get to the river. There are enough wounds and misery to satisfy the Spanish.

No one seems to be concerned about the protocols of a retreat, most likely because the circumstances of the battle's end were so peculiar. And because Commandant Dubreuil is now exhausted by his own drama, he doesn't bother to command his Spanish regiment and his collection of Chickasaw and Africans to follow the British to the river. Another time will come and further orders will materialize. Why bother?

Captain Colbert crisscrosses through the groups of his men as they walk through the small houses on their way to the river. He looks briefly at wounds and puts a firm hand on the shoulders of several of his men. He does what he can to give them some measure of comfort. He speaks in a close voice to several of the soldiers as they walk, affirming they can make it to the river and onto the keelboat. He will send runners to retrieve his brave soldiers who were killed at the ravine.

Captain Colbert spots Representative Knight standing alone in the doorway of one of the small houses. They can see it on each other's faces.

Colbert walks toward Knight, straightening his shoulders, preparing himself for a good-natured farewell, but he stumbles briefly on a rock sticking out of the dirt. In the last few steps to reach Knight, his shoulders have dropped back, his hands are in his pockets.

"I suppose that could have been successful if we had seen past their bluff and hung on to our own." Colbert has to say something. "A hooligan brigade. I suppose it's plain dishonest to assume we had the stronger bluff. Well, anyway, we swallowed it. Fish on a hook. There's little to do about it now." Colbert takes a hand out of his pocket and reaches to shake Knight's hand. "I appreciate the camaraderie, Sir."

"Captain Colbert, Sir," Knight tells him in a slowed and quiet voice, "you have nothing to be ashamed of. You were under orders from the highest command. His Majesty needed Fort Arkansas and put you in charge of securing it. You had the village, and you would have had the prize of the stockade if it weren't for the cannons." Knight puts a hand on Colbert's shoulder. "You acted as smart and as clever as the best of them. Certainly, far superior to your opponent. I appreciate the camaraderie too."

Colbert takes a moment to consider their partnership. "I have matters here, men and supplies to get off this piece of land and down the river." Colbert turns and begins to walk away. "We'll say our goodbyes at the river."

Knight stands in the spot a little longer, watching Colbert walk away to rejoin the men making their way to the river. He now feels the exhaustion in his own body and the mental fatigue of it all. Now his shoulders drop and his head too heavy; he looks to the ground.

"Thank the lord that is over. The Spaniards pulled the plot twister, smarter than I thought." As Knight says the words, a Chickasaw warrior, with a keen sense of phrasing, passes by him, headed for the river, "Never over."

Considering a response to the Chickasaw, Knight looks up at the same moment that Barbury and Hardy join him at his side. All three look at each other, grateful they made it through, but for several minutes, no one says a word.

Representative Knight speaks first. "I wonder how you could explain any of that to your father." Knight recognizes this should be a moment to be grateful they're all three alive, but he can't help himself. Ranting is his default.

"I mean, forget for the moment that we're standing here talking about a military attack by the British army on a fort on the Arkansas river occupied by the Spanish. Forget about all of that. This being some shared daydream hallucination where people actually get themselves killed, with real red blood, whatever the hell this is, what in the name of Jesus Christ can you say about the way these officers and these soldiers conduct themselves? Some ludicrous display of theatrics in a decisive military campaign. Absolute pollution of our military something."

"Stop. Please, Mr. Knight. I know you don't get how we got here and all this Revolutionary War stuff that we're stuck in, but I'm just a kid." Hardy looks down. He can't hold back tears. "You have to tell me I'm going to be alright, that around that clump of trees, or just a little farther down the river, I'll see my dad, and he'll yell at me for taking too long, and he'll say 'now let's get lunch,' then we'll get back in the Winnebago and go home. And I can, I can feed my fish and play Play Station."

Knight steps over and puts an arm around Hardy. He uses one hand to gently hold Hardy's head against his chest. Hardy turns his face into Knight's jacket and cries. He tries to hide his tears. His body is limp. The two of them stay this way for several minutes.

"Son." Knight puts his hands on each of Hardy's shoulders and pushes him back just enough to speak to him directly. "The one truth is, we don't know what any of this really is. We don't. I don't. But the other truth is that I will not let anything bad happen to you. I'm not your father, but I know what he would want me to do, and that is exactly what I promise you. We'll make it through all this, and we will get back home. This entire trip may be the most important memory you'll ever have, or we'll wake up on the other side and have no memory of it at all. People look into the past, and what they see are the stories they make up to tell. We'll just say that's what this is, something like that, stories and memories, and what's wrong with that? Anyway, it'll have to do for now. We have to get going."

Hardy uses his sleeve to wipe his face. He looks at Mr. Knight with a sense of relief and with a little more trust.

"Now how does that sound?" Knight asks him.

"That sounds pretty good, Sir." Hardy manages a smile.

"Now go get me a towel. You've soaked my jacket."

"Jeez, Mr. Knight, you and that jacket."

Barbury steps forward. "I believe the three of us share a lot in common. We need to make some decisions. Look at it simple."

"Well, Barbury, I think…" Knight doesn't want to say something foolish. "I think we could use some fresh input right now."

"Barbury and I have done some talking about paths," Hardy steps back from Mr. Knight. "And I think it's time he took off from the Captain. He needs to get free, at least from the Captain."

"That is certainly a profound consideration," Knight offers. "Something we could do."

"And what I think is that if Barbury can get on a path to get to his freedom, then we should join him and make sure he finds it. It might be what we're supposed to do. If this is some kind of puzzle, then it's the best we have."

"Son, you are by far the smartest kid I've ever known. That's what I think."

"Now, let me say this," Barbury adds. "I am not entirely sure what the two of you have been through or where you're headed. But I sure would like to see you succeed. What I know is New Orleans," a deep breath for strength, "New Orleans is my best chance, and dear God in a lightning bolt, it might be for you too. I don't see the rest of my years running around in the woods like an Indian. I have a good feeling about it. It's New Orleans."

"Okay, interesting," Knight responds.

"It's more than interesting," Hardy replies. "It's where people are, that are not stuck on this river. And they will have city ways to help people like us and like Barbury. Mr. Knight. You know where New Orleans is, right?"

"I know where it is on a map."

"But the Captain owns you; he will not let you take off in a boat with us." Hardy tells them.

"That's probably true," Knight adds. "Let me take care of that. He and I have become quite friendly. We'll get down to the river and I'll sort this out. Barbury, worst-case scenario, we might have to hide you somehow in our boat, if we still have it. Let's get down to the river and we'll sort this out." Knight motions to start walking, and the three of them walk in unison through the last of the small houses of the village.

Barbury, Knight, and Hardy have made it to the stairs cut into the bluff above the river. From here, they survey the British flotilla and the organized chaos of activity on the river bank as the British soldiers—resigned to their defeat—organize themselves for departure. Captain Colbert, in the middle of it all, is waving his arms and barking orders. No one is moving with any amount of decisiveness or speed. Here and there, soldiers put down a trunk or crate they're carrying to the keelboat to squabble over petty differences.

Representative Knight can see that Colbert has his hands full. The bateau, off to the far side of the dock, is curiously being left alone.

"This is our chance, this very moment," Knight tells them. "We have to act quickly and get mixed in with the general confusion. We need that tarp. You see it there in that small boat, the third one in?"

"I see it," Hardy answers. He can see the challenge.

"Good, now, Son, you'll need to slip in and get that tarp and bring it over to our bateau. Just act like you know what you're doing and just play along with whatever happens. Colbert is too busy to care, even notice. Barbury, you need to get down there and act as though it's all normal, and be working your way to our boat. Talk to the soldiers and let them talk to you, all normal.

"I'll be working on Captain Colbert, and if I give you a heads up, you get in that boat and cover yourself with the tarp. That has to be our plan. It's the best we've got."

In the next moment, as the three are about to get down the stairs to the river, they see two British soldiers pointing their muskets at four of Colbert's African slaves, moving them on to the keelboat.

"All right, gentlemen, are we clear?" Knight is emphatic.

"Check," Hardy responds.

"Mr. Knight, Sir," Barbury asserts, "I believe your plan is about the best we can hope for. It's a decent plan. I can see God has put me here on this river bluff, and he's given me this choice. I am determined now to get myself a future."

"We have little time. Their chaos is our advantage." Knight steps forward. "Let's go."

Down on the river's shore, Representative Knight walks in the Captain's direction. The last few steps are brisk, with his arm out, ready to shake his hand. Colbert sees Knight approach. He quickly turns back to the keelboat. "Get those powder magazines down below and stored quickly," Colbert shouts to a soldier.

"I wanted to thank you, Captain…" Knight isn't exactly sure. "Thank you for protecting the boy and myself, you know, seeing it through."

"Well Sir, it is I, who…" They shake hands. "I, who should thank you. Your council was wholehearted and filled the spaces in my thinking, and who knows, maybe one day I can make it work, produce a better outcome."

"I'm sure you will, Sir," Knight replies.

"Your council is enough for me to consider you a friend."

The two men stand at the river's edge, surrounded by noise and commotion. Their shared alliances and claims of friendship—against this background—begin to feel forced, frankly, a little dubious.

"I'm grateful for that, Captain Colbert, and honored," Knight maintains. "And I wish you the best of luck in your next assignment, or battle… wherever your command needs your expertise."

"Well, Sir, Mr. Knight, I appreciate your words."

"Well, good Sir, so I will find the boy. He's here somewhere, and we'll continue our journey." Knight puts his hand to his forehead to block the sun as he looks down toward the bateau. Is the plan unfolding?

"Yes, you continue with my blessing. Take the boy and give him a good home." Colbert's voice is thoroughly unconvincing. "Keep him safe. Keep him away from the Spanish and the gray wolves. Now let us part with that."

Knight is picking apart Colbert's words and matching them to his expression. His decision: don't ask for Barbury.

Hardy manages to climb into the pirogue and bundle up the heavy tarp. It's awkward and clumsy, but he gets it out of the boat and walks it down the shore to the bateau. Barbury is making himself look busy, sorting through baskets not too far from Hardy.

"So we'll continue on in the bateau," Knight tells Colbert, "and we'll see what's next for the two of us on this busy river."

"Yes, take the bateau. I will have one of my men outfit the boat with what you will need to get farther downriver. Down to the Mississippi, if that's where you're determined."

"Oh, that's more than generous. It's totally unnecessary. But thank you." Knight asserts, attempting to insist and back away.

"I know this river, Mr. Knight. I insist we put you with supplies."

Knight makes a quick turn of the head toward Hardy and the bateau. He shakes his head with the slightest of a 'no' signal.

Barbury casually makes his way over to the bateau, inch by inch, one greeting after another. He steps in, bends over to pick up something, and slips under the tarp, pulling it over his head.

"Then we'll call this the goodbye," Colbert offers Knight.

The two of them part, Colbert toward the keelboat and his men, and Knight toward the bateau and Hardy.

Representative Knight walks as quickly and as nonchalantly as possible. In the corner of his eye, he sees a soldier approaching, walking at the same pace, his musket held out from his body with one firm hand.

Undeterred, Knight reaches the bateau. "All right, Son, let's get ourselves into this thing and we'll shove off and get ourselves back on course," Knight announces with a loud bit of drama.

The soldier reaches the bateau as well. He's heard the announcement.

"It's unnecessary," Knight tells the soldier. "Your Captain and I discussed it, but we're fine. There's nothing we need."

"Nothing you need?" The soldier walks around Knight to his face and stands between him and the bateau.

"Mr. Knight, don't you recognize him?" Hardy asks Knight.

"I do. I do remember this soldier. It's Benedict. Isn't that correct?"

"Benedict. C-Correct."

"Well, Benedict, there's nothing we need, so thank you, and tell your Capitan good luck."

"The Captain wishes you good luck as well, and he's asked me to make sure you need nothing, particularly what's under that tarp there."

From under the tarp, Barbury hears Benedict's voice. He can only cling to the hope for a few minutes longer. The plan for New Orleans has most surely ended.

"There is no charade here, soldier," Knight coolly declares. He takes a step toward Benedict.

"Is that the case?" Benedict replies.

"That is the case, Benedict. You're either following orders or you've decided to make a point in your favor with your captain. Or more likely, you believe you're doing right by making sure there will be no slaves that could possibly disappear; all are accounted for. That could be the case. Or it might also be that there are those among us, here on the river, that are so much the racist and so full of hatred that he cannot let a man create for himself a life he can call his own. Could that be the case, soldier?"

"A strange man in a strange uniform will not g-give me his diplomacy. Only you know the place where you have come from to get here, you and this boy. And in the same turn, the slave and I know this place, and we know how to g-get where we're going. A slave does not have a life of his own unless his master says he does." Benedict rearranges his rifle in his arms. "Isn't that the c-case, Blackbird?"

"Too well." Barbury's acquiescence bleeds through the heavy cotton tarp.

"All too well. I know that to be the case." He shuffles under the tarp, searching with his hand for the edge of it to pull it off. He knows there is no resisting the inevitable. No heated words or pleading. There'll be no mercy, not one bit of generosity.

"Hardy, help me get out from under here."

"No, I will not," Hardy pronounces. "I will not get you out of there. You're under that thing until we shove off and get going down the river, far enough to be out of here."

"That's right, soldier," Knight warns him. "You believe you have right on your side. Far from it. There is more going on here than your feeble tick of perception could ever conjure."

"I see," Benedict replies. He stands fairly still but wants to show that he is obviously waiting. "Blackbird? You about ready?"

"Yes, indeed I am," Barbury replies. He pulls the tarp off enough to lift his head. "Indeed, I am."

Barbury stands and kicks the tarp away from his feet. He steps over the wooden seat of the bateau and puts a hand out for Hardy. "Now help me get out. Do that for me, will you, Son."

Knight and Hardy look at each other. Hardy takes Barbury's hand and helps him step out of the boat.

"I don't understand," Hardy tells him. "We had a pact. How can you just give up? You promised we were going to find a way out of here, back to where we belong, both of us. We had a plan."

Barbury takes a deep breath and moves closer. "Back to where we belong. I know I had a promise, and we had a plan," Barbury tells him. "How about we say we did that? You showed me, and I showed you? And how about we say just because we go different ways doesn't mean we don't share that plan? Now does it?"

"No, Sir, it doesn't mean that. I guess I just thought this was going to get easier."

"Son, it's always getting easier. You can see that."

Barbury takes a few steps toward Benedict and turns to Knight. "Mr. Knight, why don't you get the two of you down this river and get as far from this fort as you can manage. This day will not last forever."

"But we could have gone to the Capitan. I could have exchanged something. Surely there's more we can do," Knight maintains.

"Something exchanged. You see, an African is just business. I know you mean well," Barbury tells Knight. "It is the way the business of this world is conducted."

Benedict moves behind Barbury. He won't need to use the rifle. The two of them start walking in the direction of the keelboat, nearly finished with loading.

"Goodbye to the two of you," Barbury says, looking back. "Do William and I a favor. Get back on the river. Get as far as the Mississippi and don't look back. See what New Orleans has to offer. It'll be good news."

"Just not fair," Hardy says under his breath.

The two stand for a moment, one of those forever moments, and Hardy reaches out for a handshake. The two of them shake hands, the firmest grip anywhere on the river.

"Son, you are the best of company a man like me could ever have out here in this. I sure am going to miss chatting with you." Barbury gives Hardy a big smile, then turns to walk away.

Hardy watches the moment pass, but before it's too late, he calls to Barbury. "I'll see you again, probably." A good goodbye.

Colbert did arrange to have two crates of foodstuffs and other essentials brought over to Knight and Hardy. By the time they've packed them into the bateau and finish positioning their oars and getting themselves ready, they watch the last of the British boats make it to the middle of the Arkansas and turn to head downriver.

"Are you ready for this, Hardy?"

"I'm as ready as you are, probably. So, are we trying for New Orleans?"

"That is the plan," Knight attempts cheerful. It's hardly convincing. He tries a different approach. *Something has to lighten the boy's spirits.* "So, paddle hard sailor and we'll be between the devil and the deep blue sea meeting the… okay, never mind, trying to make an old sailor's joke. Let's get this going and get out of here. I honestly couldn't take another twist in this, well, whatever this is."

Representative Knight and Hardy shove off from the bank and find a decent rhythm in their paddling, and they again feel the control of their familiar little bateau. As they pull on the oars, they exchange glances and discover they're both smiling. Smiling at the proposition of what lies ahead: no more trouble between here and New Orleans, however far that might be.

After a good amount of time working the oars, they both realize they can relax a little and let the current of the river do most of the work. Mr. Knight has moved to the rear and uses his oar to keep the bateau in the middle of the river where the current is strong.

Hardy is feeling the weight of his body getting a little heavy. He puts his elbow to his knee and his chin to his palm as he watches the trees and the shore pass by.

There's a lot of bird activity on a river like this if you care to watch it. Hardy sees what he thinks to be an eagle or a hawk flying above the tree line, going the same direction as the current, coasting the wind. It's a Cooper's hawk. The hawk turns away from the river and disappears behind the trees. As Hardy looks down from the bird, he sees four men standing just near the river's edge. Standing in a clearing of the shrubs.

"Hey," he calls back to Mr. Knight. "What the hell?" Hardy spins in his seat, turning back to see Mr. Knight, who is asleep. His arm over the oar is propping him up. The current of the river is steady. Hardy doesn't wake Mr. Knight. Instead, he uses his oar in a failing effort to get closer to the men. But the bateau is quickly moving past them. In the next instant, he realizes he recognizes the men standing on the river shore. William, Jack Red-Hair, Fredrick, and the soldier, Benjamin. All of them waving their arms back and forth. They, too, realize there's nothing can be done.

Hardy yells to the men, "New Orleans, New Orleans." He assumes they can't hear him because he doesn't see any good response to it. The men change their waving gesture to an "oh well," arms stretched up. He sees William cup his hands at his mouth and yell. Hardy hears William. "Stay the course, it's down the river." But he can't be sure that he heard it right.

It's only a matter of minutes before the bateau has moved far enough that the men almost disappear. Representative Knight moans. "What are you yelling at, for Christ's sake? Some friend from Fullerton?"

"You missed it, Sir. You'll never guess. I'll tell you later."

"All right, you can do that, but for now, can we just enjoy the peace and quiet?"

The bateau is making good progress; the British and Colbert, a fresh memory. Soon they'll be a distant memory like all the rest. The bends in the river are getting easier to navigate. The Coopers hawk circles back and joins them, heading down the Arkansas River, not too far from the mouth of the Mississippi.

Chapter Seventeen

Seven Eleven jerky with a crescent moon

In the afternoon's sun, without hats, in the middle of a river without shade, and with the blinding reflection of sun on the surface, the passing hours with the dead air, the clouds given up and gone off, and the ever-present crows berating everyone in a half mile radius, it's far too much sun.

After several hours on their own, Representative Knight and Hardy believe they've found a good rhythm. The key to moving straight forward is for both to pull the oars at the same time and with the same amount of vigor, or at least effort.

Also, mastering the craft of the river means knowing when to rest and when to hit it hard. With the river stretching out for miles and miles and miles, it goes without saying, there's a long way to go.

What the two mariners don't quite realize is that being caught in the long hours of inching down the vast open monotony of the river can fill the mind with the cranky madness of toddlers needing nap time. Quite honestly, it's basic civility that first flies out the window. The stamina of a good healthy attitude is what stays the course and is the acquired skill of the seasoned, salty dog.

"You have to pull at the same exact time I do. At the same time and with the same strength." Hardy's voice is attempting patience.

"I am doing that," Knight's voice is attempting patience.

"Then why are we zig-zagging?"

"Because you're not in harmony."

"You can't say I'm not in harmony. It's two people. Both have to be in harmony."

The impatience of a twelve-year-old is somehow more sincere than that of a sixty-something diplomat who is just plain indignant when conceding the obvious.

"I think we're doing pretty good for two city people," Knight says in between pulls. "We haven't been in this boat on our own before."

"Some of the others could read the water in a way I can't see," Hardy says in between pulls. "No clue. We could get to the shore, take a break, but you know how thick these woods are."

"We're fine. Let's just keep going."

"I agree."

"I don't think we have enough experience out here to know if something is about to go wrong." Hardy is thinking out loud. Conversation helps pass the time.

When their conversation dwindles, the bateau starts the zig-zagging.

"Mr. Knight, please, we have to pull at the exact same strength," Hardy says, keeping the conversation going. "We have to get this harmonized. We have a long way to go. Try to just feel the boat."

"I can feel the boat being pulled along much faster than before. Do you feel that too?"

"I do, which is why we need to get this right."

"I don't think we can get too far off."

"I don't know about that, Mr. Knight. This river treats people pretty shitty."

"Choice of words."

"Okay. This river can be the fullest expression of nature and man working at odds," Hardy says in between pulls.

"This river is an expression of—the true, the alienation of—man from the—" in between pulls.

"Okay, now see, you're not in harmony. You're pulling us to the side." Knight speaks while he's pulling,

The tides change the river's pull on the bateau. Tide coming in pushes back on the river. Tide going out pulls everything along with it, all of it wanting to go downriver.

"Now you're not pulling hard enough... so we're turning to your side... until I pull again... it's making this harder. Mr. Knight, you're making this harder."

Across the width, with the tide going out, the river has many measures of pull, taunting the bateau with hidden agendas.

"No, Hardy, you're not pulling the same continuous strength, so I can't adjust to your changing pulls."

"Sir, you're kind of driving me nuts. Maybe just pull and we'll both not talk."

"No, if we don't compare our pulling, we'll wind up in the bushes."

"Okay," Hardy shouts, then goes quiet, except for some other words under his breath.

And still the beating sun.

Knight pats the top of his gray head of hair. "If this sun gets any hotter, we might have to use the oars with the tarp to rig up some kind of tent for shade. That tarp may come in handy."

"That's possible, but how would we paddle."

"Maybe get to a point where the current does it for us, at least long enough for a break from this sun." Knight considers pulling the Armani jacket up over his head. No, it's disrespectful.

"How about…" Knight lifts his oar out of the oarlock and holds it up just to see how it might work. "Use one oar for the tent and one to steer?"

"It's not that hot. The sun feels good."

"It's too bad we didn't grab more than these two crates," Knight says. "We should have taken the time to think this through. Let's hope what's in those two crates is enough to get us where we're going."

"Mr. Knight, we were lucky to be left on our own. Once he took Barbury back, we had to get out of there. That's all there was."

"You're right, hindsight and all that. Don't look back."

Knight takes one hard pull, then rests his oar, a little of a zig-zag. "Still, if I could replay some of it, I know what I would do to achieve better results. There are a few different ways I could have approached it. I didn't think it through. I got rushed, I suppose, which is fatal. Colbert didn't have a clue. Honestly, it's embarrassing."

Knight pulls the oar. "An incredibly unsophisticated bluff, the Halloween costumes, absolutely vulgar. At the same time, I can see how those British soldiers, boys really, would be totally unprepared for a fright like that. It didn't take much. But the adults… irresponsible."

Knight pulls his oar.

"Whatever inspired that Spaniard to cast those characters in those costumes, we may never know."

Knight pulls his oar.

"Must have been something from his regional culture, his city, town, a Spanish baroque theater. Actually, thinking of it now, it was beautiful, perfect in its own way, kind of brilliant."

Knight pulls his oar.

"But, seriously, bluffs and calculations, Washington 101, that's my expertise. I thought I had the Spanish bastard."

Knight pulls his oar.

"He knew his audience, and he delivered. Terrific theater. Overall, though, a stupid bit of story. The end of it dribbles down into a simple walking away."

Knight pulls his oar.

"How did I get so sucked into it all is the thing? Cramped down in that ditch with a toothless British Capitan. What was I trying to prove? It was an insanity I can't even begin to comprehend. Swallowed up in that ditch. What does that say about me?"

Knight takes one hard pull. This time there's not so much zig-zag.

"Mr. Knight, it wasn't theater. There were guys getting blown apart in that ditch, and shot and killed. We're lucky to walk out of there. You saw them walking back to the river. It wasn't a story to them. They weren't that much older than me, and where were they going? What's next for them?"

"I understand all that. That's why not calling the hooligan bluff is all the more agonizing. I'm not sure why I don't expect you to understand."

Knight holds the oar as it drags through the water.

"Mr. Knight, we were only there for the smallest part of it. It isn't your story to tell. You need to pull a little bit harder."

As the river pulls time along, the day keeps pace with the current. Parts of the day are longer than other parts of the day are long.

Rests, then pulls, a little bit of a zig followed by a zag.

Endless hours on the river affect rivermen in different ways. Imaginative scenarios that run parallel to the current are conceived by what their fantasies can afford. Knight's well-read imagination pulls him easily into the prose of the battlefield's memory. Soldiers caught in worlds not of their making, the troubled passage of men through time's landscape, the currents of humanity, the tide's undoing. Representative Knight's reading himself into Coleridge's Ancient Mariner, or Huck Finn's travails, could be excused by the river's current and the hot sun.

Writing himself out of the story, maintaining the proper calculation, the rests then pulls, to defeat the siren, which the river graciously provides is the riverman's true test. Failing this, one can doubtfully recover from the agonizing doldrums of endless introspection that would drown any of the uninitiated, all the way, endlessly downriver.

There are patches in the river when pulling the bateau can feel like it weighs a ton. Other patches, the bateau is light and glides on its own. The swirls and the eddies on the surface show up then disappear, points on a map that are fond of rearranging.

"If we plan on making any progress on this river, dammit, we're going to have to put our backs into it." Knight straightens up, tightens his grip, and gives it one hard pull. He immediately lets loose of the oar and puts one hand firm to his chest.

"Are you having pains in your chest? Heart pains?" Hardy asks, "We should coast for a while. I'll steer."

"No, I'll steer. You sort through those crates and see what we have to work with. It's better to know now, be prepared." Knight closes both eyes and takes several deep breaths. "Lord knows what he's put in those crates."

Hardy moves forward to get a good look at the crates. Both of them are simple, dirty wooden boxes. One of them has a top nailed shut with two or three small nails. The other, with no top, is stuffed with glass bottles and cotton bags. Both crates have black stenciled writing on two sides.

"Okay, I'll start with the one that's open. One side it says, SHANKLESS COOKED. NATURAL JUICES. PERISHABLE. On the other side, it reads,

DRIED LONG HAM. NEW ORLEANS BRAND. CASE NUMBER 4985."

"All right, what's inside? Let's not make too much out of the writing." Knight puts one arm over his head. The sun is relentless.

Hardy pulls a cotton bag out of the crate: "This says it's a one-pound bag of bromated flour. It's sewn across the top, probably to keep insects out of it." He smells it. "Smells foul, I don't think it's very fresh."

He puts the one bag back and pulls out another, "This one says, meal. Maybe oatmeal? Who knows?"

"Have you ever felt sun this hot?" Knight's chest pain has subsided; his voice has eased. "I wonder how many times that crate has gone up and down the river. How far north and back down," Knight says, switching arms over his head, "clearly, it's come and gone from New Orleans. I suppose we should consider that some sort of clue."

Hardy pulls out another. "This one has a drawstring." He fumbles with it for a minute. "Okay, this one is… opening, opening, it's tied ridiculously tight."

"New Orleans," Knight quietly muses, "I don't know how to have that conversation. Caught up in these situations, they're really just scenarios really, chapters, but really, what's the point of it? Will there be some kind of reckoning? That's the inference? I'm not wrong. Are we in the middle of experiencing the harmonic conversion? I'm not sure what that actually was, but it was a thing."

"More of the dried salted meat, the Seven Eleven stuff, could be pork. I don't smell the gunpowder on this bunch. Mr. Knight, we're either here or we're not here. Do you want the jerky?"

"What can you hope to accomplish in a dream?" Knight's voice drifts out onto the river, possibly a calculated effect.

"These look like dried peas. That's what I think, anyway."

"A dream would be the obvious. We'll close our eyes and wake up. It was all a dream, thank God. That seems a little predictable."

"Good news. This one's full of biscuits. They're hard as a rock, but they smell okay."

"I've had anxiety dreams, impossible situations, unbelievable, sometimes quite horrible... and those dreams are very real. Have you heard that term? Anxiety dream? You wake up exhausted. Sore from the physical activity and you know the whole time it's too unbelievable to be anything but a dream. And sure enough, in the end, there you are, in your bed, but you still head for the Excedrin."

"Biscuits! Mr. Knight. Biscuits!"

"You know what I think? I honestly think the people who run history are a bunch of idiots." Knight looks back and forth between the river and the crate. "We're in big history, and we're doing what we can. People are asking us for our help, so it's like rewriting the story as it goes forward. Believe me, I know how that sounds. But what else can be said? We're in it, and we're making it up as we go along." Knight turns to Hardy. "If I could find the direction of it, my purpose in it, then I believe we'd know which direction to take."

"Mr. Knight, the river only goes in one direction."

"So the story goes forward," Knight's calculation. "It's a great adventure. Looks like we'll be having biscuits."

They're actually not too bad.

Hardy digs into the crate and pulls out a bottle. "One bottle of whiskey, maybe something else. You'll like this booze. The label says, 'The King, God Bless Him.'"

"No booze for me, not anymore. We parted ways many years ago. Nothing but trouble."

Colbert had rum added to the crate for no other reason than protocol. It's what sailors drink on daily rations. British Navy rum is an eagerly anticipated ritual for generations of sailors. Why not a temporary boost in morale and surely a comfort from the noise and chaos of dodging cannonballs, grapeshot, and the tirades of the officers? Overproof rum—in half pints, good for morale.

Sailors test the "overproof" for its purity by dousing the rum with gunpowder and setting it on fire, testing if the ration has sufficient strength. Soaring temperatures below deck—in the stinking bowels of the hold—the drinking water, encased in rotting oak barrels, quickly becomes covered in a thick layer of green mold. The solution was for stronger brews to be brought on board that could withhold the rigors of longer journeys. But those were also prone to rot, so they went with an even stronger brew. Bottles of it in the crate. Knight is suspicious of any offering from Colbert, whatever its place in the daily life of a British.

"This looks like it might be water." Hardy pulls a wooden canteen out of the crate. "This is actually pretty cool. It's like some antiques my grandma used to collect. She had all kinds of old stuff, vintage collectibles."

The canteen is a standard issue up and down the British ranks, made of oiled wood, maybe twelve inches in diameter, with a cork plug. Worth its weight in gold.

"If we have to, we can rig up the tarp to collect rain," Knight offers, still looking out to the river. "And what about the other crate? Are we opening it?"

"It's probably more of the same." Hardy puts everything back into the crate. "I'll open it later. Are you as tired as I am?" He goes back to his oar and takes hold of it, but he can't quite rally the energy to start up again, so he sits to watch the water like Mr. Knight. The bateau is on its own with the current.

"This has been the longest day of my life," Hardy says, just to hear himself say it.

"I don't believe we can add up time like we normally would under normal circumstances." Knight takes off his jacket, first pulling open the lapels. "I'm beginning to see it doesn't work that way. I think we have to consider that time is different here, maybe different on the river, or perhaps off the river."

"How long were we in that ravine, ditch, whatever?" Hardy takes a long, slow exhale.

Knight pulls at the sleeves, one at a time, and then pulls off his Armani jacket. He drapes it over his head, making a small tent of it, covering his shoulders, shading his face.

"Earlier, back up the river, I was convinced this whole thing was probably something we were inflecting on ourselves. I was thinking we're not here together; we're all here but not in the same place, mentally, something like that. I know a thing or two about mental formations, at least from the side of a lawyer's defense."

Knight brushes off his pants. He looks at the palms of his hands. "When I jumped out of the boat, once I was in the water, I honestly thought I could make it to the bank and up the side. Well, I realized I could drown. I could feel that. It felt real. But that's the dream. As frightening as it is, you wake up, and it's over. You don't drown. So, I guess I would say at this point, it doesn't make any rational sense, but it just doesn't bother me anymore. Check your palms, Son. We cannot get blisters out here. We have no way to treat them, and then where would we be?"

"That's not much of an explanation." Hardy looks at one hand. "But I can see how there's really no way to explain what this is. Anyway, today I don't care."

"Are you keeping your socks dry?" Knight asks Hardy.

"I guess between the two of us, you're the one who could have a decent explanation. All I have is Harry Potter. I mean, that was a while ago. I'm way too old for that now."

From under the dark Armani, which is now a small tent in a wooden boat headed down the wide Arkansas River. In the middle of the hot sun afternoon. In the grasp of a stupor's daze, Knight continues, attempting something like discourse. "I default to Locke. It's my legal training. John Locke. Locke's gift shows us that our senses experience the world. This, you should understand, speaks to the core of our capacity to understand the world. When we engage ourselves with the tasks of interpreting what we… never mind. The essence of Locke is this: what we see and feel, this empiricism, is an honest truth, maybe an ultimate truth. Our being here in this boat and what we see and feel, well, the all of it—William and the rest, the Osage boys, the singular Niwashake, Barbury—our knowledge of them and our being here is a truth precisely because it's our experience. There's nothing more to it. What we're doing out here is its own truth, and that's it. There's no other knowledge to this than what we are doing right here, in this boat or back in that ravine, because we see it and feel it. It's real. Legitimately real." He looks over at Hardy. "That has to have sounded somewhat convincing, no?"

"Sir, I know you're a lawyer and all that. If my dad were here, he'd have the best way to explain it, the river and William, and Jack Lank-Sleeve, Barbury.

Basically, he'd say this is a big deal. He'd want me to pay attention. Then, for sure, he'd say, 'Okay, this is great. Now it's time to head home. Get your stuff. We're going home.'"

Representative Knight and Hardy sit quiet. Conversations run through their heads. The river is bending; the bateau is drifting into a considerable bend on the Arkansas.

"Everything happens for a reason," Knight's voice, drifting down the Arkansas, "even when we're not wise enough to see it. Oliver Wendell Holmes," a long pause, "insanity is often the logic of an intelligent mind over-tasked."

"That might have been true when we met up with William." Hardy's voice is a little more determined. "I've come a long way on this river since then. What people can do to each other and for each other."

"It's an unbelievable awakening to see how the Africans are treated here." Knight takes hold of his oar. "To see it here and to know it there, where we come from. A revelation, honestly, a strange perspective. It's something to know."

"What do you think is happening in New Orleans?" Hardy takes hold of his oar.

"New Orleans is the end of the river. We'll have to see when we get there," Knight tells him. "Barbury has his reasons. Those cannot be ours. Think it through."

"Barbury knows what we could never know," Hardy tells Knight, "think it through."

"Fair enough, Son, but New Orleans is not the place where slaves are given their freedom, at least not that we know of. So, what would I do? What could I possibly do there? What new role do I invent for myself? How would it be any different from all the rest I've…"

Hardy hears it in Knight's voice. It feels like the most honest he's been with himself so far. Self-respect is something he's still trying to find.

Knight steers again. "Let me steer us for a while longer. You make an inventory."

"This might be the biggest bend we've had," Hardy's confidence comes with such a wonderful simplicity. "It's almost a 180. And we're staying right in the middle of it, very cool, so the river is capable of a little sympathy. That's good to know."

The bend in the river quickly evens out, like it always does, into another long straight stretch, the woods staying thick on each side. The afternoon sun has finally eased off, transforming itself into a blinding horizon. Luckily, behind them, the Arkansas flows south-east. Representative Knight takes the jacket off his head and puts it back on where it belongs. He stands to straighten himself out and then sits back to the job of steering down the river.

Hardy passes the Seven Eleven jerky to Mr. Knight. They chew their best. It's like leather. The canteen is passed back and forth as well. Steady as she goes, the afternoon becomes early evening.

"We have to consider if we're going to go on shore to sleep for the night," the Representative speaks for them both, "if only for a little time out of the boat. Find a spot where we can safely pull up the boat and see if there's a clearing or a safe place."

Hardy calculates the passing woods, a few dark spots here and there, odd but maybe just his imagination. "Do we trust these woods?"

"I suppose to be democratic we should vote," Knight offers. "Maybe each plead our case, one way or the other, sleeping for the night, woods or boat. Of course, as an adult, I would have the deciding vote."

"Sir, there's only two of us. Get serious, Mr. Knight. Go back into those woods after all we've been through?"

"Right. We'll do this in shifts. A good-sized moon would help. I can't remember where we're at in the lunar cycle. A bit of a moon would be nice."

"We can fold up the tarp. It'll be better than nothing. The floor is dry. That's good."

"I'll take the first watch," Knight's seafaring adventurer's tone. "I can't believe how long I've wanted to say that."

Hardy folds up the tarp making as much padding out of it as it can possibly give. They both keep at the oars for quite a while longer, well into the approaching night.

The thought of another black, moonless night, by themselves, alone on the river, is a little unnerving. Finally, a sliver moon rises over the top edge of the trees.

"That tarp is looking pretty good right now, isn't it, Son?"
"Yeah, I guess."

Hardy lies down on the tarp and tries to get comfortable. So far, there's no chill to the night.

"This isn't as bad as it looks, actually." Hardy watches the sky. "The stars are coming out. Milky Way."

Just like that, Hardy's off to dreamland.

The crescent moon creates splintered light on the river, and Knight squints his eyes. He watches the shore to know his place on the river. The river itself is black as coal. The toenail sliver creeps its way to the middle of the night overhead. All the stars seem to know each other's place. They keep their distance out of respect. The sliver is definitely the leader and commands the most admiration. Soon, the sliver races to the finish and disappears behind. With both the exhaustion and the ease of the river, the night is remarkably short. And, just like that, the early morning's rose appears on the horizon, this time straight in front of them. The river begins a wide turn; the bateau is drawn into the bend.

As Hardy wakes, on top of the tarp, in the bateau's bottom, before he opens his eyes, he lists the names of the birds, far to the sides, as they begin to participate in the early daylight.

"Mockingbird, Grackle, crows, of course."

Suddenly, remembering where he is, he jerks up straight. "Was that the whole night? Did you steer the whole night? Did I help? Did I have a shift?"

"Good morning, Sailor. How'd you sleep?"

"Mr. Knight, did you sleep at all?"

Still waking up, Hardy lies back down. "I was thinking, Mr. Knight, about birds. If you listen to all the birds, it's a lot of talking at once, even from out here. If you know the call of each one of those species communicating only to each other, you can hear just the two of them talking, saying whatever is important at the time. It's like a separate channel in the noise. I was thinking that maybe that's what this is, this experience we're having, something like we're tuned into a channel, and all this is happening on this one channel, and back home, and my dad is a separate channel, maybe something like that."

"I like that you're approaching our situation like an eccentric writer, a hermit who lives in a tent in the middle of nowhere, even though I doubt we're like birds chirping at each other from a distance."

"Your first order is to sort through the bags, and let's do our best to eat a decent meal. The biscuits and the water, conservatively, and the other salted meat, the pork. That's about it, right?"

The current easily pulls the bateau. The boat glides through the mid-point of the river's bow, a change in direction.

Hardy sorts through the opened crate. He has already organized it.

"Mr. Knight, you didn't sleep. How are you going to last through this day. Take naps in the sun? I doubt we're anywhere near the Mississippi."

"You eat, Son. I'm fine. Actually invigorated. It was a beautiful, quiet night. The river was as much asleep as you were. I kept us straight and let the current do the rest, kept to the middle."

The sun is up. The day's begun. Hardy can see the Arkansas River has more floating branches and debris from the woods, more than usual. *What the heck does that mean? Are we headed into something? Out of something? This is getting somewhere?*

The bateau is pulled out of the bend, and as the river begins to straighten itself, renew its energy, the current pushes hard. The river is rushing.

"Do you feel that?" Knight says, "The pull?"

He hears the air open up around him, and he waits to hear more. "Listen, can you hear that?"

"I hear it," Hardy says. "It's an octave change, definitely. It's like I can feel the air changing."

In the rush out of the last bend of the Arkansas, which is almost a complete about face, the river's wooded edges are left behind, far to the sides. The river is no longer restrained by the woods. The little bateau is changed from a boat on a river into a ship on the widest of everything.

The Mississippi.

Chapter Eighteen

Barleycorn for the copperheads

By the time the waters of the great Mississippi greet the bateau, they've made company with rivers from the upper Montana and the Rocky Mountains of the west and with river waters from as far away as Pennsylvania in the east. A network of waters so vast it's impossible to imagine in one picture. The river splits the continent of North America in two. The America east of the Mississippi and the America west of the Mississippi. The most skilled and dedicated cartographer's task of illustrating the great river pales in comparison to the task of navigating a small boat swept along with it. The little boat bears witness to the river's brawn and swagger as it splits the world in two.

Representative Knight has never seen it, not really, and Hardy has only seen it in pictures.

"Holy freakin' shit."

"Watch your language. God damn, this is extraordinary."

"Are you scared?" Hardy asks Knight.

"I'm not scared. That's not the word I would use. But, but surely it is intimidating."

Both grab hold of the sides of the bateau for any kind of reassurance.

"What about you? Are you scared?" Knight asks.

"No, I don't think I am." Hardy parses his words. "We're in the boat. I doubt it's going to throw us overboard. What's the worst that could happen?"

"We just keep on track," Knight tells him, "and do our best to follow along."

Both Knight and Hardy sit and watch. It is overwhelming, and it takes more than a little time to appreciate the scale of it. Time is barely moving.

"Alright," Knight announces, "let's get the hang of it. You take your oar, and I'll take mine, and let's get the feel of it."

In no time at all, the bateau is already close to the middle of the river. They've discovered that the current's pull on the Mississippi is very different than the Arkansas.

"I think because it's so fat and thick, it's more steady than the Arkansas." Hardy is keeping his body and arms in a determined position to get an accurate feel.

"It's by far less skittish," Knight confirms.

Now that they're both experts.

It is indeed a marvel to be out on such a vast expanse, to be joined with it, moving at its speed, moving down toward the Port of New Orleans. So, the hours fly by, like when an experience is new. There are no other boats coming or going. The dead trees and other floating nature seem to be elsewhere. The navigating and the paddling get steady, far less effort to stay centered. Is it faster or slower than before? Does it matter?

"Who could cross this river? It would be impossible." Hardy breaks the quiet.

"Of course, they crossed it, the first explorers, the invading Spanish. More than likely, they were as overwhelmed as we are now. But that's the nature of exploration. When you discover it, you have to cross it. Neil Armstrong had to step on the moon." Knight raises his head and looks farther out to the river, the explorer that he is. "That, Son, is human nature. We have it in us to be heroes."

"But who actually crossed it first? Lewis and Clark?"

"Hernando de Soto, Son. That's the name you're looking for, de Soto. It's astounding how little they teach you kids in school."

"Why is it that people in your generation always say that?"

"There is a story." Hardy takes the challenge. "But it's a story that hasn't been told yet because nobody's looked for it. A man or a woman, a person stood on the shore, looked out across this massive thing, and thought, how to get across? He stood there with his wife and kids. He feels a great fear, but he knows he'll take the challenge. The first Neil Armstrong. Probably a group from the tribe stood there thinking about it and then he grabbed hold of their best canoe. It would have to be one big canoe. He took hold of it and said to the rest of them, We have to try, something like that. He said the great river invites me to know it. He walks a little way out into the mud, like we did, and he pulls the little boat out a bit, jumps in, and paddles across. The rest of the people are cheering for him and waving. The little canoe probably got swept into some current, maybe there was some kind of trouble, but soon enough, he makes it to the other side. He jumps out and waves at his people way back on the other side. 'We did it!" they yell back and forth. Something like that. I'd like to hear the story about the first Native American stepping up to this river, trying to figure out how to get across for the first time, the really first time. You know, like who invented the first canoe?"

"Why would you add to the history of what you don't know?"

"Mr. Knight, it's astounding how little they taught you in school."

"Mr. Knight! What's that above your head?"

Knight instantly ducks. "What, what do you see?"

"It's, it's, I don't know, it's a…" Hardy grabs the sides of his head. He abruptly stands straight up and wrestles with it, with his head jerking his body.

"What in the hell is happening?" Knight becomes panicky.

"I don't know." Hardy gives a guttural cry of pain.

Knight stands up and steps over to him.

"It's inside my head." Hardy drops to his knees and rolls around on the tarp. "I can see into the future. The future is the past. No wait, the past is the future. Oh, my brain." He's holding his head the whole time.

"My God in heaven, Son, what is it?" Knight crouches down to help.

"It's the face, no, it's the voice. I can see New Orleans. I see a bed and a bowl of cereal. No, wait, the spirit is back." Hardy throws his arms straight out and continues a crazy twisting and rolling.

This goes on for a full ten seconds. "Mr. Knight, Mr. Knight!"

"It's the voice of de Soto. He's here. He's pissed off at you for getting the history story wrong. He's going to kill you. I can't stop him."

Hardy keeps the rolling around a little longer, then stops himself, confident he's played the part well.

"You know," Knight stands. He shakes his head, "I am an elected official to the United States House of Representatives." He brushes off his jacket, pulling neatly at a cuff to straighten the sleeve. "I'm also a senior citizen."

Hardy can't help himself and bursts out with a laugh.

"I'll have you know that I am also fully immersed in a mental formation of some sort, which my psychiatrist will charge me thousands of dollars to sort out." Knight steps back to his place by his oar. He sits, head held high.

"Mr. Knight," Hardy says, "it was just…"

"No, you don't get to say a word. You've had your bit of theater for the moment." Suddenly, Knight grabs at his chest. He folds over at the waist. His body gives one, then two alarming jerks. "Water." Knight can barely say the words. "Can you get me some water?"

"Mr. Knight?" Hardy sits up.

Knight lets out a couple of agonized groans. He tries to sit up straight but can't. He doubles over again.

"I'll get the water. Hang on."

"Hurry. Please hurry."

Hardy quickly gets to the wooden canteen he's kept in the crate, but he fumbles it and drops it.

"Son, please."

Knight jolts upright. With one hand, he's grabbing his chest, shirt, and jacket in his fist. With the other hand, he reaches out across the bateau, desperate for Hardy and the water.

Hardy's grabbed the canteen but stumbles as he's getting over to Mr. Knight.

Knight grabs his chest with one last agonizing growl.

Hardy has made it over to Mr. Knight and tries to pour water into Knight's mouth while he's trembling.

Before the water can find its way out of the top of the canteen and into Knight's mouth, Knight drops his hands to his sides and drops his head to look squarely at Hardy's face. Hardy drops the canteen back to his side.

They both stand facing each other for one long, tit-for-tat moment.

"Senior Citizen," Knight says, not an ounce of remorse. "Elected Official."

"Holy shit, Mr. Knight." Hardy collapses a bit on the bateau's middle seat.

"Language," Knight tells him. Knight uses his forefingers on both hands, rapid-fire poking into Hardy's chest. "Got ya!!!"

Unbelievably pleased with himself, Knight sits and takes his oar. "Shall we continue?"

In short order, the two boatsmen fall back into their steady rhythm. The theatrics, the little passion plays, are a small dot in the vast expanse. If the Arkansas seemed to sometimes crawl, the Mississippi can almost stand still.

"Mr. Knight, there are clouds coming in. Maybe not as hot today."

"I see that." Knight turns on his seat to check all vistas. "Still, a long day ahead."

"I haven't told you about something," Hardy says, keeping his side of the paddling steady.

"What haven't you told me?" Knight keeps his side of the paddling steady.

"William on the shore," Hardy's collecting his thoughts, it's difficult to say, "and Jack Red-Hair, and Fredrick and the man Benjamin. I saw them standing on the shore after we left the dock at the fort."

"That's not possible," Knight tells him.

"He was there. They were all there."

"Why would you say that? Are you joking again? It's not possible because, as deserters, they had to disappear back into the woods and get as far from that miserable fort as fast as possible. Colbert's men were lurking around. William is too smart to get caught."

"That's true, but I saw them."

"You thought you saw them."

"And he called out, New Orleans, pretty sure that's what he said."

"Son." Knight knows the conversation's changed, "William wanted us to get to New Orleans to get off the river. He thought that the best way to get you safe and away from more of these characters who are not particularly good people." Knight shifts his position on the bateau seat. "Let me say it this way. The people we are encountering, they're all from very different worlds, all of them from worlds only they can know. And this isn't a metaphor. It's geography. Alright? Different worlds, all their own. The Osage are people we can never truly know. Their world is so far from our world, even if we knew we belonged on this trip, which we do not, their's is a place we'll never understand. William and Jack, while we believe we can know them because they're honestly sincere, good men, their place in this world is not our place." Knight bends close to Hardy. "There's a restaurant in DC and it's known as a place for internationals to meet and see each other for whatever reason, and do business. I've been there many times, and each time it's like stepping into a place where no one honestly belongs. You can call them foreigners, but that's only a shallow description. Far too different, worlds apart. But in that collection of souls, everyone knows their own place for as long as they're in that room. Here, in this place, we do not. We most definitely do not know our place here. The others, William and the rest, they do. We don't."

Hardy looks to the wooden bottom of the bateau. To put these thoughts into words is difficult. "Mr. Knight, I believe that's why we're headed to New Orleans. William knows it because he's from the same place as we are. We're here together on the river, and he knows why, and now I know why. New Orleans is going to save our lives."

The two of them sit quietly for some time.

"The thought of it doesn't surprise me." Knight looks down, He brushes off a shoe. "Downriver is more than simple river jargon. New Orleans, New Orleans, New Orleans. That has to be where this whole collection of misfortune is headed. And by that, I don't mean where the river is headed."

"It's what Barbury and William were talking about in the longhouse. I can see that now," Hardy says as he looks up at Mr. Knight. They watch each other's faces as the conversation ends.

With one quick exhale, Hardy pulls hard on his oar. "They're not only in this world. They're part of another one at the same time."

"Somehow," Knight pulls hard on his oar to get back in the rhythm, "somehow we have to beat this river to New Orleans."

The two oarsmen continue their routine. They eat biscuits and drink water out of the wooden canteen. The Seven Eleven jerky hits the spot once you get the hang of chewing it. You have to be aggressive with it.

The clouds that came rolling in earlier fill the sky, the intense sun replaced by its partner, intense humidity.

Hardy eases off his oar. It drags, spinning ripple patterns in the water. He watches the patterns on the surface, animated by the cloud reflections. Faces and animals, they pace methodically around each other. Two large bears stand on their back feet, a face off, each waiting for the first move. Then suddenly, a deep snarling growl from one of the bears. The growl echoes across the river.

"Did you hear that?" Knight asks. He's closed his eyes. "Thunder cannot be good. We've just figured out this river. We don't need any more drama."

Hardy gives it a second. He looks over at Mr. Knight, then up at the clouds. "If it does rain, we can use the tarp to get water. We're going to need it."

Darker clouds are rolling in; there is more distant thunder, this time not so distant. The wind is picking up. The bears have lumbered back to wherever they came from.

A burst of heat lightning flashes through the thunderheads straight out in the direction they're headed.

"You can't see it," Hardy tells Knight, "but we're getting some lightning."

"If the lord wants to drench us in rain after all he's put us through, then we'll take the high road."

"Mr. Knight, I'm pretty sure that doesn't make any sense."

Two or three more rapid, muted flashes through the clouds, and the thunder follows right behind, still a low rumble.

"We're definitely going straight into it." As soon as he says the words, he feels the trouble ahead. You cannot be out on a river in the middle of a storm—lightning and thunder.

Hardy watches the river's horizon line ahead, the thick of the storm, while Knight's not willing to budge.

In the distance, downriver, a line of trees moves across the horizon line. The river will turn again.

"The thunder is getting louder," Knight says, his voice a bit more engaged than moments ago. "That is a lot of thunder."

"Mr. Knight, you should sit up." Hardy's voice has sharpened.

"Why, in heaven's name? I'm finally relaxing. My poor back is trying to recuperate from the torture."

"It looks like a boat."

"A boat? Say that again, because you cannot be serious."

"Yes, I am serious, Sir. It's come around the bend up ahead."

Knight sits up and looks over the side of the bateau. "Well, I'll be damned."

"Holy shit, what kind of boat is that?"

"I'm not even sure that's a boat," Knight says, his gaze fixed. "I'm not sure what that is."

Representative Knight stands to get a better look. "It looks like a chunk of something. It's bigger than Colbert's keelboat. We'll see when it gets closer. This is not what we need right now."

"At least it's not a canoe." Hardy watches the chunk get closer. He's also watching the shore to see if there's a place to pull up and get off and get out of the way. The weeds and scrub are thick as ever.

Another flash and the pounding thud of its thunder.

"Good lord, it is a boat, a huge boat." Knight's voice wavers between uneasiness and dread. He can feel his stomach churn.

"There's smoke coming from the back of it." Hardy's voice is not panicky. He's trying to get the details, not thinking too far ahead. "Are those people? There are men on top of it, and they're waving."

"Don't tell me more British or more of the Spanish." Knight is pleading with the river. "I'll take anything, but not more deserters or whatever's worse than the military." He watches keenly as his heart thumps. The nervous stomach acid creeps up his throat.

Immediately, Hardy gets the sense that Mr. Knight will not handle this approaching situation well, not well at all.

"Well, I'm pretty sure those might look like, might even be men on that thing. Looks like nothing special. Maybe they're waving, kind of hard to tell. I wouldn't worry about it."

The chunk, the large smoking boat, coming from the opposite direction, is burning through the distance between them. The confrontation is approaching at double the speed of the river, courtesy of the river.

"The smoke is really billowing out the back of that thing." Hardy's voice has gone up one full octave. "Is it on fire?"

Knight is transfixed, queasy but transfixed.

The chunk of a boat is rushing forward.

The details are becoming unmistakable. It's not a boat, it's a ship. A ship that looks like a building, long and low to the water.

"What the hell?" Hardy can't help himself.

An overwhelming image. Dark, the whole river is dark from the clouded sun and the smoke. A dark metal building lies sideways across the river. Two huge fat pillars jut up from the top of it.

As the giant thing gets closer, the figures of the men on top of the ship are now close enough to see clearly and unquestionably, they're sailors.

"What the hell is going on?"

The large ship appeared to be approaching head-on. Now the path will take it past the bateau with enough distance between them for no serious concern. It's the incredible look of it, the overwhelming impression of this massive metal ship making its way toward them, and, of course, what will happen next?

The inevitability is upon them.

"You copperheads will be the prize of the party!"

And there it is, the inevitable sailor's voice, shouting across the river. The sound is familiar even though the words make no real sense, the language of the spectacle from a playwright's pen.

"What the hell does that mean?" Knight's already exhausted.

"Barleycorn boys, barleycorn for the copperheads." More hollers from the ship, followed by bellows of laughter.

The ship is indeed a large and very long chunk of building. A building with smokestacks and flagpoles and windows, and the sides of it are long, very long, and they're metal.

"I know what kind of boat this is," Hardy blurts out. "I've seen this in pictures."

There is one long flat deck on the top of the ship, almost the full length. Sailors are scattered down the length of it. The smoke is billowing out of the smokestacks; it spirals in the wind. It's also pouring out of holes torn open down the side of the ship, caved in holes with ripped up metal, three or four down the length of it.

"Oh, no no no… Knight looks away and takes small steps in a tight circle, not actually pacing. He starts to tear off his jacket. "I am not going to let this happen." He is stomping his feet as he speaks. "This river will not take us in that direction."

He gets the jacket off and wads it up and throws it down at the bottom of the bateau. "You pick up that oar, Son."

Not more than a hundred feet away, the white faces of the sailors in the front of the ship are beacons in the smoky chaos. Their expressions are not of a ship in peril.

"God dammit," Knight is furious, "sit down, Son, get that oar working. We're turning this boat around."

"Mr. Knight, you're losing it. You should calm down."

"We are not going down this river, not one more inch."

"Barleycorn and bark juice for the blue jackets." More hollers, now coming straight out of their faces.

Less than one hundred feet, the ship is closing in.

"I'm not doing this again," Knight yells across to the men he can clearly see. He shouts straight at them, "You're not doing this again!"

"Tow the mark sailors," one of them calls back to Knight. He's holding a glass bottle over his head. He makes a 'cheers' gesture to Knight. "Tight as a drum," with a burst of laughter. Another sailor comes to his side, arms over their shoulders. They hold each other up, "Tow the mark!"

"Mr. Knight. It's another boat, but this is the Mississippi. We expected other boats. It's not a surprise." Hardy is trying his best.

"That ship, Son." Knight is staggering in the bateau as if he were drunk. "That ship is an ironclad!" His voice is loud and mean. "Did you not get that far in your history studies? A Civil War ironclad. We're in the middle of another bit of insanity history."

Once it's close enough, it's not a surprise Representative Knight names it for what it is. The long sides of the ironclad are iron armor plates. The entire ship covered with them, impressive and unmistakable for history buffs. It's a long ship, almost 180 feet long. On average, they'll weigh 800 tons. A steam-propelled warship, fast and agile on the Mississippi. The ships are built as conventional wooden warships, then converted into iron-covered, casemate ironclad gunships. Impenetrable. It's a ship of war; the time, the place, the uniforms, the Union navy. It's low to the water, with one deck running down the length of it. Most of the sailors are on this deck. Down the length of the side are four shudders, big, metal sliding windows. Each one has a cannon sticking through it, the barrel of a large and heavy cannon. One other structure above the deck is the pilothouse, a rectangular box of iron, standing three feet high. A one-inch observation slit cut into it just below the upper tier of iron. The most impressive feature on the approaching ironclad is the steam-powered, rotating, circular turret. Inside that turret are the big guns, two eleven-inch Dahlgren smoothbores. The turret is eight layers of one-inch-thick, curved, rolled plates, twenty feet in diameter. Impressive and impenetrable.

At the same moment that Hardy says the word, "Ironclad," there's a loud boom of thunder and a burst of light close enough downriver to make them both duck.

"Not again. I will not go down another rabbit hole. We're doing fine on our own. We don't need another mayhem scenario. No more crazy twisted history."

"Mr. Knight, why not calm down, your heart—"

"You're worried about my heart, and I'm telling you, we're not where we were anymore. We're someplace else."

The ironclad is almost upon the bateau. It's clear now that the ship and the little boat will pass each other with thirty feet between them. Neither of them slow for the passing. The ironclad, still under its own power, headed upriver, and the bateau being pulled at the mercy of the current.

"Tell the other blues we'll meet again." One sailor cries out. He's calling out to Knight.

The bateau passes the front of the ironclad.

Along the entire length of it, sailors have come to the side facing the bateau, all calling out, most too drunk to make much sense of it, all revved up to full animation. Their hysteria doesn't hide the exhaustion and the terror stuck to their faces.

The dark color of the ship's iron mixes with the powder burns across the uniforms and the faces. Here and there, the Union blue coats are brushed with a mix of black and red.

From just across the trees, the far side of the river's bend, more crashing thunder.

Another rowdy joins the sailor aboard the ironclad who has connected with Representative Knight. They both stumble to the deck, too drunk and tired to stand. The sailor keeps eye contact with Knight.

Other sailors are yelling for Knight and Hardy to jump ship and come join them. They're holding out bottles of whiskey and waving their arms.

Knight throws his arms to the sky but keeps eye contact with the sailor on the deck. "Thank you, dear lord." He's shouting at the sailor, pointing at him. "Speaking for the boy and myself, we were desperately wondering if this bewildering story you've concocted for us could be any more thrilling." His voice becomes louder; he's roaring at the sailor and the ship. "And to be so graciously included, dear lord, on your behalf..." Knight moves his body and his arms back and forth between the sailor and the sky. "The odyssey you've written, how wondrously brought to life here on this most epic of stages. "Truly, a tour de force, a skillful reportage of uncanny brillance." Every sailor on the ironclad has stopped what they were doing to watch Knight's performance. Each of them slowing their animated gestures to stand absolutely still. A shell-shocked PostScript to the purgatory they're leaving behind.

Too tired to keep at the volume, Knight turns away from the sailor and from the ironclad. He drops to his seat and looks down at his shoes. "But honestly," his voice now low, he's talking to himself, "who can carry on with this bewildering nonsense? I don't care to make sense of it any longer." He rubs a small bit of dirt off his shoe. "So, we'll be on our way, and until we meet again, dear lord, you'll require another narrator, perhaps this time one gullible enough to swallow this horse shit and follow it all the way to the end." His voice is a whisper, "good night and good luck."

The ironclad is moving away at a decent speed, on its way upriver, spewing smoke in its wake. The voices of the sailors, one by one, revert to the hollers, moving off into the distance. Whiskey can provide temporary closure.

"Mr. Knight, I'm getting you the canteen," Hardy says very matter-of-factly. "Let's face the inevitable."

"What, Son, might you consider the inevitable?" Knight stares at one shoe in particular. How a good bit of polish could bring it back to its prime.

"How about… how about the Mississippi is sure full of surprises?" Hardy hands the canteen to Mr. Knight.

"No, that's not nearly enough." Knight takes the canteen. He pulls out the cork and takes a quick drink. A quick grimace from the taste of river water.

They both sit quietly.

The Mississippi, in true form, pulls the bateau through the bend.

Representative Knight sits still and looks out toward the trees along the bank jutting out into the river. He tries to pick out the individual trees; he's counting them.

"I can tell you there are several port cities on the Mississippi between where I believe we are now," Knight's voice is only slightly more engaged, "and where we're going, down to New Orleans."

"That has to be good, right?"

"I would guess," Knight's finished his calculation. "Manner of speaking, Son, manner of speaking. I would guess, around this bend, we'll find Vicksburg."

Hardy waits. He considers what Mr. Knight would want to hear. "Vicksburg?

Huh? That sounds…"

"It sounds like trouble, Hardy. This could very well be the end of this trip down the Mississippi. The look of the ship we just passed. Well, you saw it. It'll sink within a mile."

"Mr. Knight, there was always going to be more trouble before we got all the way down to New Orleans. We have the experience now. We'll get through it like we did the last time, Sir, this time better, faster."

The bateau reaches the turn of the bend at De Soto Point, a long finger of land that makes the hairpin turn. The harbor at Vicksburg is just around the bend.

"Mr. Knight, pick up the oar. We'll need to get control of this boat. We're going to be pushed out to the middle of it." Hardy's voice is full of confidence. "We'll want to get closer to shore."

Hardy back paddles and points the bateau in the shore's direction, but the boat is quickly pulled sideways. The current is relentless at the bend. Here, the river pulls the hardest to make the turn.

The turn is made. The little boat turned sideways to the river gives the two of them the ring-side seat, the full harbor of Vicksburg.

"And there it is." Knight doesn't want to see it, but he can't turn away. "The encyclopedia of history's barbarity. That Son is the inevitable." Knight's voice is at the bottom end of defeated. "The thunder of the cannon."

"Oh - my - God." Hardy is dumbstruck. "How the fuck are we gonna get out of this?"

"We're not."

Chapter Nineteen

A fleet of splinters

The whole of it would take hours to describe, never catching it all.

The fleet of ironclads—maybe nine—face south, down river. Their line cuts through the choppy waters of the harbor, a giant, fat, black snake. Each gunboat, down the length of its side, may have four, maybe six cannons—parrott rifles—facing the city on the bluff. When the parrotts shoot, they explode with a white blast of yellow fire. The eighty-pound shell flies out 8,000 yards and spits white smoke that hangs for sometime in the air. The twin smokestacks of each of the ironclads contribute more than their fair share, coughing up coal black smoke. The harbor is thick of smoke, the sun helpless against it. The shock of a blast kicks the gunboat back. It shudders an agonizing groan for a painful moment. On the opposite side of the ironclad's line, away from the city, two ships are burning, a full consuming blaze. Men in the water. There are pieces of naval debris scattered everywhere, like ice on the river's thaw. On each ship, there are a handful of Union sailors out in the open. Most, must be below. The pinging of bullet lead stinging the iron sides is loud enough to be heard at the bateau. The carbine rifles fire up to ten rounds a minute. One American flag on every one of the ships.

Up on the bluff that rings the eastern side of the horseshoe bend, the city of Vicksburg is ablaze. Large sections of it exploded with fire, the massive flames licking the smoke-clogged sky. The city hugs the river for maybe a mile. All of it an inferno. The Confederate's defense—the Vicksburg battery—stretches along the edge of the city, right down at the river. Their cannons' discharge; the same exploding flames; more smoke for an insatiable harbor.

The ironclads of the Union's Mississippi flotilla are moving downriver like every piece of everything in the harbor. A risky calculation will have the plates of thick iron fulfill their promise as the most modern of Naval designs. They will make their dash through the Vicksburg gauntlet, to come out the other side, and reconvene downriver. And what's more, they will temper their speed with some amount of hopeful precision to allow the parrotts to let loose their entire stock of munitions and bury the Confederates, their city and their sympathizers in fiery rubble.

Spread across the whole of it, the river and the battery, the fields around the city and across the hills beyond, the whole of the forty-seven-day Union campaign, extending miles to the east of the river gives the Mississippi to the Union in exchange for 8,037 souls.

Representative Knight and Hardy are paddling hard now that the panorama has presented itself. The current rushing through the bend pulls them closer to the shore side of the harbor, opposite the battery. Luckily, for once, not straight out in the middle.

They're moving downriver on the back side of the ironclads, opposite the city but totally exposed. A little boat in the circus of the iron monoliths and a burning city. It's everywhere in the harbor, and they're swept into the frightening heart of it.

"I'm going to go out on a limb here," the pinnacle of Knight's sarcastic tone, "and say this is a pinch more than we expected when we crossed the parking lot at the Winnebago."

Once the current has made the bend, it slows itself back down to its favored crawl. The bateau is too far out to get to shore and is approaching the first of the ironclads, the tail of the snake. They've entered the smoke's arena.

"We'll keep paddling, we'll go through it, and we'll come out the other side. We'll stay down as low as we can, and no one will see us." Hardy's optimism has summoned a small amount of confidence. "It's all we can do."

The noise in the harbor and the acrid smoke quickly overtake the bateau.

A blast from across the harbor, a shell from the Confederate's battery, strikes the ironclad three ships in front of the bateau. The blast is instantly followed by the deafening explosion of iron. Mangled pieces shoot into the air. Shards of the metal cut through everything in a wide area. One jagged scrap smacks the water thirty feet from the bateau, Knight and Hardy sprayed with the iron's splash.

Knight brushes off most of the water. "Operatic!" He can't muster anything more than terrified sarcasm. "Francis Ford Coppola, astonishing in scale, inspired!"

"Mr. Knight, it's not helping."

Shouting from the ironclad, sailors scramble to recover.

"Son, just as an aside, did we ever open the second crate?"

"Mr. Knight, paddle, if we can get up next to that ironclad," Hardy is yelling, "the next one up, we'll be hidden, we'll be shielded."

Three carbine bullets pop the surface water not more than three feet from the bateau.

"We're exposed, Sir. We need the cover of that ironclad."

A fourth bullet hits the side of the bateau, just above waterline. An odd plink of a sound. Shot from too far away, the hardwood keeps the bullet; it doesn't make it through.

"Holy shit," Hardy blurts. "Paddle!" Hardy is pulling hard on his oar. He keeps his eye on the ironclad ahead. If he can pull up along the side of it, they'll be out of sight to the battery.

For the next fifty feet, Hardy does his best, and the bateau reaches the cover of the ironclad. He stops. For the moment, they're somewhat safe, and he rubs his red-sore palms.

Knight has lost track of his thoughts and looks out at the side of the ironclad twenty feet to their side; black, heavy. How can that thing even float? He's dazed and charmed by the look and the scale of it. In the storm of chaos, sailors are shouting, and gunpowder explodes in all directions. The clouds of smoke move all together at their own steady pace. The patches of white and black drift across the ironclad, making an impressive silhouette.

The ironclad holds firm to the Mississippi, steady and stoic. The opposite side of the ship is fully exposed to the Confederate battery and lets loose its rain of munitions, like every angry ship at war.

Knight can feel the shudder through the iron plates as each cannon fires, one, after the other, after the other.

Hardy keeps his oar steady. For now the current is keeping the bateau steady with the iron ship.

"This is good, Son," Knight says quietly, "you did well to get us over here, smart."

"Let's not talk about it. Let's figure out what to do next."

"This is the next." Knight faces Hardy for the first time in an anxious while. "There is no next. We stay right here until these behemoths rearrange themselves, and then we see what's next."

"We could try to get closer, maybe throw a rope."

"I don't think connecting us to that hulk is in our best interest. In fact, let's avoid this whole thing."

"Sir, if we stay put and wait it out until this whole thing moves downriver, that's going to be hours and hours."

On the ironclad shielding the bateau, the cannons are slowing their repetition. One blast every five or six minutes.

"We'll make a run for it." Hardy's rattled. The chaos is unnerving. "Paddle hard and we'll get the fuck out of here."

"Son, paddling hard will not get us where we need to go, and we both know it."

They sit and wait; they stare at each other. A stalemate. It's far too loud and dangerous to come up with any convincing idea, and they both feel it. The harbor of ships and the bluffs of Vicksburg are being ripped apart.

"Hey, over there." Somewhere in the smoke, there's a voice coming from the ship. A cannon fires and the repercussion jerks the ironclad and the voice calls out again. "Get a paddle over here and I can throw a tie."

Both Knight and Hardy look up and down the side of the black iron. Oddly, there is a row of hay bales down a long portion of the upper part of it.

At some point, in the ironclad's short history of operations, there was discovered an unfortunate oversight in the design. Splinters shatter and fly when the inside wooden frame is struck by cannon shot. A serious and bloody vulnerability was hastily solved with bales of hay to catch the splinters. Given the context, it's an odd sight.

"You can't stay out there, open on all sides. The shrapnel's too thick. The splinters'll catch you." Calls the voice in the smoke.

With the smoke swirling up in the air and caught on the backside of the ship, they both know not to say a word.

Hardy sees him first, then Knight, right after.

Standing on the upper part, the pilot's deck, a sailor is waving at the two of them, trying to get their attention and let them know the danger. A remarkably young sailor, his uniform far too large for his small, blond head, a miniature figure placed in the middle of a raging, smoking, billowing collage of mayhem.

"Ignore him?" Hardy has the first reaction.

"Not ignore, turn away, look in the other direction. We haven't heard a thing. Let's be smart about this." Knight is recounting step-by-step how they were swept up into the previous river's scenarios. The deserters, the revolutionaries, the Europeans, the young tribal warriors, teenagers.

"If you recall, it was the first couple of steps, the initial decision, and we both share that responsibility. I'll admit, the first step into William's little boat, the one we are presently still in, was my mistake. I should have said we're staying on the river bank. But I let my vanity cloud my thoughts. As the adult, it was my decision, and I made that mistake. I take full responsibility." Knight looks around, breathing hard. "I am trying to impress upon you that this is another one of those moments of truth moments. Let's not make the same mistake. And I suggest you consider this scenario, here in this harbor, right here as we're talking. This comes about one hundred years after that fort, back there up the river. That's the timeline of these histories, and that's where we are. The fort was about one hundred years ago. Believe me, I know how that sounds. Sadly insane, with a ridiculous plot of some ill-conceived fantasy. A story, a movie, who knows, most definitely cross-genre." Knight bends in, "We have to think smart and do it quick." Knight sits up straight, shoulders squared. "I vote we immediately abandon and, and, and, turn away from all of this. We do not engage. We mind our own business."

"I agree. Let's keep going. Don't look at anybody. Don't talk to anybody."

They look at each other, they nod, then simultaneously the words roll out. "New Orleans."

When a cannon shell strikes an ironclad—two ships up the line—they both spin around to see the outcome. The impact blast on the ship is horrific: a loud screech of tearing metal and the deep screams of sailors caught in an unfortunate spot. It's hard to turn away, but this is happening on all sides. The Battle of Vicksburg.

Their ironclad, their barricade, is moving slowly downriver with all the rest. Mr. Knight and Hardy realize again, now with more urgency, they'll not be out of this harbor any time soon. Their position is precarious, at best. They crouch low on the bateau seat and keep their oars in the water and hang on, hoping for something.

A sudden loud snap on the inside of the bateau. Another carbine bullet strikes the wood behind them. This time, it cuts through the side of the boat.

"I thought we were protected by this hulk," Knight calls out.

"Probably ricochet," Hardy yells back.

"Make your best plan," the young sailor comes back to the side of the ironclad, "but you're in a terrible position."

"He's right, Mr. Knight. This isn't going to work. We gotta do something."

With no discussion, Hardy calls out to the sailor, "Okay, we agree. What should we do?"

"Get as close as you can to the side and keep to the middle of the ship," the young sailor calls back. The voice of a seasoned sailor, another teenager, called into duty. "Right here below where I am, not to the back by the paddle wheel."

"Sir, we can get in closer. It doesn't mean we have to get aboard."

"I don't disagree," Knight offers. "Let's just take it slow. Things have a way of escalating in these little mini panics."

Without too much effort and very little bickering, they manage to get the bateau over to the side of the ironclad. The black smoke continues its animated fury, swirling around the backside of the ship.

"Use the rope tied to the handrail on the stairs." The young sailor points as he calls out the order. "Tie up with that. It's secure enough for that boat.

What kind of boat is that, anyway?"

Once they're over to the metal stairs that lead up the side of the ship to the first deck, the hurricane deck, Hardy grabs the rope and ties the bateau oarlock to the handrail. He pulls out the slack, somewhat proud of his rope-tying first attempt.

From the young sailor, "I'm Edwards, I'm the Midshipman."

What is now between the bateau and Midshipman Edwards is a decision to be made; stay put or get aboard. There's only the stairs from the water up to the deck. A dozen steps, no more than fifteen feet. One handrail up the side.

"The child's an officer," Knight shakes his head. "That only figures, is all I can say."

Once the bateau and the ironclad are tied, the smoke becomes patchy. All three of them can get a better look at who they are. Blond-headed Edwards looks every bit far too young. Representative Knight quickly judges a kid who woefully doesn't belong. Hardy watches as Edwards ducks his upper body at the sudden surprise of a cannon blast or the clap of a carbine and how he immediately stands up straight. Hardy sees a kid who's figured out his place in this mess. Midshipman Edwards watches Hardy's face, and he quickly senses another, like himself, who's been caught out of place, has found strength because he's had to and given up wrestling with the bigger issues. There's too much going on. At this point on the river, in a situation like this harbor, these somewhat penetrating assessments come quickly.

At this distance, Knight can see deeper into the deck of the ship just above them, the deck behind Edwards. There are several other sailors passing through the erratic smoke. They're busy but hardly frantic.

"Are you coming aboard?" Edwards calls down to Hardy. The young midshipman has judged Knight, by appearance alone, as too complicated to be trustworthy. When you've been in the thick of it, judgments like this are rarely wrong.

"Stick to the plan," Knight tells Hardy. "This is a good position for now. Take it slow."

"We're going to stay here," Hardy calls to Edwards, for the time being." There's enough steadiness in his voice to sound convinced of his decision.

Up on the deck, another sailor, an older sailor, walks up and pulls Edwards to the side and tells him something definitive and deliberate. Before he finishes whatever he's telling the midshipman, he points down to the bateau, then quickly walks away.

"You should come aboard. Come up to the deck where I am." Edward's voice is more assertive. Without saying it, Knight and Hardy look at each other. They both recognize their situation is developing in a familiar way.

"Midshipman Edwards," Hardy is proceeding cautiously, "my partner and I will stay put here. We will hold here for only a short while." Hardy looks to Knight for a quick critique. "We have other business which takes us down the river."

"I see," Edwards replies, less assertive, more tentative.

"Sure," Hardy counters. "Sure you understand."

Midshipman Edwards pauses for a moment to consider his options. He turns away from Hardy in the bateau below him. He looks to other parts of the deck, possibly other sailors, possibly more senior.

"I'm sure you trust your footing," Edwards answers back to Hardy. "Sure your business is your own."

"Then we're agreed," Hardy tells him.

Edwards thinks for another minute, this time a shorter minute. "I would say you and I are in agreement, certainly."

"Good then" Knight weighs in.

"But..." Edwards stammers; he's had little experience with this type of civilian chain of command exchange, "but, well, it's the Captain. He's concerned about who you are, exactly, and, of course, your safety. He's asked me to bring you to him. It's an order, really. So you see, you'll have to come abroad after all."

"That presents a problem," Knight says to Hardy, under his breath.

"That presents a problem," Hardy calls up to Edwards.

"In one minute, maybe two, but not more than three," Knight says, as his body slumps into his seat, "A sailor will suddenly appear out of the smoke, with a rifle, and order us aboard, right at the top of those stairs."

"You're being paranoid."

"Am I?"

"Why would they give a shit about two..."

"Language."

"Why would they give two gall darns about two obvious non-sailors coming downriver in a crappy little boat with an entire city on fire and ships being blown to hell all around us? It doesn't make sense."

"Precisely," Knight says to the bottom of the crappy little boat. He lifts his arm, pushes up a sleeve on the Armani, and checks the time on a watch he doesn't have. "Three, two, one."

"You two, down below." An older sailor steps forward next to Midshipman Edwards. He's holding a carbine rifle.

"Okay, you're right," Hardy tells Knight as he reaches into his back pocket and pulls out a little pad of wire-bound paper, which he doesn't have. He makes a quick note on the pad. "Alright, you're only two points ahead. I can live with that. It ain't over." He doesn't bother to put the pencil and the notepad back in his pocket.

"You two get aboard. The Captain needs a quick conference."

"So, what do we do?" Hardy asks. He already knows the inevitable.

All four wait. They stare at each other through the awkward moment of deliberation. The older sailor, his face black with soot, turns to Edwards as they exchange their concerns without a word. Then Edwards turns and looks toward Hardy, down below, and brushes the hair out of his face. They catch each other's eyes. Both can see it's not up to them without saying a word. Hardy runs his hand across the top of his bleached crew cut and turns to Mr. Knight, still slumped on his seat. Mr. Knight looks up at Hardy, and they both know without a word.

Mr. Knight stands up and puts both hands on Hardy's shoulders. Face to-face. "This is how this is going to go," his voice is not urgent, not anxious, not a touch of sarcasm. His voice is deadpan and serious with a good amount of sober patience. Enough to put Hardy a little on edge. "We will go with the gentleman with the rifle. We will be as polite as possible. We'll speak to whomever they wish, and we will make sufficient small talk to put everyone at ease. At every encounter, we will be brief and apologetic and make our excuses to leave. We won't make recommendations or give advice. We will act friendly, but we will not be friendly; we will not show sympathy or any form of disapproval. Are we getting the picture?"

"Sir, this goes without saying. The point is, get in and get out. Vicksburg is none of our business."

"Well said, Son. You can bet there will be every effort to sweep us up into this nightmare, blood nightmare."

"I know."

Knight connects with Hardy, forehead to forehead, seasoned sailors with their own battle plan. "What do we say?"

"New Orleans!"

"Gentlemen." The older sailor up top lets Representative Knight and Hardy know there's an urgency to get aboard the ironclad. Maybe the Captain is waiting. Who knows?

They both step toward the side of the bateau and the metal steps. "You go first," Mr. Knight tells Hardy.

The significance of the first steps onto the iron ship is not lost on either of them. When the first foot connects with the black metal step, a flood of thoughts are unleashed, far too many to put into words. They make their way to the top.

Midshipman Edwards looks at Hardy. "Terribly sorry."

With a half-smile, Hardy tells him, "Don't worry."

When Knight steps up and onto the deck next to the young Edwards, he sees the face of a young sailor, even younger than he'd seen from down below. Midshipman Edwards is not sure how to greet Knight, probably the jacket. He quickly decides on a brief salute. It's awkward and quick.

The young Edwards's uniform is at least one size too big for his frame. The double-breasted, heavy, cotton blue jacket hangs from his shoulders. A double row of eight tarnished brass buttons up the front of the jacket, with shoulder straps crisscrossing his chest and a cocked hat. His blue trousers, more than a couple of holes.

Representative Knight and Hardy are standing on the deck of the ironclad. They're captivated by the size of it but more by the oddity of the massive black metal hulk that actually floats and moves on the river like a ship.

Knight looks around. He's immediately struck by the incredible danger of where they're standing, exposed. Directly across the bluffs and the battery, and the burning city on top of it all. The full view of the harbor from this height—fifteen feet, maybe more—is astounding. Never forgettable. He looks at Hardy. They both recognize the precarious place where they're standing. Around the perimeter of the long deck is a rim of the same dark iron. It's only waist high; it doesn't appear to be much cover from the carbine lead. The smoke still blows across, clouds of black and white, gray. Knight considers this height above the river a new experience. It's like being up in the clouds. A disturbing idea. Knight counts six other sailors milling around on the deck. It's unclear what they're doing up here. He grabs Hardy by the shoulder. "Come on, we're moving over here."

Knight takes Hardy and they walk over to the base of one of the two smokestacks. With their backs to it, it's better than standing out in the open. The heat coming through the iron is not hot enough to burn, but you don't stand pressed up against it.

"It's stopped," Hardy says as he's looking across the deck, particularly at the sailors, who seem to be doing nothing. Each one with a scraggly beard. The whites of their eyes seem to pop out of their dirty and tired faces, and each in a uniform of Union blue, barely blue at all.

"You're right, there's a lull," Knight says. He's looking across at the two other box-like structures on the deck, like small squat buildings. The same dark black metal, ten feet high. From where he's standing, he can see the details of the rivets. They're easily two inches in diameter, tight, regular spacing. They give the impression of such weight and strength.

"The tonnage of this thing is impressive," Knight says.

Midshipman Edwards walks over to Knight and Hardy. They both have the same thought. The boy is by far younger than the others and the only one who appears clearly focused and in charge of something. Young Edwards appears to be the brightest of the lot. Another quick assessment.

"With this break in the cannons, now would be the good time to speak with Captain Walker," Edwards tells them. He doesn't quite look them in the eyes.

Both Knight and Hardy have another shared thought. The young sailor has a pronounced, out-of-place kindness in his voice. Knight hears it and he thinks the boy is not far from his mother or family. Hardy hears Edwards's voice and knows he's giving it his best, floating through this crazy scene, at least for the moment, according to someone's grand plan.

"Captain Walker is just over here. I'll make the acquaintance." Edwards motions for them to walk with him to the opposite side of the deck.

As they walk, Knight and Hardy exchange glances. How can all that noise suddenly go quiet? And the smoke is clearing. There is a sky.

The laws of physics demand some amount of collective sigh and moment of reflection. The aggressive soldiering, the guns and the cannons, the ships and the battery, the shouting and the smoke, the anxiety and the fear, cannot go on continuously, indefinitely. The immense physicality of the lull comes from one slight hesitation, not at all remarkable, but unique none-the-less. One sailor on a hurricane deck or a hole dug into the battery's mud bank, somewhere in the spread-out field of horror and misery. One man's hesitation leads to his adversary's moment of pause. In the space of one breath, they're both waiting for the other to commit to what should come next. The pause catches hold like ripples across the river. It continues with a soldier at arm's length nearby. The unannounced break in the contest comes from somewhere but nowhere. It comes out of one moment of thought's reflection, a moment of fatigue. Who knows what the collective mind has decided or not decided? But there it is, a sweeping and sudden silence.

As Midshipman Edwards, Representative Knight, and Hardy walk over to Captain Walker. He's speaking with an officer, and they're clearly discussing particulars regarding the battery. The officer points, probably at a short row of larger artillery, the thirty-two-pounder seacoast guns.

"They've put those in place there to clean up what the others don't finish," Captain Walker tells his officer. "They're accurate and have the range. Let this abate, take its course, and then those Confederate guns must be dealt with." The Captain asks the officer to leave him; their conversation has been interrupted.

Captain Walker sees Representative Knight with Hardy and the Midshipman approaching, and he turns to get a better look. He stands stationary and waits for them to come forward.

"Captain, Sir..." The young Edwards starts the introduction, but the Captain doesn't have the time.

"Thank you, Midshipman. Take the young man down to the hold," the Captain tells Edwards. "I'll have a word here with the officer, then he'll join the two of you."

Immediately, Knight and Hardy are struck by the earnestness and the deep, considered pacing of the Captain's voice. Before either of them has time for a second thought, Edwards taps Hardy's shoulder, and it's clear they'll leave Mr. Knight and Captain Walker to speak on their own. They walk back across the top deck.

Captain Walker is undeniably a worldly veteran, as is Representative Knight, in his own way. The two men stand at arm's length, and in the heavy pause, the two of them wrestle with what to make of the other.

Knight believes he has the advantage. He can place the encounter in a timeline of events with a sprinkling of facts, partially recollected from chapters on Civil War history. Clearly, he has the advantage of knowing how the war finally ends. Walker believes he possesses a greater knowledge of the battle because of his immersion in the details, the lives of his men, an advantage Knight most clearly does not have. Walker understands the vulnerability of his ship and the damage a thirty-two-pounder can do to the story.

"I believe you have some information for me." Captain Walker goes first.

Representative Knight is neither stunned by the accusation nor is he even remotely overwhelmed by the encounter. He is, however, admittedly taken aback by the presence of this man standing before him. He'll give it a minute before he replies. The Captain's uniform is remarkable because the cuffs of his topcoat are banded in gold lace. There are inches of it stretching up the sleeve. The Captain is ranked very high in the Union's Navy.

Captain Walker has the type of face for which you cannot—for the life of you—turn away. He is older than he is old. His dark brown hair, from the top middle of his head to the back of his head, is perfectly groomed. The jowls and cheeks of his face, the mountains and valleys, are more pronounced than Knight can remember ever having seen. In a word, the man's face is striking. Captain Walker's eyes, framed by the bushy brows, are piercing, and once they find you, you are transfixed to the point of being frozen in place.

The Captain sees a man tired from the long days and the short nights preceding this moment when the man attempts to present himself as still eager for fulfillment. The man's hair and unwashed face show him to be caught out of his element. He's come downriver, but how far? The man's trousers are dirty— understandable given the crude boat—but the jacket has been kept immaculate.

Captain Walker may question the presence of this man, particularly why he is here in Vicksburg at precisely this time in the battle's dash through the harbor, but the jacket strikes him as most noteworthy. Which regiment would craft such an impressive garment? What rank is dressed?

Walker reaches over to feel Knight's jacket. "Impressive." He rubs the fabric between his thumb and forefinger.

"Giorgio Armani," Knight says with deliberately understated pride, at long last the triumph of vindication, which he's forced to conceal, for the moment. Thoughts of Alfred cross his mind. What a moment.

The Captain withdraws and recovers.

Midshipman Edwards and Hardy walk back across the hurricane deck, passing the black iron pilot house with its curved sheets of metal and rivets. The smoke is almost cleared, caught up in other winds. The lull in the cannon fire gives a dozen sailors a break. They stand around chatting with arms over shoulders or shoulder-to-shoulder. They're tired men.

"We'll go down there," Edwards says, showing Hardy the stairs leading down to a short deck. The metal stairs are secured to the same black iron at a steep angle at the very front of the ship.

Fifteen steps down and the two are standing on a wooden deck, probably forty feet across the width. It feels like the most exposed deck on the ship. Surely it is.

"New recruit?" One of three other sailors on the deck asks Edwards. They both know the cannon shelling could start up at any minute. The three sailors are passing a rolled cigarette, two measured puffs each. On any other occasion, the three sailors might have some interest in the young stranger on their ship, but not on this smoke break.

"The Captain thinks you're spies." Midshipman Edwards wants to have a conversation with Hardy. "The idea of it seems quite a bit funny. He's a good man; he's just old. He doesn't really know who we are, but he doesn't abuse us."

"That's good." The only thing Hardy can think of. Looking around, it's a lot to take in.

"Whatever side of this war you're on, that shirt sure doesn't seem like uniform quality." Edwards is looking at Hardy's hoop with hawk feathers, dream-catcher graphic on his t-shirt. It's caught a lot of attention.

"This?" Hardy pulls a little on the shirt. "No, this is from an album cover. My dad could tell you which one, maybe Neil Young. What's your role? I mean, your rank on this ship? What exactly is a Midshipman?"

"There's a nine-gun crew that runs each one of those Dahlgren cannons," Edwards tells him. He straightens up with a little pride. "We call them soda bottles. We can go down there. I am in command of the gun crew, and when the battery is on us, there's no time to waste. I have to get shots off as fast as I can organize it, with good aim too. That's my charge, my role."

Edwards and Hardy circle around each other, trying to get comfortable.

"You have to see that the battery will start up again in no time," Edwards tells Hardy. "It's a very dangerous place to be. One well-placed shell will tear open the whole side of the gun deck and shredded metal, or the splinters will tear us to pieces."

"I'm sure you're good at it, the gun crew," Hardy tells him. "How did you get here, Midshipman Edwards? This is about as far from anywhere as one can be. What's your name?"

"Bradley, from Alabama."

"When the Confederates start it up again," Hardy is thinking it through, "you'll get back down there and…"

"I'll get back down there and start it up. Yup, load 'em and fire them off. Tear their heads off and spill their guts, men, women, and children."

Hardy's eyes go wide open. "That makes you sound as old as the Captain."

"What's your name? Bradley asks Hardy, "We won't get into where you're from, but it sure ain't here. We have that in common."

"Call me Hardy."

A waft of the stink of gunpowder brings it all back into focus.

"Hardy, we're stuck in this harbor and in this war that's blowing the whole world to hell as fast as we can organize it. Don't shut your eyes, and don't let nothing get to you. Look out for yourself." Bradley takes a quick, shallow breath and walks over to the stairs that lead down to the gun deck below. He bends over and takes a quick glance inside. "There's only one thing here that needs my full attention. There are boys down there in that gun deck a lot younger than the two of us. You tell me, what business is it that puts them down there?"

Hardy stands still. "I can see this war has got you."

"It has. Surely it has."

Chapter Twenty

The stinking smell of river steam

What started as clouds threatening rain is now an afternoon sky with patches of sun.

A piece of the sunlight crosses Bradley's face, and Hardy can see a face older than his young years.

"Alabama? The south. That doesn't make sense."

"No, I'm sure it doesn't." Bradley turns to Hardy. "What makes sense is that all these men and every one of these boys down below. We're all here, caught up in this, all for different reasons. There's nothing we have in common except for being stuck on this black ship."

"But slavery is the issue. That's why you're all here."

Bradley seems to shrink a bit more in the oversize uniform. "My family doesn't have a slave. I don't know people with slaves. I've seen poor negro men and women, a lot of them, some with their kids, working themselves to death. I feel sorry for them. Money buys slaves. That's the business of people with money."

"So you're against slavery as an issue?" Hardy's voice is getting quicker.

"I'm up against my little brother and sister starving. I send eighteen dollars of officer's money back home every month. It counts up at the supper table."

"Smoke?" one sailor calls over to them.

"And you?" Bradley's voice is getting softer and slowed. "What are you thinking, rowing that little boat into the middle of this harbor? What kind of fool would do that? What's down the river that can't wait?"

"It's a very complicated story, and one I can't get into right here and now. I'm sorry to not tell it, it doesn't seem fair. We have more in common than you know." Hardy shuffles his feet, only a few steps. "Why is it that being alive in this moment right here and now feels like a long time ago and so far away that my feet don't know which way to turn?"

"Another thing we have in common."

"Bradley," Hardy faces him directly, "The older man and I need to get off this ship as soon as possible."

"I'm telling you, it's not at all safe to take that small boat out into open water. You'll be spotted, and you'll be target practice, an easy target."

"We don't have a choice. We have to try."

"Alright." Bradley puts a hand on Hardy's shoulder. "We'll put our minds to it. For now, let's get below. My crew will need to be prepared. The soda bottle will need to be primed."

With the hand on Hardy's shoulder, Bradley turns him to face the stairs going down and with a hint of a smile, "Those rebels will be about finished with their own smoke break."

Representative Knight and Captain Walker are locked into their conversation. The last of the smoke peters out and passes over them. The sailors scattered about on the hurricane deck have relaxed into their familiar at-rest. The checkerboards are quickly pulled out, and the competition picks up where it left off. Every checker back where it was.

"Sir," the Representative tells Walker, "I can assure you this conversation can go in two very different directions." Knight gathers his thoughts and takes several cautious breaths, a kind of show of strength. "The first, we can speak of what you believe I might know." Knight is speaking slowly and methodically. "You believe I might carry some reconnaissance from up the Mississippi, north of Vicksburg, which I can assure you I do not have. Or, you might believe that I carry some order from the Admiral. Admiral David Dixon Porter is the name I'm going to say. It's all I can remember from that particular chapter. Or conversely, you may think I'm a spy for the Confederacy, attempting to gain—I don't know what."

Knight waits for any sign.

Captain Walker cocks his head ever-so-slightly; with one hand, he brushes the hair on top of his head into place—which is unnecessary—and with the other hand, he takes the bottom of his coat and with one quick tug, he straightens it. "I'm willing to entertain your considerations," Captain Walker replies. "I do believe a man of your status does not simply paddle a dinghy into a battle of this caliber or suddenly drop into a harbor enraged with the predicaments of war. You've come with a purpose, and that is the goal of the conversation."

"I understand your concern, Captain." Knight can feel the confidence of his one true talent swelling up inside of him. The fine-tuned diplomatic prowess has finally found a true purpose, a worthy moment. Not one reservation could possibly keep him from continuing to press the conversation. He continues. "The other direction of this conversation, Sir, which I have no shame to admit, is that myself and the boy are indeed dropped into the middle of this harbor, the battle, and the war." Knight pauses for a short moment. There is no good reason to go on with this. And then he does. "Dropped and paddled from a place so far and distant from this Vicksburg harbor, it cannot make sense to you. I'm not describing far upriver, and not another country, but a different time and a different place, called California, on the far west coast of the Country, the United States." Knight believes he's dropped the bomb. Let the chips fall.

"Let's stop this right here," the Captain says, unperturbed. "Let me sort this through a little further. You're not gold miners; you're not dressed for it. Gold is being brought east through regular channels. You do not appear to be with the railroad; you'd have no business on the Mississippi. You could be sneaking around for the Democrats, but they lost their power and answer to the Republicans and Mr. Lincoln. Plain and simple, you're not dressed for politics. You could be sent by the southerners of California, but for what purpose? They don't have slaves, and they have very little business in this war. I'd say you're two back-country folk out scouting deer and got caught up in the current at De Soto Point, but you're not even carrying rifles." Walker stops for the moment. He stands quietly, running through other possibilities. "Sir, for the life of me, I beg your honest pardon," Walker continues. "I haven't even asked your name."

"That's quite alright. I can see you're busy here, preoccupied. My name is Franklin Knight. I'm newly elected to the United States House of Representatives. From the great state of California. And currently, myself and the boy are on our way to Washington, DC, as we speak, at this very moment."

"Washington." Captain Walker lets the word hang for a moment.

"And you're traveling by dinghy, going south on the Mississippi."

When Hardy takes the last of the steps down into the gun deck, he can see the size of it. Its low ceiling; the space inside is a hundred feet deep, maybe more. It's dark, smoky, and crowded. A thin veil of black, oily soot covers most of everything. The gun deck smells of burning coal and the steam from the engine. There are easily a hundred sailors sprawled all over the deck, mostly lying or sitting on the floor. An incredible quiet, which is immediately strange. So many men packed into such a tight space, and no one saying much at all. A few grumbles here and there, a bit of broken laughter, a crowd of men at rest with nothing more to say.

And the cannons, five equally spaced, down the length of the deck, each with the muzzle end projecting out through a square opening, all aimed at the Vicksburg battery.

"It's best not to breathe too deep down here," Bradley tells Hardy, "unless you're under one of those air shafts."

Roughly square, the shafts are open to the air above. They're also the main source of light for the gun deck. There are three down the length.

"Found yourself a friend, did you, Midshipman?"

"This will be one of the two fools who came up on us in the rowboat."

"Try your best to ignore these stinkers," Bradley says to Hardy, no attempt at all to conceal the words, "and keep your money close; they'll take the bills right out of a shot-dead's body before it's even cold."

"Don't listen to the Midshipman, Son. He wants you to think we're getting paid for this."

"No no no, listen up; he'll tell you exactly where to put your money. He's a hundred percent above board."

"Absolutely. When the boys start up with the laundry, hand your money to the Midshipman, one hundred percent trustworthy."

It's immediately a sight. Hardy can't exactly tell who is talking, all their faces blackened, and they're all smiling and pushing on each other. It's immediately kind of wonderful too. They're older than Bradley. Hardy can see now that there are groups of men gathered around each of the cannons. At this cannon—the one closest, it must be Bradley's cannon—sitting and lying, uniforms as dirty as the faces, their bodies so cramped together it's like one large mass of a body with maybe eight different heads.

"There'll be no laundry for you, Winston." Words from another voice, very much younger than the others. Hardy catches the face, pulled from side to side by the hugest of grins. He sees the face of a boy, a free slave African kid, a sailor for the Union Navy, maybe ten years old. The face next to him, another boy, maybe younger, they could be brothers. Looking around, these two are not nearly the only young boys spread through the deck.

The guy, Winston, picks up a scrap of cloth, probably laundry, and throws it, hitting the young African boy in the shoulder. The boy breaks out into a laugh and throws it back. A lot more shoving and pushing.

The two young boys were most likely swept into the war with the surrender of Fort Sumter. President Lincoln called for volunteers, and they came—75,000 of them. The greatest numbers were the recently freed and runaway enslaved. In most instances, they were immediately put into service.

In the below decks of an ironclad, the gunpowder has to be carried by hand, up from the safety of the powder room on the lowest level of the ship, up to the cannons on the gun deck. The youngest of the volunteers—ten to fourteen years old—are put to service because of their size. These boys can scramble, dart, and weave throughout the decks carrying leather bags of powder, sometimes two at a time, and stay clear of the other heavy action by the rest of the gun crews. With equal parts affection and respect, their lives devalued and disposable; they're called the Powder Monkeys.

Captain Walker and Representative Knight have turned away from each other to look out to the harbor, or wherever, to avoid heated words. Both of them, knowing the conversation is not nearly concluded, turn back to face each other. Patiently, they take another moment for the tone to lower and become a little more conducive to their mismatched concerns. Every few minutes, one will take a quick look at the harbor, cluttered with ironclads, debris, and the clearing remnants of choking smoke. Or a quick look to Vicksburg, a city on fire, on top of the bluff where the battery's cannons are idle. But for how much longer?

"Captain Walker." Knight's determined there's only one direction out of this conversation, and off this boat, confront it head-on. "Might I ask your Christian name?"

"Certainly, Franklin, Cornelius, Cornelius Walker."

"Cornelius," Franklin steps into it, "I'd like to be very direct. I believe, given the circumstances, direct is best."

"I would not disagree with that. Please, Franklin, speak your mind."

"Cornelius, the boy and I are from the future. There, I said it. It's done."

"I see," Cornelius says, remarkably unperturbed. He's decided the best way to conclude this conversation is to let the gentleman reveal his mission with his own hand-picked words and convict himself with their incredulity.

"As a sensible man," Cornelius proceeds slowly. "I would say that sounds more than a little outrageous, but as a judicious man, I would ask for some type of evidence."

"There is no evidence, Cornelius, nothing more than the words I use to convince you."

"Then keep talking, Franklin, please, convince me."

"I can tell you, Cornelius, how this battle in the harbor ends. I can tell you what your victory has already accomplished. You've taken the Mississippi and brought this war, America's most horrific war, you've brought it to its end." Knight watches Cornelius's face. "Here in this harbor, your victory gets you the Mississippi, which gets you to Gettysburg. A place you know by its name but not by its infamy. Gettysburg gives the Union her victory."

Cornelius gives Franklin his due pause.

"Franklin, those are powerful thoughts and surely a sentient prediction. Tell me, are these visions come to you in a dream?"

"Sir, they're not visions. Maybe I wish they were."

"I see."

"You should sit over there," Bradley tells Hardy. He points to a spot about ten feet to the side of the cannon and against the back wall, out of the way. The recoil from a fired Dahlgren will kick the cannon back ten feet, a dangerous place to be standing or sitting. "Keep your feet up under you, or you'll trip somebody running through."

"Got it."

"Let's get up," Midshipman Edwards tells the men and boys surrounding his cannon, their cannon. In a calm and everyday voice, "Let's run through the drill. Get it loaded." A good amount of relief comes from getting back to the business of the gun and its loading. Less time for thinking.

There are a couple of grunts to get back on their feet, but they all quickly move back to their crew positions around the cannon. You can't feel it, you can't see it, but it's in the air. You can sense it. The lull in the shelling is nearly finished.

The first few minutes, the men are lazy to get to their places. With the last one of them up and in position, the six men of this gun crew stand ready. They turn to the Midshipman and wait. They watch Bradley's face for a sign.

He tells them, "Get it right." The gun crew stands ready, and he calls out, "Silence." A striking voice from such a young man. He waits for the sailors to stop the chatter, and with the one word from Edwards, "Load," they start again the serious business of loading the cannon.

The first crewman stands at the back of the cannon, the soda bottle end, and he cleans the vent, a small hole in the iron, and puts a thumb over it to cover it. He wears a heavy leather thumbstall. The next man worms out any debris left in the barrel with a long pole. They call it the worm pole. The next uses a wet sponge on a long pole to put out any remaining embers down the long barrel.

The next, the dry sponge pole.

The young powder boy is called to the front of the cannon. In his leather bag, brought up from below, the ten-year-old carries a small, silk-wrapped bag, nine pounds of gunpowder. It's loaded into the cannon and pushed tight with another, different pole; all of these poles hang just above the crew.

With the powder loaded, Midshipman Edwards calls for the shell, which the young boy retrieves from another bag he's brought with him. An eight-inch exploding shell, an odd looking, strangely futuristic cylinder of metal.

The shell is shoved carefully down the muzzle of the gun and pushed into place by the rammer. This man stands as erect as a body can get, his face stone-cold sober. He steps into his position and gingerly shoves the bomb into place with his long pole.

The hand spike, a four-foot pole sticking out of the back of the carriage of the cannon, down low to the floor, is swiveled left to right to put the cannon back into its aim. Edwards steps forward and uses a small wheel, just under the soda bottle, to raise the cannon's angle up to a perfect aim at Vicksburg on the bluff.

The next of the crew steps to the back of the gun and uses a twelve inch long, stiff needle of brass—brass doesn't spark against iron. He primes the gun by punching the needle into the vent. The needle tears open a hole in the silk powder bag. He reaches back into the leather bag and pulls out a stubby, short metal needle, the friction primer. One end of this primer needle is wrapped with a metal wire, which connects to a long, thin rope attaching the friction primer to a lanyard, easy to grab hold of. He carefully sticks the friction primer down the same vent hole. The gun is primed and ready.

When Midshipman Edwards calls for the gun to fire, the lanyard is given a hard quick jerk. The metal of the friction primer sparks against the iron of the vent hole, the spark finds the powder, the powder explodes, and the shell shoots through the long iron tube of the cannon to fulfill its duty at Vicksburg.

For now, the crew stands ready, stationary and still. The crew is primed. Most of the men look down. There's no need to confirm that their job is done. They wait for their Midshipman's order. Edwards waits to hear from the Capitan above deck.

From the Vicksburg battery, a blast catches the Captain and the Representative off guard. Walker with a flinch, Knight with a pronounced duck. The shell strikes open water.

"Sir," Knight is becoming less tolerant and more bewildered by the Captain's attention. "It appears your Confederates are waking up. Do you not have other business than this conversation?"

Walker postures.

"Captain," Knight's voice has soured, "what exactly can I help you with?"

"If you're associated with the Confederate, I'll need you detained," Walker's voice remains inquisitive and levelheaded. "But I'm sensing there's more going on here."

"Captain Walker, the boy and I will need to continue downriver as soon as possible."

"A bold request given the circumstances." Walker shifts his weight, an odd angle, an awkward bend at the waist. "Any urgency in a situation such as this can only be the predicament of a larger strategy."

"Captain, you cannot see the situation from my perspective." Knight feels he's done his best.

"Representative Franklin Knight," Walker rolls his words, "your perspective is what struck me in the first occasion of our shared words." Walker folds his arms across his chest and looks out to the harbor. "And now I see clearly why it is imperative you conceal yourself. For the very reason my wife Abigail and her infuriating circle have tried for years to convince me. It's true you are not from here, Sir. You're not from any one place at all. You are an intermediary between the world of the living and the world of spirit."

Knight's jaw drops.

"The spirit speaks through you, I will say, and you're here to relay messages from spirits regarding this feat in the harbor. Which is what you have done, in so many words. Words being secondary to those mediums who have been chosen to channel the energy of the message. Not in so many words."

"Captain," Knight cuts him off. "Sir, you're going in the wrong direction."

"Perhaps that is true," Walker digs a little deeper, "Your urgency to get downriver is to secure an appointment with another in this chronicle. Your messages from the spirit world are not for my company at all."

"Again, way off." Knight crosses his arms across his chest.

"In league with the Fox Sisters of New York." Walker thinks it through. "I would not have pinned that to the map, but now I see the evidence."

In the storied legend, two of the three Fox Family sisters heard a "rapping" on the bedroom wall of their upstate New York house. The sisters claimed the entity creating the sounds was the spirit of a peddler named Charles B. Rosna. Poor Mr. Rosna had been murdered five years earlier, apparently, and buried in the cellar, ostensibly providing context to the story. The two young sisters used the rapping to convince their older sister and others that they were communicating with spirits.

"I can see," Captain Walker continues, he's seen the evidence, "that your type of channeling has no use for the seánce tables, trances, or the Ouija. Not at all. You're a traveler who has no need of these earthbound instruments."

"Captain, it's a wonderful idea." Knight has no other choice but to go with it. It gives the kind of intrigue that really elevates a story like this. "And you! Look at you, the Captain of this iron ship in this furious Vicksburg battle, still able to recognize the spirit world that surrounds all of this. A testament to a man of your rare caliber."

The Fox sisters became the celebrities of the Spiritualism movement, claiming to allow a spirit to control their bodies and speak.

"The spirits are using your mind at this very moment?" Walker insists. "You're being influenced by their thoughts. You see, I am not the novice in this area, Franklin. I see, despite your contradiction, that you are delivering a message. An honor for me to be the focus of the spirits' attention."

"Captain, you're so far off, you make my story seem like a novelist's first effort. As amusing as this episode is, I need to let you know we'll be off this ship and on our way."

"So I ask you, Franklin," Captain Walker continues, "and please do me the honor of being direct about it. Do the spirits favor the Union in the harbor or the Confederates on the bluff? Tell me direct."

"Captain Walker, I will do you the honor as you have requested. Despite what the spirits are telling me, I correct myself, channeling through me. It's the boy who is the medium. I am merely his protector here on the river. He is the one who must get downriver. It's an urgent situation. I hope you can see that, Captain."

"I cannot know the particulars, Sir." Walker shifts his position. "The boy in the story is an accuracy which doesn't add up, very suspicious. Spirits can be mistaken like all of God's children. My wife has shown me this, and I have many encounters to show me the proof of it. This being yet another, but very suspicious." The Captain unfolds his arms and takes a step back from Knight.

"Captain Walker," Knight can't help himself, "it's clear to me now the spirits have given me their final judgment. You've gone quite insane and lost your fucking mind."

"Pleasantries aside," the Captain finishes the encounter, "you and the boy will be kept below until this next round from the battery concludes, one way or another." He raises his arm to get the attention of a sailor standing on the opposite side of the hurricane deck. The sailor walks quickly to the Captain's company and waits for the order.

The Fox sisters' story ends with the eldest of the three sisters confessing it had been a hoax. She publicly demonstrated their method. The many congregations of the movement were left chagrined. The last of it, the addendum, she attempted to recant her confession the next year, but reputations were ruined, and in less than five years, they were all dead, dying in abject poverty.

Hardy watches the hustle bustle up and down the row of Dahlgrens. Each crew following the same drill, the same succession of poles, the powder boys, and the leather bags with their shells. At nearly the same moment, every man in every crew on the gun deck stops and stands at attention, a relaxed attention. This pause in the shelling, a welcome reprieve to the otherwise long day of priming and re-priming the Dahlgrens, shot after shot. They've been at this for hours.

When the two powder boys from Bradley's crew finish their task, they quickly get out of the way of the others and come straight over to Hardy, curious to know who he is and why he's here. Something different in the routine.

Without any pause or introduction, the two boys slide in right next to Hardy, one on either side. The three of them sit packed tight, shoulder-to-shoulder, against the wooden wall of the ship across from the cannons. They're out of the way.

Each boy puts his leather pouch down next to him, right up against his side. One hand across it to secure it, keep it where it is, ready to jump back up at a moment's call.

With the whole deck at attention, voices are kept low.

"Who are you?" The first boy begins. He's keeping his voice low. He is keenly aware of the anxious tension on the deck.

"Yeah, what are you doing down here?" The second boy, keenly curious.

"Are you a friend of Midshipman Edwards?"

"Are you Alabama too?"

"Hang on you two," Hardy tells them, keeping his voice low as well, "slow down, I'm not from Alabama. We can sit here for a minute and talk, but this whole situation looks like it's going to get very busy at any moment."

"Yeah, it will. We know what we're doing."

"We're in between."

"Okay, sure," Hardy tells them. He can't really find the words. The whole of the scenario is so amazing and impressive. And intense. He's stunned.

He's also surprised the two boys came over. Their job in the crew and their responsibilities with the explosives is so dangerous. The three of them sit and think for a moment.

"Where are the two of you from? Where's home for you?"

"We're contraband." The two are quick and ready to respond to anything put to them. "Yeah, we're contraband."

One of the two boys may be slightly older. His voice is slightly older. Both of them equally bright, confident, one a little bit weary.

"We're from different places before this." One after the other.

"Before we took up with the Navy."

"Two plantations up the Mississippi."

"Two. Then, lucky for us, they started this war."

"It is darn sure lucky for us, cause we're gettin' paid."

"Yeah, and I'm gettin' paid more than you."

"You know it's not true. Pay attention, the Midshipman is getting a look on his face."

"I know what I'm doing more than you."

"How many powder bags you have left?"

Hardy grabs a break in the crosstalk. "So the two of you are freed slaves? Is that what you were before this, this ship?"

"Freed, that sounds good."

"Yeah, that sounds good, not as good as this."

"Nah, we're not with the freed. We ran off."

"Contraband with the Navy is as good as it gets."

"Better than anything."

"But the two of you," Hardy keeps it low, "you're just kids."

"Navy doesn't care."

"Yeah, we just told them we were older, and they didn't care. They have this war, so they don't care. Good for us."

"Darn good for us. We do laundry and some deck scrubbing and make even more. Darn good for us."

"So…" Hardy finds himself overwhelmed by the two boys, the scene, and all the explosives. It's hard to believe it all. "So you two have been friends for a long time?"

"Yeah, we have, since the beginning."

"What do you mean, the beginning?" Hardy asks.

"Since we were little kids. We're brothers. Are you saying you can't tell?"

"Elijah, knock it off. I told you."

Hardy can tell now that the one boy is older. His voice and his manner are just plain older.

The older boy turns to Hardy. "He keeps saying we're brothers, but we ain't."

"We are, and you know it," Elijah says. They've had this conversation probably hundreds of times. It's nothing to get worked up about now. "You can say what you want to this man here, but you know it."

Hardy turns to his left, "You're Elijah." He turns to his right. "So, what's your name? You don't have to tell me if you don't want to. You think I'm a man?"

"Marcus, up the Mississippi." The boy to the right tells him quickly. He's diverted his attention back to his Midshipman.

"Sure you're a man," Elijah says. "Compared to me and Marcus and the rest of the monkeys down here, you're a man. And you got yellow hair. We ain't seen that, so you must be."

"It's not really yellow."

"I just asked you, and you didn't tell me back." Marcus leans forward to ask Elijah directly, "How many powder bags you have left?"

"I have two. That's how many I'm supposed to have."

"Alright for now." Marcus sits back against the wall. "I'm just taking care for you."

"Let me ask you this," Hardy starts up again. "If you're both runaways from the plantation, why not keep running and get off this ship? It's so dangerous here, you could get seriously hurt. Why not keep running, like to New Orleans or some city where you would be better taken care of?"

"Mister," Elijah snaps back, "you're crazy."

"We don't want to be on our own," Marcus says, finally slowing himself down. "The Navy is the best we can get. We're just boys, Mister; we don't know how to take good care. How would we eat? We don't have family to show us all that."

"But surely on the plantation they gave you meals, didn't they? And the plantation must surely be safer than this. This is a battle being fought here. Men are getting blown apart. You've seen that. You must have. How can a plantation be worse than this?"

Both boys look down.

"The suffering," Marcus says. His voice separates from his breath.

Elijah doesn't speak.

The three sit still and quiet for a moment. A long moment.

Across the deck, there are only a few clinks and clanks every so often. The entire group of sailors on the gun deck are waiting for it to come. Any minute.

Hardy throws his arms behind the shoulders of the two boys and pulls the three of them together. "I'm just glad I got to meet you, Marcus and Elijah. I don't think I've ever met two sailors braver than the two of you."

"Yeah, we're brave," right away from Elijah.

"Yeah, we're brave." The same words from Marcus are very different. They're heavy and touched by the sadness.

"New Orleans," Marcus says, "I have heard of it. I'll bet that's where you're headed, isn't it?"

"It is where I'm headed. I'm not from here, like the two of you. I have to get to a place where I am supposed to be, or at least be going in that direction. Does that make sense to you?"

"Makes no sense at all," from Elijah.

"I understand," Marcus tells Hardy. He reaches behind his head to take Hardy's arm off of his shoulder and puts the arm back on Hardy's lap.

"Elijah and I don't have a direction, so this is good enough for us two."

Marcus reaches behind Elijah and takes Hardy's arm off of his shoulder.

"You have your direction," Marcus tells Hardy, "and you should get to it, and I mean right now. This shooting will start by my next words, count on it, and you'll be stuck even more than you are now. It'd be best to get up and get up to the deck above and right off this ship while you still have the time."

"I think you're probably right," Hardy tells them. "See how smart the two of you are."

"I'm smarter than him."

"You're not smarter than me, but you are smarter than Winston. That man got kicked in the head by his own mule."

Both of the powder monkeys—the two boys, Elijah and Marcus, from two plantations upriver, who could be brothers—share a giggle.

"I wish there was a way," Hardy says quietly, "a way for you two to come with me. I'm traveling with an older guy. He's up on top talking with the

Captain, but I know he'd want you to come with us. We're going downriver, no matter what."

"You think you know how to get out of this harbor?" Marcus asks Hardy.

"I know we can get out of this harbor. I just know it. And I know it would be better for you two to come with us to New Orleans. It's a city where they treat kids like you, African American, black boys, freed, runaways—they'd treat as equal. Equal as these days get."

"I told you he was crazy."

"It's not crazy, Elijah," Hardy says. "It's why they're fighting this war. To get black people free."

"We know that," Marcus tells Hardy.

Hardy turns his attention to Bradley, twenty feet away on the other side of the cannon. He tries to get his attention by watching his eyes and waiting for a moment when he looks back.

He watches for several minutes and can see that Midshipman Edwards has his hands full. Hardy abruptly stands up and turns to face Elijah and Marcus.

He stands facing the two boys for several minutes. He stands, considering how he can bring the two boys with him. Why he would do that, and then there's Bradley and the others in the gun crew, and Mr. Knight. Where is Mr. Knight?

A cannon shell strikes the river and explodes a mountain of water fifteen feet in front of the ironclad. The concussion shock smacks the ship.

On the hurricane deck, Knight and Captain Walker are hurled backward, and they roll and slide across the deck, backwards twenty feet. The explosion showers the deck with harbor water.

At the bow end of the gun deck, sailors are thrown backward, hitting either wood or iron. The cannons, every one of them, are shoved back several feet.

Hardy is thrown against the wall, where he had just been sitting. Elijah and Marcus still sit.

Midshipman Bradley is violently thrown against the iron of the Dahlgren. He lies on the deck's floor beside the cannon.

Representative Knight struggles to get up. His legs can barely hold his weight. His knees—in piercing pain—won't let him stand straight.

Captain Walker, a few feet away, hasn't yet tried to stand. He rolls off his stomach to face upwards, still dazed and deafened by the shock.

Bradley, on his back, puts a hand to his chest. Maybe a broken rib.

All around, sailors roll and twist, trying to get back up. Most are able to stand.

Hardy quickly checks to see how badly the two boys might be hurt. At first glance, they seem okay. Mr. Knight, where is he?

Hardy bends at the waist and pushes Marcus next to Elijah, as close as possible. "I'll be right back. Don't move." He quickly straightens up and looks around to see other damage. Stepping over sailors on the wooden floor, he immediately makes his way to the steps leading up to the hurricane deck and Mr. Knight. He takes one quick look back at the two boys and Bradley on the ground, who looks back at him—for that one instant.

The second shell is a direct hit to the ironclad at the rear of the ship. It catches the paddle wheel. A massive white hot explosion rips open the side of the ship. A deafening blast and the shrieking torn shards of iron shoot through the gun deck, striking walls and cannons. The entire back half of the deck is instantly filled with a blossoming ball of fire.

The shock and pain of torn skin are the first cries from the sailors all across the gun deck, the first sound that follows the cracking thunder of the blast. Blood screams of instant agony. Sailors too close, their shredded bodies carpet the deck's floor. Farther back, sailors look to their bodies to discover torn arms and legs, bodies sliced by the shrapnel iron and wooden splinters, fired out in all directions like miniature spears. Those sailors still standing have their uniforms streaked with fire, hair and skin burned. Farther still from the blast, Midshipman Edwards's crew are blown down hard, burned, cut, and bleeding. The guy, Winston, lies face down, his back an open wound. His body doesn't move. He can't possibly be alive.

Bradley—already lying flat on the deck—escapes the shrapnel but not the splinters. The moment the concussion boom dies and the fireball passes over, he bends his neck forward to look to his legs, peppered with splinters, mostly small, except for the one. Elijah peeks his head out of the tight ball he and his brother have made of themselves. Too far to the side, the fireball only grazed them. The back of Marcus's uniform jacket is blackened. He cautiously looks up. He's looking for Hardy; he sees Midshipman Edwards on the ground by the cannon; his face is white; the trousers of his dirty blue uniform are turning a dull red. Bradley's back arches rigid, his fists clenched tight, his face quickly distorted with grimace. His jaw clamps his mouth shut tight. He will not cry out.

Marcus pokes his head up from the arm he has over Elijah's shoulders. Just enough to see Hardy lying on the stairs leading to the upper deck, his body face down on the stairs. His legs are twisted. Awkwardly wrong. The back of his t-shirt and the back of his head singed black. A piece of wood, like a table knife, sticks out of the back of his bare arm above the elbow. He doesn't move at all.

The blast end of the ship begins to drop. The gun deck's floor is becoming a ramp. The ironclad is taking water, now the stinking smell of river steam.

Representative Knight and Captain Walker are witnesses to the blast's fireball strike. They're far enough to the front and low enough on the deck to escape the violent barrage of shredded metal and splintered wood. A vertical column of fire and black smoke erupts from the ripped open side of the ship.

Captain Walker finds his footing and gets up to look around. Across the deck, the pilot house appears intact. Above, the thirty-foot smokestacks are in bad shape. One is split and leaning badly. Its black coal smoke pours out of a jagged tear only a few feet from its base. To the back of the ship, the paddle wheel is destroyed. Its iron housing is ripped open. What's left of the paddles are a tangled mess of lumber.

Like a stroke victim in the first minutes realizing life has survived, Knight sits up in the pure shock of the moment. He raises his arm to put one finger to his temple and keeps it there. Walker begins to hear again. The ringing deafness recedes slowly to reveal the calling out wails of pain, scattered cries from shattered men.

The back-and-forth shelling between the Vicksburg battery and the Union flotilla has returned to its full glory and stays steady. The city on the bluff, engulfed in flames, the acrid smoke its blanket. The ironclads in the harbor are moving downriver, still at their steady pace. Captain Walker's ship swings wildly toward the western shore of the river. The ship is crawling toward shallow water and the mud flats.

Hardy! Knight's only thought.

The Representative stands; pain and shock are nothing. He strides across the deck toward the stairs going down. As he passes through the thick of the coal smoke, it chokes him. He bends at the waist to cough it up and spit it out. He keeps going and reaches the stairs. One hand on the railing, and one step at a time, he's down to the short wooden deck at the front of the ship. There are several sailors there, huddled, holding each other up. Knight turns to the stairs leading down to the gun deck below…

Marcus pulls himself up. He looks quickly down his legs and across each arm. He grabs each shoulder of Elijah's jacket and pulls him up and presses the boy against the wall. He holds him there while he checks his body for anything, any cut, any hole, any blood.

The two of them have made it through the blast. Only the jacket has been scorched. They both look around the gun deck, and the sight of it all is too much. They can't move. What should they do?

Guttural moans come from every direction. Sailors get to each other to see what can be done. Tourniquets are torn out of uniform jackets, and the cloth of their trousers torn off below the knees. Anything nearby will do.

Two of Midshipman Bradley's gun crew reach him and immediately start pulling splinters where they can and put pressure where blood is steady.

Marcus and Elijah, without speaking, know what needs to be done. Marcus pushes Elijah toward their Midshipman, and when they reach him, the two crouch down and put palms on wounds. Keep the pressure.

Marcus looks to Hardy over on the stairs. His eyes widen and with one panicked gulp of nasty air he puts each of his palms to his little brother's hands on Bradley's wounds; he pushes them hard and then pulls himself away from Elijah to dash over to Hardy. One step away, he stops. He sees the one splinter in the arm, but that's not enough. Suddenly, at the top of the stairs, right above Hardy, a man appears. The man has rushed to the top of the stairs, but now he stops. He's not a sailor. There isn't a uniform. Marcus knows who he is.

Hardy, face down on the stairs, lies still.

Knight sees the splinter, but it's not enough to keep him down this way. So still.

Without taking the breath, Knight's lungs heave with sudden air. Without thinking, thoughts rush in. "No!" Knight's shout is not a wail of sorrow but a boardroom bark of insistence.

"Do something," Marcus says softly.

Representative Knight feels the hesitation. Hardy will shift his weight or make a sound. But he doesn't move. Knight takes the steps down slowly to his side. He sits on the short metal step and puts both of his hands on Hardy's back. He stays that way for another moment. The back of Hardy's head is singed but not burned.

In an instant, Knight starts to do what's necessary. "Come up here. Take his arm," he commands the boy below. "Hold it straight out as I turn him over. Don't let that splinter touch the step."

Marcus quickly grabs Hardy's forearm and holds it straight out. Knight takes Hardy's shoulders and lifts the weight of his body to turn him over. The stairs are a difficult place to turn him, but that is exactly what they do. Hardy's body is wedged into the stairs. Marcus holds his arm out. The splinter touches nothing. Hardy's arm is bleeding badly.

All around them is chaos, with the loud hissing of steam pouring out of the hole torn open on the far side of the gun deck. The melodic moans of the men come from everywhere as the iron ship veers into the river's mud.

Knight bends to put his ear close to Hardy's mouth.

He's breathing.

Knight puts his hands on both sides of Hardy's head, first his temples, then his cheeks. "Son, come on back," he says quietly, close to Hardy's ear. He taps lightly on his cheek. "Come on back."

Only the loud hissing steam.

Chapter Twenty One

Sittin' ducks

Hardy's head jerks forward. His eyes flash open. Wide and blank. He takes one huge and deep breath. His jaw clamps shut. His mouth is closed tight and holds it in. His chest swells full and stays that way. Then he blows it out, loud as the steam.

"There you are." Knight throws his arms around Hardy's shoulders.

"There you are, Son." Knight kisses the top of his head. "You came back to us. Do you know where you are?"

"Representative Knight, you're here," Hardy says, working his way through. "Is my dad okay?"

"Sure he is, Son. He's back at the Winnebago with Alfred. They're waiting for you."

"Sure they are," Hardy says with soft confidence. "I should give him a call."

"We'll do that."

Knight moves his arms under him and lifts his weight. "Don't let that arm touch a thing," he tells Marcus.

"We're going to give Buddy a call, but let's get down off these steps and take a look at you." Knight shifts his position to lift Hardy at the shoulders. "Can you stand, Son?"

Hardy pulls himself up off the steps, and Knight lifts him the rest of the way. They manage to get off the steps and down to the wooden floor of the deck. Knight gently puts Hardy's head down on the deck and moves to straighten him out. As Knight is circling Hardy's body while straightening his legs to get him flat on his back, he looks over to the steps. Two of the dark iron steps drip with Hardy's blood. Way too much blood.

"I know what to do about this," Marcus tells Knight, his voice much older than the young boy Knight sees.

Hardy is looking straight up, watching the blurry cloud of smoke and steam pass over.

"I know him," Marcus tells Knight, still holding Hardy's arm out straight. Slowly, Hardy's head drops to the side; his breathing, shallow and low. His eyes slowly blink a few times. With the last one, they stay closed. Knight quickly moves close, face-to-face.

"Son, we need to get you fixed up," Knight says quietly.

Hardy stays still. A moment passes.

His breathing low, "I thought we were in New Orleans," he tells Knight, his voice halved, his eyes still closed.

Another moment, then he turns his head slightly and opens his eyes to see Mr. Knight. "I saw the people there. They were happy to see I finally made it. I told them we had come a long way. They knew that already."

Knight takes hold of Hardy's chin and holds it tight. "Son, we need to get you fixed up." He looks up at the steam and takes a heavy breath, then yells out. "So we can get off this fucking boat!" Knight's voice mixes with the rest of the shouting from all over the gun deck.

With that, the stinging pain of the splinter begins.

"Shit." Hardy can feel it now. His body tightens, and he lifts his head. "Fucking holy shit," he says, looking directly at Knight, "this really fucking hurts."

Knight looks over to the young boy Marcus. "Okay, let's get this splinter out."

"Yes, Sir." Marcus carefully puts Hardy's arm down on the deck. He turns and dashes off in the direction of the ripped apart ship. He quickly becomes one of the many bodies crisscrossing through the smoke of the crowded gun deck, sailors doing what they can to patch bloody wounds and stop the flowing blood.

Knight moves to take a closer look at the splinter and the damage it's done. "It's not as bad as it looks." Six inches stick out from each side. It's bad.

Hardy's sharp groans, coming with every short, rapid breath, are dampened by his clamped-tight jaw. "Well, that's good," is barely heard.

Mr. Knight holds Hardy's arm out. No unnecessary moves. He looks to see both sides—the front and back—of the arm. It is worse than he thought. The spike of wood has penetrated the back of Hardy's arm, in the muscle midway between his elbow and shoulder. The opposite end is sticking out way too far. The splinter has shot through Hardy's upper arm, and it's still bleeding way too much. Knight will give Marcus another minute to see what type of medical tool he might bring, but Knight looks around to see what others are using for bandages. He needs to get the splinter out and clean the wound. He's looking for anything he can use.

"Are we getting it pulled out?" Hardy grimaces. "Should we call 911?"

Knight rubs Hardy's forehead. "Sure, we are. I'm getting a better look, then we'll see what needs to be done."

Marcus appears out of the bodies and smoke and slides in next to Knight and Hardy. He's carrying three dull metal tools. Knight can immediately see what Marcus has brought will be of no use. They're filthy, and frankly, they're frightening.

One tool is a capital saw. Clearly, Marcus has seen amputation. The other two tools are just no use.

"Son," Knight has to shout at Marcus to be heard, "we need alcohol and bandages."

The immediate look on the young boy's face tells Knight all he needs to know. Sterilization hasn't yet reached the Mississippi.

"Whiskey!" Knight calls across to Marcus. "The officers must have whiskey somewhere on this ship."

"Yes, Sir," Marcus shouts back, "in the quarters. But for right now? Don't you want it for after?"

"No, Son, right now. Go as fast as you can and bring as much as you can carry. Whatever the rest of these sailors are using for bandages, grab some of what they have, and, Son, you need to hurry."

Without saying a word, Marcus turns and darts back into the melee.

"Alright, Hardy, we'll give that young man another minute to get what we need." Knight will keep talking slowly and quietly. "And then we'll get on with getting this piece of wood out of your arm; get it wrapped up. We both know I can't paddle that boat of ours by myself."

"No, Sir, you sure cannot." Hardy's voice trembles. Knight hears the panic in his voice. Hardy knows what has to happen next.

"So," Knight continues calmly, "the young African boy and the two of you were talking." He gives it a moment. "That boy is far too young to be here in this harbor. What kind of sense does that make?"

"It doesn't make any sense, Mr. Knight," Hardy says quietly, talking seems to help.

"As soon as we get your arm cleaned and bandaged, we'll take that young man with us. That's the best we can do for him."

"And his brother." Hardy's voice is drifting.

"And his brother. We'll get both of them off this ship and back where they belong, out of this." Knight lowers his voice. "We'll be back on our way down the Mississippi and back on our trip, our adventure."

Knight realizes he can't wait for the whiskey; there might not even be whiskey. The splinter has to come out. He again looks at both sides of the wound, entry and exit. There is no way around it. There's no easy, painless way. Knight again moves in close to Hardy to speak softly and as calmly as possible. "Son, there's no easy way."

"I know that, Mr. Knight." Hardy takes longer and deeper breaths. "There's no ambulance or doctor."

"No, there isn't."

Knight looks around, and he picks up a piece of wood a couple of feet away, a much larger splinter of wood.

"Son, your arm is bleeding way too much with that splinter stuck in there. We have to pull it out."

"I know that, Mr. Knight."

"I'll pull it out, and you bite down on this piece of wood. We don't need you biting your tongue off as well, do we?"

"Don't worry, Mr. Knight, I've seen Netflix westerns."

Hardy reaches up with his other arm and puts a ten-inch piece of wood sideways in his mouth and bites down hard. There are sharp points on the wood that prick his tongue. His heart is racing, and his breathing turns shallow and fast.

The thought of water and cleansing crosses Knight's mind until he realizes the futility of it. There is no clean water. He takes Hardy's arm in both hands and holds it to feel the weight.

Through his tight jaw and the wood clamped tight in his teeth, Hardy cries a muffled scream. His mouth closes tighter around the wood, and his breathing through his nose is loud and fast.

With one hand, Knight uses his thumb and index finger to clamp the arm, just at the spot of the splinter.

The guttural cries come from deep in his throat, the instant agony of unbearable pain. His back arches rigid.

With the other hand, Knight gently, firmly takes the splinter between his thumb and finger and pulls steady. A little harder. Steady, a little more. Steady, almost done—it's out.

Hardy's muffled scream is too much to bear.

Knight takes a deep breath, drops the splinter, and pushes with both palms on the wound. The bleeding is quickly much worse. Hardy's rigid, arched back eases a little.

They both stay still for a long minute.

Mr. Knight, with both palms squeezing Hardy's arm, is on his knees with his head down, waiting through the minute. The Representative's eyes begin to fill with tears. One or two run down his face. His breaths are heavy sighs. It's unbearable to see the young man in such pain.

Hardy is heaving fast breaths through his nose, the wood still clamped tight in his teeth. He's twelve years old; he's too young for a cinematic moment of bravery.

He starts to cry very hard, and it's painful to hear. His sobbing trembles from his chest, and his body rocks with each gulp of air. He knows the pain will begin to fade, but it doesn't.

There's nothing more to say. Hardy lies in excruciating pain, crying inconsolably, lying in agony on the wooden floor of the ship just torn apart on a river where he doesn't belong. Mr. Knight at his side.

Marcus appears, and he quickly kneels next to Knight, holding a tin can in one hand and a cotton cloth in the other. He waits for Knight to see he is there. He knows what has just happened. Knight sees the young Marcus out of the corner of his eye; he sees the can and leans over, holding Hardy's arm firm, and he smells the can and what's in it.

"Son," Knight says quietly to Hardy, "there's one more step in this."

Without fuss, Knight takes the can from Marcus and gives it one last smell. He puts the can to his lips, tastes it, and spits it out.

He brushes Hardy's forehead, holds his arm more upright, and pours a quick, steady pour of the whiskey into the open wound of Hardy's wounded arm.

A growling, raspy groan is let loose from Hardy's neck and chest. Loud, excruciating, and unbearable. Hardy's back jolts up off the deck, arched farther up than before, more rigid than before. The muffled scream moves up Hardy's throat, up to his clenched jaw and gritted teeth. The cry of pain explodes out of his mouth, a wailing yell of cry and howl, a full, long exhale of a jagged roar adding to the crying and tears.

The wood stick in his mouth drops to the side. His breaths are furious and shallow, more than before. The wail of pain and the stinging through the rapid breaths. Too much to bear.

Every half-dozen breaths, the crying wail is broken by a deeper breath. Again and again. An impossible stinging, a whole body of stinging.

Hardy puts his other arm over his face and covers his eyes. He cries into his arm and his covered face. He stays that way.

Another sudden explosion rocks the deck, this one not as loud, not as bad. River water has met the fire and hot metal of the ship's engine. A blast of gray steam rolls through the gun deck. The back of the ship inches deeper into the Mississippi.

Hardy hears the explosion and pulls his arm away from his eyes. In the ceiling above, the patterns in the wood with clouds passing through. Some far away country. The place where people watch the sky, a dreamy place, high above. The clouds chase each other off to someplace farther still; the awful smell, the shouting, and the ship, the ironclad, the harbor. The river.

Hardy looks across to see that Mr. Knight is right there beside him. He's bandaged his arm. Knight leans in and tells him as calmly as possible, "Son, we're getting off this ship. Let's try to stand up."

Hardy runs his hand across the bandage on his arm, touching it only lightly. He can feel now that he is reaching the other side of it. The worst might be over, the stabbing sting of it is dying out. He tries to lean forward. Knight helps him lift his upper body off the floor. Looking around, he sees Marcus sitting beside Mr. Knight. He looks deeper into the deck. Groups of men huddled over other men, lying on their backs, through the clouds of steam and smoke. On the farthest side, smoke billows up out of the ship.

Bradley.

Hardy turns to Knight. "Where's Bradley?" Then he remembers and turns to Marcus. "Where's the Midshipman?"

"He's by the cannon, Sir," Marcus tells him, "with Elijah and the others."

Hardy lifts one leg at the knee and tries to push himself up to stand. It doesn't work; he doesn't yet have that strength. Knight gets behind him and lifts under Hardy's one arm, and with that, Hardy is standing. Feeling his weight and breathing deep to put himself past the pain, he takes one step and then another. Knight helps him from behind until he realizes Hardy is walking in the opposite direction from the steps to the deck above.

"Son, we're going the other way. We're going up, and we're getting off."

Knight says it only once. He can feel the determination in Hardy's steps. There is more happening here than he knows. Slow steps toward the cannon; already from this distance, Hardy can see Bradley lying next to the cannon. He doesn't move. The young boy Elijah is next to him on his knees with his head down.

Hardy tries to walk a little faster. Knight helps him. They reach the back side of the cannon, and Hardy stops.

Marcus and Elijah look at each other. They don't exchange anything other than a familiar recognition of the obvious. Hardy waits. He looks at the young Elijah. Why is that little kid even here?

The ironclad moans as the ship's hot engine is twisted by the cold river.

He takes the last steps toward Midshipman Bradley lying on the deck. He stands next to him, and he tries to get down on his knees. Mr. Knight helps him down.

Hardy kneels there, lost in the moment. Can a moment of time take back what has already been given?

Hardy reaches out and puts his hand on Bradley's chest. He keeps it there. There is no sigh of breath. Not a beat of heart.

He straightens Bradley's coat with his one hand and brushes off the lapels. Quietly, carefully, he brushes soot off his young friend's forehead, the hair off his face, and lets his hand stay there, feeling the skin. A still deeper sobbing in his breath shudders his body; he drops his head, leans forward, and puts his face sideways on Bradley's chest. He says only to himself, "I want to go home."

In the next moment, Hardy is changed. He stands. He shrugs off any help from Mr. Knight, and turns to Elijah, still next to Bradley. "Come on, get up; we're getting off this ship; you're coming with me!" He turns back to Marcus, who has watched it all. "Get your brother, you're both coming with me."

Hardy moves to gather the two boys, taking them by the shoulder with his good arm. Neither of them say a word. Knight is part of this. He follows what Hardy has decided for them all.

The group takes determined steps to the stairs leading to the upper deck. Hardy keeps them together, and when they reach the steps, he lightly pushes Elijah to go up first, then Marcus. When the two are most of the way up, he turns to Mr. Knight and motions a 'you go first' with his one arm. Knight climbs the steps. He follows.

Hardy struggles to get up the stairs to the deck, but the pain in his arm is nothing to the determination pushing him forward. He steps out onto the short deck. It's higher off the water than when he and Bradley were there. The whole deck is an uphill slope.

Out in the open, the harbor is still hurling metal between the ironclads and the battery. The pungent smoke and the stink of powder still blow across all of it, and the fires on the Vicksburg bluff haven't diminished in the least. None of this insanity is lost on either Hardy or Knight. The Union flotilla will continue until they make it past the battery. The Confederates will not hold back until the last of the ships are out of reach. There might be a better time to get off this ship and head out on their own, take their chances, but neither Hardy nor Knight care to consider the option.

There are half a dozen sailors with blackened faces and torn uniforms standing next to the waist-high iron barrier around the deck. They're watching the front of the boat slide closer to the shore of the river.

One sailor sees Knight, Hardy, and the two powder monkeys come up from below. "We'll run aground in no time at all," he cries out.

"Then we'll just admit," Knight announces to the group, "that God has given us his plan." In an instant, he regrets the words.

"I get what your thoughts are telling you, whoever you are," the sailor calls out, "but it's the Capitan who calls to abandon the ship."

Representative Knight looks at Hardy, tired and in too much pain. He can see what must be done. Knight takes Hardy carefully by the shoulder and moves him away from the rim. He pulls Marcus and Elijah to stand next to Hardy, all out of harm's way, at least for the moment.

Knight walks over to the sailor, who's shared comments on the situation. "Indeed, it's the Capitan who calls it," Knight tells the sailor in his diplomatic, power voice. "I rank with the Captain, and I give orders of my own."

"Yes, Sir," the sailor complies, along with two or three other sailors standing there.

"The small boat, brought up and tied to the ship," Knight delivers.

The sailors nod.

"I want that boat brought right here to the front of the ship, and I need that to happen right away."

"Yes, Sir," their immediate reply, in unison.

"Do we know the whereabouts of the small boat?" Knight is now in full command. "The bateau, if you don't know the name of it."

"Yes Sir, tied just at the back, starboard."

"Then that shouldn't take long at all."

"No Sir," in unison.

"Let's hustle men; there's no extra time. We'll all need to get off this ship, an order I can call as well as the Captain."

Three of the sailors scramble up the slope of the black iron, up to the deck above, not using the steps. They make their way to the back, where the bateau is still securely tied, avoiding the burning steam.

One sailor still standing on the short deck turns to Knight, "This ship will run up the shallow water in no time at all. There won't be enough water to float your bateau, Sir."

"You have no idea how flat the bottom of our little bateau is," Knight tells him. A smile crosses his face.

Representative Knight walks back to Hardy and the two young boys. He's taken charge of the situation. Stands for a moment, collecting himself, straightening himself, he scans the river shore and the harbor, organizing the priorities of the plan in his head, preparing to tell each what they will do. He looks at the three boys, and in the beat of a heart, his sudden determination turns to nothing. The two young African kids, so unbearably young, no worldly business being here, tired and dirty and no idea what will come next or what to do next. Their Midshipman has been killed. His body lies just down below. And the look of Hardy. He needs food and a bed. *If his father were here, that would be the first order of business. And he needs serious help, serious medical attention, and where in God's name to get it? Let me think. Jesus Christ, it's New Orleans. It really is New Orleans.*

"This is what we're going to do, guys." Knight bends to their level. "We're going to get in the bateau, and we'll skirt through the rest of this harbor without being spotted, and we'll get back to the business of getting down this Mississippi River, all the way to New Orleans, all four of us. That is what we are going to do." He straightens himself, shoulders back. "The sailor is bringing the bateau up alongside of this miserable ship, right over here, and we'll climb down to it and be on our way. No goodbyes, and certainly no words with the Captain Walker, wherever he is."

All of them are quiet for a minute.

Hardy sits. Marcus helps him.

Elijah, the youngest, takes a quick look at his brother, "Sir, Marcus and myself cannot get off this ship and go down in a little boat with you."

"Yes, you most certainly can go downriver with us. You have no other place to go."

"Sir," Marcus steps in, "my little brother and I cannot go with you because we belong here."

"I'm not discussing this, Son. You'll come with Hardy and I. It's in your best interest. Look at this ship. It's a disaster, and you're… you're not…"

"We were with the slaves," Marcus says to Knight, a decidedly confident young man. "We're free now, with the free slaves. That doesn't mean much, not to you. For sure it can't mean too much, but to us, it means a whole lot. We are part of this army, and we belong with the war, and with this ship, and these other sailors. This is the place where we belong. You go off wherever you think you'll be better, but my brother and I won't be going with you."

Knight is somewhat astonished by the boy, but he won't insist. "You are a brave young man, both of you."

A sudden thud comes from the front of the ship, and the entire hulk shudders to a stop, stuck in place. The mangled ironclad has met the inevitable Mississippi mud.

Everyone on the deck rushes to look over the side, except for Hardy.

The ironclad is more pointed toward the shore than parallel to it. The shrubs along the bank are twenty to thirty feet from the deck. The water is shallow. It's difficult to tell how shallow. It's a swirling, muddy current.

As the group stands, calculating the mud versus river water depth, several more sailors come up to the short deck. They're wearing bandages and lean heavily on each other. The gun deck below is clearing out. Most of the sailors have made it up to the hurricane deck. Knight looks up to see them lined up along the side, all of them waiting for the call. The smoke and steam still pour out the back of the ship, Captain Walker nowhere in sight.

"That's it then," sailors are saying. "We're sittin' ducks."

"If we wait for the Captain, we'll all be blown to hell."

"Sir." Knight hears the sailor's call from the hurricane deck above. He's pulling the bateau by rope along the side of the ironclad, toward Knight and the front of the ship. Knight moves to get a better look.

There it is. "That miserable little boat never looked better." Knight turns to Hardy. "It's all in one piece."

Hardy gives Mr. Knight the slightest of a smile, the best he can do.

The back of the ironclad is sinking deeper into the water and the river mud. The steam hisses and billows. Great clouds of it cut across the side of the ship facing the shore. The sailor pulling the bateau has brought the little boat almost directly under where Knight stands waiting. The sailors lining the side of the ship are silhouetted in the gray smoke. They're waiting. No one seems to know exactly what the wait is for or how long they'll wait. Suddenly, toward the middle of the ship, one brave sailor makes the first daring move against the river, the mud, and the sinking ship. He gets himself over the iron rim of the deck and slides halfway down the iron slope, and he jumps.

The poor man is immediately stuck in the mud up to his waist.

The entire crew, facing the shore, is stunned by the sight of it. The first moment is dead silence. No one moves. The breeze seems to have stopped itself, so the steam sits stuck in the air. The sailor in the mud turns his torso to face his comrades, throws his arms in the air, and shouts out, "Come on boys, pigs in the pigpen!"

The audience immediately rips into hoots and hollers, sidesplitting laughter, pushing and shoving, men bent over at the waist unable to contain the full belly laughs, an absolute pandemonium of hysterical laughter. Knight can't believe it. What an unimaginable scenario. What this world is made of, his only thought.

And then, as if that weren't enough, the hilarity subsides, if only just a little, and another sailor makes the plunge, then another, and another. All of them stick at various heights depending on their weight. One portly sailor, almost to his chest. Several of the sailors start to toss the bales of hay into the river, and then they jump on them. The bales help a little, better than no bale.

Knight turns back to see Hardy sitting with his back up against the side of the ironclad, his head down. At that very moment, he knows time is now the issue. He turns back to see where the bateau is tied and how to get to it. The little bateau is still floating in maybe twelve inches of water, hard to tell.

Within minutes, dozens of sailors are trudging through the Mississippi mud to get to the river's bank. They've made a row of hay bales, and they pull themselves along. They're making it to the river bank and getting up the side. In no time, several of them are standing on firm ground, and they help the others behind them.

As Representative Knight walks back to Hardy, Marcus stops him to give his final words. "Sir, get your son off the ship and take him down the river as far as you have to, to get some kind of help. I've seen this before, and it's gonna get worse. You probably already know that."

Knight puts a hand on the young sailor's shoulder.

"That's exactly what I'm going to do. And what about you and your brother? Shouldn't you jump with the others?"

"We'll go see to the Midshipman, then we'll see what is best for us. Don't you worry, me and my brother know how to get off this ship when the time comes for us."

"I believe you do, Son. I believe you do."

The two of them walk the rest of the way over to Hardy and Elijah.

"You two find a place for yourselves," Knight tells them, his last words.

Knight lifts Hardy under the arm, and Hardy stands, ready to get down to the bateau. He pulls slightly on the arm of Knight's jacket to help pull himself away from the two boys. The time is now to walk away from the brothers. "Goodbye," his only word.

Knight and Hardy walk to the side of the short deck, climb over the rim, and inch their way down the slope of the ironclad, ten feet, to reach the bateau. Hardy steps in first. The little boat takes his weight as familiar as family. He steps to the back, and with his one hand, he takes hold of the rudder. Knight steps in and quickly sits down on the middle seat, takes up both oars, and readies himself for the routine.

Both Marcus and Elijah toss the rope down to the little boat, and they both stand for a minute, then disappear back into the ship. Knight watches them, and as they turn back, he looks up to see Captain Walker looking down. The man has not one expression on his face. Not animosity and not farewell.

Knight looks over to Hardy, and he starts to paddle, pulling on the oars with the full of his weight. He's able to pull the bateau away from the mud flats and back into better water. The Mississippi current hits the boat and sweeps it along downriver. He keeps the boat as close to the shore as he can manage without tempting the mud. Already he's passed one ironclad that has slowed itself for some reason and found a good place to hide behind another, the next in line. He'll keep the bateau in rank with the flotilla and skirt around when he can. Good speed, and they pass the last of the ironclads. Open river ahead.

"Look at that, Hardy," Knight says into the air. He turns on his seat to see the reaction. Hardy watches the city as they pass. There appears to be fewer flames, but smoke still billows up like dark, low-hanging clouds. The bateau crosses the line. Vicksburg, now and forever behind them.

The bateau is out of the harbor. They're on their way back down the river. When they come out of the horseshoe bend, the river picks up speed, a welcome relief to Knight. He's already got sore palms from the rough wood.

The all of the ironclads is less now. Soon a memory, a story stuck in the mud with all the rest. For now, it's hay bales to New Orleans.

Chapter Twenty Two

Ripples on the surface

"There's still more to it." Hardy's voice is low. The words stick in his ragged breath.

Knight hears the resignation. "I see them."

Less than a half-mile ahead are the rest of the Union ships holding their position. An astonishing sight, the huge wooden sailing ships, the Union Navy's sloops of war, masts shooting up in the air, a dozen or more giant sails on each, cannons sticking out every which way.

The bateau moves steadily closer. Mixed in with the sloops, a dozen or more "double-enders," the Union's newest gunboat. Every bit the size of the big sail ships, the double-enders have massive paddle wheels on each side of the ship. The sails take the wind, and the giant wheels allow the boats to back out in reverse, which proves a critical adaptation for low-water rivers. The ships give the Union the advantage.

Soon enough, the river pulls the bateau into the scene. Each one of the magnificent ships holds the fluttering American's flag beating at the wind, the most striking color throughout. The scale of it all is testimony to every history book's full-color illustration. An overwhelming impression. The black harbor and the filthy ironclads have nothing to compare. Knight paddles the bateau with his full determination, but the sight the river offers here is an exhibition beyond. He keeps to the urgency but is overwhelmed by the spectacle.

Get past all of this military, Knight's mantra. He keeps watch as they pass alongside, but he keeps to the oars. Every look out to this flotilla is followed by a look back at Hardy at the rudder. His face turning whiter as time passes, but Hardy can't look away either.

As the bateau makes progress, Knight's idea to skirt past the fleet—on the Louisiana side of the river—stay out of the mud, and go unnoticed or at least unchallenged is made all the more possible by the many other small boats mingling with the monsters.

With the sloops and the double-enders at anchor, the generosity of the Mississippi pulls the bateau quickly through. Without the slightest confrontation, the Union Navy, preoccupied with its well-deserved glory, is disappearing behind them. Knight and Hardy exchange one long and deep look into each other's faces. What a relief. Not another chapter of insanity from these big ones. After all of the episodes, bound as participants, what more could this river possibly have demanded or offered in sympathy? An unbelievable relief.

Confident with the progress, Knight eases off of his routine. His arms are tired. "Is there anything we want to say about the ships and the sails?" Knight floats the offer.

"They were cool."

"They were cool," Knight takes a deep breath, "an impressive bit of closure, that's about all I would say as well."

"You've got to be hungry," Knight says, looking back to Hardy, still holding the rudder.

The current is keeping the bateau in a good position, down the middle. Knight lets the oars dangle for the moment, and he digs through the crate.

"Let me guess," Hardy tells him with a bit of lifted spirit, "biscuits, Seven Eleven jerky, and water."

"Be grateful for what we have," Knight tells him, although sarcasm is a good sign. "You have to admit, the longevity of this so-called food is impressive."

"Sir, that's the trademark of every Seven Eleven. The food lasts forever."

Both of them are grateful for a moment of humor's reprieve, but it can't last.

"Mr. Knight," Hardy lets go of the rudder, "my arm is getting worse; the pain is really bad." He looks at Knight, then closes his eyes; his voice is strained. "What do you think is gonna happen to me?"

Knight can't piece together what to say. There's no point in conveying worst fears. Then he studies the bandage. It's more blood-soaked than a half hour ago. "You're going to be in a lot of pain, Son. It's going to hurt for a while longer, and then it will get easier. It won't hurt as much. You'll be fine."

Hardy takes a bite and pulls hard on the jerky. He tears off a bit. "You know, in all of this time, that's about the worst try at convincing I've heard come out of you," he says with his mouth full.

"That may be," Knight lowers his voice. He slows it down. "But, I think you're a strong young man, and your body will fight off the pain you're feeling right now. It'll get better. It has to."

"Okay, if you say so."

"Son, the reality of what is happening here, the bigger reality, if that's what we're calling it now, this trip down the Mississippi, this Mark Twain fiasco, the reality is that you have a nasty wound, and it's probably going to get infected. Lord knows if we even had clean water. The reality is that we don't have access to antibiotics, not here on the river. With a little luck, if we make it down to New Orleans, they will have discovered it by the time we get there. I think we both know how that sounds. If they have the antibiotics, then we're in good shape. If not, we'll clean the wound, keep it clean, and your strong body will win. You're going to be fine."

"Okay, if you say so."

"Look, you wisecracker, eat, drink some of this filthy canteen water, chew your Seven Eleven jerky, and try not to think too hard."

"Got it," he says with his mouth full.

Mr. Knight takes a stick of the dried pork, the jerky. He feels his hunger, but the jerky is only a distraction, at least for this moment.

The last of the bright sun is dropping behind the river shrubs. The air temperature drops with it. Both Knight and Hardy chew the jerky for an interminable amount of time before even entertaining the swallowing.

"God, this jerky," Hardy says, "it's cardboard, it's actually plywood."

"You know," Knight tells him, "we're going to be fine. We really are."

"I know we are, Sir. When we get down to New Orleans, and I get the antibiotics, and we get off this river once and for all, we'll get back on the road to Washington, DC, and I'll head back to Fullerton with my dad."

"That is the plan, Son."

Knight can finally swallow. Unbelievably, the tarp is still with them. Knight steps over to it. It's still folded up in the front of the bateau. He spreads it out on the wooden floor and tries to fluff it up and make it more comfortable. "I want you to lie down here, and we'll call it a night."

"Yes, Sir."

Knight helps him lie down and pulls the edge of the tarp over him.

"Not too bad, right?"

"No, Sir, not bad at all."

Quiet.

In the deep quiet of the river's evening, Hardy hears the sharp, rapid knocking on a dead wooden door. Pileated woodpecker.

After no time at all, Knight can hear Hardy's breathing has gone off to sleep. He stays the course with the oars, keeping the bateau headed straight down the middle.

All is well. Let me put my head down for just a minute. Knight puts his head to his lap. He's able to find a comfortable position, just for a minute.

The light of dawn brightens the darkness of closed eyes. Knight can sense the night is over and morning's begun. Before he's swept back into what the river will want from him, he wades through the thoughts, wanting their own consideration. Washington, of all things. What to do about Washington.

The anticipation of parading his victory among the colleagues he imagined would be envious now feels petty and one more miscalculation. *What's wrong with me, is the familiar refrain to this never-ending ending… Am I incapable of seeing any realistic way forward to get wherever it is I thought I wanted to… Oh no, no, I will not cave in to this anxiety, the whole back-and-forth, up-and-down. That's what needs to stop, give it up, and get down this damn river. Washington will be a problem when the time comes. Leave it there. Get up, get back on the oars, focus on the oars and the river.* Shame will be there later, where it always is.

Representative Knight opens his eyes to a golden-rose Mississippi River sunrise, somewhat of a relief. The valley, flat as hell. The color stretches across forever.

What the hell am I going to be able to do?

He raises his head and sits up. The bateau stayed down the middle. They're not hung up in the shrubs or stuck in the mud. Knight turns his focus to Hardy. "You're awake."

Still wrapped in the tarp, he's put his good arm up on the side of the bateau. Thinking of Jack Lank-Sleeve, he's leaning over the side just enough to watch the sunrise patterns on the water. Hardy turns his head slightly toward Mr. Knight, and with a troubled half-smile and a very tired and raspy voice, "Yeah, I'm awake," is the best he can do.

"Okay, that doesn't sound good." Knight lets out a tired exhale and shakes his head. "Let me take a look."

He steps across and squats next to Hardy, pulling the tarp back a bit. He helps Hardy turn back into the boat and gently takes his arm.

"Ow, ow."

"Okay, okay."

Clearly, the bandage has done all it can. It's done a good job of keeping the wound contained, better than expected, but it needs to come off.

"We're taking this off."

"Okay," Hardy says quietly.

Knight puts his hand on Hardy's forehead. He doesn't say a word. Surely a fever.

Whatever the anxieties Knight had at the first touch of sunrise, they're gone now. In a series of quick and decisive moves, he stands, takes the canteen, and gently gives Hardy water. He carefully but quickly unwinds the bandage around and around his arm. The serious redness has expanded at least an inch outward from the actual wound, maybe more. The front of his arm appears worse than the back. Both are red and obviously infected.

"Well, it looks pretty much how I thought it would. I mean, you have a small hole in your arm. It goes all the way through. It's going to look bad, it's going to get a little infected. We knew that. Worse before better."

Knight decides to not pour canteen water on it and puts the canteen down. He considers one or two other options for the briefest of a moment. And then suddenly, the conviction of one singular decision strikes hard, never before this clear-headed and this obvious. With not an ounce of reservation or the slightest tinge of doubt or hesitation, he stands and then pulls at the cuff of his jacket, then at the arm, then the collar, and in an instant, his Armani jacket is off. He's holding it with both hands. The weight of it still feels perfect but now irrelevant.

"Forgive me, Giorgio. It looks as though you've found a higher purpose." Without a second thought, Knight pulls the jacket inside out and finds a seam in the silk lining of the inside pocket. He starts to carefully pick at the seam, then tears it, ripping the silk, and with a couple of hard yanks, he rips a good portion of the lining completely out of the jacket.

He tears the silk into a long strip and carefully but quickly winds the bandage around and around Hardy's arm. When he's tied it, "There, that's done."

"Son, you're going to lie there and not move around too much, and I am going to get us down this blessed river as fast as I can. There will be nothing between us and New Orleans and a decent doctor, and that's all there is to it."

"Okay."

Knight looks at the woebegone jacket he's tossed to the bateau's wooden floor. It won't do. He picks it up and turns it right side out. Without the lining, it's lighter but still relatively intact. He slips it on, straightening the fit. It seems only fair.

Knight takes to the oars like he hasn't before. One strong pull after another. Not another word. Blisters be damned.

Hardy lies on the tarp for quite some time. It's not too uncomfortable, but a worn-out body with a rising fever is no match for worried thoughts. What to think about the violent parts? *When people you care about die so suddenly with such violence, it sucks you in. You can't help but feel part of it. What could I have done? Now they're gone.*

With the body aches of a fever rushing through him, Hardy inches over to the side of the bateau and sits up slightly to look down at the water and out across the river. There is nothing else floating down the river, no other obstacles, no new chapters, only a lackadaisical, midmorning, absent-minded current.

If there's something to be said, it would be the river's feeling generous. It could be the river decided to leave the bateau alone this morning. Only the river knows what it will want in return to close the distance to New Orleans.

Sunrise patterns are the ripples from the bateau.

When the surface turns dark, the ripples are dark; the patterns have turned dark. There are clouds coming in.

Maybe the pain is better, not so bad. It's hard to tell. It feels like a lot of time is passing because each ripple has its own set of ripples. If you look for it, you'll see an entire network of ripples, waves of ripples, some joined and some going off.

Rivers of ripple waves connecting ripple rivers. Each one of the rivers has its own patterns, patterns of rivers connecting other rivers. It sure feels like a lot of time is passing. Just below the surface of that one river's ripples, there's a light-colored shape, kind of an oval shape. It looks like it's keeping up with the bateau; that's not at all surprising; it's probably joined in and it's headed downriver too. It sure looks like it is. What is it? five, maybe ten feet out from the side of the boat? The shape—the top part of the shape—is poking through the surface. It's what? a few inches high? It's a fin; holy shit, that's a big fish. If you think about it, the river's got to be full of fish this big. You're gonna find very old fish in a very old river. That fin must be some type of carp or catfish, poking up through the surface, making its own ripples. The ripples of the bateau are crossing through the ripples of the fish, which is probably a carp. Those are complicated patterns. You cannot count those; don't even try. They come in sets of ten, ten by ten. Those merge with the other sets of ten, then other sets of ten. There are overall shapes to the sets of ten. These are changing, so don't even try to count those. Of course, not at all surprising, there's another tip of a very large fin, another carp could be catfish. That figures. The ripples from that fin are joining all the other ripple waves. Look at that. When they come together, they make one large V across the surface, about the size of the bateau. It's another boat going down the river. Two Vs headed down the Mississippi. That's pretty great. Morning is a decent time. Not surprising, now there's five or six, no, definitely five; they're all keeping up with the boat. It's hard to tell how fast we're going. The two very large fish, pretty sure they're carp, are joined with the rest of their partners. It's like they're all watching the boat out of the corners of their eyes. Holy shit, of course, the big one jumps out of the water and splashes back in. It might be the biggest one. The river must be moving along pretty quick, I guess, because a fish that size is swimming pretty quick to jump out like that, and to keep going, the river's gotta be really moving. Not at all surprising. There goes another one, probably carp, now another and holy shit, another. They're jumping through the surface and then get right back in formation, which makes sense, like a pack of dolphins, leaping out of the water and smiling across at ya as they keep going. They've gotta be strong to keep that up.

Hardy tries to take hold of the tarp to pull it over him like a blanket. His body is shivering. That tarp is heavy.

In a situation like this, you're supposed to follow certain guidelines. If we're all going together downriver, there should at least be some kind of hello, or some kind of very-large-carp greeting, maybe a good morning or a how's it going?

People in boats have to break the ice.

"How's the water today?"

Okay, one of the fish leaps right out of the water, so it seems to work. That feels right. Wait for a response. Maybe, maybe not, maybe not right away. They're very large fish, probably carp, and they're busy with their swimming, although, on second thought, the river is probably doing most of the work.

"The water is terrific."

I knew they'd say hello. Wow, okay, not at all surprising, not at all, when a fish that size leaps out of the water and she says, the water is terrific, she has got to keep her part of the conversation short, she's up and back pretty quick.

"Where you headed?"

Of course, right away, the next one. She is polite, but she sounds a little rushed.

"Let me guess."

This one's a little more friendly, that makes sense. They're a team, or they're just close friends.

"New Orleans?"

Okay, that's just downright crazy, but it's a nice gesture to be that friendly, but it's kind of personal to ask that. But we're all headed that direction, so I guess it's fine.

"Why would you ask him that?"

Okay, they talk to each other when they're out of the water. Maybe it's easier to hear each other.

"You know where he's headed."

"I don't like your tone."

Okay, I don't get this. Why the arguing? Maybe they're just kids, maybe teenagers.

"Well…"

"Well, yourself…"

Given the abrupt turn in this conversation, you'd expect very large carp to start all kinds of foul-mouthed name-calling. So, what now? That's it? They're just gone? Back down under? Not even a goodbye or a good luck?

"Sorry, it's not a good time."

There she is, and a wink. Now that is a nice gesture, that's really nice, and just like that, gone. I guess they all just go back to what they were doing. It's

"How are you feeling now?" Knight watches Hardy stare out at the river.
He hasn't moved in a while. He doesn't look well, not at all.

After a few minutes, he asks again, "Son, are you feeling any better? Or
pretty much the same?"

Knight gives him another minute.

"I'm here." Hardy's voice comes from farther off.

"Whatever place we pass, we're getting off, and we'll get to a doctor
wherever that is. I'm thinking now that we must have passed Natchez last night.
We should have seen it by now."

Hardy pulls himself into a tight ball, knees up to his chest. The tarp feels
too heavy to pull up for a blanket. It's freezing cold.

Knight alternates the oars, several hard pulls, then with the rudder,
correcting his position. Keep it straight and down the middle, like we've done
all along.

He won't let himself give in to the frustration. *Can't there be one little dock,
one little town? We're making good progress, but we're stuck, and there's no way
of knowing how much time we have.*

"Let me feel your forehead again. This fever has got to be going down."
Knight steps over to Hardy and crouches down to put his hand on Hardy's
forehead. Burning up. He reaches over to the scraps of jacket lining and tears
off a piece.

"Let's see if we can bring it down."

Knight rolls up the piece of cloth. He reaches over the side of the bateau to
feel the water, the temperature. "Unbelievably neutral." He dips the rolled-up
fabric into the river. It has to be cooler than his body.

"Son, I want you to lie back down on the tarp. I'm going to put this cool
cloth on your forehead. We'll bring your temperature down." Knight helps
Hardy lie back down. "You just watch the sky and listen for the birds. You tell
me the names of the ones you hear."

"Mr. Knight, birds don't have names."

"Sure, they have names. You've told me a bunch of them. I can't remember them, but we'll look them up when we get back to the Winnebago. How's that sound?"

Knight puts the cloth on Hardy's forehead, rolled up and across the width, so the water runs down the sides of his head and not down his face. "Now, how does that feel?"

"It smells."

"Well, Son, some of this we'll just have to tolerate, won't we?"

Knight keeps the cloth in place for several minutes, then dips it again in the river and back on Hardy's forehead. There's no way to know for sure if it's working.

"This is definitely working." Knight's voice rings with conviction. "You see, we're making progress."

"I like it when you talk like that." Hardy's voice feels better. He sounds better. "You're just not very good at it."

"Aha, so we are feeling better. Maybe this is working."

The two of them stay where they are for a while. Knight changes the water in the cloth every few minutes. The clouds that were moving in earlier in the morning are patchy now as they move across. The type of sky that makes it difficult to lie flat and look up. One second, there's no sun, and the details of the clouds show their progress. The next second, the sun breaks through and tries to blind you.

"Mr. Knight," Hardy can only speak when the clouds block the sun, "I think we should consider that we're… We should consider that we're here, that we might be here."

"Son, don't think, don't talk, just lie there and think about nothing. You might fall back asleep. That would be a good thing."

"I mean, like city limits, maybe we're already in the city limits of New Orleans."

"That could be, but we're not going to think about that right now, and you're not going to talk anymore. Think about nothing."

"Mr. Knight, can I ask you something?"

"No, you cannot."

"Mr. Knight, why is everything so complicated?"

"Hardy, I'm telling you, don't think and don't speak."

"Sir, I'm not thinking, but maybe New Orleans is not a place. I mean, it is a real place. I guess it's real, I've never seen it, but what I'm saying is that maybe for us it's not supposed to be a real place."

"Son, I really need you to stop." Knight dips the cloth in the river again and puts it back on his forehead. "Things are complicated because we make them complicated. I assume it's the way we prefer it."

"Do I prefer it?"

"You're a young man. Young men prefer the simple and straightforward. Me, I'm an old man. The world piles up around me, and it would bury me if I didn't sort through it all, over and over. I have many piles spread all over the place. You, you have one pile, its straightforward and direct. That's part of the reason old people don't really care for young people. We're jealous of the straightforward. We want it back."

"So the point is, you can't get it back. That's right, isn't it?" Hardy keeps his eyes closed. The sun is cutting through a big part of the open sky.

"That's right, you're right. But on the other hand, think of all this time we've spent going down this river. If by some miracle we would have come straight down with no problems whatsoever, starting with when we first met William and all the way down here at New Orleans, a young man's straight and forward, think of all those complications we would have missed."

"But, Mr. Knight, we've almost been killed more than a couple of times."

"That's right, you're right. You see, Son, it's complicated. See how that works?"

"Mr. Knight, I can see why you love Washington. I'll bet you're gonna be good at it."

"You know, Son, I really appreciate your saying that. You more than anyone else. With all we've been through, those words mean a lot to me." Knight takes the cloth off of Hardy's head and decides it's enough with the river water; it hasn't done what he had hoped. The temperature is not going down.

"Just lie still. I think the river water is doing the trick. You're cooling off. That's what we want." Knight uses the cuff of his jacket to dry off Hardy's forehead. He sits, thinking it through. What are the options?

"You're going to be fine. I can tell. I don't want you to worry. We'll get to the doctor's office soon. How does that sound?"

"That sounds good, Mr. Knight. Maybe you could keep talking a little while longer. I like to hear about the complications. It's interesting."

"Alright, I can do that. I love the sound of my own voice. That's an old saying, but maybe I have it reversed: I can't stand the sound of my own voice. Either way. This trip to Washington now with a bonus complication, to say the least. I don't think either one of us could dream up something more complicated. I wouldn't even know where to begin. And now, to think about Washington, D.C., I don't even know what I would do there. Why I wanted to go there in the first place. To be important, that's what I wanted. What I thought I wanted. It's a place where important people get together and do important things that other important people recognize as important. I wanted that for the longest time. If you're with important people, then you're important. And after all of this, I don't think I'm the same. Do you think you're the same? After all this? I'm elected, but it doesn't mean the same as it did. Not after all this. There you go. That's another complication."

"You're a complicated man, Mr. Knight. Everybody likes that about you."

"Well, that's a nice thing to hear. I'm not so sure it's what I would want people to like about me. I suppose it's better than simple man, although I'm not sure why it's better."

"It's better because you're in politics."

"That's true; I am. I represent, I'm a representative. With all my complications, what I do is represent? I represent you, dear boy. The complicated man represents the simple, straightforward Hardy. Only a complicated man can see the inherent problem with that equation."

"William's in politics."

"You can absolutely say that William is in politics. That's exactly what he is. And oddly, that's why we both like him the way we do."

"He isn't complicated."

"Son, I told you no more talking from you."

"I like it when you get annoyed." Hardy's voice has taken on a deeper rasp, his words are thick with effort. "It's what I like about you." His eyes are closed even when the clouds pass over.

"William is a straightforward man who's been put into a complicated situation. He is doing what he sees is the right way forward. Part of why he feels that way, why he's out roaming these woods and the river with the others who are straightforward and stuck in the same complicated situation, is because their people in politics, their representatives, can only see the complicated. And if that's all you see, then that's all you know. William sees more, so he is the traitor. And he sees his representatives caught up in a world of perpetuating complications. We call that hypocrisy. And William sees that as treason, traitors to the straight and forward. That, Son, is a complicated situation. And where I fit into this equation, I can't even begin to straighten that out. But I will tell you this: William is the smarter man. It's what we like about him. Which makes me think I may be too far on the side of the hypocrites. The people we've come across on this river appear to me as remarkably straightforward. Certainly compared to the important people in politics. Anyway, we're not having the 'summarize the journey and reevaluate your life' conversation."

Knight looks down at Hardy, asleep on the tarp. He's put his arm over his eyes. "And there you have it. The complications put the straight and forward to sleep." That is certainly profound enough for anyone.

Representative Knight has spent a lifetime talking his way in and out of every imaginable type of complicated situation. Hardy's fever, out on this river, he's helpless. He can hear Hardy mumble in a shallow sleep. A fever dream is more than disheartening. Knight drops his head. He can't see an option. *Get to the shore?* Miles from anywhere. *Paddle harder, keep at it?* The river stretches out to the horizon.

The Representative hears a familiar sound from above. He looks up to see a half-dozen crows barking at each other as they pass over. It actually appears as though they're hovering, convening above the bateau, a boardroom meeting.

If you could speak crow, you could shout out and ask how far to the next city, or port, or whatever is ahead. *They certainly know how to get where they're going. Are we talking hours or days? Then again, they're cantankerous enough to give you bad information. There's something about the spirit of the crows. Hardy would know the exact species. Or look it up.*

There's a sound coming from behind the bateau, back up the river. A mechanical sounding sound, a mechanical buzzing. A mosquito buzzing in your ear from almost a mile away. Knight turns on his seat to see what can be seen of it. There is something there.

He stands to face it, get a good look. "Good lord, a boat."

Immediately, he's overwhelmed with relief. His entire body feels the boat coming this way. His lungs can feel the air again.

Knight turns to look at Hardy, still asleep on the tarp. Do not disturb.

He puts his hands to his hips and watches the boat intensely. It is coming closer. Don't look away, it could disappear. It might disappear. Don't let that boat disappear.

The closer it gets, the deeper the buzzing. It's not as high-pitched as before, more of a droning than a buzzing.

Definitely two people sitting, one near the front and one at the back.

The little boat is getting closer. Knight counts the minutes.

The crows share their parting thoughts—they don't seem very spiritual—they move off, gone behind the trees.

The little boat is getting closer. It's easy to forget how wide the Mississippi really is. The little boat is getting closer, but it's coming up far to the side of the bateau. It's sticking to the side, fairly far from the middle.

At a quarter of a mile, Knight prepares himself for whatever it's going to take to get their attention. Waving arms and shouting. What if they don't speak English? Surely they speak English.

He can't wait any longer. The boat's close enough. Knight starts by waving his arms above his head. Starting with the simple every man's gesture, the universal call for help. He keeps at it for a full couple of minutes. The little boat is certainly close enough to see that it's not an arbitrary hello gesture. It's getting closer. It's going to pass far to the side. Knight looks down at Hardy asleep. It doesn't matter. He calls out to the little boat. "Over here, we need help." His first thoughts are that they can definitely hear him. They're not that far away. But they don't seem to hear him. "A call for help, out here on this river, and they don't respond? What the hell?" His waving arms are as aggressive as waving arms can get, all over the place. "Over here, goddamn it, I know you can hear me. We're in trouble. I have a sick boy here. We need help."

The little boat keeps a steady pace. It's nearly opposite the bateau. Not any change in speed or direction. The boat is clearly not going to come over. It's not going to stop.

"Over here, goddamn it. This boy needs medical attention. What the hell is wrong with you?"

Knight stops the waving arms. There's no point to it. He watches the two figures keep their attention straight ahead. They don't seem to turn to look at all. There's nothing left to do. They're not going to stop. Knight lets the swear words fly. You motherfucking assholes, sons of bitches, fucking backwoods inbred hillbillies, on and on, not at all creative, the worst of the simplest worst. No effect whatsoever, not even a simple recognition.

Hardy has changed his position on the tarp, but he stays lying on his back with his eyes closed.

The figure in front of the boat watches straight out ahead, and the figure in the back is holding on to a steering handle. In an instant, Knight recognizes it, an old Mercury motor. He can see clearly now what he didn't notice before. The little boat is aluminum. It's a small fishing boat with a gas motor. About as common as a boat can get.

Knight drops to his seat. A blank stare, a blank mind. He takes several long breaths. He can feel his heart slow from the violence of minutes ago. His head drops farther. His shoes, a familiar comfort, what maintenance might they require. The mosquito is fading into the distance. The little boat is making good time downriver, already out of sight.

When Representative Knight's thoughts return, the underwhelming shock is how unfazed he is by the timeline of the fishing boat, or whatever you want to call it, what it means about where he is now in river time. What was before an exploding fury of confusion and frustration is now merely the satisfaction of having a pleasant way to think about it: the timeline of the river. It has a charming note to it. It feels definitive, and there's no other way to respond to it other than to submit to it. It should be a comfort. Anyway, it doesn't matter. It would have mattered. It doesn't anymore. One more: "Where are we now? Why is this happening?" seems more than a little redundant. Frankly, fatigued. He's been on the river too long to be shocked by this again. It most certainly does not feel like being swept up in the marvels of a wonderfully mysterious universe. Amateurish. Knight puts one finger to one small bit of mud on his shoe and swipes it off. He raises his head, one heave of a long breath, and he stands up to assess what's to be done. The river is not a marvel; it's an adversary that will not defeat him. Not with the boy, and not today.

Knight's mind is now scrolling through the new propositions that the Mercury motor presents, foremost of which is antibiotics. This changes everything. A renewed urgency but now with a target. Any Mississippi River doctor anywhere along this stretch—probably not too far above New Orleans—is going to have antibiotics.

Staying the course straight down the middle of the river, all the way to the city, may not be the best plan. There might, in fact, be a small town along the river. Surely there is. Any small town is better than trying to make it all the way down. Probably. But where to pull off? Paddle to the side. The scrub is nothing but consistent. You'd think the river would have some patch of farmland butted up against it. So far, it hasn't.

Knight puts it on hold and bends down to check Hardy's forehead. It's not one degree better. He moves in a little closer to listen to Hardy's breathing as if it will give him a sign of what to do next. It's what you do in a situation like this. Hardy's breathing is so shallow, it's barely at all. The lowness of the inhale feels barely enough. His exhales are raspy. Knight moves in closer still. He wants to hear clearly in one ear the sound of Hardy's breath. He stays there for a moment. He listens to understand. There's a flutter in the breath, the rasp in his breathing is the air being dragged across what has accumulated in his lungs. Knight can hear it clearly now, the details of it, the complications of it, in both of his ears. Both ears?

Knight slowly lifts his head. The rhythm of the rasp is not only in Hardy's breathing. His breathing has brought another rhythm. As he lifts his head away, the rasping sound is pronounced. It's there. In an instant, Knight lifts his head and turns to look upriver. And there it is, another motor, another boat.

About a mile upriver, another small fishing boat. Representative Knight stands erect to face it. He squares his shoulders back and spreads his feet. He'll hold this position for however long it takes.

The little boat is making steady progress. It's still too far to wave arms. Knight stands for several minutes longer, waiting for the little shape of the boat to present itself. The buzzing hum of the outboard carries across the distance. When it gets louder, the boat is getting closer.

There are moments in this short, stubborn vigil when Knight loses the razor of his focus. *What if they don't respond? The people on this part of the Mississippi don't give a shit about other people. The bateau is too uncommon. We look like foreigners. Country people hate foreigners, by God, it's actually true. Where's that fool Walker when you need him? Get some sailors out there and take that boat. It's definitely another fishing boat. There are two. Two people. Aluminum.*

It's time to wave. It will not be wild and crazy, it's going to be steady and continuous. Knight waves his arms above his head in a regular, steady rhythm. *That boat is coming straight at us.*

A little less than a quarter of a mile and it's a man and a woman. Regular looking people. *That boat is coming straight at us.* Knight lets his waving get a bit sloppy so he adjusts. Steady and as non-dramatic as possible. Simple, everyday, arm waving river communication. He checks the Armani, brushes it, straightens it, look sane and presentable.

At this distance, the details begin to present themselves. The woman in front is older, an old woman, an elderly woman. Gray hair, parted in the middle, down to her shoulders, just above her shoulders. A very pleasant face, actually very pleasant. A sleeveless top of some sort, which makes sense in this weather. The woman is sitting patiently. She doesn't seem to look away. Where she is sitting, she is blocking the view of the person, maybe a man, in back at the motor.

In a quick gesture, the elderly woman raises one arm and puts her hand up, palm out. Only for a quick moment. Perhaps a "stay put" gesture. It's not clear. It's enough.

Words to describe Knight's relief cannot possibly do justice. Weight of the world lifted. Hope on the horizon. There is good in the world after all. There is a goddamn God. Any communication is a blessing. Knight doesn't relent his arm waving. There's nothing certain about any encounter on this river, but his heart is beating faster.

He looks down at Hardy. He's excited, and he wants to wake him, but Hardy is still asleep, which is good.

The boat keeps coming. The elderly woman doesn't have much of an expression on her face. It's not a big whopping smile, but it's not threatening either.

A hundred feet away and the boat shifts its direction, a slight pivot, a slight rotation, a better approach to the side of the bateau. This changes everything, makes all the difference in the world. They're coming. There will be help.

From where Knight sits, as the angle of the boat adjusts, the woman in the front is moved aside to let the man in the back slowly reveal himself. There's a loud, floral-patterned shirt, a decent pair of sunglasses, and a beard. The man's a little overweight.

"God in heaven." Knight's arms drop to his sides, one long, long breath in, and with the exhale of the river's air, his head drops, chin to his chest. His limp body drops deflated to the bateau's wooden seat. At long last, it's finished. One last passing moment, the little boat on the mighty river, and with the new breath. He stands again, he looks straight up into the clear of the sky, a brightening whips across his body and finds a truly humbled grin roll across his face, grateful forever.

It's Buddy.

Chapter Twenty Three

Gravestones and history books

An overwhelming sense of impossible relief. Heaven has shined its light, but thoughts trickle back, practical concerns, not out of the woods. Most of what must happen now is passed to Buddy. There's nothing more to say about Buddy. Buddy will do whatever is necessary, whatever it takes.

"Where's my boy?" Buddy's first words. From where he sits in the fishing boat, he can't yet see Hardy asleep on the tarp.

Representative Knight uses both palms to quickly whisk away the slightest of tears from his face. Solace and joy. He calls over to Buddy, twenty feet away, "He's right here. He's asleep. He's been hurt. He'll be okay."

Buddy immediately cuts the motor and guides the boat but half stands to get a look into the bateau.

"What do you mean, he's been hurt?"

In the last ten feet, he maneuvers the fishing boat; it slides in directly side-to-side with the bateau. The elderly woman grabs hold. She holds the two boats together with both hands.

"He's asleep. He's been hurt." Knight is now keeping his voice low.

Buddy quickly gets himself into position and steps over. When his weight shifts to the bateau, it wobbles. With the other foot in, it settles. None of that concerns him. He keeps his attention on his son lying on the tarp. Hardy is curled up asleep. It's a lot of noise to sleep through, but he's curled up like he usually sleeps.

When Buddy steps one leg over the middle seat to get to his son, Knight throws his arms around his broad shoulders and the loud floral print. "My God, you have no idea." Knight's tight hug throws them both off balance. The bateau wobbles. When Buddy steps the rest of the way over the seat, it settles. With one arm around Knight's waist, Buddy pulls him in. Both men are overcome with relief. Everything about this world has changed.

With Buddy's weight in the bateau, the ordeal of it all is truly over. It's ended. There's a trauma to an ending like this. With his one arm, Buddy can feel the whole of the Representative's burden. He is weak; he is a hundred years old. Buddy's relief is cautious. His attention is with his son lying on the tarp. Knight can feel this, of course he can. He lets his arms slide off Buddy's shoulder.

With the last two short steps, Buddy has finally reached Hardy, and now that he's here, he's all business. Buddy crouches down. He feels Hardy's forehead with his palm, then gently rolls him a little more on his back to get a first look at the wound, wrapped in the silk of the jacket lining. An odd design of fruit orange fabric with a near-perfect circle of dried blood. Buddy can see Hardy is not in grave danger; the fever is treatable, the wound, we'll see; but it's a relief.

Buddy can see his son is exhausted from this trek down the river, whatever this has been. He could not have slept well in this rotten wooden boat. He pokes lightly on the tip of Hardy's nose. And again. And one more time, finally, a grumpy exhale. One eye first, then both squinting to look up at the face silhouetted in the blinding light of the day. The face in shadow is too dark to see, but immediately, "What the hell, Dad, where have you been?"

Buddy reaches behind Hardy and pulls him close. His arms wrap around him. Hardy is stuck in the tightest squeeze, the most grateful heart ever seen on the Mississippi, in the whole history of the river.

Hardy buries his head into his dad's chest. He's finally safe, and the river is over. His short, rapid breaths can't hold it back, the emotions and the all of it. The overwhelming all of it bursts out of the twelve-year-old young man, an experience he has no way to control. He's powerless and suddenly helpless. His father is here. Hardy cries into his dad for the longest time, until his words can make it back. "I knew you'd come. I knew you'd come." Hardy lifts his head and wipes his nose with the back of his hand. He looks up at his father. Buddy is shaken. His world has made it back. His eyes are closed. He's doing his best to hold it in. "Dad, it's okay. I knew you'd come."

Buddy puts his hands on Hardy's shoulders and pushes him back to look him in the face. "Hardy, you had me so worried. Don't you ever pull a reckless stunt like that again. I mean it."

Buddy takes a deep breath, his head drops, and he lets a long breath out. He's had his own ordeal.

"Son, you really had me scared."

"I know. I know that, Dad. I knew you'd be worried. I kept saying that. You don't understand, Dad, it's the longest story."

"Well, you can tell the whole long story on the way home, because that is exactly where we are headed, and I mean directly, after we get this arm looked at."

"No, Dad, you have to hear this. You don't get it. Mr. Knight and I, we're like time travelers."

"Alright, I promise you can tell me the whole story, but let me look at that arm. I have to pull that bandage off. I need a good look."

"Dad!"

"Son," Knight's parental tone, so befitting, "your father's right, take care of the immediate business, and when the time is right, you can sit together, and you can tell him the whole long story. Perhaps not all of it."

Knight sits back down. The weight of his body and the feel of the bateau's wood are changed. His feet and legs are cramping, his knees are wrapped in a dull throbbing pain, and his arms and shoulders feel useless. The tightness in his chest is at medium, but he can feel it waiting to grab hold. Representative Knight is truly out of steam. He's turned the very real corner. With the river's blessing, the elderly gentleman has become the old man. He can hope to recover, but it might not come, not in full. When the weight of a man's body is dragged down the hill, this far and that fast, it's very difficult to get back up. Knight sits. The story has changed.

Buddy unwinds the silk bandage and peels it off Hardy's arm. He's a little more "get the job done" than "careful and gentle."

"Doris, can you toss me the water bottle?" Buddy calls over to the woman in the fishing boat.

"I'm Doris," she says to Knight, with a wary smile, then she tosses the plastic bottle to Buddy. It's a Gatorade bottle filled with tap water.

Knight glances at her. He doesn't really want to get to know another person, not right now.

Buddy squeezes the water bottle. He uses the slight pressure stream to rinse the puncture wound. "Does that hurt?"

"Yes, it hurts, Dad, it hurts." Hardy's voice has returned to a mumbled, tired twelve-year-old.

"I know it does. I'm sorry. I think it's best to let it get some air. We don't have a clean bandage, anyway." Buddy puts his hand under Hardy's head and lets him lie down on the tarp. "I want you to stay still and don't talk too much."

Hardy closes his eyes. The sun is still very bright, but there's too much to tell. "We got in a boat with this guy, William. Did you run into him? You would like this guy, Dad." Hardy's words barely make it out.

"You got in a boat. I see you got in a boat. You're lucky I could find you. This river is about as wide as it is long. No more talking."

"It's such a long story, Dad."

"I love you, Son, let's get back to the Winnebago. Then you can tell me your story. I know it's a good one."

The two small boats move with the ever-steady current.

Buddy turns to Representative Knight and Doris. "We really only have one option here."

"Buddy, you're probably right." Doris's voice is a little rough, a little masculine, deep, and a little raspy, but the words are delivered with a distinctly casual grace. She's immediately a kind person. "But in a situation like this, we'd best talk it through."

"Probably only one option." Knight feels the need to be part of it. "I'm sorry. Who are you?"

"Sorry, Mr. Knight." Buddy turns to Knight, he's getting ready to get going. "This is Doris, sorry, I don't believe I know your last name."

"That's alright," she looks across to Knight, "Mr. Knight, you call me Doris. That'll be enough. It'll be fine. This is my boat. I offered to guide Buddy down the river, to lend him a hand."

"Well, that's…" Knight can't finish it.

"Yes, she did," Buddy tells him, "and I'm very grateful. Mr. Knight, is there anything of value in either of those crates?" He waits only a very short moment for Knight to offer anything back, which he doesn't. Buddy steps over to the crates and sorts through the cotton bags and the bottles, then picks up the wooden canteen. It is a remarkable object. He pulls out the cork and smells the water. "Foul." he puts it back.

"Buddy." Doris is merely putting words to the obvious, mostly for Knight's sake, to keep him included. "I assume your plan is that we all get in my boat and we get back to the path that cuts up through the bank. Is that what we're thinking?"

Buddy takes hold of one edge of the tarp. He feels the weight of the cotton to see if it has anything to offer. It might be of use.

"What are your thoughts on towing this wooden boat?" Buddy asks Doris. He genuinely wants her opinion. "It's heavy. It'll be a considerable drag."

"I would say I don't think the river has too many more surprises, but that would be a fool's mistake. We tow it." She reveals a little more of her river-self. Buddy can hear it, and Knight is reassured when he hears it.

"Alright then, I'm going to need some help lifting my son into your boat. I want him out of this, whatever this boat is." Buddy isn't rushing, but he wants to move it along. "I don't trust this old, wooden..."

"Let me help you." Knight steps over to Buddy and waits for him to lift Hardy by the shoulders. "I'll put the tarp in the boat."

Buddy moves behind Hardy and lifts his weight to see if he can stand.

"Dad, I can do it."

"You have to step over the side into the other boat."

"I know that." Hardy stands on his own and takes short steps to the side of the bateau. He thinks for a second. "Okay, you can help me get over."

Buddy, with the look of a father's patient impatience, steps over to Hardy and lifts him up in his arms and steps over into the boat. Knight quickly gathers up the tarp. He steps over and spreads the thing out like the bed it's been. Buddy gently lays Hardy back down and feels his forehead. "I want to get moving."

Doris pulls the bateau backward, one arm after the other. She pulls the dead weight of the bateau far enough back to use a rope in the fishing boat and tie to the front of the bateau.

"Alright, Buddy, it's tied off."

"Alright then," Buddy announces as he sits down on the metal seat next to his son. "Let's get back up the river."

Doris takes a quick pull on the motor cord, and it starts right up. It sputters, then loud and steady.

"Hang on one minute," Knight announces. "I think it would be better if I were to take a seat in the bateau. You know, spread the weight around."

"Seat in the what?" Buddy will only give this a minute.

"In the wooden boat, I should be in the wooden boat. Doris, if you could pull it over, I'll just jump in, and we're off."

"Yes, Sir," Buddy tells Knight, "that's a smart idea."

Doris pulls the bateau back into position. Knight steps in and sits quietly down on his familiar seat. "Okay, I believe I'm good to go," he tells them. The truth is, he can't suddenly change boats. It's testing fate. There's a predictability with the bateau, a trust. It deserves to see it through until the end.

Doris throttles up slowly to take the slack out of the tow rope. Then steadily more gas until they reach a decent speed. There shouldn't be anything more between where they are now and the spot on the river bank where the path cuts through the woods. Nothing more than river water. Doris is steady on the motor, clearly a veteran. She knows what she's doing. Buddy sits next to Hardy. He's checking his cell phone for service; nothing yet. Hardy is lying on the tarp. It's more comfortable than it appears. He's watching the sky. The sun is not nearly as bright now. It's more of an afternoon sun than a sun at noon. And Knight can't stop thinking about this path up the bank and through the woods. Something he missed, some little clearing in the scrub, between Vicksburg Harbor and wherever we are now. *Why exactly are we going back upriver? That's not been the goal for the longest time. You gotta trust Buddy, but the Winnebago is a long time ago. New Orleans is the other way.*

A "V" formation of geese is crossing the river behind the boats, low to the water. There's a lot of loud honking between them, even over the sound of the motor. They seem well organized and seem to know what they're doing.

"Canada Geese," Hardys says without looking over.

Representative Knight sits quietly still. He sits in the middle seat of the bateau. Alone in the bateau, after all this time and all the people, it's the strangest thing. Certainly unexpected. His thoughts are racing with worry, but he doesn't want them to be. Not one thing on his list has a decent, logical explanation, definition, or a simple way to put it aside. *Back through the woods? It's just not possible. Where on the river is this fantasy path back through the woods? It can't be, and it certainly can't be done. I cannot get myself back through those woods. Sit. Watch the river. Sit and just watch the river. It is rather remarkable to see the trees go by this fast. After all this time, plodding along, barely more than drifting. Stuck to the river, pushing this boat, inch by inch.* Knight lifts his hands to look at his palms. They're red and sore. *Surely there will be blisters. They'd be here by now. Maybe they'll come later. Probably soon. It's not natural to go this fast. It goes against nature. Poor William, if he had seen this motor, imagine the look on that poor man's face. What I would give to see the look on one of those Osage drunks.* A slight little snicker leaks out of his heaviness at just the same moment Buddy looks over to check on him.

"Mr. Knight? Is everything all right with you? You feeling okay?"

Knight gives Buddy a polite nod. He's not going to raise his voice over the motor.

"I got a signal," Buddy announces. His voice is upbeat. For Buddy, it's upbeat. He takes a deep breath, looks down at Hardy, and immediately gets busy with the phone's GPS. This changes everything, speeds up everything.

Doris watches Buddy's body language to gauge his success. She keeps the motor at a steady speed. The bateau is quite a drag.

Buddy makes a quick gesture with his fist in the air. "Got it." He turns to Doris, "2.3 miles up." Doris nods.

Probably because the sound of the motor is so constant, it keeps Hardy's attention on the afternoon sun and the feel of the boat's speed. His dad, right next to him, is working his phone. *That means we'll be out of this boat and off the river before you know it. Mr. Knight has got to be freaking out about this whole new part and this new stranger. Doris, what an old name, old-fashioned.*

"A young boy has got to be awfully tired from a long day like this one." Doris's voice carries through the sound of the motor. She's not speaking loudly. She's only a few feet away. Hardy hears her voice, and it's a familiar comfort. He doesn't look in her direction. He's squinting at the sky.

"What you have experienced would make an old woman like me very tired indeed."

"I guess it probably would."

"It must feel strange to have another person swoop in with another boat."

"Strange, not really strange, not anymore. Another boat, and another stranger."

"You are right to keep your thoughts to yourself. It won't be much longer on the river, not much longer."

"It feels like I've been on this river my whole life."

"Not too much longer. You don't belong out on this river, do you, Son?"

If I hear that one more time, Hardy won't say it out loud.

"Doris." Buddy's voice is focused. He leans forward. And he shifts his attention between the river bank and his GPS. "Right up there on the left. We're looking for any bit of clearing."

Doris slows the motor and guides the boats closer to the shore. A substantial clearing of any kind doesn't look promising.

Buddy stands and points to a spot. "There! We'll have to make it work."

"I see it, Buddy. We can make that work."

The front of the fishing boat glides into the mud and brushes against the stiff scrub. They've come to a stop. The bateau slides in next to the fishing boat. Representative Knight watches both Buddy and Doris as they figure the logistics and the ropes. There's nothing he can contribute. He's remembering the last time the bateau felt the river mud—a very different place.

Hardy sits up to watch. His thoughts are choppy with fatigue and fever and the aching pain in his arm. He watches over the side of the boat to see how deep it is, and he notices the small sapling a few feet away. It must be an oak sapling. This one has only the one leaf. It's a little too far out. Seeing it shifts his attention—is there something more to know? This gives him a little more energy, and he stands up to see what he can do to help, then quickly sits back down, this time on an aluminum seat.

Buddy and Doris get the ropes and everything else ready to step over on to the river bank, what there is of it, just under the overhang of the scrub bushes.

"Up through there is a state highway, the closest one," Buddy tells his son. He looks over to Mr. Knight to make sure he's included. This will be tough for Knight. "I can't tell you exactly how far, but it can't be that far."

"You can use the oar from the wooden boat." Doris's experience gives her some advantage over the scrub. "You can use it to clear the brush in front of you. You'll come to thin woods once you're past the scrub."

"And how far is the Winnebago?" Knight asks Doris, but he would prefer if Buddy would offer the plan of what is to happen next. "Do we know if it's very far? Is it where we left it? Because that makes little sense, well, in terms of distance and where we were, all of that."

"Mr. Knight," Doris politely interrupts, "I recommend you come with me. We'll take the boats to a spot downriver. That's what makes sense. I can see that. I'm sure you can too. You would be a big help."

"Sir," Buddy can't imagine getting both Knight and Hardy through the woods up to the highway. "The Winnebago is quite a way from here. You can help her get the boats back. She'll need your help. I'll be getting Hardy to the nearest hospital or doctor's office, whatever is closest. You'll meet us there. In no time at all."

Buddy lifts his phone back out of his pocket and calls 911.

He holds his phone to his ear, waiting for his turn to speak. "Yes, ma'am, I have a twelve-year-old with a bad puncture wound in the arm... no it's not... yes it is... yes, very red, very infected... no he isn't, but that's what I'm afraid of. If it's alright, I would like to have a paramedic..." It's happening faster than he thought it would, "County 33 at Pendleton, a rest stop. I'll do my best to stay on the line."

Buddy ends the call, there's too much to do. "This all has to move quickly." He looks at Doris, Mr. Knight, the ropes, the scrub, and the bateau. "Doris, let me know what you need help with; get yourself ready to go."

Buddy reaches over and grabs an oar out of the bateau. He steps over to the front of Doris's fishing boat, throws one leg over, and carefully puts his weight on anything solid, testing the mud to find any solid footing. The mud proves to be only a few inches deep. "I can make a hole in this wall."

Buddy uses the oar to chop at the bushes. He swings it like a baseball bat and then like an axe. In no time at all, he's made an opening that he can carry Hardy through. It looks thinned out on the other side. The scrub is not nearly as tough as it looks. After all this time, not nearly as tough. There's no time to consider the implications of it; all those times, not nearly as tough.

Doris is the type to get organized quickly. She checks the tether rope to the bateau and steps back to the motor. She sits and waits for the others.

"Mr. Knight, is there anything you will want from the crates or anything in your boat?" She gently nudges with the lightest touch. She won't rush him.

Knight realizes the brevity of the situation. Everything is about to change. There will be goodbyes. He'll hurry to get himself ready, but he will not be rushed. With Doris's question, he first considers how she's asked it. But before that consideration, there is the way she looks. Who is this stranger, really? The light cotton blouse, short-sleeved, a pleasant cornflower blue pattern. It's nice. It's gentle. The way it's cut at the waist is very pleasant. Baggy denim pants are a smart choice, obviously. It's her glasses that are so striking. Just the right touch of masculine. This woman is confident and capable. She can be trusted.

"Doris, Dear, I can assure you there's nothing in this little boat I can't live without." Representative knows there's nothing much to salvage in the crates. He considers the canvas bag that William left, stuffed under the back seat, and brings it to the fishing boat. With that, Knight stands and steps over into the aluminum boat. He sits down next to Hardy on the aluminum seat. They look at each other. There might have been a wink exchanged. The sun is still fairly bright.

Ten feet in front of the fishing boat, in the hacked-back scrub bushes, Buddy has made a good enough hole he can get Hardy through. He'll have to carry him through this tangle until they get to the other side, where the thick thins out. The scrub is not as tough as it looks. Buddy climbs back into the boat and stands next to Hardy and Mr. Knight, he's breathing hard, but he's easily patient. He looks off downriver. He'll give his son the moment. Everything is about to change. He knows there will be goodbyes.

Hardy sits, looking straight ahead. He can feel it all around him, this exceptional moment. He'll be getting off the river. Mr. Knight will get back out to the middle of the river. It's the best current, and he'll keep going downriver. He'll be leaving, going off without him. He'll get the rest of the way without him.

Knight can hear the thoughts spinning through Hardy's head. It's not right to let the boy have to conjure the first words. These are adult words that need to be exchanged.

Knight looks up to Buddy. "I can't tell you how honestly grateful I am that you found us, that you found Hardy. He needed you to come at that exact place at that exact time."

Representative Knight stands to face Buddy directly with a smile. There won't be time, and there won't be words to get it all in. "It's been an incredibly long story, a truly long trip down this river. I just couldn't begin to know where to start. And I have to admit, I thought it was an ending. And then you came, and thank God you did. I hope someday you let your son tell you the whole of it. It's quite a good one. I know that he'll be fine, Buddy, because you're the man that gets it done. Take care of our boy."

"Representative Knight, it's you that needs to know how grateful I am. You saved my son." Buddy throws his arms around Knight. He holds him there until he's sure it's enough. The loud floral and the tattered Armani. The two men feel it's enough. They break away, and then, the most vigorous of all handshakes that there's ever been in the whole history of the river.

"Mr. Knight," Buddy needs one more. He can't let the moment pass. "You will be alright. You're a strong man. I know there's still more ahead. You'll get to where you're going."

Knight reaches across to Buddy and pats his shoulder, the older man to the younger man. With that, Knight turns to Hardy and sits down next to him.

He puts his hand on Hardy's forehead. The temperature does seem to be going down.

"You see, things have a way of getting better." As Knight says the words, he feels compelled to recognize the sincerity of strength he has discovered in himself, a changed man. It feels different. "You'll need to get through the woods up to the highway." Knight waits. He can sense Hardy is sorting his way through the significance of the moment. "I won't be going with you. Your father will take back that job."

Hardy folds his arms across his chest, and he looks down at the bottom of the boat, the aluminum boat. He takes a deep and difficult swallow. "Is it really over?"

Both of them sit quietly. The words hang in the air in front of them. Is it really over? They will evaporate, gone in a moment. Is it really over? When the moment passes and takes with it the burden of the river's menacing trials, the words float off into the breeze of the afternoon sun.

"We held our weight." Knight graciously takes his turn. "We beat back everything they could throw at us." He has to measure the spaces between his thoughts. "We joined with them, we fought with them, and we fought against them." The words connect the spaces. "We found truly good people, good honest, decent people. They found us."

"They made us one of them." Hardy's voice is still low.

They both give it time. The longest pauses have their own measure.

When the weight lifts off to its proper place, they both feel its passing.

Hardy looks up and over to Mr. Knight, and with the biggest grin that could ever fit on a twelve-year-old's face, he lets fly the end of it: "I don't understand it. I don't think we're supposed to, so that's that."

"Dear Boy, I certainly don't know why it was us or why it was me." Mr. Knight looks at Hardy and uses a lot of hand gestures. "All those people, place after place, just keep moving through it? Boat after boat? Honestly? Keep going down the river, down the river? Was that the point of it? It still seems way too close to a Samuel Clemens story, a very personal one. I don't remember it being a tragedy."

Hardy almost jumps with energy. He stands and faces Mr. Knight and plops both hands on his shoulders. "I'm pretty sure William and Jack made it to where they were going."

Knight looks back at him with a grand ole smile. "Nobody knew more about this river than William. And that man was more cantankerous than any politician I ever met, and I've seen the worst of them."

"I've never been there when somebody died." Hardy steps back. "I guess most people have. I never have. I could see what was happening. I mean, I understand why it was happening, but it still doesn't make much sense."

"Son, those are questions people wrestle with their entire lives. Let's not forget them. That's what you do now. That's the way it's done.

"I understand that, Sir, gravestones and history books."

Hardy takes another step back. He knows what it means to have the conversation end.

"Mr. Knight, the fat lady with all that white powder..."

"Good lord... she was... she was... I can't find the words. Over the top. Far too much."

"All I wanted was to close my eyes, but I couldn't look away. I wonder what happened to her?"

"Another question we'll leave behind for now."

A burst of a laugh rips out of Hardy's mouth. "She didn't care much for your Armani jacket, which still looks pretty good, Sir."

"Of course it does." With that, he reaches to shake Hardy's hand. Not the slightest hesitation, Hardy wraps his arms around Mr. Knight. In that moment, Representative Knight feels the blessing the young boy has given his life. To travel down the length of a river with this young man places him in league with those who have been brought back to life by the trusted love of those younger. There's little more to say.

"Mr. Knight," Hardy isn't ready to let go, "will I ever see you again?"

Knight takes Hardy's shoulders and holds him away just enough to look him in the face. "Don't think of it that way, Son. You will go on, and you'll hold on to the memories of this time we spent on the river. And when you're an old man like me, those memories may step aside. You may lose some of them, but they'll always be right beside you. They'll never leave. They make you who you are."

The two of them stand side by side for one minute more.

"Mr. Knight," Hardy's voice slows down, "thank you for getting me to New Orleans. I mean, I know we're not totally there, but William and those others must be grateful for what you did. I know it."

"I know it too, and you are most deservedly welcome."

Doris yanks the cord on the outboard, and the motor roars ready.

"Is the bateau tied?" Knight asks Buddy.

"Sir, you won't need it," Buddy tells him.

"I can't leave the bateau."

"Dad, he has to take the bateau. It doesn't belong here."

Buddy steps over to his son. "Then the little bateau boat will finish up this last stretch and get where it belongs. It's tied and ready to go."

Buddy turns his back toward his son, and Hardy jumps aboard piggyback like he's done a hundred times.

"Sack of potatoes," Buddy says, like he has a hundred times.

Hardy looks back one last time to Mr. Knight, a simple twelve-year-old's, "Goodbye."

"Not goodbye," Hardy says. "I'll see you later."

Buddy steps up to the front of the fishing boat and then carefully, one leg at a time, steps over the side.

"Jesus Christ, this river mud stinks," Buddy says, one leg at a time.

"Goodbye, river." Hardy calls out to all of it.

With a few more steps through the mud and up through the opening, the scrub closes behind them.

No further words necessary. Doris throttles into reverse and backs the fishing boat away from the shore, and in no time at all, the tether rope snaps tight and the two boats are making decent progress to the middle, where the current is strongest.

"So, you've been headed to New Orleans for a good piece of time?" Doris knows small talk is the best way to start any trip on the river. "This river eats up time. Some people have spent a good part of their lives moving up and down this river."

"I'm sure that's especially true without an outboard motor like this one." Knight appreciates the small talk.

Chapter Twenty Four

Notes for the story

Representative Knight is more than content to do nothing. The steady drone of the outboard is soothing, but more than that, it gives him the sense that he's beating the river. Speed on the river, after all, is the measure of winning.

It's not long before he notices the other small boats, maybe half a dozen. It's only a little surprising.

"Apparently, we're not alone." Knight feels the tone of casual conversation sets the appropriate mood. "It is curious that we're all about the same size and going in the same direction. Don't you find that odd?"

"Well, Franklin, on a stretch of the river like this, that's what you're going to see."

"I won't ask why. I find it reassuring, actually."

"I'm glad to hear that."

Doris's lightest touch on the motor handle keeps the fishing boat straight down the middle.

"Shall I tell you a story about boats on a river?" Doris's lightest touch, a very pleasant way to pass the time.

"Why is it I knew you would want to tell that story?"

"Probably because you're a wise old man."

"Old, yes."

"Well, I'll tell it. How's that?"

The outboard won't be going any faster or slower for a while longer.

"It's the story of two boats, each the same size, small and steady like us. Each has just the one person at the motor, each making decent progress. After a certain point, one boat starts stopping, pulling over to get a good look at all the interesting things you'd find up and down a river, all the way down to the destination. One stop after the other. The other boat doesn't stop for a thing. This boat barrels along, straight down the middle, steady as she goes. The one boat gets to the destination sooner, the other more than a bit later. The boat that arrives at the destination first misses everything along the way, doesn't see a thing, only the river. And the boat that gets there later misses the celebration of the arrival and everything else that has happened at the destination, doesn't see any of it. You have a choice; which boat would you choose for your trip down the river?"

"Alright, I get it. I understand the proposition, a kind of Confucius Says parable. I wasn't expecting that, but alright. A bit of a cliché, isn't it? Let's see, you're always in the boat you need to be in. No, we're all in both boats, and each has its own story? Okay, frankly, I can't remember, but it's a fairly pedestrian answer that I do remember. Nothing a little more rigorous?"

"You are one of the crusty ones, aren't you? I like that about you, but it goes like this: time on the river, Franklin, is only meaningful when it is remembered many years later. When it's become a part of you, where you've started and where you chose to arrive. Our lives have a kind of meaning when they're measured. We've seen what we needed to see."

There's only the sound of the outboard for a little while.

Knight turns slowly to look back at Doris. They watch each other's expressions and wait. In the next instant, they both burst out laughing, a real knee-slapper.

"The deep voice was perfect." Knight can barely say the words. "Perfect delivery. Tony award."

"Clearly, I'm not great at Confucious parables. I'll admit it. I don't think they're called that. I knew you'd see right through that one." Doris pulls herself together. "Alright smart ass, let's put it this way: you were in the slow boat, and you haven't even reached your destination."

Knight turns back in his seat to face forward.

"The river gave you what you needed to see. I guess we could say that."

The river is full of stories. I believe we all know that.

Knight sits still, eyes straight ahead, downriver.

A little more time passes, with the motor's very pleasant drone, and Representative Knight is thinking how Doris's conversation is the perfect way to pass the time, the sweetest touch.

"Some of these stories on the river, Franklin, look like grand, big histories."

Doris's voice is only a little less theatrical. "A lot of big drama. Tribes at war, battles for big, worldly ideals, the ones that change the world. Some are so small you barely even notice them. You noticed them, didn't you, Franklin?"

Doris waits. She gives Knight the moment to catch up.

"Still with me, Franklin? Okay, here goes another one, I swear, I'll try my best. I'll make it as cinematic as possible. I know you appreciate that. It goes like this: two tribes, two nations, battle for territory. They have been in this battle for a very long time. The tribes will risk everything for the dream of the greater good. They believe if they succeed, they will have their greater good, and their nation will live in prosperity. But a nation is only a dream. It is the people who are the living.

"To reach the dream, the tribe must be the first to arrive. They cannot stop along the way. The greater good is the dream's destination. But the people have their own stories in the dream, don't they? Their own stories to tell. Without all the little stories that you barely notice along the way, the history can't be told." Doris waits for only a short minute. She knows Franklin is poised with some kind of response. "How about that one? Any better?"

"Doris, Dear, honestly, I'm not going to commit to better or worse. Clearly, with your abilities, that would be foolhardy and, quite honestly, shortsighted. It's charming and a beautifully crafted parable, which you'd like us all to ponder, hoping we see ourselves in its foretelling." He turns back to catch her smile. "But you are gifted, I'll give you that. Not everyone can pass time so graciously."

"Son, my back is killing me." Buddy stops for a break. He holds on to the trunk of an oak for support.

"Dad, I can walk. I'm better. It doesn't hurt as bad. I don't feel so spaced out, like I did in the boat."

"Let me look."

Hardy slides off his father's back, and Buddy takes a good look at the arm.

"It isn't as red, not as inflamed as before. That's good." He feels Hardy's forehead. "Not as hot as it was before. That's good."

"Then let's go," Buddy tells him, "I want to get up and out of these woods as fast as possible. The paramedics will understand that we're coming up from the river. They'll wait for us, but let's not keep them waiting too long."

"Dad, you can't rush through the woods. Every inch of these woods right here will tell us the straightest path. You have to see the signs. You have to know what you're looking for."

"Alright, I believe you, Mr. know-it-all, but let's keep moving. You read the signs, and who made you so wise?"

Knight sits quietly facing forward. He still can't quite imagine what is out beyond the trees lining this stretch of the river. Probably something familiar but unexpected. The edge of the woods have become the edge of the world.

"How are you, Franklin? What are you thinking about?"

"Well, Doris Dear, I find it remarkable what an outboard motor brings to this. I don't know, this part of the story, I guess I'd say. My father had a Mercury outboard. It wasn't very big. It was bright red. The word "Mercury" was in white, bold letters, not like the Coca-Cola script letters, it just looked powerful. He loved that thing. In the winter, he'd store it in the basement. We went fishing many times in a boat much like your fishing boat. That was a long time ago. To this day, I can't remember what happened to that old Mercury. I didn't even remember it until now."

"I'm glad you remembered it now, Franklin. It's a nice memory. I wish I could say I loved this motor, but it's a rental."

"I don't think I ever showed my father how grateful I was for those fishing trips, for everything he did for me."

The steady hum of the motor is soothing. It adds to the hums of the other boats. None of them seem to be in much of a hurry.

"Did your father ever tell you how grateful he was that you went fishing with him? I'll just bet he did. I'll bet he has a whole story to tell about the fishing trips on the river with his son."

Doris has no other concern in the world. They'll get there when they get there.

"Franklin, your father's story of his fishing trip with his son is your story to tell. Your father's story becomes your story. Isn't that a wonder? History doesn't tell true memories because those memories are always other stories told. Isn't that a nice way to put it?"

"It was the heart attack, wasn't it? That's why I'm here with you."

"It's never one thing, Franklin."

"I should have cut the cholesterol."

"You know the old saying, when your number's up."

"Again another cliché, honest to God, Doris, what does that even mean?"

"Honestly, Franklin, I have no idea. Some Las Vegas reference, the roulette wheel, fortunes lost. But Franklin, your story on the river is a wonder. It probably should be told, don't you think?"

"Thank you for saying that, Doris, but it's not a story. It's just what happened. And thank you for bringing the bateau along."

"Of course, for sure someone else will put it to good use."

"Dad." Hardy slows his walking. The woods have become a little too much. "Can we stop, just for a minute?"

Buddy turns back and puts his palm on Hardy's forehead. "Not good. We're pushing too hard. We need to slow it down. But we need to get to the parking lot. It can't be much farther."

"Dad, we'll get there. I just need three minutes."

"Just three? What are you, a doctor now too?"

Buddy sits down cross-legged on a spot heavy with leaves. He pulls lightly on Hardy's arm to sit. They sit next to each other. Sitting quietly in the woods is good medicine.

"Dad, did you know some tribes hang their enemies in these woods? They hang them upside down by one ankle in these trees."

"Son, sit quietly," Buddy tells him. "We'll have to start up again in a minute. If I have to carry you, then I will."

They sit quietly for a few more minutes. The birds, without any amount of consideration, carry on with their noisy business.

"What's that?" Buddy is doing his best to be patient. "Some type of thrush?"

"A wood thrush. They're not quite endangered."

Hardy looks over to a spot of sunlight on the forest floor. "If we get stuck here for very long, there will probably be potatoes in there. They're not very deep."

"Okay, that's it." Buddy stands and lifts Hardy up beside him and sets him straight. He puts one arm around his shoulder, avoiding his wounded arm, and takes a fair amount of his son's weight. They set out again for the parking lot. It has to be just ahead.

It turns out that it is only a little farther than Buddy thought. There it is, the clearing in the woods, the edge of the parking lot.

Buddy is still helping Hardy walk, and at the exact same time, they step onto the gray pavement.

The paramedics are already here. That's a relief. Buddy tries to walk a little faster, but Hardy can't manage it.

"Let's get you some attention."

Buddy takes a moment to look around. There's more activity than he expected. There are two paramedic trucks, one bigger than the other. Buddy is more than grateful to see them both. He's relieved. This will get easier. The Winnebago looks fine; there is no issue with that. The highway, only a couple hundred feet away, has sporadic traffic. For some reason, the sun feels hotter out here. Next to the bigger paramedic truck, there are a few people standing around what looks like a hospital gurney. It looks more than a little serious. You can tell by the way they're standing and how they're not really talking. He takes a few more steps, moving Hardy along with him.

One of the paramedics steps out of the back of the smaller truck and makes a beeline for them. He's a man, maybe in his mid-thirties. He's wearing blue scrubs, what you would expect. He's half smiling and half hurrying to get to Hardy. Something about him, he's immediately a good person. Before he even reaches them, "You were smart to get your son back up from the river and get that arm looked at," he says walking toward them. "Probably not serious, but we'll take a look."

When the paramedic reaches them, he puts an arm around Hardy and quickly moves him over to the EMS truck. Hardy doesn't say anything. He lets it happen. When they reach the truck, the paramedic quickly starts the routine. He sits Hardy down on the edge of the back of the truck. The wound is washed and dressed. He has various plastic bottles with various fluids. It all happens very fast.

"As soon as I found him, I started back." Buddy looks down. He's not comfortable showing this much emotion to a stranger. "He's never been in this much trouble before. With the Representative and all."

"Well, I'm glad I can help. I wouldn't worry. It doesn't look too bad, maybe a stitch or two, probably not."

The paramedic wraps another temporary bandage around the arm. He reaches across, and Hardy can't help but look closely at the man. His black hair, a decent haircut, and some kind of silver chain around his neck. He seems like a very nice person. He has the letter "D" tattooed on the side of his neck, a small, black letter. Hardy thinks to ask about the tattoo, but the paramedic finishes with the bandage and steps back.

"This will keep it clean until we can dress it properly," he tells Buddy. His voice is reassuring and familiar. "You did good, Son. You should be proud of yourself. I'm really sorry about your friend, the elderly gentleman…"

Before the paramedic finishes his words, Hardy looks up at his face. There at the back of the EMS truck, it all stops. Everyone and everything, in one silent, frozen moment. He stares at the man's face, reading the man's face with shock and wonder. The thoughts of what must be impossible flood his thinking. Hardy stands and starts the walk across the pavement toward the others at the gurney. The paramedic follows, with Buddy behind them both.

The sun feels colder than five minutes ago.

When Hardy is halfway to the others, one of them walks to meet him. They meet in the middle. It's Alfred. His last few steps are hurried, and when he reaches Hardy, he throws his arms around him. Alfred doesn't have emotional strength. He's strong in other ways. He looks Hardy in the face. It's clear he's been crying.

"For sure, he's gone to another place." Alfred can barely speak. "He's too good a man for Washington."

Hardy lets Alfred hug him, but he doesn't say a word. His body is limp. Not so much from the shock. It just doesn't feel all that unexpected. It's confusing to hear, the sense of it is hard, the how and the where. Where exactly on the river? And how long? It's not something you're going to figure out by standing here and thinking it through from beginning to end. It will get unscrambled later on. A piece of it will jump out, and the whole of it will start to make sense, more than it does right now.

Alfred brings Hardy over to the gurney. They both stand quietly for quite a while. The paramedic, with Buddy, walks up behind them. Representative Knight lies peacefully on the ambulance gurney. His body is half covered with a white sheet. It's difficult to describe his expression. Peaceful. Annoyed.

Hardy turns to the paramedic. "Was it a heart attack?" He wipes tears off his face with the back of his hand. "He got chest pains, but I thought they were going away."

"Son," the paramedic tells him, "it's never one thing."

Hardy reaches over to pull the sheet down a little farther and brushes off Mr. Knight's Armani jacket and buttons the buttons. With one last tug at the bottom, the jacket looks just like Mr. Knight would want it to look. That jacket, he never took it off. Maybe the once, it is a nice jacket. Mr. Knight would want him to think that. The thought brings a smile to his face. We'll call it a little bit of a grand ole smile.

Buddy steps next to his son and puts one arm around his shoulders. "I'm so sorry, Son, I really am."

"It's alright, Dad. I know he's busy with something. I don't think he wanted to go to Washington anyway. He's doing something with somebody, some great project, or, I don't know, something he thinks is a great project."

"For sure, he thinks it is," Alfred adds. They all share a little chuckle.

The paramedic steps over to Buddy. "Sir, we need to wrap this up. I don't mean to keep you from saying your goodbyes. There will be time for that later, but we need to get going."

Hardy takes hold of the sheet, just to hold it. There's more to say, but he won't say it here. He stands very still, but his breathing has a deep rhythm. There are tears on his cheeks, but he's not crying. He's holding the sheet just a little longer. All the thoughts running through his mind start to fly off on their own. He doesn't need them. Hardy puts his head gently down on Mr. Knight's chest. Just for a moment. It's not a goodbye. It's a "see you later" that only Mr. Knight can hear.

The steady hum of the outboard is the only thing he can hear. Representative Knight looks back and forth across the river. He's counting the small boats, all headed in the same direction.

"This bend in the river must be the tightest, widest turn on the whole of the Mississippi."

He turns on his seat to check on Doris. She's as steady as the day is long.

"And you don't find it the least bit odd that we're all, however many dozens of us there are, we're all going the exact same speed? Not odd?"

"Not odd, Franklin. Don't think of it that way."

They exchange goofy smiles.

"I could insert a charming old saying here, but you can see how bad I am at that," she tells him. "I'll watch the river, keep our boat headed straight, and mind my Ps and Qs. You should turn around. You'll like this one."

As the little boat turns through the bend, Knight turns back, facing straight ahead, and he sees it. The colossus of all lettered signs, suspended as if in midair, held in place by a grid of rust-iron girders, high above the dirty brown docks, enormous letters. Who knows how high they are. The Port Of New Orleans.

He quickly spins back to see Doris's face. To catch her expression, she gives him one big smile back, big and wide, her whole face, a grand ole smile.

The flood of thoughts and emotions, all the time and the people, the trust they put in him, the agreements made, the last and final push, the test of his determination, all of it floods through him. In spite of it all, he's persuaded the Mississippi to bring him to the port.

Franklin drops his head, his shoulders, and his chest, heaving with breaths he can barely take. He looks down to his shoes one more time, just a touch of dirt, maybe river mud. One finger wipes it away.

To say he is proud that he has finally made it and beaten the river would not do the moment justice. Also, it wouldn't be accurate.

"I wish Hardy could see this," Knight says as he looks up to watch the huge, perfect letters. "Somehow, I believe he'll see it."

Knight sits up straight, shoulders back. He brushes off the Armani, a bit of dirt, but otherwise it's in very decent shape. You cannot underestimate an Armani. It'll go the distance.

"That was the longest trip I believe I have ever taken and will ever take."

"I'm sure it was a challenge." Doris keeps the lightest touch on the motor's throttle. The little boat makes it back to the middle where the current is strongest. "Franklin, I could tell you that you will want to remember this trip and that you'll want to tell this story, but I believe you already know that."

"Doris, I am so incredibly grateful for all that you and all the rest have done for me and for the Hardy. It's important that you know that."

"You're an intelligent and considerate man, Franklin I know you are grateful."

The aluminum fishing boat with the wood bateau tethered securely behind passes under the monumental sign. Both Doris and Knight agree it's even more impressive from directly underneath.

"It's the size of the pyramids."

"It would dwarf the Titanic."

"I'm still a little confused how those hooligans put all that costuming together. They must have had help." Knight is looking up at the enormous letter "N" in New Orleans, and can't keep himself from sorting through a number of the inconsistencies. "And the Captain Colbert, how he got so stuck in that ravine, with his training... I don't think we ever actually heard what they called that horrible jerky, but I'm glad we had it. We called it the Seven Eleven jerky. All the names and faces, honestly I'm going to have to start taking notes on this. Did it all start and end at the river? I can't trust my memory." He looks back at Doris. "You do know how old I am."

Representative Knight takes a quick look around, as if there were a convenient stack of paper. Any boat on a river can double as an office. He remembers William's bag. Thank God he brought it! He grabs it and digs through it, pulling out the small book, thinking there might be extra paper. On the dirty leather cover of the book, in dirty gold-embossed letters, "The Life and Strange Surprizing Adventures of Robinson Crusoe. Daniel Defoe." What a charming idea, thinking of William, such a wonderful character, but no paper.

"Here you go." Doris hands Franklin a small spiral notepad. "I knew you'd be needing this. I have a pen, so don't worry."

"Isn't that kind. There are a few holes here and there, particularly at the end of it." Franklin flips through the little pad, looking for who knows what. "It seems you spend time with people, you share something inextricably profound, and then off they go. Where is it that people go? How do you ever bring people where they're supposed to be and keep them there long enough so everyone can make sense of it?"

"It's always a little messy," Doris tells Franklin as she finds the pen in her loose denim pants and hands it to him.

"I certainly hope I can patch the holes and put together a decent ending. I assume Hardy made it back with that poor arm, but I have no way of knowing. How could I know that? Don't you feel that presents a problem?"

"Tell it the way you remember it, Franklin, or the way you would like people to remember it. People will forgive you if you can't patch the holes. Why wouldn't they? You're part of the story. You'll do your best. I wouldn't worry too much about it, Franklin. People love to read other people's stories, and the story ends differently for everyone.”

Such a kind and thoughtful way to put it.

“And just think, Franklin, you were part of the history. Think how lucky you are. Every history is a story always told for the first time.”

Representative Knight doesn’t hear her, of course; now he’s very busy with his notes and the notepad; a possible preliminary outline might start with chapter notes. He’s so focused on the story he doesn’t notice the New Orleans sign is now behind him.

The paramedics step forward to wrap it up. Time to go. Alfred will go with them to the hospital. They all give each other their parking lot goodbyes. Buddy tells Alfred he’ll take care of the Winnebago and return it to the rental company.

The paramedic tells Buddy that he and his son will go in the other EMS truck to a different part of the hospital. Hardy may not even need stitches, a decent scratch but a minor wound. They’ll take a look. He checks to see that the gurney is properly secured, closes the back doors, and comes back around to Hardy, standing with his father.

“I’m sorry I didn’t get there a little sooner.” His reassuring and familiar voice. “It wouldn’t have made much difference. He was gone before I got there. He was lucky you were there. That’s got to count for something.”

The paramedic makes his way to the driver’s side door and climbs in. As he buckles his belt, he calls out the window. “You’re a good kid. I’m sure everything will go well for you. I know it will.”

Hardy smiles back with a simple thank you.

With that, the paramedic truck pulls out of the parking lot rest stop and out onto the Interstate.

The driver of the smaller EMS truck leans out of his window, and with a wave, he calls to Buddy and Hardy. “You should get in. We should get going.”

Buddy and Hardy climb in the back seat. The driver looks into the rear-view mirror. “You guys set? Make sure the buckles are secure. It’s not very far, just down the road.”

“Sure, we’re good,” Buddy tells him.

Right away, even before they’re out on the highway, the driver is full of questions. He’s either naturally chatty or it’s been a long shift.

“So what happened to you, Son? How’d you get so scratched up?”

Hardy waits to see if the question will dissolve into the air blowing in as they leave the rest stop and get out on the highway, which it doesn't.

"What kind of trouble did you get yourself into? I'm so terribly sorry about your partner, your friend. Was he your uncle?"

"Well, Sir, the trouble I got myself into is part of a long story, but essentially I got blown up in a Navy ironclad ship. It was up at Vicksburg Harbor. Know where that is? The Confederate battery?" Hardy feels pretty sure he's said enough to get the conversation going.

"Well, dear God, in a lightning bolt, Son, that sounds like an exceptional story," the driver calls to the back. "That sounds serious enough and dangerous too. It looks like you came out of it okay. I'm sure you're going to be fine, so it turned out okay. Wouldn't you say."

"Yes, Sir, it turned out okay."

BOATS ON A RIVER

The Author

In New York, Mr. Balk was represented by American Fine Arts,
Colin de Land. In the Middle East, Mr. Balk established media arts
programs at universities in Bahrain, Abu Dhabi, and Jordan. He
served as the Director of the Digital Media Department of Bangkok
International College for a decade. In Bangkok, Mr. Balk created the
streetwear brand Splinter Group.
Mr. Balk currently lives in Richmond, Virginia.

The collective is not a grouping of individuals.
The individual is more and less than a component of the collective's
objectivity. The collective cannot see the individual. A community of
individuals is a fiction the objectivity requires. The field periodically
uses the fiction of its objectivity to justify its effort
to keep out the weeds.

Mr. Balk exhibits artwork in international exhibition
and distribution circuits.

A shot of whiskey never hurt a coke.
A dollop of fiction never hurt even a sliver of history.
It's a remarkably civil compromise.

Winter 2023

www.ingramcontent.com/pod-product-compliance
Lightning Source LLC
Chambersburg PA
CBHW040853010826
48978CB00013BA/1004